"Amanda's story is the heart of the book. An unconventional, courageous woman, she develops an interest in the new art of photography. . . . Shreve uses her well-honed storytelling talents to make it a memorable journey."
—*The Orlando Sentinel*

"Ambitious . . . Uplifting . . . This is Shreve's best novel so far—elegantly plotted, gracefully written, and moving. . . . She has succeeded in chronicling the lives of five generations of women while letting the history fall, like a mural, behind the women's lives. The result is literature, not a supermarket historical saga."
—*Bangor Daily News*

"A marvelous novel . . . Shreve has constructed a multigenerational family saga that never plods, grows stale, or falters. The opening scene immediately establishes the power and tension of her story. . . . Shreve explores the wonder of personalities and genetics, the astonishing accommodation and resiliency of women, the courage and dignity of true love, and the surge of change that has driven this unlikely century. An enveloping, rewarding, and heroic tale told with great skill and much heart."
—*Booklist*

Also by Susan Richards Shreve:

A FORTUNATE MADNESS
A WOMAN LIKE THAT
CHILDREN OF POWER
MIRACLE PLAY
DREAMING OF HEROES
QUEEN OF HEARTS
A COUNTRY OF STRANGERS

DAUGHTERS OF THE NEW WORLD

Susan Richards Shreve

IVY BOOKS • NEW YORK

Ivy Books
Published by Ballantine Books
Copyright © 1992 by Susan Richards Shreve

Library of Congress Catalog Card Number: 91-8146

ISBN 0-8041-1123-5

This edition published by arrangement with Doubleday, a division of Bantam Doubleday Dell Publishing Group, Inc.

Manufactured in the United States of America

First Ballantine Books Edition: April 1994

10 9 8 7 6 5 4 3

For
Po,
Elizabeth,
Caleb,
and
Kate
and
for
Timothy

WITHDRAWN

TABLE OF CONTENTS

"Your photographs . . . if arranged in sequence . . . create the illusion of time in this century—like a motion picture . . . each frame persisting in the eye until the next image arrives so the eye is tricked into seeing continuous motion . . . Our lives have changed so quickly, your mother's and yours, my mother's and mine, faster and faster, from a still photograph to a silent film to a camera with ninety frames a second. It seems today as if there is only time to dip into the moment and briefly stop the motion."

Excerpt from a tape to Amanda Steward made by her grand-daughter Eleanor on the fourth of August, 1972.

ANNA

ONE: NOVEMBER 18, 1890

"AMERICA," ANNA JERMYN said from the ship's deck where she lay wrapped in a gray wool blanket, concealing with her longer, broader body the body of her dead mother. "So, Papa, we are here and you said we would never be."

"New York," her father said dully.

The skyline of New York floated in brown square blocks just at the end of Anna's vision and she squinted her eyes against the bright glare of the distant noonday sun.

"New York is not America," her father said as if he had memorized all of the information about his new life in advance. "And besides, we are not all of us here."

"Well, I am," Anna said.

"And I," Fiona, the youngest, small for her fourteen years, said as she held tight to her father's hand. She could not bear to look at Anna or imagine her mother suffocated by her weight.

"And I," Roger said. He kept his eyes fixed on New York City as the ship moved closer and the buildings grew.

The Jermyns had left Liverpool in mid-October 1890, had left three older sons behind in the village of Parkgate which was their home because the sons had good work as butchers in a shop belonging to their uncle. But Thomas Jermyn, himself a butcher in Wales, had been born with dreams, inherited now by his angelic Anna, and he could not settle. Always he wanted to be someplace else. Rome or London or Paris—someplace where the days were interesting and the work did not smell of blood. So when Anna, working as a kitchen maid with a family in London, met the Stewards from America and their handsome son and they offered Anna a situation, paid for her passage, and even had a dress made for her out of silk as a gift for several favors, Thomas Jermyn knew it was a sign from God.

"We are going to America," he told his wife and younger children.

Maria, his wife, had no interest in America. She had heard from cousins that it was a dangerous place to be and did not wish to go. Although not strong physically, she was strong-willed. But she could not deter her husband. By September, they had packed what possessions they were taking, said good-bye to their sons and other family, and left for Liverpool to meet the ship which would take them to America.

On that journey, Anna, soft-bodied and sensual at sixteen, with full lips and large wide-set eyes the color of green olives and the broad forehead and small peaked chin of a da Vinci woman, sat in the back of a carriage with her mother on a seat intended for one. The journey was long and her mother, usually reserved, talked and talked about everything—the man she had wanted to marry who did not like adventures, the firstborn baby daughter who had died, her secret wish to be a dancer and how she danced in the barn even now when everyone was working. It was as if she knew in advance she must say everything, her whole life, because she would not have another chance.

The deck filled up. So many people had died, especially in the last days on the ocean—more than half, a ship's steward had said. So many still were ill.

"You must be grateful to have made it," one of the stewards said to a grim and pale Thomas Jermyn.

"Of course," Thomas said. He did not mention his wife, nor did the ship's steward, who had witnessed Maria Jermyn's swift leaving in the last few hours. Just that morning her breath had been observed by another steward as shallow as the breath of a bird. The steward might have presumed she had died and been thrown overboard like the others but was a man of too much sensibility to inquire. He did, however, ask Mr. Jermyn about Anna, who lay under the blanket at her father's feet.

"Ill is she?"

"A bit," Mr. Jermyn said.

"She'd be better off standing if she can," the steward

said. "She'll catch her death on the cold planks." He leaned down over Anna.

"Are you quite ill?" he asked.

"Not to death."

He touched her face. She could tell he liked the look of her but she didn't like him with his long oily hair and bad-smelling breath.

"Come on then. Get up," he said, reaching for her hand under the blanket. "Look at New York City."

"I can see it from here," Anna said, her heart beating hard in her chest. He was looking at her with too much interest. She glanced at her father but he was staring straight ahead at New York. Roger as well. Only Fiona, her black eyes wide as a rabbit's, stared down at Anna and the ship's steward leaning over her.

"What are you hiding there, pretty girl?" he whispered to Anna, his breath putrid, undissipated by the cold air.

"Nothing," Anna said.

"Nothing?" the steward replied. From underneath the blanket, he pulled a long strand of Maria Jermyn's gray hair. "Yours?"

"Leave me alone," Anna said quietly.

"I will," the steward said. "I wouldn't want to bother so beautiful a girl as you." And swifter than she could stop him, he reached under the blanket, took hold of her breast, and with the other hand dragged her just enough so the body of Maria Jermyn, her face almost concealed by the hood of her cape, was exposed.

Fiona buried her face in her father's woolen coat.

"Don't look," Thomas Jermyn said in warning to his son.

Anna jumped up, took the gray blanket which had dropped, and wrapped the body of her mother in it.

"How long has she been dead?" the steward asked. Anna did not reply.

The crowd of passengers whose attention had been fixed on New York City now moved away from the railing and gathered around the small drama of the Jermyn family.

"She'll have to go overboard," the steward said. "It is the rule."

"Not here," Anna said. She had covered the body of her mother, rolled her tight in the blanket. "We're almost in New York."

"It's the rule," the steward said.

"Papa?" Anna asked.

Thomas Jermyn did not turn around.

"Please, Papa."

"I am sorry, sir," the steward said. "It's the rule."

"I know," Thomas Jermyn said.

"She will not go in this cold river," Anna said and sat on her mother's feet. "Fiona, sit down with me."

Fiona, her eyes covered with her hands, sat down.

"Roger?"

"I cannot look," Roger said.

"Coward," Anna said.

The steward reached down to take hold of the body of Maria Jermyn but Anna, bright with anger, kicked him hard.

"You have no right," she said.

The crowd murmured in sympathy and pushed in closer to Anna and Fiona.

"Let her be," one man said.

"We're almost at the port," another said.

"Not in the river," a woman said. "It's different than the sea."

"Leave her alone."

"Have it your way then," the steward said, but he had hold of an edge of the blanket. With a great pull he yanked it from under Anna and the body of Maria rolled out.

"Ship's property." He dropped the blanket overboard and walked away.

Anna wrapped the cape tighter around her mother.

"She would hate for anyone to see her dead," Anna whispered to Fiona as she covered her mother's face with the hood. "It would humiliate her."

Hours passed before the ship was finally tied at the pier and the passengers were allowed to leave. In that time, Anna and Fiona sat guard.

"When we get off," Anna said, "we will carry her between us."

* * *

Anna had actually known about her mother's dancing before the ride to Liverpool when her mother had been confessional. Once she had come upon her mother dancing on her toes to the church bells of St. Sebastian's.

"Why don't you dance always, Mama?" she had asked.

"I can't. It would be terrible for a woman who is a wife."

"What kind of woman dances then?" Anna had asked.

"A bad woman," Maria Jermyn had said somberly. "A very bad woman."

The ship docked in the East River and the immigrants were transferred with their luggage to Castle Garden, a former entertainment hall which was the processing center for new arrivals, near the Battery at the tip of Manhattan. Anna was protected by other passengers sympathetic to her plight as she and Fiona carried their mother, wrapped in her cape, tied like a bundle, and entirely covered, between them.

The crowd let Anna and Fiona go first off the gangplank onto the pier.

"What are we going to do?" Fiona asked.

"Bury her in America," Anna said. "We'll find a place. Someone will help us."

"No one will help us," her father said. "We are strangers."

But Anna was right. By nightfall, with the help of a passenger's brother who had connections with a priest, the family of Thomas Jermyn had buried their beloved mother in a small Catholic churchyard in exchange for Thomas's gold watch and all of Maria's jewelry except her locket, which Anna had taken and hidden in her underclothes.

The next morning, gray and windy in New York City, Anna Jermyn boarded the train for her situation in Washington, D.C., dulled by an irreparable grief which would last her life but stirred as well by the promise and wonder and excitement of the New World.

TWO

In London, Anna had discovered that she was beautiful. Not conventionally beautiful like the women she had served in Mrs. Barclay's dining room or in the parlor for afternoon tea, with their porcelain skin and long narrow lips colored to perfection, their voices tinkling in harmony. But she had passed the great mirror in the main hall of the house at Harrington Gardens where she was a kitchen maid, had lingered there with her reflection. Her face was fuller, richer than theirs, and even Anna was momentarily arrested by the sight of herself. She knew that her presence in a room had a certain power: she was treated differently from the other servants.

"An angel. You are an angel," Mary, head of the Barclays' kitchen, had said to her. "You turn the stomachs of the men to pudding."

In Rhyl with her family, at the small farm just beyond the village, she had been Anna the butcher's daughter, wilder than the Welsh girls who lived in town because, according to the gossip, the butcher had married a Roman Catholic girl of Sardinian descent, the child of a British sailor and his Italian wife, who had a streak in her which showed up again in Anna. But Anna was expected to marry a shopkeeper's son when she turned seventeen, to have her own little cottage and raise babies, her life too occupied with responsibilities to permit the indulgence of wild streaks.

It was her mother's idea that Anna go to London to find a situation when she was sixteen, working at the sweets shop.

"You have possibilities," her mother said while making bread with Anna one afternoon.

"What possibilities?" Anna asked, her mind possessed with visions of royalty since she was small. "To be handmaid to the Queen of England, I suppose. I've dreamed about that."

"I don't know which possibility. I simply feel it in my blood," her mother said. "Not to be handmaid to the Queen of England."

Anna had been in the employment of the Barclays for only two months—working in the kitchen, polishing the silver and the brass, serving, making small cakes and vegetable dishes—when the Stewards came from America. With their arrival Anna knew something in herself she had not known as a girl in Rhyl—the possibility her mother had felt in her blood.

The Stewards, three of them, had come on holiday: a physician from Washington, D.C., his English wife, and a son, William, himself a physician, dashing like the hunting pictures Anna had seen in the Barclays' library. The Stewards were excessive people, louder than the English Anna had known, familiar, even personal, and their presence in the Barclay house had stirred her.

"Aha, a Welsh beauty," Dr. Steward had said the first evening while she was serving soup. "That's a contradiction in terms."

"I'm part Italian," Anna had said. She could not believe her own ears at her transgression. "From Sardinia."

Later, Mrs. Barclay had spoken to her sharply and said she would not be permitted the privilege of serving anymore. But the Stewards complained of her absence in the dining room.

"Where is the Sardinian flower?" Dr. Steward had asked and Mary had reported to Anna in the kitchen.

"You must be the Sardinian flower," Mary had said. "I don't know of such a flower in England."

By the third night, Anna was serving again and this time when she leaned over the young Dr. Steward to serve his soup, he blew the hot wind of his breath in her ear and she had to struggle to keep her composure.

At night, she lay in her small bed in the room behind the kitchen, a black cat with fish breath purring hard at the bottom of her bed. She could not sleep, shivering with the excitement of possibilities for a future she could not imagine even in her dreams. For her dreams never went beyond the one in which she was handmaid to Queen Victoria and was kissed by a palace guard in uniform with gold braid at his shoulders and a bristling face roughing her cheek.

Her family was poor and not entirely respectable because her mother was Roman Catholic and foreign, but they had a small property and subsisted. Their future, if dull, was at least predictable.

Nevertheless the house was full of stories—her father's about distant places with long horizons, unfamiliar in England, whose soil grew promises in abundance like wheat, her mother's of the rich forbidden secrets, housed in the safe shell of catechism and incense, the lyrical Latinate Mass, transforming the spirits of young women to romance and, darkest of all the secrets, sexual flight, although to name it was a sin. So, unlike the other girls in Rhyl, Anna Jermyn was full of restlessness.

Now she sat very straight on the horsehair seat of the train clattering to Washington, D.C. Across from her, an older man with a full, speckled beard sat, one hand on his crotch, reading a book held in front of his face so she could not see his expression. She was aware, however, that from time to time when she wasn't looking he dropped his book and let his eyes wander to her full breasts, tear at the cloth, and burn through the flesh.

The young Dr. Steward had kissed her hand when he left for Southampton and the ship back to America.

"That was inappropriate for a gentleman to kiss the hand of a servant, of course," Mrs. Barclay had said to her later. "I hope you won't be ruined by America."

"Of course," Anna had said, smiling to herself behind the accustomed solemnity of her demeanor. For young Dr. William Steward had done more than simply kiss her hand. His head bent over, his hair falling just enough to shield the gesture, he had slipped his tongue between her fingers and touched her palm.

She was wearing the plum-colored silk dress the Stewards had had made for her, with lace at the throat and her mother's locket resting just between her breasts. The cape in which her mother's body had been wrapped hung loosely at her shoulders. On the long trip she imagined her arrival in her mind's eye.

The young Dr. Steward would be walking briskly, handsomely, toward her as she disembarked carrying the carpetbag with all she owned—one dress, a camisole, a velvet skirt her mother had made, her mother's blouse (the one she had died in), a small book of poems which was the only book she had remembered to take from the cottage in Rhyl, and a bag of sweets Fiona had given her for the journey.

Her cape flying, her long hair falling loose of its pins, she'd be walking to meet him, flushed with the damp November air and her pleasure at seeing him. Would he kiss her? Would he lean over, abandoning the acceptable distance between them, and kiss her lips?

The older man said he was getting off the train in Baltimore. Was she traveling far? To Washington, she said.

"Why are you traveling alone?" he asked as the train was coming to a stop.

"Don't women in America travel alone?" Anna asked. "I had thought there were not so many rules of behavior as there are in England."

He leaned forward, put his hand gently on her knee.

"There are rules," he said, "or I would not have behaved myself so well on this long journey face to face with you."

She blushed and did not look at him as he disembarked.

The young Dr. William Steward did not meet the train. Louisa, who did the ironing and laundry at the Stewards', was there with a young, speckled, unattractive man whose name was not given and who drove the carriage through a light wet snow down Pennsylvania Avenue to Georgetown, where the Stewards lived in a large house on N Street several blocks above the banks of the Potomac River.

THREE

Dear Mama, Anna wrote on the 23rd of November, 1890, sitting against the wall on top of the coverlet of her small bed at Dr. and Mrs. Steward's house on N Street.

Today is your birthday. It is a gray morning with a thin mist like the north of England—even the smell in the garden is the same. Louisa, the laundress, older than I am and quite sullen, tells me Washington is a swamp, that the houses sink by the fortnight into the mushy ground full of rats who have a fancy for swamps and the garbage we put out back. Sometimes, she tells me, the rats scramble into her bedroom behind the kitchen and run across her feet at night. As you can see, Louisa does not have an optimism about our lives on earth and I wish she did not live in the room across from mine, crabby and stormy-minded as she is.

My room has a small bed and a dresser and a picture of a plump French girl holding a bunch of tulips and looking forlorn. There is one window and since the room is slightly below ground, I imagine it is the perfect place for rats to invade if the dreadful Louisa is right about them, as I suppose she is, given her peculiar turn of mind.

I have not seen the young Dr. William Steward since I arrived, which surprises me very much since he certainly indicated in London that he would be greatly pleased to have me in residence close by him. I have, however, seen more than I wish of an unattractive gentleman, if you can call him that, called Arthur who drives the carriage and keeps the horses. I was in the carriage house putting out the garbage last night, not realizing he was there, and after I did my chores he tried to kiss me without a word, not hello or how are you or isn't it a pleasant evening, which it was. He just took me flat against him and kissed my lips. So I was forced to bite him and he told me he would spit on me if I did such a thing again. I said likewise to him about the spitting and the kissing as well.

Sometimes I feel a great secret power at being a woman. Sometimes I feel outraged. I would like very much to know Dr. William Steward better, however, as he is a real gentleman and would not take advantage.

On the subject of kissing, night before last I came upon Mrs. Steward kissing a young man from university who had been at the house for dinner—young enough to be her son surely. I was walking into the library with coffee for the ladies after dinner and there were no ladies, just Mrs. Steward and the young university man together in a shadowed corner of the room.

"Never mind," she said to me, breaking free of him, quite composed she seemed, although the young man was certainly not.

"Just put the coffee here," she said.

Later that evening, she knocked on the door to my room, came in, lit the gas lamp, and sat down at the end of my bed. I was surprised and touched as well by her forwardness.

"I feel I should mention something to you about this evening," she said. "I expect you to keep your counsel of course." Her voice was very soft. "The life of a lady is not satisfactory and so I take what small happiness I can, whatever the consequence. Do you understand?"

I said I did but I don't.

She said I speak very well for an uneducated foreigner. I told her that I spoke no differently than any Welsh girl except musically because of my Italian mother and the Welsh, of course. She said Americans speak plainly, even educated Americans. She is right about Americans. They speak plainly, and poorly as well.

I cannot sleep at night for the turbulence in my body. I know it is because you are dead and Father, Fiona, and Roger are going to Wisconsin to look up Father's cousin. I will not see them for a very long time, I suppose. Fa-

*ther has turned black as coal with your death. I had al-
ways thought he was the one with a lightness of spirit,
but it must have been you all along sunning the sky.*

*I want something to happen soon, right away. I wish
you were here to explain to me what it is I'm longing
for.*

*Yr. loving daughter,
Anna*

Anna folded the letter, put it in an envelope, and tucked it
into the pocket of her carpetbag. Then she turned out the
gas lamp, climbed under her covers, and imagined ladies
and gentlemen kissing against the trunks of trees, hoping
to put herself to sleep with such pictures before morning.

FOUR

THE YOUNG DOCTOR William Steward arrived on Sunday of
the second week Anna was in residence at the Stewards'
house. He was not alone.

"Her name is Elsbeth and they are betrothed," Louisa
said smugly. "Just last week it happened."

Anna was beating the egg yolks for custard.

"They will marry in June, so Dr. Steward says. June
twentieth on a Saturday," Louisa said. "Her parents are extremely well-off."

"That's very nice," Anna said weakly. Her legs had
turned to water with the news of young Dr. Steward.

"Miss Elsbeth's family will give the wedding," Louisa
said. "They live in Richmond and have quite a bit of land
for a garden party."

Louisa was what Anna's father would have called pale
red Irish—blue-veined and fleshy. She was bad-tempered
and remote but Anna would have liked to be friends with
her. Sometimes Anna left the door to her room open, hop-

ing for conversation, but nothing had happened between them; by her demeanor Louisa was almost contemptuous.

This Sunday afternoon, however, was different. Louisa was taken by the new circumstances of Dr. William Steward.

"He has brought many young ladies here. Some quite beautiful, I'd say. And he is dashing, don't you think?"

Anna nodded. She had forgotten the number of eggs she'd cracked into the blue pottery bowl, how much milk to add.

"But this is the first one he's been respectful of. Watch him at the table, how deferential he is, how sickly sweet," Louisa said. "I think she looks like a donkey."

She looked like an ordinary dark-haired lady with a small face and bright pink cheeks, not particularly pretty, although she was elegant in her brown velvet costume and her voice had a pleasant melody to it, not too high.

The young doctor smiled at Anna when she brought in the first course.

"So you've arrived in Washington," he said politely, and there were acknowledged murmurs around the table as if he had made an original observation.

"After all, he is thirty-five and it's time he got married," Louisa said when Anna returned to the kitchen with the plates for the first course. "He's been to jail, you know."

"I didn't know," Anna said.

"Well, he has. He's very hot-tempered," Louisa said. "Once he got into a fight in a hotel and the police took him to jail for that because they couldn't calm him down. And another time he turned over a carriage on Pennsylvania Avenue because he'd had an argument with the driver." She sliced the lamb for the main course. "But he'd had quite a bit of brandy, too."

Louisa heaped the potatoes and vegetables on the serving platters. "What's more—and you can't let on you know a thing about this or I'd be killed for it—he has a child nineteen years old already. From a serving girl who came from Ireland, County Cork, and used to have your room in fact, and he seduced her when he was only sixteen and in university. I know it from a confidential source."

She handed the platters to Anna. "Now you take in the main course."

In bed that night, Anna couldn't sleep. The night was black and starless outside her tiny window. The room was cold and damp and smelled of roasted lamb, and the evening weighed on her as if it had substance. She longed for home.

At home in Rhyl, her mother would be alive, unwasted by the sea journey to America, making supper in the kitchen, Fiona and Roger setting the table, churning butter, her older brothers playing the fiddle while she worked, and they'd be singing in the golden-shadowed light from the lamps.

She had made a mistake to come to America. She had dreamed beyond herself, and her hopes had fallen like snow into a ravine between her and what she hoped to be. In England, when they met, the young Dr. William Steward had made a promise. Or had he?

She knew nothing of men. She had been kissed only once by Sam Boller behind the sweets shop and once, which did not count at all, by her uncle, who should not have been kissing his nieces but he did and had a reputation for it so the nieces knew to stay out of his company.

She had thought the young Dr. Steward would save her. Lift her out of the ordinariness of her daily life to some other place. This house, perhaps, where she would be in the seat of the dreary Elsbeth eating bread pudding on a silver spoon.

"Anna?"

She had not even heard the sound of shoes along the corridor.

"Yes," she said quietly.

"It's William."

He opened the door to her room and the light from the hallway fell across her.

Her heart was beating so hard she could not speak.

"I was very glad to see you today but I couldn't express my pleasure with Elsbeth and my parents at the table for Sunday lunch."

He spoke in a loud whisper. Even Louisa in the room across the hall could have heard him.

"I'm sleeping." It was all she could think of to say to him.

"Oh, I see." He sat down on the bed. "Talking in your sleep?" He took her hands and kissed them.

"No," she said.

"No?" He laughed softly. "No what?" He leaned over, holding her hands lightly beside her head, and kissed her on the lips. "No kissing?" he asked when he had lifted his head.

"Just no." She scrambled up. "You have a betrothal." She pulled the coverlet off the bed and wrapped it around her.

"What difference is that?"

"It is a difference."

He took her waist and pulled her toward him, kissing the ends of her fingers.

"Please leave," she said.

"Leave? I have only just come." He pulled her next to him.

She had a moment's hesitation. Sensing it, the young doctor took advantage, grabbing her breasts and pulling her against him. Perhaps if he had been less brash.

"If you won't leave, then I will," she said.

"I thought you were fond of me," he said. "You gave that impression."

"I was," she replied. "I am."

"Then." He took hold of her face.

Instinctively, without a thought of repercussions, she slapped him.

Then she opened the door to her bedroom, walked down the corridor to the kitchen, and stood by the fireplace still smouldering with the red embers of the evening's fire. She heard his footsteps down the corridor and up the back stairs behind the kitchen to the second floor.

Back under the covers of her bed, she left the lamp on. The shadows danced eerily across the wall and she felt disengaged, as if her mind and body had separated with the young doctor's arrival in her room. Her body was restless, full of longing, but what her mind knew of William Steward's visit was clear. The only power a young servant girl with uncommon dreams could have was to refuse.

It was almost dawn, time to begin the preparations for the day, before her body finally settled into the small cup in the mattress and she fell asleep.

FIVE

MONDAY MORNING WAS particularly dreary, too dark to call day, gray-black with a steady rain and cold, when Anna walked with Louisa to the market on Wisconsin Avenue. It was like a midwinter day in England when the spirits of the people on the streets rose to compensate.

Louisa, taller than Anna, clumsy, mannish in her gait, slipped her arm through Anna's and they walked along for some time in silence, their bonnets shielding them from the rain.

"So I see Dr. William Steward has taken a fancy to you," Louisa said finally.

"What do you mean?" Anna asked.

"I'm not foolish. There he was in your room last night. I heard him come."

"Oh, that," Anna said, flushed with embarrassment. "Nothing actually happened."

Louisa laughed. "Oh, yes. I can imagine nothing happened."

The houses in Georgetown were built side by side with shared walls to contain the heat, brick with long windows on either side of the entry doors. This morning because the weather was dreadful, the carriages had been brought around front and the horses were rambunctious in the cold air, prancing, splashing Anna and Louisa as they walked so that by the time they reached Wisconsin Avenue where the markets were, they were covered with mud.

"He is betrothed, after all," Anna said.

"So?" Louisa shrugged. "How else are you going to have a gentleman unless he is betrothed or married, I wonder."

"That isn't having anything."

"Tell me." Louisa gripped her arm tighter. "What really happened?"

"Nothing happened," Anna said. "And that is the truth."

Louisa's arm slackened in Anna's.

"Before long you will see that you can trust me," Louisa said angrily. "That I am altogether trustworthy. And then you'll tell me what really happened to you."

At the vegetable market, Arthur was buying apples for his horses.

"How's Miss High and Mighty?" he said in Anna's ear as he left. Anna bought apples, potatoes and snap beans, figs and raisins, as much as she could carry, while Louisa was at the butcher's. Then they went to the bakery together, sat in the corner at a small table in the window overlooking the shoppers on Wisconsin Avenue, and had cake and coffee. Louisa knew everyone—the shopkeepers, the people on the streets, the small children with their nannies, the char cleaning the bakery floor of mud.

"After all," Louisa said, "I have been with the Stewards for ten years."

"And you'll stay forever."

Louisa shook her head. "I don't know about forever but I'll stay until I'm forty, I suppose, or fat or old. Why do you ask? Are you ready to leave already?"

Anna brushed the drying mud off her skirt. "Not yet. But I won't stay until I'm forty."

"What's to do with a life but work in a house? You have to eat."

"Ladies marry. At least in Wales they do."

"The only man at the Stewards' to marry is Arthur and I'd as soon drop dead," Louisa said. They paid for their sweets, gathered their packages, and headed home.

Anna could tell that a secret confession was brewing by the nature of the silence between them, the way that Louisa looked at her. But they had almost walked to the corner of N and 30th Streets where the Stewards' house was before Louisa spoke.

"You see, I have an arrangement."

"What do you mean?" Anna adjusted her packages.

"The elder Dr. Steward." She shrugged, considering, and then said coyly, "He is very fond of red hair."

Louisa pulled a lock of red hair out of her bonnet and ran it through her teeth. "You see?"

Anna giggled. "I do," she said.

"For ten years since I first came to work, he has been visiting me. Always he comes when one of his patients dies and he's full of sadness. Sometimes I pray for an epidemic of influenza," she said. "So now you understand?"

Anna nodded.

"And now you can tell me what happened when young Dr. Steward came to your room."

Anna hesitated. She did not want to disappoint Louisa, especially on the verge of this new friendship, but she shook her head.

"Nothing at all," she said.

"Very well," Louisa said crossly, walking up the back steps which led to the kitchen. "If that's the way you're going to be." She put her packages on the kitchen table. "Just leave the marketing here." Her voice was frozen.

"I'm sorry to have offended you," Anna said, taking off her bonnet and brushing the wet hair off her face.

"No offense whatsoever," Louisa said.

"It's lovely what you told me about yourself."

"It's not lovely at all," Louisa said. "It's my life."

All morning they worked together in the kitchen and then in the laundry, washing and folding. Louisa was cordial but for the moment at least the friendship was closed.

When Anna went to her room that evening, exhausted by her restless night and her failed attempt at friendship, a note had been pushed under her door.

"Dear Miss Jermyn," he had written. "Please forgive me. Yours, Wm. Steward."

She put the note in her carpetbag, turned off the gas lamp, and fell asleep fully clothed on top of the bed.

SIX

ON ANNA'S HALF day off, she went to a teahouse Louisa had shown her on P Street with a book about medicine she had borrowed from the Stewards' library. But her mind drifted from descriptions of the body, the digestive system with detailed pictures in color of the stomach and esophagus and intestines, the mysterious glands. She put the book down and ordered strong tea and a strawberry scone, took the stationery from her carpetbag, and started a letter.

Dear Mama, she wrote on the 12th of December, 1890.

> *Last night I slept fitfully and dreamed of drowning. The ship on which I traveled had tipped over and I was hanging on to the side of it for dear life. Louisa, whose friendship with me began and finished yesterday, came to my room to wake me and said I had been screaming out. She insisted I was screaming "William," which is the name of the young doctor she would like to think is filling my mind. I doubt it was William I was saying. But he is the subject of my letter to you. He would like to have me as a convenience, now and after he marries as well, which he is doing the 20th of June in Richmond, Virginia—a lady called Elsbeth who is plain-looking and well-to-do. If I were to agree to such a thing, I'd grow old and fat in this situation because, Louisa tells me, there is no one to marry of interest in Washington at all, except gentlemen already married, and that, to me, is a life like death.*
>
> *So this morning, raining as if the world is ending, I decided—and you will be proud of me to read this—the only power a girl has with a man is her virtue and so I will keep mine.*
>
> *I am reading medical books and presently I have quite a thick one about the workings of the body to*

*study on my days off. I would prefer a situation in the
office of a physician to cleaning and cooking.*

*In my dream of you, you were alive but I had left you
in Wales in the kitchen with your hair down and it was
not gray but the color of chestnuts as I remember it as
a child.*

*It gives me great pleasure to write these letters to
you.*

*I have heard from Father, who tries to be light-
hearted. Fiona and Roger are fine, he tells me, going to
a school in Chester, where they have moved in with his
cousin. The address is c/o Jermyn, Sheboygan, Wisconsin, United States of America. There is a large Welsh
community there.*

*I am thinking of cutting my hair to my shoulders and
wearing it down.*

Yr. loving daughter,
Anna

She took another piece of stationery from her carpetbag.

Dear Dr. Steward,
    Thank you for your note. It was kind of you to write.
*Presently I am studying medical books on my half day
off and in the evenings. I would appreciate it if you
would let me know if you hear of a position as a doctor's assistant. I have a temperament for medicine.*

Yours,
Miss Anna Jermyn.

She dropped the letter in her bag, paid her bill, wrapped
her mother's cape around her shoulders, and went back out
into the weather. At least, she decided as she hurried down
N Street, late for the preparations for supper, she no longer
had the temperament to be a handmaid to Queen Victoria.

SEVEN

THE YOUNG DR. Steward was a man of obsessions. Even as a child, he fixed like a crazed dog, so Mrs. Steward told Anna in confidence, using those exact words when she realized over the Christmas holidays that the Welsh servant girl had become the object of her son's extreme affections.

"Sometimes I worry about his sense of balance," she said to Anna, who recognized the warning.

The quality was attractive. It gave him an intensity, a sense of danger, and in spite of this tendency to excess, or perhaps because of it, he was a remarkable surgeon. He had a reputation not only in Washington but in the Northeast, where he was asked to speak on developments in surgical procedures, especially bacterial infections and anesthesia.

Ever since he had finished medical school and set up practice with his father in Georgetown, he had lived on the first floor of a modest row house across the street from Georgetown University Hospital since he kept such long hours. But at the beginning of January he moved, to all intents and purposes, back to his parents' house on N Street.

"So he can look at you every night at dinner pretending to be engaged in conversation, I imagine," Louisa had said to Anna, not without sarcasm. It was perfectly clear to everyone—his parents, his sisters, poor Elsbeth arranging for her trousseau to be done up in silks from Paris.

Anna was perplexed. She could feel his eyes fly after her when she served dinner or happened upon him in the library when she was dusting or on a walk after supper. Once in the corridor behind the kitchen, she found him opening the door to her room.

"You startled me," he said.

"I should think so." She opened her door and he followed her in.

"You can't," she whispered. "Louisa's in her room."

"Damn Louisa."

"You oughtn't be here besides." She sat down primly on the bed.

"I've a perfect right to visit."

"But not in my room," Anna said.

"Then what can I do to persuade you?" he asked, leaning against the door so she couldn't push him out. "How can we be friends?"

"As I told you, I have been studying medicine on my own. These books—" she indicated the large stack of books in which she had been reading about the developments in medicine, particularly about drugs like quinine and the use of morphine and opium, quite common in England but not in the United States. "You could give me a position as your nurse. I know a lot just from the reading I have done."

"I don't want you for my nurse," he said, crossing his arms over his chest and holding the door closed with his foot.

"Then," she said with a quick coquettish toss of her head, "you could ask me to be your wife." She laughed gaily and pushed him out of the room. "Now leave quickly before I tell your father that you are showing signs of mental trouble."

The Stewards had been physicians in Washington since the Civil War. They were comfortable, not wealthy but socially secure. Since the election of Benjamin Harrison as President of the United States in 1888, when the elder Dr. Steward was appointed physician to the new President, their lives had changed dramatically, suddenly graced by circumstance during a time of ease and wealth and conviviality in Washington. Certainly they did not wish to sacrifice the pleasure of their association with the White House to some romantic whim on the part of their only son. So plans continued for the wedding in June in Richmond in spite of the long lovesick countenance of the young Dr. Steward.

Dear Mama, Anna had written.

Today is the first day of the new year and snowing. The snow piles up here soft as silk, although it does not

*last very long because, according to the young Dr. Stew-
ard, Washington is below sea level and the humidity is
such that everything is damp and flimsy. Dr. Steward is
teaching me a great deal lately about ladies and what a
life in a large house is like with servants and supper
served by someone else and parties. He knows he ought
to marry the perfect Elsbeth and live the life designed
for him. But he is not sure his heart is in it.*

*I am studying medicine. Here there are many women
who are doctors, even colored women, quite strange in
this country, which made the colored slaves and then
fought a war about it. I do not know whether I will be
able to qualify for medical school since I had so little
school in Wales, but there are possibilities in America.
One does not have to marry to escape the life of a servant, but it is preferable.*

*I have heard from Father in Wisconsin, which is lo-
cated far to the north and west. He has found a small
farm which he is homesteading, close to his cousin. The
Welsh settlers do not bother to speak English and long
for home. So they should have stayed home is what I
think. I don't know when I will see Father and Fiona
and Roger again—Wisconsin is so far away.*

*I have developed nerve. You would be pleased with
me.*

> *Yr. loving daughter,*
> *Anna*

Later Anna believed the brain tumor removed on the fifth
of January, 1891, from the left side of the brain of the Secretary of War altered the course of events and sealed her
fate. The first operation to remove a brain tumor had occurred in England in 1882, but the operation had not been
performed in America until the Secretary of War for President Harrison lost his sight and, suffering from terrible
headaches, went to the young Dr. William Steward, who
agreed in spite of the high risk and chance for failure to
perform the first brain tumor surgery in the United States.
There was great excitement in the medical community because the surgery was new and the patient important.

When he died on the operating table, with a story in the newspaper the following day and plenty of gossip among the city's physicians, the Stewards, particularly the elder Dr. Steward, blamed the arrival of Anna Jermyn deviling his son's susceptible heart.

"I did the best I could," the young Dr. Steward said. "He would as likely have died if another doctor had done the operation."

But his father was convinced that William's unsettled state of mind was responsible for the death of the Secretary of War.

Anna overheard the violent argument upstairs from her own bedroom, where she was reading a large medical book, memorizing various bacteria and their treatments. She turned off the gas lamp beside her bed and lay very still, certain the young doctor would come to her when the shouting stopped. Which he did do, full of excitement and resolve.

"Anna," he said, loud enough for Louisa to hear, as she told Anna the following day. William Steward sat down beside her on the bed.

"I want you to marry me," he said.

She sat up, pushing him away gently.

"But you already have someone to marry in June."

"I have just now written her a letter telling her I am sorry for this reversal."

"You have done that?" Anna asked.

"I have. And I've just spoken with my parents."

"I overheard you speak to your parents from here," she said. "They did not seem enthusiastic about your conversation."

He kissed her hard on the lips, pulling at her nightdress.

"Please," he whispered in her ear.

"No," she said. "No. No. No. No. No."

EIGHT

THE SEATS ON the train from Washington to Chicago were made of horsehair and the backs had a slight concave curve, which made the long autumn journey across half the United States uncomfortable. William spoke very little. Anna considered his fine straight features in profile, the darkness of his countenance, the way he situated himself on the seats, constantly changing position as if the bones themselves were seeking readjustment to a sudden new life. He was a stranger to her.

They had been married the past winter on the first of February in Alexandria, Virginia, by a justice of the peace, attended by the justice's wife and his fourteen-year-old daughter. No one in the Steward family expressed an interest in being present.

"He's ruined for Washington, you know," Louisa had said to Anna, who had continued to work at the Stewards' until the end of February since, according to Mrs. Steward, her passage to America had been paid and she owed them time without recompense. "You can't be the son of the President's personal physician and marry a servant, especially when you are already betrothed."

Anna shrugged. "He had a choice," she said.

"You trapped him," Louisa said crossly, deeply, displeased at Anna's good fortune.

"As you say, I am a servant and he is wellborn, so what power have I to trap?" she asked, kneading the dough for cinnamon rolls.

"You have the power of sex," Louisa said.

Dear Mama, Anna had written several months after her marriage.

> *You may be disappointed to learn that I am married to the same young doctor I have mentioned to you who was betrothed to someone else. We may not be able to*

*remain in Washington because William's father is a man
of considerable importance and he is humiliated by this
marriage and William's behavior to the other young
woman, called Elsbeth, quite plain and, he says, dull as
well.*

*I find it odd to be married, not at all as I imagined,
rather lonely. I don't know whether I love him or if that
is even important. Sometimes I don't care for the smell
of him in the bedroom especially and he can be sullen.
In fact, his moods are like thunderstorms. They go from
sunny to a terrible blackness without warning. I do not
know whether I am responsible for these changes or not,
or whether we humans simply slip through the world as
isolated souls. I am feeling much older than seventeen.*

*It has occurred to me that love between a man and a
woman is too mysterious to count on or to expect. I feel
certain that William loved me more because I was unat-
tainable. Now we are together, his feelings are different
than they were. I feel like an animal, alternately curious
and on guard, sensitive to scents.*

*I wonder, did you love Father? Actually love him as
we read about in stories?*

Yr. loving daughter,
Anna

*P.S. I would not of course ask you such an imperti-
nent question if you were to actually read this letter.*

The plans, insofar as the young Dr. Steward had been able
to make plans, had been to live in the small house across
the road from Georgetown Hospital until the clouds lifted
on their marriage. And then one evening in the parlor after
supper, the elder Dr. Steward, in the company of several
family members, had said, "Given your present circumstances, you might as well be living with the Indians."

"I think that's a splendid idea, Father," William replied
in a cold temper. "I would very much like to live with the
Indians."

That evening he told Anna.

"We are moving West to work with the Indians," he
said.

"I didn't know you had an interest in the Indians," Anna said, astonished.

"I have just discovered my interest this evening," he replied.

And so, as Anna wrote her father, they were swept out of Washington like floor dust.

NINE

THE SECRETARY OF the Bureau of Indian Affairs suggested northern Wisconsin around Lake Superior, where the Chippewe had settled. There was a small town called Ashland in need of a surgeon and especially in need of a hospital for the Indians on the Bad River Reservation just west of town.

Ashland, in the heart of Lake Chippewe country, was founded at about the same time as the LaPointe Treaty in 1854, when the Chippewe chiefs signed an agreement to divide their land and set up reservations. Though remote and very cold, the town had become, by the late nineteenth century, a shipping center for iron ore from the Gogebic Iron Range and for timber as well as brownstone quarried nearby. There were four railroads serving the town, which was built on a plateau above the shore of the icy blue Lake Chequanegon, and only one hospital, which was understaffed. The Chippewe of Bad River Reservation refused to come to town for medical attention.

"We want our own hospital," the young Chippewe spokesman called Hole-in-the-Day, the son of the former chief, said.

The land where Anna and William Steward settled in the autumn of 1891 was extraordinarily beautiful, peppered with spring-fed lakes, dark blue spruce, and cedar forests.

The house into which the Stewards moved was a large but unpretentious clapboard farmhouse on the edge of town with a cleared path through a forest of blue spruce down to the lake, where Anna walked in the late evening, long after supper while she waited for William to come home from the hospital. The northern light made pale yellow ribbons through the trees, stripes of silver on the lake. It was a strange landscape, like a still life with a blue cast of shadow from so much water and sky, conveying a sense of human diminishment and isolation.

From the start, the plan was to make the house into a small hospital for the Chippewe who lived on the reservation and for William to do surgery at the hospital in Ashland until the hospital was opened in their house.

"Turning our house into a hospital can be your charge," William said to Anna.

Anna was pleased with her charge. During the long, lonely afternoons, when she worked without help to set up the hospital, she would pretend she was a physician with imaginary patients in crisis whose lives she could save.

She set up a parlor and bedroom downstairs for herself and William and turned the bedrooms, eight in all, into hospital rooms for the Indians. When news of the Stewards' arrival had gotten around, however, the Indians expressed no intention of leaving the reservation for a hospital in Ashland.

"You'll have to persuade Hole-in-the-Day," people in Ashland told Anna and William. "The Chippewe think of him as their physician."

Hole-in-the-Day was young to be a leader of the Chippewe—in his early twenties with a small daughter and a silent, pretty wife.

"She is like you," Hole-in-the-Day said to Anna just after they met, when Anna remarked on the loveliness of his wife. "Only you are from another country and have hot blood."

He was tall for a Chippewe, long-legged, with a dark, rectangular face, intense and handsome; he was trained by his grandfather as a shaman, a man of spirit, a medicine man. He had a dignity about him, an impenetrable wall, which disallowed the common dismissal with which the white men treated the other Indians at Bad River.

William traveled daily to Bad River between surgeries

in Ashland to examine patients on the reservation. Always Hole-in-the-Day accompanied him, not with hostility or even curiosity but as if he were required to witness what the doctor did. It was nevertheless a gesture of distrust.

"You have people who are dying and could be saved," William said to Hole-in-the-Day one afternoon following the death from gangrene of a young man whose life could have been spared if he had agreed to allow Dr. Steward to amputate his leg.

Hole-in-the-Day shrugged. "They do not want to leave the reservation."

"He can't be persuaded," William said to Anna after one of their visits to Bad River. "I have known stubborn men like him."

He rode with Anna seated in front of him on the horse, his hands holding the reins across her lap, through the dark pine forest, damp and rich with the smell of evergreens. "If the Chippewe don't want a hospital, I will not be the one to force it on them."

"Let me talk to him," Anna said.

"To Hole-in-the-Day?" William asked. "It would be inappropriate for you to go alone."

"What could happen?"

"Anything could happen," William said.

But Anna went to see Hole-in-the-Day alone.

It was an early June morning, brightly sunny and cool. William had left with the carriage for the hospital in Ashland before light. Anna put a blanket on the back of her horse, bridled him, and took off across the fields, along the lake to the pine forest which marked the boundary of Ashland and through which a horse path had been made to Bad River Reservation. Riding at a slow canter through the dark woods, she felt wicked, as if she had embarked on an adventure of betrayal.

The path opened onto a clearing, a large field of low grass with cabins scattered, a few wigwams, and small clusters of Indians walking with baskets and cooking in front of their wigwams. There was a pervasive silence which Anna had noticed the other times she had been to the reservation with William, as if their arrival had been announced in advance and the Indians had fallen silent in reaction. She slowed her horse to a walk as she passed a group of five or six older women; one she recognized as Grandmother Yellow Flower, Hole-in-the-Day's mother, a small, sharp-eyed, distrustful woman poised for trouble.

"Hole-in-the-Day is there." Grandmother Yellow Flower nodded with her head. "Where is the doctor man?"

"I have come alone," Anna said. She slid off her pony and walked along with the women.

"He'll be coming soon," Grandmother Yellow Flower said with disdain.

"Not until the afternoon. He comes after he finishes at the hospital. I have come to talk to Hole-in-the-Day."

"He is working," Grandmother Yellow Flower said.

"I'll wait."

Anna followed the path in the direction Grandmother Yellow Flower had pointed, past two wigwams with children playing in the dry dirt, past a cabin where a baby was whimpering, up a long hill to another cabin where she could see Hole-in-the-Day standing against the sky. Her heart took flight.

She stopped less than twenty yards from the cabin where Hole-in-the-Day was attending the birth of a baby and leaned against a tree. He had seen her. He didn't catch her eye but she could feel that he had seen her, and she leaned against the tree with her face in the sun feeling beautiful.

Grandmother Yellow Flower had followed her up the hill. Anna could hear the old woman scuffling but she didn't turn around until she was right there beside her handing her a plum from the bowl she carried.

"You'd better eat this. He will be a long time," she said and cocked her head examining Anna's face. "You have too small a nose."

"That is because I'm Welsh," Anna said. "The Welsh have small noses."

"It does not look right," Grandmother Yellow Flower said. "It looks like a bump instead of a nose." But she was smiling a broad, toothy smile, full of mischief, and she announced that she would tell Hole-in-the-Day he had company.

"I'm not company," Anna said. "I've come on business."

"I'll say the girl with a bump for a nose is here on business," Grandmother Yellow Flower said. "And he will say, No. Tell her to go home."

But Hole-in-the-Day didn't tell her to go home. When Grandmother Yellow Flower spoke to him, he walked toward the tree where Anna was leaning. Behind him, Grandmother Yellow Flower stood facing Anna, the bowl of plums still in her arms, and a woman came out of the cabin, a young woman who wore her black hair loose and to her waist and who had a look of interest on her face which Anna could recognize even from that distance as a curiosity between two women about a man.

"Hello," Hole-in-the-Day said. He took the plum still uneaten from her hand, ate it, and pitched the seed behind her toward the trees. "You have come about the hospital?" he asked.

"Yes, I have." She shifted her weight and looked up at him. "My husband is ready to open the hospital now, this week, for people at your reservation who are too ill to stay at home."

"Do you know about medicine?" he asked, his arms across his chest. He was a great deal taller than she was and he looked down at her with a private amusement.

"I have a medical book I read at night before I go to sleep. But I didn't study medicine in school. I didn't finish school."

"I didn't finish school either," Hole-in-the-Day said. "I didn't even start. But I know about medicine from my grandfather."

"Then you could help us with the hospital. That's what we've been sent to Ashland to do. Start a hospital."

He shrugged. "I will work with you," Hole-in-the-Day said. "If you want to make a hospital, the Chippewe will come. But I will not work with the cold-eyed doctor."

Anna smiled up at him. "I have made a hospital," she said. "You should come and see it."

"Tomorrow I will come see it," he said. "Or next week."

When Grandmother Yellow Flower called to say, "Hurry, the baby is coming," he had already turned away from Anna, headed back to the cabin, and she mounted her horse, trotted through the reservation, and then galloped along the path to Ashland, her one hand clinging to his mane, her hair flying.

"Hole-in-the-Day said he will come visit the hospital tomorrow," Anna said when William came home that evening.

"He did not tell me you had gone to the reservation today when I saw him," William said with an edge.

"Maybe he forgot I was there."

"No, Anna," William said. "I don't think he forgot."

That night, William made love to her, softly at first and then on and on into the early morning until her legs ached.

"If it's a baby you've been wanting, you should have one now," he said in the morning as they were dressing.

She smiled at him and said nothing. She had been wanting something, she thought, perhaps it was a baby after all and she had mistaken the desire for something else.

TEN

Dear Mama, Anna wrote in May of 1893.

> *The bumblebee ought to be too fat to fly with tiny and transparent wings bearing the weight of the enormous body, but it flies easily—not fast but without great labor. I became a bumblebee.*
>
> *The baby born April 1, 1893 was two babies, both boys, called James and Robert. James was too small to survive more than a few hours but Robert is extremely well and fat with cinnamon-colored hair and bright red cheeks. I am grateful for this child familiar to me as William is not. Sometimes at supper I look at him across*

the table—and he is quite handsome to see—stirred by his presence but wondering whether we have met before, whether he is a man I know as a casual acquaintance, so foreign are we to one another.

He has disgraced his parents by marrying me. He tells me he will not go back to Washington ever.

Yr. loving daughter,
Anna

AFTER THE BABY, William became unpredictable. He was alternately gentle, almost soft, and violently temperamental.

Once, late at night, he opened the window of their bedroom and threw his black medical bag, his overcoat, and a print of Washington in 1800 out in the snow. Anna pretended to be sleeping. By the time she woke in the morning, he had already retrieved his belongings and brought her a cup of hot coffee with milk. Another time, after he had been called to the hospital in Ashland for an emergency surgery in which the young woman, injured on her horse, had died while he was operating, he came home to find Anna in the rocker by the fire writing a letter to her mother.

"It is disturbing these letters you write to your mother," he said hanging his coat on a hook in the entry hall. "She is dead."

"Of course she is dead. You don't think I am imagining her alive, do you?" Anna said softly. "I simply like to write to her as a kind of diary."

He had gone into the kitchen, lit the fire under the kettle, and come back into the parlor, his sleeves rolled up, his hair disheveled, a look on his face she had not seen before.

"I want you now," he said and lifted her out of the rocker. He pushed her on her back on the thin rug by the fireplace and came down on her with a kind of desperation.

That night, after he had gone to bed, he asked her not to have Hole-in-the-Day work with her at the hospital.

"But you know I work with him at Bad River during the

mornings while you're in surgery," she said. "He comes with me while I visit patients."

"I know you work with him at the reservation," William said. "I just don't want him to come here to the hospital, to our house."

The hospital—Anna's hospital, for the making of it had been her work—had been receiving patients since just after the June morning in 1892 when Anna had asked Hole-in-the-Day to allow the Indians to come to the hospital she and William had started in their home. By 1893, two resident nurses shared a bedroom in the back of the house next to the kitchen and one young doctor on regular duty lived in a small cottage nearby. Anna worked at the hospital in the afternoons and at Bad River most mornings of the week. After William left for surgery, Anna would strap Robert on a board as the Chippewe had taught her to do and ride with him on her back to Bad River, visiting patients not ill enough for the hospital. Usually she was joined by Hole-in-the-Day and sometimes Grandmother Yellow Flower.

Dear Mama, Anna wrote on the first of April, 1894.

> *Robert is one today, chubby and blond—with perfectly round, wide-set eyes. Occasionally when I look at him, I see the memory of your face in his.*
>
> *We are together all of the time—he and I—like twins. In the mornings we go to the reservation where I visit the ill, and in the afternoons we take a long walk by the lake and come back for tea with the nurses.*
>
> *I cannot tell you how happy I am to have this baby boy. Complete is actually the word, as if I had parts of me missing before he was born.*
>
> *William loves him but he is too intense to be a father. He worries about strange things, like Robert's talking. Why doesn't he develop a vocabulary sooner and isn't he bowlegged and was there high intelligence in my family or is there some chance with Robert of limited accomplishment? It makes me cross. Usually I don't let on; however, yesterday when he brought up the subject of the intelligence of my family, I did say we had suffi-*

cient intelligence but not enough to be mentally unbalanced as happened with the Stewards. Today we are not speaking.

> *Yr. loving daughter,*
> *Anna*

Dear Mama, Anna wrote in the summer of 1894.

I have not actually told you about William except to say that I do not know him well.

He is very dark, thicker than Englishmen tend to be, much taller than the Welsh, with a strong carriage—striking to look at, and I find myself quite soft in his presence. But he has a deep melancholy—we go days without talking—which, he tells me, is common amongst American men. He knows no idle conversation.

> *Yr. loving daughter,*
> *Anna*

Dear Mama, Anna wrote in September 1895.

Day—I mentioned him before—Hole-in-the-Day—a name which suits his lightness of temper—is a big conversationalist. We spend many hours together at the hospital.

I am at ease with the Indians. Like the Welsh, they have a fierce individuality which stands in the way of cooperation. So they are difficult and stubborn. Day tells me I am beautiful as evening.

Evening in Wisconsin leaves me out of breath—the way the light falls on the lakes and the trees, especially the blue spruce. You feel diminished by such height and space, incomprehensible, unlike little Wales. I am not unhappy but I would not like to die here. There is too much sky.

> *Yr. loving daughter,*
> *Anna*

Dear Mama, Anna wrote in November 1895.

I ache for another child but William says no. There is too much work to be done, he says, now that we are building a new hospital, a real one, large and closer to

*the reservation than our house is. We should wait until
Robert is older, he says.*

So we are careful and I don't argue with him.

*I seem to be in love with Robert. He is a determined
little boy and cheerful. He marches around the reservation just in front of me, refusing my hand, and in the afternoon he likes to go to the site of the new hospital and
watch the men, mostly Indians, clearing away the trees.*

*Sometimes, I feel that it is Robert to whom I am mar-
ried. Although I certainly love William, he is preoccupied and only occasionally and surprisingly does he
turn his attention and then we talk in the old engaging
way we used to talk.*

*It isn't good for me to be the one responsible for our
move out here. The weather is cold and though the land
is beautiful, it is hard land to live on, particularly the
winters. And there is none of the glory that William used
to have in Washington being a surgeon for the rich and
important. Just hard work.*

> *Yr. loving daughter,*
> *Anna*

Anna did not write again for a year because the winter in
Ashland was particularly difficult, cold and windy, and although there wasn't any memorable event, the long days
were taken with hard work. In early March, Anna got
pneumonia from which it took her months to recover to
full health.

Dear Mama, she wrote in the fall of 1896.

*William has asked that I not spend time with Hole-in-
the-Day. It is unbecoming, he says.*

*Last week I was in attendance when Hole-in-the-
Day's wife had a new son called Flat Mouth, born
breech with some difficulty.*

*I hear from Father that Fiona has married a 2nd
cousin called Ralph Thomas and that Roger is sullen
and speaks only Welsh.*

> *Yr. loving daughter,*
> *Anna*

Anna started letters to her mother. There were among her letters many unfinished ones, but there was so much work to be done, especially at the reservation, where she was loved, and at the hospital, where she was looked to as in charge since William was often in surgery and remote besides, that she had very little time for anything but Robert and her work.

Dear Mama, she wrote in the spring of 1897.

I lost a baby this month, very early, but it was nevertheless upsetting—even for William, who had adjusted to the idea of another baby with some pleasure.

Robert plays with Day's baby boy, Flat Mouth. The name is ugly I think, but the boy is a striking baby with huge black eyes and a handsome face, already formed and he's not yet a year.

I have been attending the illness of a Chippewe girl, age six, who died last night. For days, since we knew she was probably going to die, I have sat with her mother by her bed.

I cannot imagine the death of a child. How can a mother want to go on afterwards? I do not believe in God as you did. Why, I wonder, don't I? You took us faithfully to church and said our prayers with us. But so it is. Death is death to me. Except I write these letters to you, and that faithfully.

> *Yr. loving daughter,*
> *Anna*

Dear Mama, Anna wrote in December 1897.

The earth as far as I can see is white, white over the trees and houses, over the lake, frozen and scattered with snow, and it ought to be beautiful but I am unsettled by so much whiteness.

I am no good at geography but I wish I could see where I am in relationship to Wales, to Rhyl, to New York where you are buried in St. Thomas R.C. Cemetery.

Do I exist, I sometimes wonder, if you cannot see me?

> *Yr. loving daughter,*
> *Anna*

Dear Mama, Anna wrote just before Christmas 1898.

> *There is an epidemic of influenza in Wisconsin, not just Wisconsin but everywhere according to the newspapers in Ashland. I have a sense of foreboding as if the air is flapping with invisible dangers.*
>
> Yr. loving daughter,
Anna

Anna had spent the year of 1898 hoping to have another child, but she did not conceive. William was unpredictable in temper and he had little time. He often came home late after she had fallen exhausted into bed and got up while it was still dark to dress for the day's work. Anna began to treat Robert as a confidant—Robert and Day—and as Robert got older, he replaced her letters to her mother as a listener. She wrote less than she had, although one spring afternoon, particularly damp and English, after reading a letter from Fiona about their mother, Anna took a pen and paper, did a line drawing from memory of her mother's face, and put it in a frame beside her bed.

ELEVEN

ONE THOUSAND FOUR hundred and six people died, mostly white children, some Indians, in an epidemic of diphtheria in Ashland, Wisconsin, which began on the 20th of December, 1898, when James Roswell, age eight, son of Abigale and John Roswell, was the first citizen to be diagnosed.

Diphtheria strangled children with an inflammatory lesion which in fatal cases formed in the pharynx, larynx, and nostrils a thick, leathery blue and white membrane composed of blood clots, bacteria, dead skin, and white blood cells. The disease was caused by a club-shaped bacillus which created toxic reactions involving primarily the heart and peripheral nerves. In the 1890s the Germans developed a vaccine which involved injecting the patient with the toxin of a disease to build up antibodies against it. Dr. Steward knew of a serum that could prevent death, but the epidemic struck Ashland and the Bad River Reservation so unexpectedly and traveled so swiftly that a supply of serum ordered from New York did not arrive in Wisconsin in time to save the lives of the children.

William put up the Christmas tree on the 20th of December in the main parlor of the hospital, and Anna decorated it with candles, ornaments, berries, and painted pine cones. The house smelled of pine and hardwood burning in the fireplaces in the parlors and the kitchen. That night the nurses played Christmas carols on the piano and everyone who was ambulatory and was well enough to sing, even the Indians, sang. Just after six P.M. James Roswell was diagnosed by Dr. Steward at home, where his family sat in a circle of premature mourning around his bed, and at nine William arrived with the news. Walking into the warm parlor to the singing of carols, he motioned to Anna, who stood by the piano with Robert sitting on her shoulders.

"We've had the first case," he said with a kind of desperation.

By the morning of the 21st of December, twenty people had been diagnosed by the physicians at Ashland Hospital. Ten of them were dead by afternoon, four of them Chippewe at Bad River.

"Don't take Robert to Bad River," William said.

"Is he any better here?" Anna asked.

"If we protect him," William said. "We need to keep him in our quarters away from everyone."

The first night of the epidemic, William changed his clothes and put a handkerchief over his face before he took Robert on his lap to tell him a story.

"Hole-in-the-Day's daughter is one of the cases at Bad River," William said after Robert had gone to bed.

Anna's throat caught.

"Did you see her?"

"I was there this afternoon."

"How bad is she?" Anna asked.

"She is bad," William said. "There is no such thing as good. She is like James Roswell was when I saw him yesterday, and this morning he is dead."

Anna put the kettle on the fire.

"I don't want you to go to the reservation tomorrow either," William said.

"Of course," Anna said.

"Don't even leave these rooms to go upstairs to the hospital. I have never seen such a contagious illness."

That night, Robert woke up fretful in the middle of the night, and Anna rocked him, sitting with him in her lap long after he had fallen asleep. His head was perspiring just under the neck.

"Come to bed, Anna," William called. "You'll catch your death."

"I'm warm enough," she said.

She didn't want to put Robert down, didn't want to relinquish his small firm body against her chest. When she did finally put him down, she pulled his cot over as close to her side of the bed as space would allow.

She could not sleep. Outside the moon was full, the trees were silver, and the wind sounded against the window. It should have been too cold for germs, she thought.

"William?" she said finally.

He was not sleeping.

"I was at Bad River yesterday with Robert and he played with Day's daughter. They sat around the fire in the wigwam and played a game with spoons and the kettle making music."

"There's nothing to be done for it," William said.

She pulled the feather comforter under her chin and stared into the darkness. "William?" she said, reaching for his hand. "She kissed Robert." She turned over on her side. "Did you hear me?"

"I heard you," William said. "Stay here. Stay in our quarters until it's over. That is the only thing to do. And don't think about what has already happened. What is too late to change. Of course Robert has been exposed. We've all been exposed. It's a matter of strength," he said. "And luck."

"He's very strong, don't you think?"

"He seems strong," William said.

They lay awake without speaking. Sometime in the middle of the night, one of the nurses knocked on the door to their quarters to say that Morning Sun, old and ill with pneumonia, was having difficulty breathing. But by the time William got to her bed, Morning Sun had stopped breathing.

At dawn, before the light, the day just beginning to brighten, Hole-in-the-Day arrived at the hospital and banged on the door to the Stewards' quarters. Anna answered the door.

"My wife is ill," he said, out of breath from riding. "My daughter has died in the middle of the night."

William pulled on his trousers and a coat.

Anna put her hand on Hole-in-the-Day's arm.

"It is very bad for everyone," he said darkly.

All day, Anna sat in her parlor with Robert, playing with him on the floor, reading to him on the bed, conscious of his breathing, the color of his skin, the temperature of his forehead, the light in his eyes. When one of the nurses brought lunch, Anna, wary of germs, gave Robert only peeled apples and bread from the middle of the loaf. During his nap, she lay down beside him and held his small plump hand in her own.

Lying like that, his head next to her shoulder, his hand in hers across her stomach, she was aware of the start of fever. At first she thought it was the heat from the fire. She got him up, carried him into the parlor away from the fire. She noticed, with a sinking heart, that his back and neck were very hot.

William came home at four and Robert was sitting beside Anna's rocker on a blanket, playing absently with blocks that Day had made for him. William put the kettle on, took off his shirt and his trousers, and put them in the hot water Anna kept on top of the stove to boil.

He came into the parlor. "What has been happening since I left?"

"I have been inside with Robert, as you said we should," Anna said. She did not say that Robert had been complaining of a sore throat, that his usual cheerful disposition had given way to crabby complaints, that he refused lunch and tea.

"It is making me ill to be inside," Robert said. "There is nothing to do all day and I have no friends here."

"Until the epidemic subsides, you have to stay inside," William said.

"What is the situation today?" Anna asked.

"I don't know how many have died today. Many. Hole-in-the-Day's wife—she is lovely. Do you talk to her often?" He sat down on the rocker.

"Almost never. She knows me, however."

"I'm sure she knows you," William said with an edge. "Her husband is your dear friend."

"How is she?" Anna asked, avoiding the implication.

"Already the film is over her eyes," William said. "She said to me, 'Take the covers off my eyes so I can look at you.'"

Robert stretched facedown across his mother's lap.

"It is too hot in here," he said. "Could we put out the fire?"

"Hot?" William put his hands on Robert's forehead. "Have you been checking?" he asked Anna.

"Yes," Anna said.

"And is your throat sore, Robert?" William asked.

"It was too sore for lunch. The apples scratched my throat," Robert said.

William listened to his chest and throat with a stethoscope. He picked him up and carried him to his bed.

"Put on some hot water," he called back to Anna. "And you, Robert," he said, "will have to stay in bed for a while."

William went into the kitchen where Anna was making a pot of tea. "Why didn't you tell me immediately when I came home?"

"I was afraid," Anna said. "And I was hoping it wasn't true."

"Well, now we have reason to be afraid," William said.

"You heard a rattle with your stethoscope?" Anna asked in a thin voice.

"That is what I heard."

"You are sure?"

"Listening for rattles is all I do lately," William said. "Of course I'm sure."

The days following swam together in Anna's mind, one bright watercolor day after the next, the weather deceitfully cheerful and sunny. Christmas came and went without a trace.

Hole-in-the-Day's wife died on the 24th of December. One hundred and fifty-seven was the count of the dead by Christmas Day, with hundreds more sick. Some nights William did not get home at all.

But Robert hung on, his breathing labored, his temperature flying up and down. Anna soaked his head and back with cold towels. Sometimes he drank some water and tea although it hurt him to swallow. All day Anna rocked him in the chair by the fireplace, telling him stories, singing him the songs her mother had sung to her, singing in Welsh, the familiar thick sound of the language like warm oatmeal in her mouth.

And then late in the afternoon of December 29, he died. When William came home for tea at four, bone-tired, exhausted by the daily losses, Anna was rocking Robert in the chair by the small fire, and William knew, before he even took off his overcoat, that his son was dead.

Later, Anna thought she must have known as well. There was a moment when her singing became louder and she didn't look down to check the child's breathing as she had been doing.

All that evening, William was sweet with Anna. He wrapped the child in a blanket, laid him in his cot, and slept with Anna in his arms. But sometime in the middle of the night, he lost his sense of balance. Anna, sleepless, heard a sound like the cry of an animal and saw William jump out of bed, open the window in their room, take Robert in his blanket out of the bed.

"No," she shouted.

"We have to kill the diphtheria," he said. "Kill it in the cold. Or we'll all die."

"Please," she said. "Give me the child. I'll take him to another room."

In the morning William left early, just as the sky was turning, and with the help of an orderly who worked in the hospital Anna buried Robert alone. They walked in silence down the path behind the hospital, through the dense forest of blue spruce, and the orderly broke up the frozen ground with a hole large enough to bury Robert in a shallow grave. Then Anna took her mother's cape from around her shoulders and laid it on the ground to protect him from the weather.

TWELVE

SPRING CAME EARLY in 1899, a clear wet spring with sharp rains and bright sunny afternoons reflecting silver off the lake, soft morning winds sweeping the lingering smell of death across Lake Superior and out of Ashland, Wisconsin.

In early February of that year, Anna and William moved into the new hospital, in a wing on the second floor with a view of the lake. They had adjoining single rooms, a bath with a bathtub—a luxury they had not had in the house on the lake—and a common room they could use for reading or conversation, although they had little time for either. What they did, well into the night, was work, William at the hospital and Anna with him at the hospital or on the reservation, where the population which had survived was weakened by the ravages of illness.

When they began to sleep at the new hospital, they pushed the single beds together in one room and slept with their arms entwined across the divide. But one afternoon in late March, Anna returned from the reservation to find the rooms single once again, with a note on her bed from William: "I have developed insomnia and ought not keep you awake. W."

It was not, Anna knew, the insomnia, although he had difficulty sleeping. It was her insistence on another child.

"Please William," she would say at night as he lay on his back, lifeless between his legs. "I need another baby. I can taste it."

"You lost that one baby in the womb," he'd say. "It was a bad sign."

"Look at the babies you deliver from women who have lost many babies," Anna said.

"They can be spoiled. Mrs. Austin had a damaged baby. So did Mrs. Pearis. Leave well enough alone, Anna."

"Please," Anna would beg him.

"Besides," he said to her one night while she sat silent in the darkness on the bottom of his bed, "I have shown evidence of madness."

That of course was true. On one occasion, she had found him in the operating room in the middle of the night looking for the ether.

"You don't understand," he had said to her. "I have *got* to go to sleep."

Another time he had cut his clothes in careful strips and dumped them in the incinerator.

"I don't want anything from before the epidemic," he had said. He blamed himself for the deaths.

Anna attributed his mental slippage to pressure and had concealed her hunger for a baby in her work at the reservation.

Hole-in-the-Day, reduced by the epidemic to one child, the son called Flat Mouth, his wife and daughter dead, worked with Anna. They had been wary of each other, formal since early in the months of her pregnancy with the twins. But after the epidemic they fell together, working side by side like husband and wife.

At night, lying in the single bed, listening to winter charge her window, to the impatient unsettlement of her husband in the adjoining room, Anna fell asleep imagining Day unbuttoning the wrists of her dress, kissing her arms on the inside veins, and she would kiss her own wrists.

"Hole-in-the-Day should have training as a physician,"

she said to William. "He could take care of the reservation himself. He knows a great deal."

"He hasn't been to school at all, Anna."

"Then you could train him," Anna said.

"You train him," William said. "You know about medicine."

So she did. She taught Day the way to bring a fever down, the way to prevent dehydration, to dress a wound, to perform minor surgery, to administer ether, to diagnose high blood pressure and heart failures, tumors, strokes, to use heroin as a cough suppressant, to provide women with the vegetable compound Pe-Ru-Na for the discomfort of their menses, to inoculate against typhoid and smallpox. They went from house to house, delivering babies, tending to influenza, intestinal infections, to superficial wounds, to the growing alcoholism on the reservation.

With the first soft promise of spring, the windows of Ashland opened, letting in the air. Pallid and arthritic from a long confinement in a small space, the families in the houses emerged at the front doors and stood in their gardens on the first warm day of the year.

On the first of April, a day too warm for coats and glittering with a young spring sun, Anna went to William's bed just as darkness fell.

"Please," she said to him. "I have waited long enough."

He did not reply.

She took his head in her hands and kissed his lips.

"Have you forgotten?"

"I can't," he said. "I cannot bear to have another child."

She stood, straightened her dress, brushed her hair falling from its pins off her face.

"I mean to have a child, William," she said.

It was not late, just before nine in the evening, and she went to the barn behind the hospital where the carriages and horses were kept. She hitched up her horse to a single wagon and rode off full of purpose to the Bad River Reservation.

Hole-in-the-Day lived in a wigwam, one of the few remaining at the reservation. He wore full Indian dress and spoke Chippewe, although he could speak English fluently. Unlike the other men Anna had known, broken by change, romantics by temperament like her father and William, Hole-in-the-Day survived reversal without the price of energy. There was something original about him which had caught her attention from the beginning, some internal sense of himself which did not have to do with being an Indian, she thought.

One night when her single bed was still beside William's and they slept with their arms wrapped around each other, Anna had asked William if he believed in God.

"Of course," he said. "Of course I do and you do as well, Anna," he said, as if to not believe was a failure of manners rather than of faith.

She had lain awake that night listening to the hollow corridors of the hospital echoing, the occasional high-pitched cry, remembering God as He had been to her in Wales when she did believe and He was substantial.

"The Chippewe believe that life after death is the same as life before it, only permanent," she said.

"We are not Chippewe."

"I wish I were. I wish for such clarity."

"And what pleasure is there in permanent happiness?" William asked.

"It doesn't matter whether it's true or not. Who's to say? No one comes back to tell us, after all," Anna said. "But the illusion matters. Otherwise you lose your energy."

Dear Mama, she had written that night when she couldn't sleep.

> I used to sit between you and Fiona at church and you would be sleeping through the sermon, weary from taking care of us all. Fiona would be playing house with her fingers on her lap and I'd be sitting listening to the timbre—not the words of course—of Mr. Mervyn Jones, dreaming of God.
>
> He was a large and handsome man with big hands and a splendid voice. And fearsome. That I liked in particular, knowing as I did that His terrible temper would

*be waged at my adversaries, never at me. I believe I
was in love with Him for several years until I was
twelve. There was a power I felt at once stirring and
safe in His imagined presence which I have felt since
with Father when we lived in Rhyl and before you died,
occasionally with William at the beginning, and now I
feel very much the way I did as a child with the Indian
called Day whom I have mentioned to you.*

   *I am quite sure that Father and Roger, who still go to
church very regularly, according to Father's letters to
me, do not have these complicated feelings about God.*
                                       Yr. loving, daughter,
                                       Anna

Hole-in-the-Day was outside his wigwam reading *The
Principles and Practice of Medicine* by Dr. William Osler,
which she had taken from the Stewards' library in Washington and later given to him.

"Waiting for me?" She sat on the ground beside him,
lifted her knees, covered by her long skirt, and tucked
them under her chin in a gesture that struck her as provok-
ing, "Did you expect me?"

"I am not surprised to see you," he said.

"What do you think I've come for?" she asked, coquettish.

He shrugged. "Something," he said. "I don't know
what."

"Where is Flat Mouth? Is he here?"

"Sleeping at his grandmother's," Hole-in-the-Day said.
He leaned against the wigwam and looked out at the darkness.

"I want a baby," Anna said. "Is that what you expected
from me?"

"I have felt that from you," he said softly.

She leaned against his knee. "William tells me no. He
says he won't."

He ran his finger down the middle of her face, across
her lips.

"Please," she said. "I feel I will die of emptiness."

When her son had died, she had wanted to make love,

not the awkward sweet grapplings as had happened between her and William but terrible lovemaking, hammering against one another like warriors. She wanted William
to pull out her hair until she was bald, to dig his fingernails into the soft flesh of her cheeks. And they did make
love for days, as if his spending of sperm knew no natural
limitations, as if he would use up all of the energy of a
lifetime of lovemaking in that one week, be done with it
for life.

Anna took Day's face in her hands.

"Can we go inside?" she asked.

"It is too warm," he said, gently taking her hands, folding them together in her own lap.

"I am a Chippewe at the center," he said. "Marriage is
not sacred for us as it is for you. If it doesn't work out, we
return to our own clan and divide the children. There is no
shame. But death is sacred." He hesitated. "Do you hear
horses?" he asked.

She listened. "I hear something," she said. "Maybe it's
a horse."

"It could be your husband."

"Never," Anna said. "He would never come after me.
Finish. You were telling me about death."

"There is a ceremony about the death of a wife if you
are married and living together. It is sacred. You know the
bowl which I carry with me full of food to give to others,
especially children. That is a part of the year of mourning.
And for a year, I am faithful to my wife."

"What would happen if you weren't? Who would know?"

"I would know," Day said.

Anna was standing in the door to the wigwam when the
horse they had heard in the distance galloped through the
reservation and stopped in the darkness just short of Day's
tent. She heard William's heavy breathing, heard him clear
his throat.

"Anna?" he said.

"Yes?" she replied, her heart beating in her ears.

"Come home," he said.

They made love that night and the next and the next, tear-ing at one another's flesh, biting their lips bloody as if gentleness were too dangerous to their uncovered hearts. And out of those nights came the beginnings of a baby.

THIRTEEN

THE END OF the century in Ashland, Wisconsin, was celebrated in the last week in December with drinking and dancing in the beer halls, dancing in the streets, wandering musicians, a parade of carriages and decorated horses, of Indians from Bad River in full ceremonial dress, and costumed replicas of the French fur traders on floats on Lake Superior. On the last afternoon of the nineteenth century, the lake, thinly frozen, glittered with toy sailboats and steamers, tiny warships and paddleboats made for the occasion. In spite of the weather and the swift approach of evening, everyone in Ashland was on the street, stirring with excitement as if they could actually sense a wind change announcing the ferocious energy that the twentieth century would bring to their lives in the New World.

Anna Steward, weighted with child, danced with William to Scottish bagpipes on the lake just behind the house where they used to live, now occupied by Welsh settlers who had moved in for the winter, sleeping under the blankets left by the Stewards, eating from their dishes.

She and William had moved back together in the same room at the hospital. She had made curtains and hung pictures. On the long afternoons of autumn, careful with herself, not working on the reservation until after the baby, she had made a quilt for their bed and one for the baby. She spent hours naming. Daniel, Martin, Anthony, Christian, Timothy. She tried them all with Steward for the sound, settling finally on Daniel, although she was quite sure this baby was a girl. She hoped it was a girl. She sensed that William could not bear the cost of another son. Miranda, Helen, Maria, Mary, Beryl, Meryn, Serena, Caroline,

Eleanor, Amanda. Steward was such a serious-sounding name, she thought. So English. It needed a melodious Christian name, she told William, who was not engaged with the naming of this child. She had known an Amanda when she worked in London—a tall birch tree of a girl, a marvelous girl who worked in the kitchen and wore her dark hair long and straight, like a silk slip around her face.

"Do you like Amanda Steward?" she asked William. When he had come to her full of the power of his man-hood, when the baby was made, she had fallen in love with him again. Even his face changed to her eye, taking on a new dignity and handsomeness.

Dear Mama, she had written.

> *Can it be possible that these changes in the heart have to do only with a kind of power—that I fell in love with William in the first place because I didn't wish to be a servant but a lady and when I didn't get to be a lady as indeed I didn't—you would know if you could see life on the edge of the universe here—the feelings slipped away. Then I wanted a child and the feelings for him flew back when he gave me what I wanted. I must be a more gentle-hearted girl than this, but I do wonder about the source of feelings, their undependability. Attraction is strange and elusive.*
>
> > *Yr. loving daughter,*
> > *Anna*

The evening of December 31 sailed in like an actual ship—they could see it hurrying across the lake as the sun set behind the dancers, and since the day had been partic-ularly sunny for early winter, they could feel it as a deep chill. Anna pulled William's face to hers and kissed his lips.

"I doubt you thought you'd be ending the century like this—in such a town with such a wife."

He put his hand against her face.

"No," he said. "I imagined to live day after day as I al-ways had."

"And are you sorry?" she asked. She shouldn't have done so—she knew that—for what was he to say? If he was sorry, what good to tell her? And was she sorry? she wondered, pulling her head back so her wool bonnet did not scratch his face while they were dancing.

"I may not be able to stay here much longer, William," she said.

"Not through midnight?"

She shook her head.

But she did stay, dancing comically in the beer hall, her belly full of child, turned to the side, balancing precariously, taking turns with the Indians from the reservation, but not Day, who did not dance but walked about with Flat Mouth on his shoulders drinking.

The last four months with William had been strangely settled, even personal. They went about their daily lives, speaking very little, but at night after supper in the hospital dining room, they sat together in the common room through long respectful silences—sometimes he took her hand—as if they could actually touch a part of one another.

"Do you ever think of Elsbeth?" Anna asked once.

"I do," William answered.

"What do you think?"

"Not what you imagine. It didn't bother me when my mother wrote to say that Elsbeth had married. I simply wondered what kind of life it would have been, what children, what house. Would we have had Sunday dinners with my parents unto death?" he said. "The only thing that ever bothered me with a woman was the night you went to Hole-in-the-Day."

Snow began to fall just before midnight, a fat wet snow blowing off the lake, making puddles on the warm cheeks of the revelers, and Anna wanted to stay up all night warmed by the conviviality, a girl again locked in by the spirit of friendship this spectacular night as she had been in the safety of her family in Rhyl. Just after midnight, she beckoned William to leave, knowing by the weight on her that the baby had fallen, was engaged, and would be born by morning. They walked the long mile slowly back to the hospital, William in a rare expansive humor protected by the blue-black night as if he had a second sense that this moment, walking through the soft snow luminous with a young moon, attached to one another, familiar as they very seldom were, was the best that life on earth had to offer and he ought to make acknowledgment. He ought to tell his wife that he loved her, that she had been a good and strong wife, beautiful to look at and cheerful, and that he admired her, which he had not had occasion to do with the women he had known in the carefully pruned society of Washington, D.C.

Just before they reached the hospital, he kissed her, licked the snow off her nose, off her cheeks, and kissed her long and hard on the lips.

The baby girl was born in the late morning after a difficult labor, a round-cheeked, black-haired girl with dark eyes open when William first handed her to Anna.

William could not stop the bleeding. He tried to force the contractions but the flow of blood seemed to increase. He got cold towels, gave her a new medication recently available to force the blood to clot. He was concerned and got another doctor and together they stood over Anna, perplexed. At noon, they gave her blood, and gradually through the day her condition improved.

"Do you like the name Amanda?" She seemed impervious to the seriousness of the situation.

"It's a fine name," William said.

"Amanda Steward," she said. "Would you prefer Eleanor?"

"Amanda is lovely."

"Or perhaps something more formal, like Margaret or Josephine."

"I'm pleased with Amanda," William said, abstracted.

"You could call her Josie or Jo if you chose Josephine. What do you think?"

"I like Amanda."

"Then we'll call her Amanda."

It snowed all day and through the night the first day of the twentieth century in Ashland—a lakefront snow, wet and graceful, gathering on the branches of the trees, mak-

ing lace filigree gowns of the blue spruce, accumulating
on the ground so the earth was a sea of white, substantial
in appearance but deceptive. Too damp and airy to last the
sunlight.

Anna drifted in and out of sleep, her black-haired
daughter swaddled in a blanket, sucking fiercely when
William put her to the breast—Anna hadn't the strength to
lift her—sucking her mother dry without regard.

Anna did not recover. Her appetite changed. It was as
though her daily world were a proscenium stage which had
been moved away from her, a little at a time, beyond her
reach, a part now of the horizon, and she was reading her
life as a script. She lived as if drunk or tranquilized, sweet
with William and her tenacious daughter, isolated by a
general weakness which had overtaken her since
Amanda's birth. Although the life of her mind had an extraordinary clarity, like the particular brilliance of color on
a gray day, she was and knew she was slipping out of the
world.

Dear Mama, she wrote in early March 1903, a month
before she died.

> *I believe I am dying. Did you know when you were
> dying? My mind swims around in my skull, a small slip-
> pery fish, bumping into the cranial bones, sliding be-
> tween the folds of brain.*
> *What surprises me is that mostly I think of you instead
> of Amanda and like to pretend I am a child again and you
> are alive working in the kitchen in Rhyl, which smells of
> sweets baking in the oven.*
>
> > *Yr. loving daughter,*
> > *Anna*

AMANDA

ONE

THE SUMMER OF 1913 was hot and still, hotter than any summer in memory. There was no breath of air off Lake Superior. The lake was motionless as a swamp pond and green with algae. The thickness of the air portended trouble.

The Indians who knew about weather warned of a storm which scattered the earth in its path, sweeping like a giant broom. The white men were unsettled, brittle with one another, bad-tempered. Even the children in Ashland and on the reservation had fallen into a state of wary somnambulance, lying with their feet in the creek facedown on the bank, impatient with their daily summer work.

On this particular July morning, Amanda and Flat Mouth lay on their backs on Amanda's bed in the hospital where she and her father still lived, their feet against the wall, bickering back and forth as they did night and day, hot weather or not, a warm convivial bickering just enough to keep the sex at bay.

Amanda was long-legged, slender, flat-chested, built like her father, like a boy, with fine high cheekbones, her mother's dark olive eyes and black hair, which she wore loose, cut just below her ears in a square cut like an Indian boy. After all, as she told Flat Mouth, she may as well look like a boy since she was one.

Flat Mouth was tall, over six feet by the time he reached fifteen, and handsome with a strong angular face, already the face of a man, and deep-set black eyes. He wore his hair in a short mane and had a high-bred stallion's way of flipping it off his forehead. He suited the willful Amanda Steward exactly.

"A Man," he called her.

She loved him more than anyone on earth.

She was uncomfortable with her father. He was formal, still uneasy with the expansive temperament of the Northwest, particularly so since Anna died. He didn't permit personal conversation.

Once when Amanda was small, unaware of the cost of conversation for her father, she had asked him to tell her everything about her mother—how she had smelled, how it had felt to touch her cheek.

"I cannot talk about her," William Steward had said. "Don't ask me again."

When Amanda was nine, in a spurt of domesticity, cleaning her father's room, she discovered that he kept a nightdress which belonged to her mother and slept with it, hanging it in the morning on the back of the door next to his own.

One night between Christmas and her eleventh birthday, she was lying in the dark wide awake when her father came very quietly into her room, fully dressed, just back from final hospital rounds. She pretended to sleep. He lay down on top of her covers, breathing unevenly for what seemed a very long time. Then he got up and went to bed. She could hear him taking off his boots.

Amanda and Flat Mouth had been together since the first time she remembered him, when he was six and his deep black eyes had sailed toward her like airborne marbles. He'd put his face flat against her face, flesh to flesh.

"Girl," he had said to her, deeply earnest. They had been sitting at the bottom of Anna's bed, Anna still alive then, floating on her white pillow.

"Boy," Amanda said. "I am a boy."

"No, treasure," Anna said to her. "You are a little girl."

"Wife," Flat Mouth said smugly and he slapped her left hand with his right hand and her right hand with his left and pushed his head into her soft belly like a puppy.

When Anna died, Flat Mouth stayed. Sometimes he slept on a bedroll beside her bed or ate supper at the hospital or, later, when they were older, he spent the morning with Amanda and Dr. Steward doing rounds. He, like Amanda, gradually learned the simple tasks of attending to the ill. They washed them, brought them meals and medicines, combed their hair, sat on the ends of their beds and talked. He taught Amanda to ride a horse going at a full gallop without her hands on the mane, to shoot, to skin and clean an animal. He taught her secrets and the Chippewe brought her into their warm and predictable world as if she were a beloved pet.

Her life with William Steward, however, had complexities she did not understand. He was too quiet. She felt an unspoken request in the air and her reaction was a stubborn temper. She refused to go to church ever, and when she was thirteen, on her birthday in fact, she refused to go to school again.

"I can see and hear," she said. "And I can read. What else is there to learn as long as I keep my eyes open?"

"If you lived in Washington, you would not be permitted to behave this way," her father said.

Flat Mouth's long legs were propped against the wall, Amanda's next to his. As they lay there, silent in the oppressive heat, Amanda, dressed like Flat Mouth in thin cotton trousers, flung her leg, almost the length of his, across Flat Mouth's leg, took his large brown hand in hers, and gently bit the knuckle.

"I have bad news," she said.

"Don't tell me," he replied. "I have no interest in bad news."

"This is terrible news."

He pulled his hand away and covered his ears.

"My father is making me move to Washington, D.C.," Amanda said. "Soon. In August."

"Making you move to Washington?" Flat Mouth said.

"To go to school," Amanda said.

"I thought you were strong," Flat Mouth said. "I thought you were as strong as me, as strong as a man." He jumped up, flipping her off the bed. "I didn't know that a man could tell you what to do."

"I am only thirteen and he is my father."

"You are just a lot of big talk," Flat Mouth said standing above her, his voice extremely quiet. "I am sorry to tell you we cannot be friends if you move to Washington, D.C. I don't have friends so far away."

"I will be back summers. Maybe even for Christmas," Amanda said.

"By summer, I will probably be married," Flat Mouth said.

"You are too young to be married," Amanda said.

"I am almost seventeen," he said, "and Chippewe marry early."

He opened the door to Amanda's bedroom located in the south wing of the hospital, just beyond the dining hall for the patients and staff. The corridor always smelled of food cooking.

Amanda followed him to the door.

"I hate you," she said quietly.

"Christians don't hate," Flat Mouth said with a toss of his head. "That is what I heard from your father."

"I am not a Christian," Amanda replied. She watched him walk down the corridor, his long arms swinging. "Good-bye forever," she said.

She heard the door shut to the side entrance of the hospital and then the pounding of Flat Mouth's pony by her window. She closed the door, took a box out from under her bed where she kept the letters Anna had written to her mother and a few pictures, none of Anna but one of Amanda when she was small and some of the reservation with Flat Mouth and Hole-in-the-Day. She found a piece of stationery and a pen and sat down at her table.

Dear Flat Mouth,

You probably will not be able to read this because you are an Indian and can't read and write very well, but I am writing to tell you that I plan to kill myself before we have an opportunity to see each other again.

                              Yours sincerely,
                              Amanda Steward
                              formerly A Man

TWO

THAT NIGHT AMANDA barely slept. She lay in the dark, wearing a camisole and long slip which had belonged to her mother—and pretended that cool air from the open window blew across her body.

She had ridden to the reservation with her letter just after supper but Flat Mouth was not there. Only Grandmother Yellow Flower was sitting in front of the wigwam, her eyes heavy in the heat.

"This is a letter for Flat Mouth," Amanda had said.

"I will read it first," Grandmother Yellow Flower said taking the letter from Amanda. "And then I will give it to him."

"It's in English," Amanda said.

"I read English," Grandmother Yellow Flower said sharply. "I just don't like to speak it."

"I think you are lying," Amanda said.

"Only white men lie," Grandmother Yellow Flower said.

All evening, Amanda had sat in her room, sometimes wandering through the corridors of the hospital or out the side door to the stables, waiting for Flat Mouth. But he never came.

Now half-sleeping in the steady heat, she heard her father come down the corridor, pass his own room, and come into hers, slipping quietly through the door. A shaft of light from the corridor crossed her lids and vanished. She closed her eyes and lay very still.

"Amanda?"

She did not reply.

He sat on the chair in her bedroom and took off his boots and she knew with a chill that he was going to get into her bed. She did not know what to do—whether to speak to him or pretend to sleep. Surely his intention was not to be noticed.

He climbed into the bed beside her, lying on his back, his head on her pillow. She could feel his warm breath, the antiseptic smell of him.

"Amanda," he said softly.

She stretched, made a small moaning sound in her throat as if her sleep had been invaded but not intercepted.

Perhaps, she thought, she should wake up now. But then what would she say? "Hello, Father. Good evening. Or is it morning? What are you doing in my bed?"

She lay for a long time and waited for something to happen. Somehow she knew that this time something would happen. There was an insistence in his presence beside her. But the night went on and on, her father beside her, breathing irregularly. Finally, in spite of her discomfort, a certain sleepiness overtook her and when he did reach over and very gently take her breast, she stiffened in surprise.

In a swift movement, he leapt out of bed.

"What happened?" she asked as if she had at that moment awakened, not wishing to allow the dark knowledge of his transgression to be between them.

"You cried out," he said. "I came in to check on you."

She did not question his dishonesty.

"It's so hot," she said lying back down on her pillow. "I don't sleep well in the heat."

"Are you all right now?" He reached over and laid his hand on her forehead.

"Fine," she said and closed her eyes. He opened the bedroom door.

"Amanda?"

"Yes."

"You should keep your door locked at night," he said. "I am worried about strangers."

"Chippewe?"

"White men and Indians both," he said.

After he left, Amanda could not sleep at all. The night sounds of summer outside her window, crickets, a bird flapping in the trees, the sorrowful owl, were like loud cymbals in her ears. She covered her head with a pillow to soften the noise and from time to time, until she finally fell asleep, she touched her breast where her father had touched her.

THREE

LATE THE FOLLOWING morning, a charcoal storm gathering over the lake, no news having arrived from Flat Mouth, Amanda went to Bad River. She rode her father's stubborn horse at full gallop the way Flat Mouth had taught her, her legs tight around his girth, the reins looped on his neck.

The roads of the reservation were empty. Here and there a young child squatted on the ground in front of a cabin or a mother carrying a child walked slowly down the road, dulled by the heat.

No one was outside Hole-in-the-Day's wigwam. Amanda dismounted and tied her horse to the trunk of an oak tree which shaded the wigwam with brittle, heat-dried leaves cracking in the slight wind.

"Day?" she called outside the wigwam.

"Come in," he said, although he did not look up. Flat Mouth stone cold was there as well. He told her to be quiet, his grandmother was sleeping; his grandmother, although lying on a grass mat, was not sleeping at all but rather was wide awake, her eyes on Amanda.

Grandmother Yellow Flower was a small plump woman with white straw hair braided in two coils around her ears and skin black with age and weather. Small-boned with tiny hands and feet and features more delicate than common among Chippewe women, she was warm and generous but not entirely to be trusted. Too mercurial for that, too involved in the lives of other people.

"You have come to see Flat Mouth about the letter." She spoke in Chippewe.

"I have come to see Day," Amanda said.

The grandmother gave a quick toss of her head to indicate disbelief and reached over, taking hold of Amanda's ankle.

"Sit down," she said pulling Amanda toward her. "You are too jumpy. Always here and there. It gives me a bad stomach to watch you." She checked the bottoms of Amanda's feet. "Hard as rocks. Your mother would not like to think of you without shoes."

"Her mother would not bother about shoes in the summer," Day said. "She—Anna—was not an ordinary white woman. Do you remember her?"

"Her face? Yes," Amanda said. "And she was soft."

"She was my close friend," Day said. "My closest friend."

What Amanda knew of Anna came from the letters she had discovered in a cupboard in her bedroom at the hospital, hundreds of them tied in packets, organized in boxes; she read them over and over when she should have been doing her lessons. She had memorized paragraphs. Some letters she had separated and kept in the drawer beside her bed. One she had slid under her mattress with a strange belief that the letter was actually her mother and she could, by keeping it under her while she slept, assume the life of Anna Steward.

Dear Mama, this letter read.

> *It is so different to have a daughter than sons. I find myself expecting a miracle of Amanda, that she walk early and speak in sentences. I gave no thought to that with sons. I am less indulgent with her.*
>
> *Daughters must be raised to a world in which no one will take care of them except themselves. Sons are cared for from birth to death.*
>
> *She is a miracle.*
>
> > *Yr.˙ loving daughter,*
> > *Anna*

"I was speaking about hard feet, not her mother," Grandmother Yellow Flower said. "Your mother had a better disposition than your father."

"Be quiet," Day said to his mother. "You have never learned what business is yours and what belongs to other people."

"So," Grandmother Yellow Flower said, "why have you come to see Day and not Flat Mouth?"

"I have come to tell him that I have changed my mind about killing myself."

"I am very pleased to hear that," Hole-in-the-Day said.

"You knew that I was thinking of it?" Amanda asked. "It was in the letter that I wrote."

"I did not read the letter you wrote," Grandmother Yellow Flower said.

"That is because you cannot read, Yellow Flower," Day said. "You looked at it for long enough hoping the words would sing their meaning in your ears."

"And what did Flat Mouth say when he read the letter?" Amanda asked, sitting next to Day at the bottom of the bedroll.

Many times, since she could remember, she had been at Day's feet with Flat Mouth leaning against her. Many times, they had spent the day when she should have been in school, had eaten supper at Grandmother Yellow Flower's cabin, had listened to stories in the evening.

"Ask Flat Mouth what he said," Hole-in-the-Day said. "Perhaps he will answer you."

"Will you answer me, Flat Mouth?" Amanda asked, her voice thick with feeling.

"No," Flat Mouth said. "We are no longer friends."

"People are like weather," Day said running his fingers through Amanda's short-cropped hair. "Sometimes like today, after the long heat, there will be a storm. So bad that a man can think of nothing but the storm, nor remember what it was like before when the weather was fine."

"I don't understand," Amanda said.

"Do you remember the month of June?" Day asked.

She nodded.

"How the days were cool with a bright sun and the air smelled of pine?"

"Yes," she answered. "It was beautiful every day."

"You can remember those beautiful days even in this awful heat with the dust thick in your mouth?"

"I think I can," Amanda said. She didn't understand. Day seemed to announce a death.

"I have to go," she said nervously, not wishing to hear bad news. "I have to leave now."

Flat Mouth had his back to her. He was making something. She could not tell what, but he was always making something, his hands could not stay still.

"Wait," Grandmother Yellow Flower said as Amanda ducked out of the wigwam. "Your feet are too hard and I must fix them."

She opened a small bottle in which there was a liquid the color of tobacco, with a strong, almost putrid, smell.

"I have to go," Amanda said.

"You must stay until I fix your feet."

"Please. I'll be late."

"No. First your feet," Grandmother Yellow Flower said. "Then home."

Amanda sat down.

"Oil," the grandmother said. "For your feet." She pulled Amanda's bare foot from under her long skirt and rubbed the oil on the bottom. Then she took the other foot.

"Pine oil," she said. She put the bottle to her nose. "Terrible," she said and smiled.

Amanda stood up, the dust sticking thickly to the bottoms of her feet.

"I hate you," she said quietly to everyone, but she meant it for Flat Mouth.

On the way out of the wigwam, she stopped where Flat Mouth was working so diligently, leaned over him, and spat a little silver nickel of saliva on the top of his head.

FOUR

ON THE TRAIN to Washington, D.C., in late August, the earth lush with a week of heavy rain, Amanda Steward stopped speaking. She made the decision boarding the train in Ashland that she would not speak at all until she returned.

"Are you going as far as Washington, D.C.?" the conductor asked when he collected her ticket.

She smiled and nodded.

"You change trains in Chicago to the B and O," he said. "Are you from Washington?" he asked. "I was born there."

She shook her head no.

"Where are you from?" he asked pleasantly.

She pointed backward toward Ashland, put her fingers to her lips, and shook her head to indicate she could not speak.

"Oh, I'm sorry," he said. "I didn't realize."

"But you can hear?" the blue-hatted lady with a small beak nose sitting across from her in the compartment said.

Amanda nodded.

"Most ones I know can't hear if they can't speak." She settled into the bristly cushions of the train. "I have four daughters all grown," she said. "And one is hard of hearing. Born that way."

Amanda pressed her face against the window of the train. Perhaps, she thought, she should be deaf as well.

Outside the window, the state of Wisconsin expanded to the horizon and in spite of her great sadness at leaving, her anger at her father for sending her away, she was excited. In her pocket was a letter from Flat Mouth. TO A MAN. GOOD-BYE BUT NOT FOREVER. In her satchel were her mother's letters and a pen from her father's desk which she had taken to have something with her which had been his. She pushed up the blind to uncover the window entirely, let in the light, and she stood, her hands framing her eyes, looking at the world.

"Don't fill up the whole view," the blue-hatted lady said.

Amanda moved to the right.

"It must make a big difference hearing," the lady said, "but I ask myself why if you can hear, can't you talk."

The train slowed, sometimes stopped, at crossings and then Amanda caught a whole scene in the frames she had made with her hands: outside of Arcade, Wisconsin, a funeral behind a large farm, the family carrying a casket between them. A small girl, barefooted with a large straw hat flopping over her eyes, sitting backward, her hands on the rump of her pony watching as the train rumbled by. An old man with two sticks, walking with his three-legged dog, a mangy gimp making his way down the track.

"I change trains in Chicago for Washington as well," the blue-hatted lady said. "I'll be glad to help you with your things. You have quite a lot to carry. You must be going to Washington for a long time."

Amanda shook her head yes.

"I like to talk to you," the lady said. "I have never in my life spoken with a mute and it's much simpler than I would have thought."

Chicago roared into view, black against the clear blue sky, strong and masculine, and Amanda was thrilled by it as if the city were male. She was by nature an observer, not unreflective but easily moved by the object itself without translation, like the sight of Chicago.

On the train to Washington, the blue-hatted lady asked to be in her compartment.

"I have to watch out for you," she said. "Who would imagine a girl your age, traveling alone. Even if you could speak," she said. "And you can't," she concluded, pleased with her powers of observation.

On the second half of the train ride, Amanda slept or half-slept, her eyelids alive with the pictures she had seen from the train. She could, she thought, ride everywhere on the train, all over America, from place to place, stopping in cities for supplies. There was a comfort to the movement of it, to the bold engine chugging on and on, even to the foolish blue-hatted lady going on like a ticking clock. She did not want to arrive in Washington, to see her grandparents standing severely at the end of the platform, to be closed into the grand house on N Street without escape. She was very glad she had decided not to speak.

Amanda's room in Washington had a canopy bed with lace, lace on the bed skirt, silver frames, boxes, brushes on the vanity, pictures of young girls in bonnets on swings with flowers in their hair. Next to her room was the sitting room where Dr. and Mrs. Steward sat after dinner in the evening.

On the first night, sent to her room to unpack, Amanda stood beside her bed and listened to their conversation.

"William said nothing about her problem in his letter," Mrs. Steward said. "What do you think, darling?"

"I think she won't speak," Dr. Steward said.

"I don't agree," Mrs. Steward said. "I think she can't speak."

"Then we'll have her examined," Dr. Steward said, "but I think you'll find she was speaking perfectly normally when she left Ashland."

Amanda hung her dress and her skirts in the closet. She put the box of her mother's letters with her father's pen and Flat Mouth's note under the bed. She put on the blue beads Grandmother Yellow Flower had given her and went into the sitting room.

"Don't mention the speaking," she heard her grandfather say. "Ignore it."

Her grandfather, a long pole of a man, was seated stiffly in a straight-back chair, his legs crossed, his hands folded—like her father in appearance but assuming less space, his gestures abbreviated. Her grandmother was a powder puff of a lady, her hair in curls around her face, her peach dress puffed at the hips.

"You look so much like William," Mrs. Steward said. "Not at all like your mother, who was quite short."

"Anna was small, Emily," Dr. Steward said, "and lovely in the face."

"She was not fair-skinned." Mrs. Steward could not help herself.

"She was of Italian descent, I understand," Dr. Steward said.

Dear Father, Amanda wrote in her mind. I don't like it here as you might have expected. My grandparents are unpleasant, particularly my grandmother. I no longer speak. I plan not to speak again for a year until I come home.

"We have made arrangements for you to attend the Sidwell Friends School," Dr. Steward said. "It is a Quaker school with a liberal point of view which should be agreeable for a girl who has grown up uncivilized."

"They haven't been informed about your problem," Mrs. Steward said.

Amanda smiled.

"Your grandfather is going to make arrangements for a doctor to see you."

"But you can hear perfectly well—is that correct?" Dr. Steward asked.

Amanda nodded.

"And this problem just developed?" Mrs. Steward asked. "Your father never mentioned it."

Amanda sat very straight, her hands folded, her feet together. She had seen portraits of young girls seated so, holding a single rose, a domestic long-haired cat. And in her mind's eye, she saw herself. She discovered she could shut out their voices entirely of words so she heard them speaking as if she was half-sleeping—the sound and not the sense of them.

Later, she wrote to Flat Mouth sitting under the lacy canopy—she could see herself in the glass on top of the bureau and she looked at that distance like a boy. She could pass for a boy, she decided, if that became necessary.

"Of course, darling, you will have to grow your hair," her grandmother had said. "No young lady in Washington wears hair like a boy's."

Dear Flat Mouth, she wrote.

> *I no longer speak. That began when I left Ashland and now I see much better than I have ever seen— perhaps because I am not speaking, perhaps because every minute I am seeing new things.*
>
> *Everything I see is a photograph, squared off with dimensions. Next time I am home, I will get a photograph of you.*
>
> *Yr. loving friend,*
> *A Man*

Amanda's days in Washington had a comfortable regularity and she was lonely but not unhappy. It gave her pleasure not to speak, a sense of power.

She made a friend called Pauline at school, also a poor student, a lively warmhearted girl pleased to have as a friend so boyish a girl as Amanda Steward, with the added curiosity of being mute. Mr. Sidwell had told the Stewards his concern about Amanda's continuing at the Quaker school since she did not seem at all interested in scholarship nor did she complete her lessons except art, and although she read voraciously, it was never the assigned material. The Stewards, however, insisted that Amanda remain.

Finally, disturbed by Amanda's poor adjustment, her grandfather, who was not a man noted for his sensibilities but who was fond of Amanda, fond of her independent spirit, bought her a camera. He had noticed, as he told his wife, that she paid attention to things around her.

"She has, I believe, an unusual eye," he said.

Dear Flat Mouth, Amanda wrote in late January.

> *I have a camera. It is black and heavy, the size of a rock only exactly square, like an accordioned box. Have you seen one?*
>
> *I look at things through a square glass slightly larger than my eye and what I see is fixed in place, just as I have seen it, forever.*
>
> *Mostly I take pictures of people because people do not last.*
>
> *You would hate it here.*
>
> Yr. loving friend,
> A Man

FIVE

In late May before the close of school for summer holidays, already warm in Washington, Amanda heard from Flat Mouth about her father, a simple piece of news but disturbing.

Dear A Man,

> *It is May here and the weather is fine and cool.*
>
> *My father tells me to write to you news of Dr. Steward which we have from Grandmother Yellow Flower who has it from the man who lives in the house—the old hospital, where your family used to live before your brother died.*
>
> *Two nights this spring your father comes on foot from the hospital and sleeps in their garden waking before the sun but they have seen him. It is too cold yet to sleep out of doors.*
>
> *My father thinks you would want to know this news.*
> > *Yr. friend forever,*
> > *Flat Mouth*

Amanda had not seen her father since August, although there were letters once a week in his large scrawl with news of the hospital and recommendations for a useful life, always a postscript. "Please reconsider speaking," he would write.

After January, he no longer mentioned her speaking.

Her grandfather had taken her to a physician at Georgetown Hospital who had attended the lectures of Sigmund Freud at Clark University in 1909 and who suggested that Dr. Steward take Amanda to Europe where they were sympathetic to Dr. Freud's method of analysis.

"If it's her mind and not her throat, we won't bother," Dr. Steward said.

Once the physical concern was dismissed in early October, the subject of speech did not come up. Louisa reported to Amanda that Dr. Steward had said it was quite pleasant to have a woman in the house who didn't speak.

At Mr. Sidwell's school, Amanda Steward was a force. The boys in particular were drawn to her. They had never known such a girl and were tantalized by the fact that she was mute. It seemed to their somewhat sophisticated and southern sense of the world that her absence of speech made her capable of anything, and she was the subject of notes of a sexual nature passed back and forth.

Even before the letter from Flat Mouth, she had been worried about her father. His letters since January had been irregular—sometimes once a week, sometimes three weeks went by, and he was a man of deep compulsiveness. Once he had called her "my darling" in a letter and on several occasions he omitted a salutation. Two days before Flat Mouth's letter, she had received a blank piece of paper carefully folded in the envelope.

On the third Sunday in May, just before lunch, the house warm with the smell of beef, she gathered the letters from her father and took them to her grandfather who was sitting with the newspaper in his study as he usually did before the Sunday meal and after church. Her grandmother was there as well, fragile since a bout of pneumonia in the winter. Amanda put the letters on his lap and sat down across from him.

"Letters from William," he said to his wife, leafing through them. "Strange like the ones we've had lately." He folded them, put them back in their envelopes, handed them to Mrs. Steward. "I don't know, Emily. I don't like what these letters suggest."

"I don't believe he is well," Mrs. Steward said. "We should send Amanda back to Wisconsin and go ourselves as soon as possible."

The train to Ashland took days. There had been a crash between Cleveland and Chicago so the Baltimore and Ohio crept along while track work was done. There were flash floods in eastern Wisconsin from the storms. But finally on Monday, the first of June, a strong, cool, sunny day with the clear fresh scent of pine in the air, Amanda Steward arrived at the station in Ashland.

Her father stood alone at the end of the platform, stood there as she got off the train with her large satchel. He made no gesture to walk toward her and she saw the change immediately, a train car away from where she stood, the alteration in his face, the way he held his long frame—a sudden onset of age.

"Hello, Father." She embraced him. "Hello. Hello." The

first words she had spoken to another person in ten months and they rang, tinkled like triangles, sounded in her ear like cymbals.

"Hello, Anna," he said to her. "I have been waiting for a very long time."

She did not correct him.

She put her arm through his and they walked through the station house full of people she knew, not well, but the faces of her childhood.

"Hello."

"Hello."

"I don't really care for Washington a bit," she said in response to one question. "It's too claustrophobic."

"Hello."

"Hello."

"Hello."

"I have been with my grandparents," she said to someone else who stopped her. "Just for a visit. Now I'm back home."

William Steward had a new Ford motorcar, black with leather seats, very handsome.

"I purchased it while you were away," he told Amanda opening the door for her. "I am the last doctor in town to have an automobile, my dear," he said as if she were a stranger.

She wanted to ask him if he actually knew where she had been, if he knew she was his daughter come home again, but she didn't. On he talked about his new automobile and its mechanics.

They drove through the familiar streets, past the shops of Ashland, the beer halls—it was lunchtime and the streets were spilling with activity—down the road to the hospital and into the main gate, but just as Dr. Steward pulled up to the front door, he changed his mind.

"We'll take just a little drive through town," he said. "You've been away so long. You'd like to see the whole of it."

He didn't drive to town at all. Instead he took the road by the lake, a narrow road which wound around the lake, past the white frame house, now painted yellow, where the Stewards had lived until the diphtheria epidemic. He stopped the car.

"Remember?" William Steward said.

Amanda was not certain what she should do. She reached into her satchel for her camera. "I have become a photographer," she said.

"I don't want pictures," Dr. Steward said. "Someone else lives here now so it is not our house, but look in the front window. Remember when we used to sit at night and watch the weather off the lake?"

Her heart fell. "I never lived here, Father."

A look of perplexity crossed his face.

"Our bedroom was there at the front so you could see the lake," he said.

Amanda leaned back against the seat of the new Ford motorcar.

"I know," she said. "I remember now."

It was evening at Bad River, the first day of Amanda's return. She had come after eating supper with the staff at the hospital, which had been strained because of her father's deterioration.

Hole-in-the-Day was there and Grandmother Yellow Flower, unchanged. In fact, nothing had changed whatsoever; even the wigwam where Day lived was exactly as it had always been and smelled sweetly of baking bread.

Amanda leaned against a tree and Flat Mouth pulled her hair out of the bun in which she kept it now. Her grandmother had insisted she grow it long. He pulled the long black hair through his teeth, smiling.

"So you have changed to a girl," he said.

"I haven't changed at all," Amanda said. "What has changed is my father."

Day nodded solemnly.

"His brain has gone," Amanda said.

"He should not have left his home," Day said. "People should stay where they belong."

"His home is terrible. That is where I have been all winter."

Hole-in-the-Day folded his arms across his chest.

"He thinks I am my mother," Amanda said.

Day ran his long rough fingers across her face. "In the eyes, you are your mother," he said.

It was a clear starry night, the blue color of midnight. She turned to Day.

"I suppose you heard I didn't speak in Washington, D.C."

"I heard," Day said, a rare slow smile spreading across his face. "Flat Mouth told me."

The hospital was dark when she came back. Her father's room, even the main reception room, were black except for a small light where the all-night attendant was sitting.

Amanda slipped between the sheets of her bed and, lulled by the familiarity of her own room, by the slight dampness of the lake, the smell of pine, she was asleep before another thought surfaced to her conscious mind.

Dear Mama, her mother had written, one of the first letters after she arrived in Wisconsin.

> *I have been searching everywhere for signs of Wales here and today passing by a house with the windows open, I smelled the sweet butter smell of shortbread baking.*

> Yr. loving daughter,
> Anna

SIX

Amanda, in a profound sleep, did not hear her father, did not hear him open the door or come in the room until he had fallen across her, his giant frame the weight of an ape, his stiff gray hair straw against her cheek. His breath in her mouth was whiskey and tobacco. She scrambled from underneath him and managed to turn on her stomach, to pull her body free. In the process, he fell off the bed and lay on his back, breathing in starts, his hand, his long slender fingers across his groin.

The night nurse was in the bedroom almost at once.

"I heard him fall," the nurse, unfamiliar to Amanda, said.

Gently, she took him by the hand, herself kneeling on the floor beside him, all the while talking.

"Hello, Dr. Steward," she said softly. "It's Miss Barclay again."

"Hello, Miss Barclay," her father said.

"I'm going to help you to your room," she said putting her arm firmly around his waist.

"This is my room," he said. "I live here with my wife."

"I'm Amanda Steward," Amanda said, standing, brushing the long hair out of her eyes.

"I know," Miss Barclay said.

"Just now we'll go to the bed in the room next door," she said, "until tomorrow."

He started to go with her like an old man, leaning on her slender shoulder, and then he straightened and turned toward Amanda.

"You are Amanda?"

She nodded.

"Amanda," he said.

"Yes," she replied.

"I heard that you were coming," he said. "But you have grown into a woman. I thought you were Anna."

He turned to Miss Barclay and in a strained voice insisted, "I thought she was my wife. You know I wouldn't have come in her room if I had not thought she was my wife."

"Of course," Miss Barclay said.

"It's confusing to me how these things change," he said meekly.

"It is very confusing," Miss Barclay agreed.

Amanda followed at a distance and stood in the doorway to her own room. She watched Miss Barclay help her father into bed, cover him with a sheet, turn off his light, and shut the door. From her pocket, the nurse took a ring of long brass keys, turned one in the lock, and closed her father in his room.

"We don't know what else to do," she said wearily to Amanda.

"Does this happen often?"

"He wanders every night, sometimes inappropriately dressed, and then other times, usually in the day, he seems to be of sound mind." The nurse was a small-framed British woman with a heavy northern accent, crisp but warm. She touched Amanda's cheek. "You live with your grandparents, I understand."

"No," Amanda said. "I spent this year with my grandparents. I live here. I have lived here all my life."

"The doctors have been thinking that perhaps you ought to take your father back to his home in Washington, D.C. I'm sure they'll talk to you about it in the morning."

"I have come back to Wisconsin for the summer," Amanda said fiercely. "Probably for good."

"That's very nice," Miss Barclay said, evidently not wishing to become involved.

Amanda sat in the chair by her bed for quite a long time, her body an ocean wave of weeping. Finally, she turned out the light, climbed into bed, and fell asleep. She heard the shot but in her sleep, at a distance of years. It did not even wake her, so deeply weary was she.

What woke her was the confusion in the corridor. People were running down the hall, talking back and forth, calling for Dr. O'Roarke, shouting down the corridor, Dr. O'Roarke, Dr. O'Roarke. And he was coming down the hall. She heard the heavy boots and then there was silence. She lay in bed on her back, the covers under her chin, her eyes closed, the light off.

She knew before Miss Barclay and Dr. O'Roarke knocked on the door.

"Miss Steward."

"One moment, please," she said but her voice did not register in the air. There were no sound waves, as if finally the studied muteness had taken hold and she couldn't speak.

"One moment please," she whispered.

"Amanda. It is Dr. O'Roarke."

She did not know Dr. O'Roarke. He had come this year from medical school in Boston. Her father had told her about him. "Can you imagine," he had written, "an Irish immigrant, a doctor?" There were three new young doctors in Ashland, her father had told her. The town was booming.

"Miss Steward, excuse me, it is Dr. O'Roarke."

She opened the door to her bedroom.

Dr. O'Roarke was young, red-haired, with soft brown spots on his face, an ashen pallor. "I'm sorry to wake you," he said. "You know Miss Barclay?"

Amanda nodded.

"Did you hear the gun?" he asked.

"In my dream," Amanda said.

"It was not a dream," Dr. O'Roarke said. "Your father has shot himself."

SEVEN

IT WAS DARK outside but with the feel of dawn, the sun just under Wisconsin, about to slide over the horizon, and Amanda dressed quickly in her old pants, tight now at the hips, a buckskin jacket, and flew down the corridor although the doctors, two of them, and several nurses outside her father's room called out to her and one—she heard him—hurried down the hall after her. But she didn't stop. Out the back door of the hospital, across the lawn to the stables. She got her father's horse and headed to Bad River.

They were sleeping when she peered under the flaps of the wigwam—Hole-in-the-Day on one side on a bedroll, his broad back toward her, and Flat Mouth a large lump in the sunken center of a hammock.

All day they sat together, Amanda in the center, Day and Flat Mouth pressed up against her on either side, like animals huddled in a storm. She felt her body sink into theirs, travel out of herself, no longer her burden to support for this moment. Sometimes they talked, mostly Day, and what he said was spoken with the force of spiritual truth.

"Your father did not wish to live with his brain scrambled," Day said. "What he did was brave. Not to give trouble anymore."

"He came to my bed last night," Amanda said.

Day shook his head. "That was a sign, A Man," he said. "Not the truth."

She stayed with Day and Flat Mouth all day, into the night, without returning to the hospital, and no one came for her. Grandmother Yellow Flower brought supper and they sat in silence eating the bread and vegetables. She rubbed Amanda's face with the petals of red poppies and showered the crumbled poppy in her hair.

Amanda didn't know how to feel but what she did feel seemed inappropriate. Not sadness. She had no such feelings for her father, nothing like the warm rush of blood in her veins for Day and Flat Mouth. She had fondness and respect. She was pleased to have had him as a father, as if he were a picture of a man, unfamiliar as flesh. But when she saw him broken, when his life presented a kind of danger to her, she was not sympathetic. She wanted him away.

"It is not wrong to think that," Day said to her when she told him what she was feeling, that she should be struck dead for terrible thoughts. "We are animals of course and must fight to stay here."

She was inconsolable but without grief.

"I will spend the night," she said to Day after dark. "Tomorrow I'll go back to the hospital."

Day made her a bedroll next to his.

Late, after Day was sleeping, Amanda, unable to sleep, went to Flat Mouth.

"I want you to come for a walk with me," she said. "I can't sleep."

He got out of the hammock and they crept out of the wigwam.

"Tomorrow I will have to go back to the hospital and

everything will be different. I will go again to Washington and this time maybe for good."

She took him by the shoulders and, standing on her toes, she kissed him on the lips.

"I want you to show me everything."

He put his fingers between her lips, separated her teeth.

"There," he said. He put his tongue in her mouth over her teeth, deep in her mouth. He touched her breasts slowly, along the sides, under her shirt. He took her nipples. And they kissed for a very long time, standing, then lying on the damp bed of pine needles, their bodies meeting as they kissed, no longer confined by the limitations of skin. She touched him, long and hard and straight, surprised by the size of it. Not even her occasional daydreams could have imagined the size, and she wondered how it would be possible that such an enormous weapon could find its way inside her.

"Show me," she said.

"You take it." He closed her hand on him. "Now put it in."

"Have you done this before?" she asked.

Flat Mouth nodded. "But you are my best friend," he said softly.

She nestled her face in his neck.

"I can't find where to put it," she said. And gently with his hands, he opened her and put himself inside.

For a long time, they lay very quietly on the pine needles, their lips together, his breath sweet cornbread, his body wet with perspiration.

"It hurt," she said, "but I am glad."

In the morning before the doctors from the hospital came to collect her as she knew they would do, she took pictures of Flat Mouth. He sat in front of the wigwam solemnly, his hands folded in his lap, his face without expression, ill at ease.

"You must smile, Flat Mouth. You must look like you look to me." She turned her lips up, wrinkled her brow.

She took pictures everywhere, of Day and Grandmother Yellow Flower and the pines and the village, even after Dr.

O'Roarke had come. Once she caught Flat Mouth off guard but mostly he held himself stiff and looked darkly into the camera.

They could not say good-bye. When the time came for her to leave, he jumped on the back of his pony and rode away.

"I'll see you, A Man," he called.

Grandmother Yellow Flower and Hole-in-the-Day walked her, locked between them, to her horse.

"You may stay with us," Day said.

"I'll be back," she said.

Perhaps she would be, she thought, but what she knew with a sense of inevitability was that now she had to return to Washington. On the ride back to the hospital, next to Dr. O'Roarke, she still felt the force of Flat Mouth's body imprinted on her own.

Amanda was in Ashland for less than two days. The arrangements made by her grandparents were that she should return immediately with the body of her father. And so she did. On the third of June, she left by train once again. In Chicago, she stood on the platform while the attendants carried the casket to the Baltimore and Ohio baggage car and then she boarded the train herself, wide awake, combative, alert to survival.

EIGHT

WHEN ON THE sixth of April, 1917, the United States Congress finally declared war on Germany, lives in Washington, including the Stewards, went through a sea change. There was a hurricane of excitement. Workers for the war effort flooded in, and the houses of the small southern town filled to include them. The air shimmered with pride and the feeling stirring was of a party, not a war. Dr. Steward was appointed by President Wilson to provide instruction in emergency surgical procedures to the doctors and nurses who would be going to the front. Mrs. Steward, in keeping with the national spirit of generosity, opened her house to boarders, filling six empty bedrooms. And Amanda fell in love with Lincoln Draper, the first boy at Sidwell Friends School to sign up to fight. In fact, he was the only student at Friends to go to war in the first year of America's involvement, antagonistic as the Quakers were to war, intent on peace as a matter of belief, and Amanda, seventeen, grown taller, even slimmer, in the years since her father died, fell desperately in love with him.

"If you go, I will follow you," Amanda said to him in the weeks before he left for training camp in July.

Lincoln Draper was a tall, slender, black-haired, sculpted young man, expanding easily to heroic proportions. He was, like so many other American boys of his time, believing, innocent, and virile.

Most of the young women at Sidwell Friends, already taken with Lincoln's frank good looks, were won by his grand gesture of patriotism. But he was Amanda's from the moment she locked her long arm through his and whispered that she would follow him anywhere.

"To Germany, to France," she said walking home with him in early May, a light spring breeze lifting her skirt. She was exactly his height and bold in a western manner, unfamiliar in the South. She brushed his black hair off his collar and ran her tongue across the back of his neck.

"I have never met such a girl as you," he said to her.

"You have never kissed?" she asked, guessing he had not—boys at Sidwell Friends, properly brought up as they were and in the dark shadow of Quaker principles besides, did not kiss until after high school.

"Of course," he said. He implied there had been much more to his life than kissing but she had won him, whatever tall adventures he invented about his past. He was hers for the days before he shipped out to training camp in Texas and hence to France.

Amanda was possessed. She did not even recognize herself in the mirror, so crazy in love was she, stunned as if struck by electricity, her brain spinning. Not even the strong dark face of Flat Mouth slipped through her daydreams. His regular letters to her once or twice a week since they had separated continued to come but were dropped unopened into the box of Anna's letters. She could not eat anything. She seldom slept.

"You don't believe I'll go to France," she said to Lincoln. "But you'll see."

Since the death of her father, she had lived in the house on N Street as if without a childhood of losses, so complete and impenetrable was her defense. She was to graduate in June of 1917 from Friends School, although she had been unremarkable as a scholar, barely passing her courses. But she had already earned a small reputation as a photographer, winning a national contest for provocative photographs of Negro poverty in the shadow of the Capitol. She had built her own darkroom in the basement of the N Street house and most afternoons when the other girls from her class were at the sweets shop or flying around the streets of northwest Washington in the rumble seat of a Ford motorcar, Amanda was experimenting with new processes of development. She had adjusted to the life expected of her as the granddaughter of Dr. and Mrs. Steward. She kept her hair long and in a knot, dressed in long skirts and high-necked blouses, even hats and gloves, and, insofar as was possible for a long wheat sheaf of a ranging girl, presented a demure countenance. She had become a stranger to herself.

Until Lincoln Draper as a soldier crested the horizon of her vision, she was unfamiliar in her own skin. And so the romance with the lovesick boy she had claimed had only something to do with Lincoln Draper. It was as well a love affair with herself.

They had a little more than a month for lingering over coffee at the sweets shop, for wandering the back streets of Georgetown, the small alleys, the flushed wet gardens of the parks, for kissing behind the stables, long lingering kisses, painfully sweet. It was unbearable for Amanda to imagine his departure. She thought she would die of it.

Lincoln suggested that she go to Europe as a photographer.

"Surely we'll be sending journalists and photographers

now we're involved. The English have been since the beginning."

"But women?" she asked.

Lincoln shrugged his shoulders.

"Or you could go as a nurse," he said.

"No," Amanda said, the idea spinning into focus in her mind. "It is a very good thought, Lincoln. But I'll go as a man. A male photographer."

NINE

THAT EVENING BEFORE dark, mid-May and raining, the smell of lilacs floating through the window, Amanda tried out for the part of a man. She stood in front of the long mirror over her dresser in her grandfather's trousers, which fit her exactly except for the bagginess in the belly, his high-collared blue-striped shirt and black suspenders, pulled her hair back leaving a floppy lock across the forehead, and lit a cigarette she had taken from Louisa's room, holding it casually between her thumb and forefinger. She had not smoked before.

"I am pleased to meet you," she said extending her hand to the image of herself in the mirror, but the voice was too high. She started again.

"How do you do. I'm Sam Dane, photographer from the Minneapolis *Morning Tribune*." She had to stand straight, she thought, and not let her hips tilt. "How do you do. I'm Sam Dane, photographer from the Minneapolis *Morning Tribune* and I am prepared and honored to go to France to photograph on behalf of the war effort." She took a drag on her cigarette, blew the smoke out slowly, clouding the mirror. Not bad, she thought.

She practiced casual conversations, sitting in a chair in front of the long mirror, her right leg crossed like a man's, her arms flung over the back of the chair, her eyes lowered. She practiced smoking, standing, her shoulder lowered, one hand in her pocket.

"I'm from Madison, Wisconsin," she said in her rehearsed baritone. "Sam Dane. Samuel Dane."

"I used to have a girlfriend," she said to the mirror. "Josephine. Josie Banks. But she married another man in Madison."

She got better and better. She learned to inhale, to blow smoke rings, to maintain the register of her voice without cracking. She learned a mannish gait, her arms swinging, just so, almost military in appearance. Sometimes she even felt like a man. Alone in her room practicing in front of the mirror, she could forget her own name.

"What's the matter with going as a nurse?" Lincoln asked her the day before his departure for Texas. They were lying in the damp high grass in an open field behind Dumbarton Oaks.

"You'll find me good as a man. I practice in the mirror," Amanda said leaning over Lincoln, her hair down in a tent over his face. "And I'd be a bad nurse. I'm terrible with blood."

"You're sure there are no women photographers in Europe?"

"I've looked into it. So far, absolutely none. I read in the paper that they hope to send the first group of American photographers in June, although some are already there." She stretched out in the grass. "Don't worry, darling. I will be there. If you are going to die, I will die with you," she said.

"I am not going to die," Lincoln said, put off by her dramatics.

The actual fact of dying had not occurred to either of them, only the poetry of it, as if death could be locked in the rhythm of language, repeated and repeated to eternity.

They rolled over in the high grass, clinging to each other until they were wet to their skin in the cool air.

"Let's marry before you leave," Amanda said, her eyes shut to the high afternoon sun.

"Now? I leave tomorrow," Lincoln said, always literal,

smart in his studies, charming, boyish, but lacking the imagination of a survivor.

"Now. Like this." She turned his head toward hers, their eyes so close to shut out sight, their lips touching.

"I Amanda take thee Lincoln to be my lawful wedded husband, to have and to hold, to love and to cherish." She touched her finger to his lips. "You should say it first to me. That's the way it goes."

"I don't know the words."

"Haven't you ever been to a wedding?" she asked impatiently.

"I didn't pay attention to the words."

"So then you repeat. I Lincoln take thee Amanda to be my lawful wedded wife."

"I Lincoln take thee Amanda to be my lawful wedded wife."

"To have and to hold. To love and to cherish."

"To have and to hold. To love and to cherish."

"Now," Amanda said. "Do you have my ring?"

Lincoln looked stricken.

"Your ring? I didn't know I was to have a ring for you."

Amanda turned over on her back, covered her eyes with her damp-sleeved arm.

"I thought you would have something permanent to show what we have meant to each other—in case we never see each other again."

"I will see you before I ship out to France. Nothing will happen to me in training camp. I promise."

Amanda turned her head away.

"Perhaps something will happen to me. Especially now I have to leave home and become a photographer," she said. "I could even be murdered for pretending to be something I'm not."

"I'm so sorry, Amanda." Lincoln touched her cheek. "That was cloddish of me not to have thought of a ring."

They parted at the entrance to Dumbarton Oaks, their faces flushed with kisses and tears.

No one was home when Amanda returned except Louisa busy with supper in the kitchen and bad-tempered as

she had been ever since Mrs. Steward had taken in
boarders.

"So he's gone," Louisa said without particular sympathy.

"He leaves tomorrow morning for Texas."

"True love. I forget what it was like. Time-consuming,
that's how I remember it."

"Do you remember my parents' courtship?" Amanda
asked, taking a spoon of mashed potatoes.

"That I remember very well," Louisa said.

Once when Amanda had first moved back to Washington, after her father's death, she had asked Louisa about
her mother.

"She was beautiful and brash," Louisa had said.

"What is brash?" Amanda asked.

"Brave and nervy," Louisa replied.

Amanda had considered. In Ashland, people had described her mother as lovely and generous and warm,
words appropriate to a lady. Brash was a new possibility.
She began to think of her mother as brave in warrior
terms, courageous in battle.

"Your mother," Louisa said, testing the pork roast for
doneness, "captured your father as if he were a flag."

The vision of her mother capturing her father pleased
Amanda as much as the news of her brashness had when
Amanda was younger.

Upstairs on her bed, there was as usual on Tuesdays a
letter from Flat Mouth. This time she opened it.

Dear A Man,

*It is six weeks since I have had a letter from you and
always before you have written so I have a letter every
Tuesday morning unless it is snowing.*

*Has something happened to you I wonder. There is a
telephone at the lumber camp where I am working since
Christmas and if I do not hear soon, I will find you by
telephone.*

Your friend forever,
Flat Mouth

Dear Flat Mouth, Amanda wrote.

Something has happened to me in the last six weeks which is like a sickness but one from which I will eventually recover.

I will write you about it when the diagnosis and my future is more clear.

I must tell you that I'm going to this war in Europe as a photographer but I have first to leave home and disguise myself as a man since I can't do this kind of work as a woman. I am taking on the name Sam Dane.

I wish you happiness and if this strange sickness had not had me in its grip, I would have written.

> *Love forever,*
> *A Man, in fact.*

A knock came to the bedroom door and it was Louisa, flour on her apron, on her hands.

"The lovesick soldier is in the parlor to see you," she said.

Lincoln, flushed, breathless from running, was pacing back and forth in the parlor when Amanda came downstairs.

"Can we go outside for just a moment?" he said. "In the garden."

She led the way to the back garden, out of sight of the kitchen window where Louisa was standing.

"I have brought you something," he said, so pleased he could hardly contain himself. "Put out your hand."

She put out both hands.

"Your left hand," he said triumphantly.

He took it in his own.

"With this ring, I thee wed."

And he placed a small gold band set with dark rubies, several of them, perfectly round, across the top of the ring.

"I stole it," he said.

"Stole it?"

"From my mother's jewel box. Wear it always as a token of my love," he said, for once in charge of the drama of the moment. "Good-bye beautiful Amanda. Good-bye."

At the gate, he turned back.

"If you happen to see my mother anyplace," he called, "hide your hand."

TEN

AMANDA, AS SAMMY Dane, had careful plans which took up the rest of 1917.

Dear Flat Mouth, she wrote at the beginning of September 1917.

> *All that I am going to tell you from now on until I go to the war is private, even from Day. I write it to you because if I die of this plan, someone will have known my life up until its end. Otherwise I feel as if I have never existed.*
>
> *I wish I believed in God, or several of them—the latter more convincing to me but unfortunately I don't.*
>
> *Plan for Sam Dane: Photographer.*
>
> *This summer (cool, breezy with a fine Wisconsin sun, unheard of in Washington) I am taking photographs which indicate I am first professional and second courageous facing danger without shirking in order to convince the newspapers and magazines of my skill. I have so far taken one photograph of a murder on S Street in Georgetown. I came just after the killing of a prostitute (I have permission to use my grandfather's motorcar. I lurk around the police station and follow the police cars when they receive an emergency call.*
>
> *Which is the way I arrived at the murder on S Street.) I got a very good close-up shot of the dead prostitute, quite daring because her skirt flew up when she was shot, revealing a gun in a holster just under her garter and no other underwear. Her face was particularly clear in the photograph, her eyes wide open in surprise. And then the police caught the suspect, a young man, maybe twenty, impeccably dressed. The close-up I have of his face is one of complete boredom.*
>
> *I should mention that by a process of developing, I*

*have learned to alter the exact picture taken—otherwise
the* Washington Post *newspaper would not have published my picture on the front if it had been obvious the
prostitute was not wearing underwear. But there it was
with my byline,* SAMMY DANE, *and a story about how the
bored young man had known the prostitute too well.*

*I am building a portfolio to get a job at a paper or
magazine and then that job will send me as a correspondent to the war.*

*So far, I have one bar fight scene which I took in Bal-
timore and several still shots of poverty in Washington,
particularly amongst the Negroes, as well as a picture
which the* Washington Post *bought of a dead baby put
out in the trash behind a tenement. I was wandering
around this very poor section of the city (dressed
scruffily as a man, of course) and there was this terrible
smell in the alley which I followed to the trash bin. I
opened the trash bin and there was a baby—maybe two
months old. So I called the police. According to a story
I read in the* Post, *no one claimed the baby, but obvi-
ously someone put him there and killed him first.*

*In April, I plan to have enough pictures in my portfo-
lio to find a regular job so I can be properly bonded
and sent to war. Meanwhile I have a post office box in
Georgetown in the name of Sam Dane. I haven't
changed into Sammy yet as I'm still living with my
grandparents who have already put up with me as a
mute and I imagine will draw the line at a change of
sex.*

*I am taking lessons in flying an airplane from a
young pilot who leaves soon for France. I'm glad he's
going because at the end of each lesson, he seeks pay-
ment in romance, a barter which I have so far refused.*

*I have not had such a sense of excitement since we
were children together at Bad River.*

Love forever,
A Man

Lincoln Draper left for France in January, later than
planned because he was selected for special training as an

officer. Amanda saw him once for three sweet and painful days in the autumn and then he was sent to Florida to complete his training.

Almost daily, Amanda received notes of deep and abiding love comparing her to a variety of flowers, particularly tropical ones.

Dear Lincoln, she wrote crossly after one of the letters.

> *I am not like a rose hibiscus. I have black hair and sharp features, even angular, very dark eyes. Do you remember me? Maybe the stamen of the hibiscus but not the petals.*
> *Isn't there anything going on in Florida at all?*
> *I of course love you forever—*
>
> > *Amanda*

Lincoln didn't write for several weeks, even after letters from Amanda imploring his forgiveness. When he finally did, it was to request the return of the ring.

> *Dear Amanda,*
> *You may or may not recall a ring I gave you with rubies—real ones, not small either—which was my mother's.*
> *Please return it to her.*
>
> > *Yours,*
> > *Lincoln Draper,*
> > *Captain, United States Army*

Dear Captain Draper, she wrote back.

> *I will not return the ring, you boobie. It's my wedding ring from my loving husband and people from his background do not so easily get unmarried.*
>
> > *Love forever,*
> > *Your rose hibiscus*

He came home once more before he left in January, looking wonderful in uniform, brave and somehow sad, his face still full of boyhood. They had dinner at his family's house, an evening of merriment until his father, a congressman from Illinois, whose dark countenance had gone unnoticed throughout the meal, got up to make a toast.

"It is a real war," he said when everyone was drinking down their champagne. "We forget that here in the United States."

Lincoln's letters from France were of a different character than his romantic letters from training camp—less frequent, terse, with only an occasional burst of boyish sentiment.

Darling, he wrote in May of 1918.

> *Give up your plans. It is terrible here beyond belief.*
> *Love, Lincoln*

But Sammy Dane was already in place.

Amanda had researched carefully the possibilities for war photographers. She knew her chances were small even as a man. There were only fifty official photographers in Europe at the time. In the summer of 1917, the American Expeditionary Force had been established as a press center in Paris, Chaumont, and Neufchâteau. Censorship was tightly enforced.

But early in June 1918, under pressure from the press who could not cover the vast expanse of the war effort, General Pershing cabled Washington to announce that the General Staff was now authorized to employ civilian photographers for photographic operations if circumstances warranted overseas. The cable published in the *Post* went on to say that photographers should be accredited and bonded before leaving the United States, that they agree to pay all expenses, to submit all work to censorship, and to attend to their own print development.

At dawn on the ninth of June, Amanda Steward left home. She had practiced this morning for months.

She had clothes which had been Lincoln's old trousers and shirts packed for Sammy Dane in a valise under her bed. She cut her hair with a razor just above the ear, flattened her breasts with a rectangular cloth tied tight, and two hours before the Steward house was stirring, she left by the back steps, softly in stocking feet. She took a taxi to Union Station, boarded the train for New York City, and was beyond Baltimore before anyone in the household noticed her absence. In fact, they might imagine she was off taking pictures in the early light and not begin to worry until supper. By then she would already have made contact with *Leslie's* magazine, which had published three of her photographs—one a picture of a young doughy-faced boy flying toward manhood in his United States Army uniform, drinking a whiskey at a bar, and two were at the Red Cross, one in particular a very old woman, thin as a sparrow, her hands arthritic, rolling bandages. By the end of June, she would be a bonded civilian photographer and experienced pilot in France.

On the train, she wrote to Flat Mouth.

Dear Flat Mouth,
   I'm off to war. I will love you forever

                                             Sam Dane
   p.s. Check the magazines, particularly Leslie's, *in Ashland for my pictures.*

ELEVEN

ON THE TROOP ship, there were as well as soldiers six other civilian photographers and a veteran, Clifford Bones, called Blue, a Texan from Dallas who had been in Europe since 1915, twice injured and now on a mission following the Second Battalion replacement troops for men lost in the Battle of Château-Vieux in February 1918. He was a small, squarish, swarthy man, middle-aged, saved by a kindness in his warm attentive eyes, the eyes of a domesticated pet. He took an interest in Amanda.

"Quiet sort of guy, aren't you?" he asked on the second day out, gray and stormy, the smell of vomit heavy in the air. "How old are you?"

"Eighteen," Amanda said. "On the thirteenth of September."

She had a simple story for Sam Dane so as not to confuse the facts. He was from Madison, Wisconsin, the youngest son in a large Roman Catholic family. He had been taking pictures for Wisconsin papers for five years and had come to Europe to work freelance. He did not have as much experience as the other civilian photographers on the ship, but what he did have which impressed Blue Bones considerably was a new DeRam camera, which freed the photographer from setting the exposure or manipulating the film plates. And training as a pilot.

"Major Palmer will be very pleased to have you," Blue said. "Even though you're young. There are no new cameras available in Europe and almost none of us with the press knows how to fly."

Mostly on the long tumultuous journey with dark wintry days and nights of such turbulence that she was roped in the bed, Amanda resisted Blue's gestures of friendship and those of the others, feigning seasickness, lying against the stack of the steamship on the bottom open deck, overwhelmed by the bold danger of what she was doing.

What had been a kind of game, a theatrical production with the illusion of reality and not reality itself, now on the rolling troop ship, a pin prick on the Atlantic Ocean, became serious. Amanda was cold to the bone, disoriented by seasickness and the surreal look of soldiers in the bluish light of stormy days; she wondered if she were going crazy. Who was Lincoln Draper to her and did she love him to the end of the world as she had told him? Why was she following him to war, she asked herself, anxious to iron flat her mind, to think in a linear and analytic manner, to remake the world around her as sane, to still the wild bird trapped in her skull. Whose legs are these, she thought looking at her long legs in Lincoln's trousers stretched out in front of her. Whose arms but the arms of Sammy Dane. These hands belong to a young man who will be eighteen on the 13th of September, who believes in God.

She had forgotten to stuff her pants. She looked down at

the flat trousers across her belly and wondered what Blue had thought when he looked at her—what had the others thought. Was he asking himself, Who is this man built like a woman but a woman dressed like a man? And if he asked her, she would laugh and say of course. After all, they wouldn't send her back to America now.

Blue was standing on the deck, the last day out, looking at her.

"Why do you want to be here?" he asked. "You don't seem to be the type."

"It was never a choice," Amanda said. "I've known I was coming for a year. I've just been waiting for the rules to change so I could come as a civilian."

"Have you seen much?" Blue asked.

"I have seen death," she said. "Murder."

"What you will see in Europe is horrible beyond pictures," he said. "The photographs are censored so as not to upset the people at home but even so, no picture could possibly contain the horror."

"I have seen Jimmy Hare's pictures of the Germans and one of the Americans inspecting a field of dead Germans."

"You can't re-create the mud in pictures," Blue said. "Or a gas death."

"I thought the weather had been better."

"The fields are still mud. Mostly it's rained for a year and it swallows you. I've seen it. I was a kilometer from the front and a group of Germans moving low to the ground with guns hit soft wet earth and WHOOSH. They were gone. Swallowed. Nobody will ever see them again, lost in the center of the earth." He lit a cigarette and gave it to Amanda. "Are you afraid to die?"

"I don't know," she said. She wanted to tell him that she knew about death, her parents were dead, but that was Amanda. The parents of Sam Dane were just fine in Madison, Wisconsin.

"It is easy for a photographer to get around in Europe," Blue told her. "What is not easy is the job itself of facing down death."

Among the letters from her mother, Amanda had recently discovered one half-written, folded up with another, unsigned.

Dear Mama, her mother had written.

> *When you were alive, I felt I could do anything because you were here. Now I don't know the limitations of my life.*

On the train from Le Havre to Paris, Blue Bones sat next to her, their arms touching. He had bought a newspaper and was translating it for her. Seeing his large competent hand around the paper, Amanda felt a rush.

"Where will you stay?" he asked.

"I'll find a room, I suppose," she said.

He invited her to stay at his flat, a small three-room place, he said, on the Left Bank, which he shared with two other journalists from Providence, Rhode Island.

It was early morning when they arrived. "Raining as usual," Blue said. "It rains most of the time." And he showed her Paris. At lunch, they drank too much wine and he walked her up the hill of Montmartre so she would be sober enough to face Major Palmer.

Major Palmer was in charge of the press section of G-2 intelligence. Until recently he had been the foremost correspondent in Europe as representative of the American press services—Associated Press, United Press, and International News Service. He had become something of a hero in the hard-bitten press corps for turning down the job of chief correspondent of the *New York Herald* at a very high salary when General Pershing offered him a commission as a major in charge of press intelligence. He subjected photography to strict censorship, rejecting any photographs which could give information to the enemy or cause anxiety at home, such as American corpses or hospitals or for that matter a naked soldier in bed at a whorehouse.

"This kind of thing won't do while you're here," he said of the photographs Amanda had brought in her portfolio along with her falsified credentials. "They're too explicit and provocative."

"I can fly a plane," she said. "And I have my own camera." She showed him the DeRam camera which could be used easily from a plane because she didn't have to reload after each shot.

The major considered. "If you're any good," he said, "that will help."

He filled out the papers necessary for Amanda to travel freely as a photographer within Allied territory.

"Blue will tell you, you're on your own, Mr. Dane. So far, no dead photographers, but who knows." And then he laughed.

"I don't know if anyone has ever told you this," he said, "but you would make a good-looking woman."

"No," Amanda said coolly. "No one has ever told me."

The flat, just off the river Seine, third floor, was sparsely furnished with four cots, a dining room table with stacks of old newspapers and magazines, a bowl of pipe tobacco, discarded fruit pits, and two mangy tabbies sleeping on the newspapers.

"You are welcome to stay as long as you like," Blue said. "I've been here three years and we go in and out, out sometimes weeks at a time."

In the bathroom, Amanda looked at herself in the mirror. Sammy Dane needed a haircut, she thought, but otherwise he was intact and she was aware of being as comfortable with him as she had been years ago as a young mute girl in Washington, D.C.

"Do you have a girlfriend?" Blue asked Amanda when she came out of the bathroom.

"No. I used to in high school but we drifted apart." She lay down on the cot.

"I haven't had a girlfriend for years—just women in and out. Too unpredictable, this life," he said. "I used to have a wife." He sat up on his elbow and looked at Amanda. "You need a haircut, buddy," he said. "I'll do it if you like."

Later while Blue was cutting her hair, his hand on the back of her neck, on her face, tugging at the hair around her temple—she wanted him to cut her hair all afternoon—she asked how she might find Lincoln.

"My cousin is a captain with the Second Division," she said. "He has been outside of Paris. I have a letter. Can you find soldiers?"

"He may have moved, probably has since your letter, but you can find soldiers. Just call headquarters or Palmer could help you."

Later that night—no one in the apartment except the two of them—Amanda felt Blue Bones looking at her.

"You know," he said finally. "There's something odd about you, buddy—soft. Though that isn't exactly what I mean. Maybe young. Or boyish. That's the word."

"Well, I am only eighteen."

"Yeah, you said." He lay on his back on his cot and smoked one cigarette after the other. "So tomorrow I go to the front. That's where the group of soldiers on our ship is off to and I follow them."

"What's it like close?" Amanda asked.

"Terrifying," Blue said. "You could come along."

"Tomorrow I'm going to find Lincoln," Amanda said. She reached over and took Blue's cigarette. "Mind?" There was something provocative in the gesture.

In the middle of the night, restless in the cold apartment, Amanda woke up to Blue covering her with a blanket.

"Thank you," she said softly, not in the voice of Sammy Dane at all. "I was freezing."

TWELVE

CAPTAIN LINCOLN DRAPER was camped forty-five air miles east of Paris outside Belleau Wood, with the Second Division, Third Field Battalion, twenty-five thousand men in two brigades, one army, one marine, and one thousand officers stretched out in camp below the wood.

In 1918, the front line ran from the North Sea between

Dunkirk and Ostend down the middle of France north and east of Paris. Belleau Wood had been the hunting preserve for the ancient château of Belleau and was a densely planted wood with slender trees, no undergrowth for protection, and high ground scarred by crags and gullies. At the southeast corner of the wood was a small village called Bouresches held by the Germans. To control the wood and thereby access to Paris, the Allies had to push the Germans back and retake Bouresches. To the south, the Third Division at Château-Thierry was holding at the Marne.

Lincoln had seen action already on three occasions, in February, late April, and May, losing a large number of the Third Field Battalion at Dormans and then again at Château-Thierry, but in mid-June new troops full of youth and boisterous enthusiasm had arrived from the United States, and so in high spirits they waited for orders to fight.

Major Palmer had arranged for Amanda to go by staff car with Blue, who was headed to Château-Thierry at the Marne. He knew Captain Lincoln Draper, he said, and admired him for his courage. He was pleased for Sam Dane to go to Belleau Wood.

"They ought to advance on Bouresches in the next two days," Major Palmer said. "And the conditions should be good for photography—high places, woods, and open fields. If the weather holds, you might get something." He gave Amanda a stack of photographs before she left.

"Look at these, Mr. Dane," he said. "These are the kinds of pictures getting through the censors and printed back home."

She dropped the photographs in her camera bag, which she had been provided along with camouflage, a helmet, a gas mask, and a machine gun.

"You know how to use it?" Major Palmer asked of the gun.

"Yes," Amanda replied.

"So you have trained," Blue said in the car on the way northeast of Paris.

"No," Amanda said. "If you mean the machine gun."

"Here," Blue said, taking the gun from her. "Have you ever shot anything?"

"Rabbits." She and Flat Mouth had shot rabbits one summer when Flat Mouth was learning to shoot.

"Well, if you can shoot rabbits."

"You think I'll need it?" Amanda asked, hoping her voice sounded firm and casual, unconcerned.

"Of course you'll need it," Blue said.

They didn't talk during the ride, about three hours by car over rough terrain, through Allied territory in which there were certainly German troops.

Amanda imagined her meeting with Lincoln full of humor when he saw her as a young man in a helmet, imagined their shaking hands—what else could they do, of course, in the company of strangers? He would be astonished to see her and it pleased her to think of it.

They took photographs along the way, passing fields, burned-out mud ponds, the buildings leveled, the vegetation gone. They stopped at the phone board, an operation center close to the front, and arrangements were made for a private, slightly injured in an earlier battle, to be with Amanda. Blue got out of the car when they arrived at the outskirts of Belleau Wood and stayed with her until she met up with the private, a boy no more than eighteen, a deeply polite southern boy from Georgia who had shrapnel in his shoulder from the day before and couldn't fight.

"See you back in Paris," Blue said then, giving her a mock punch, and Amanda had a sudden longing, a sense of abandonment, as if her mother whose death she had not noticed when she was a child could die again and again, at surprising moments with almost strangers like Blue Bones, to whom she had become inadvertently attached.

"See you, buddy," she said bravely.

She climbed into the car with Hunter Conaway, for that was the name of the impeccable southern boy.

"I have orders to take you to Château-Thierry on the Marne where there's fighting," he said.

"I thought I was going to Belleau Wood. Is that where we are?" she asked.

"We're three kilometers from Belleau Wood," he said. "But we can't go by daylight. There are Germans all around us here and the woods are full of thousands of our men waiting for orders. If we were to go in now, we might give away the plan."

"What's the plan?"

"I don't know. We don't find out until it's about to happen. But I know the woods are full of more men than I've seen in all my time here, which is going on nine months, mostly on the front."

He drove the car in the direction of the river Marne past devastated fields, wheat fields sheared by battle, trees half-burned. His eyes traveled the sides of the roads.

"Germans," he said with disgust.

"You've seen some."

"No sir," he said. "But they're around here."

"Will we be coming back to Belleau Wood? I have a cousin."

"Tonight. God willing. Once it's dark we'll come back, park the car, and walk the last kilometer into the woods."

"Maybe you know my cousin."

"Captain Draper. He said you were his cousin and he'd see you tonight. Sam Dane. Right?"

"Right."

"My father's name is Sam. Samuel Conaway III but I was named Hunter for my mother's family."

"How is Lincoln?"

"Fine. As far as I can tell, sir. He seems fine. He's a quiet sort of man but he'd do anything, you know. Anything. The men respect him, more than a lot of the other officers. He doesn't turn his head."

"What do you mean by that?" she asked.

"He doesn't run. Mostly out there we're all scared as chicken shit. Given a way out, a lot of us will run. I have. But he doesn't. Maybe he isn't scared. Maybe he likes to fight."

"Maybe," Amanda said. "But I don't remember that about him."

They stopped the car in a valley surrounded by low hills which overlooked the Marne and climbed to the top of a particularly high hill, not a mountain but the climb was long and the view quite extraordinary when they got to the top. The day was clear and blue over the river, over the

French and American troops spread along the river, flat and treeless in the valley except for some low underbrush which had survived the years of fighting. Behind them clouds were gathering.

"Later, it's going to rain. I'm glad I don't live in this country. All it does is rain but it'll be good for tonight. I have a feeling we're going forward tonight," the young man said.

They sat together all afternoon watching the fighting in the distance and smoking until Amanda's cigarettes were gone. Occasionally they spoke and she took pictures, but only for the sake of appearance since the private had gone to the trouble of bringing her to the front. She was too far away for the pictures.

"Mostly the soldiers move in small groups like four or five," Hunter said to her. "I thought it would be like the pictures I've seen. The whole army marching forward against the enemy. Like the Civil War. And horses."

"Are there a lot of casualties?" Amanda asked.

From the vantage of the hill above the Marne, the battle seemed unreal.

"A lot were killed yesterday when I was hurt. I had a buddy called . . ." He stopped. She knew he couldn't bear to say his friend's name.

"Are you afraid all the time?" she asked.

"Yes sir," he said in his soft melodic voice.

Amanda laughed. "I'm only eighteen," she said. "You don't need to call me sir."

At dusk, Hunter said it was time to leave. There was a warm even-tempered rain falling as darkness settled in and they drove back to Belleau Wood in silence.

"Now you've seen the war," Hunter said.

"I don't feel as if I've seen it. More as if I've read a book about it."

They parked the car off the road in a clump of trees with two other cars and walked, off the road, through a field to the edge of Belleau Wood.

"I'll tell Captain Draper you're here," Hunter said. "You wait here."

She waited in the dark sitting on a large rock and for a

long time he didn't come. No one came. She heard the sounds of voices but muffled, as if people were speaking back and forth underwater. She found a cigarette deep in her side pocket and smoked it. The darkness was pure, unalleviated by light—the stars covered by a thin fog, and she could not see at all into the small forest where the Second Division was in camp.

Lincoln was there beside her before she even realized someone had come out of the trees.

"Follow me," he whispered. He walked across a small clearing into a wood and then he took her hand.

"I came," she said. "You didn't believe I would."

"Shh," he said. He put his hand over her mouth. Then he put his lips over her mouth, kissing her deeply. He pulled her to the ground.

"Don't you have breasts anymore?" he breathed into her ear.

"Tied up," she said.

"And your beautiful hair." He ran his fingers through her short hair and kissed her eyes, pulling her across him.

"I hope there's something of Amanda Steward left in Samuel Dane," he said unbuttoning her trousers.

She laughed. "See," she said. "I'm stuffed." She pulled the small wad of cotton cloth forming an irregularly shaped penis in her trousers.

"You are an embarrassment," he said, licking her cheeks, her eyes, her ears.

"Then you are surprised to see me."

"I am enchanted," he said in her ear. "I only wish I could see you."

The rain kept up through the early night, a light sweet rain, soft on their naked bodies. They lay in one another's arms under a bush, sleeping in fits, their lips together.

"We have orders to move at three A.M.," he said. She didn't know what time it was, only that there was a change in light. The rain had stopped and the dark had lightened with a sense of coming dawn.

"You come back with me now and we'll find Hunter. My men are in the first group out." He kissed her fingers.

"What does that mean?"

"It means we're marching on a town at the other side of the wood held by the Germans—thousands of us in a surprise attack going straight across an open field. It will be amazing. We haven't had orders like this since I came."

"Where will I be?"

"On the edge of the wood, behind us actually, with Hunter." He touched her lips. "Shh. These woods could be full of Huns."

He pulled her against him with such a longing she could feel him to her bones.

"Good-bye, sweet Amanda."

"But won't I see you tonight? Or later? After the battle."

"Tonight," he said. "Maybe. Depending on orders." He laid his palm against her cheek. "Be careful, Sammy Dane."

THIRTEEN

FOUR A.M. ON the 30th of June, it was foggy and cold as the Second Division moved out of camp. Amanda stood with Hunter at the far end of the wood.

"What will we do?"

"Watch from here at first. Then go closer."

"All the way to the fighting?"

"That's what you want, isn't it?" Hunter asked. "That's what other photographers have wanted."

"Right," she said. Her stomach turned over.

"You've used one of these?" He indicated her machine gun.

"Sure," she said.

He looked over at her curiously. "You've been trained, haven't you?"

"I'm a trained photographer, if that's what you mean."

"No. I mean trained to take pictures in action while there are shells falling all around you."

"No," Amanda said. "I haven't."

She had been in France seven days and she knew nothing except the small details—the apartment with Blue, the conversation with Major Palmer, the night with Lincoln, the landscape. Nothing else seemed to have a reality, even her view of the fighting at the Marne and now the sharp sound of artillery in the thin dawn. She was afraid because she knew she ought to be, not out of any real sense of fear. Which was lucky. Later she understood that the absence of emotions had protected her all that terrible day when the Second Division died like ants on their way to victory.

She followed Hunter through the wood, an oasis of protection in the middle of a vast, desolate wheat field whispering in the rain.

At the edge of the wood, Hunter stopped and they could see in the beginning dawn the long stretch of field.

"This is going to be amazing," Hunter said quietly. "I haven't seen the kind of attack you're going to see here." He was a soft-faced boy with flat features, fair speckled skin, and always a look of youthful surprise in his face, as if he had learned the look by heart for war.

"Tell me what I'm going to see."

"As soon as the fog lifts—feel it now on our faces? Well, as soon as it lifts just a little so we don't kill our own men, that field is going to be a sea of Yanks."

Hunter couldn't stand still. He readjusted his helmet, checked his gun, paced back and forth in a small arena.

"I wish they'd start," he said. "I'm going crazy."

And even as he was speaking, the woods opened up and the field was full of soldiers, almost in formation shoulder to shoulder. A tempest of machine gun fire shattered the air. On and on the men came, out of the woods, filling the field until they were stretched from one side to the other. Then as quickly as they filled the field, the lines were pockmarked with fallen soldiers.

Amanda grabbed Hunter's arm. "It's crazy," she said. "Hundreds are going to be killed."

"But we're going to win," Hunter said fiercely. "We're going to win this one. Let's go. You want to see the real thing. This is it."

"Out into the field?"

"Across the field where the war's being fought. I want to see us win."

She tightened the strap on her helmet and followed Hunter across the field, shells falling on them like hail. They ran to the left flank of the Second Division into the blaze of enemy fire, the wheat peppered with crimson poppies underneath her feet. Ahead of her, Hunter dove into a trench dug just at the edge of Belleau Wood. Shells pounded on her helmet; she didn't know whether or not she'd been shot as she fell into the trench beside Hunter.

There was a dead American in the trench. His face was concealed by the position into which he had fallen when he was killed and Amanda did not realize he was dead until the soldier beside him with eyes so blue they shone, lights on his blackened face, shouted to her above the noise, "DEAD." They had to move him to make room for another doughboy who came into the trench on all fours, shot in the leg, bleeding in the face. When they moved the dead soldier, his head fell back. He had died screaming.

"His name is David Spike," the blue-eyed soldier said. "Private David Spike."

Awkwardly Amanda took two shots of David Spike, feeling that she was violating the young soldier, feeling sick at the sight. But it was her job to take photographs, she told herself when the horror of that day slid back to her in the weeks that followed. One picture was front on and showed his teeth, his tongue, the way he died with his mouth open. The second was at an angle with his face in profile and the blue-eyed soldier leaning against the side of the trench, his machine gun cradled, his head in his hands.

They were in the trench for a long time, the machine gun fire unrelenting, the twenty-five thousand men charging on and on across the fields.

"Stay down," Hunter said to her. "You'll know when there's a break in the firing."

Twice there was a break in the advance. Suddenly the woods spilled no more soldiers and the machine gun fire from the German side became intermittent, tentative.

"A trick," Hunter said to her. "To make the Germans think we're finished."

"But we're not?" Amanda asked.

"The woods are full of men. We could go on all day."

The sun, not yet over the horizon, created a yellow fog. Amanda left the trench to take pictures of a line of soldiers, eight doughboys on their bellies lying on the field pulling forward toward the trenches. She got two pictures of the doughboys: one as they crawled forward and, much later after the day's attack was over, she walked through the corpse-strewn field and the same eight doughboys were dead, killed in a line of rifle fire. It was the first picture of the eight living soldiers which was passed by the censors and published in *Leslie's* magazine. The second picture, of the doughboys dead, was too damaging, too disturbing, Major Palmer said.

"Do you have a girlfriend?" Hunter asked. They were lying face to face on the ground.

"No I don't," Amanda replied.

"I do," Hunter said. "Mary Louise. She's very beautiful."

"I wish I did," Amanda said politely.

Again at dawn, the field was empty except for the corpses and the injured from the first attack, and they waited in the trenches in the strange silence, interrupted occasionally by gunfire, by the sound of the wind through the wheat. Then they heard orders.

"Go kill," she heard an officer shout near her. "What's the matter with you anyway? You want to live forever?"

The air swarmed with excitement and the human blanket rolled out of the wood again, across the wheat field, swept by machine gun bullets, the wheat blowing, waving in the storm of metal. All down the lines of thousands, men were folding but the general glorious sight was the sea swell of soldiers advancing on the German wood.

Amanda had moved out of the trenches into the shadow of the wood facing the American advance. She was photographing the victory when out of nowhere, out of the trees, a German soldier appeared with a machine gun and shot Hunter. It happened in slow motion.

Hunter moaned and folded to the ground. Amanda's instincts were quick. She shot straight toward the wood where he was standing. She was still shooting after he had fallen, the adrenaline burning her body.

Hunter was on all fours, moving toward her, his head down and blood flooding his face.

She knelt beside him.

"I see white," he said.

"You're hurt."

"I'm all right. I'm breathing," he said. "But everywhere is white."

"Hold your head up so I can look at it," Amanda said.

He did. His face was covered entirely in blood and his eye was gone.

Amanda covered her mouth.

"My eye?"

She didn't reply.

"Did you get the Hun?"

"I think."

"Go take a look."

"There might be others."

"Not likely. If there were others, he wouldn't have shot me like that. I turned around and there he was, already hurt by the way he was holding his stomach, and he shot me," Hunter said. "Go look."

The German was dead, riddled with machine gun fire, his head thrown back, blood coming from his mouth.

"You better hide me," Hunter said when she came back. "Pull me under some low brush until the fighting's over and the medics come out."

Amanda pulled him under a low bush, covered him with leaves and branches, climbed under one herself, just at the edge of the poppy field, to wait.

"It won't be long now," Hunter said.

The doughboys were still coming out of the Allied wood, wave after wave.

"The Germans can't last," he said. "We simply have too many men."

What was left when the battle was over was a field of smouldering cropped wheat and wasted soldiers flattening the pockets of standing wheat. The medics came first with their litters to bear off the damaged living.

At dusk, Amanda saw the picture which passed the censors. It became in the years to come one of the famous photographs of the Great War, called *Fraternity* in the exhibit in 1925 at the Smithsonian and in the history books. *Fraternity* by Sam Dane.

One of the officers, young himself and alone, walked through the littered field. At each body, he stopped, knelt down, touched the dead soldier's face with the palm of his hand. The picture Amanda captured was of this officer on his knees, his own face ravaged, holding the wrist of a dead boy whose hand had been blown off.

Later that night, young men in the hundreds removed from the field were buried in Belleau Wood. But in spite of the terrible losses, the spirit of victory was clear.

"I killed a German," she said. She had no particular feelings about the fact of it. She had been a young man in war and had done what was necessary to survive. What she did feel besides relief that the day was over was a keen sense of understanding of soldiers who, because they were young and men, had to be in this war and do it bravely.

Dear Flat Mouth, she wrote when she got back to Paris.

> *I am glad to have been a man. Now I have a new and profound respect for men I did not have before.*

After nightfall, starlit and clear, Lincoln pulled Amanda roughly to the ground with him, tore off her clothes, and they made desperate love.

FOURTEEN

LATE SUMMER 1918 was the turning point of the war with Germany. Three hundred thousand American soldiers full of spunk and irreverence arrived by the month in Europe and in spite of the heavy Allied losses, the Germans had no second string and could no longer compete.

By September, Amanda was settled in the flat in Paris with Blue and a Negro pilot from Columbus, Georgia, Eugene Bullard, the only colored pilot in the First War. He had flown at the beginning of the war for the French Foreign Legion, winning the Croix de Guerre, but when the United States entered the war, Americans had to join their own forces and Bullard was benched for the duration because he was Negro. Sometimes in August and September, he flew with Amanda so she could take photographs over the front, especially along the Marne. At the end of September, word came from Major Palmer that the Twenty-seventh American Division and a division of Australians had orders to break through the Hindenburg Line at the St. Quentin Canal, a large and important campaign, and Amanda went with Eugene Bullard to St. Quentin Canal.

She did not feel well when they took off from Paris. She had not been feeling well, but on this particular morning she was lightheaded and nauseous. Bullard on the other hand, bad-tempered at being sidelined by the Americans, was up to trouble. He didn't want a photographic mission. He wanted to fight.

Amanda had not seen Lincoln since the victory at Belleau Wood. The Second Division was fighting along the Marne, had in fact pushed through the German line and moved it well east of the center of France. Occasionally Major Palmer gave her word of Captain Draper, and Blue had seen him. She thought about him always, dreamed about him, but in the past tense as if he had already died. After she witnessed close up the Battle of

Belleau Wood, the loss of lives, after she had seen the face of the dead soldier in the trench with her, she could not imagine Lincoln surviving.

Hunter, who had lost his eye the week after Belleau Wood, was in a hospital in Paris waiting to be dispatched to the United States and she visited him there several times a week when she was in Paris, took cigarettes and read him chapters of Dickens.

She had been in contact with her grandparents, with her grandfather actually, who wrote her news from home addressed to Sam Dane in care of the American Expeditionary Center. He did not mention her swift departure from Washington or her life incognito and only once he made an oblique reference to her present life and then in admiration of it. "I would like to have known your mother," he wrote. "I was quite taken with her when she was in the employ of our friends in London. The Stewards have a temperament for science but are not noted for their creative imaginations." Her grandmother did not write at all.

On the flight to the Hindenburg Line, flying at dawn and in the rain, Amanda was too sick to photograph. Bullard flew the plane north to south at one thousand feet along the St. Quentin Canal, where the aerial view of the fighting was quite extraordinary. From Verdun to Flanders there was fighting, but every time Amanda put her head up to look out the window, she was sick again.

"You probably have one of those French diseases," Bullard said, anxious to stay with the plan. But by the time they reached the line where the Twenty-seventh American Division was holding, Amanda was clearly too sick to complete any kind of mission. The cockpit smelled of vomit and even Bullard was ready to turn back.

"I had that sickness once after I got hurt in Verdun," Bullard said. "It won't last long."

But what Amanda had was a different sickness.

At the beginning of September, she thought she was pregnant. By the morning of the Battle of the Hindenburg Line, she was certain.

* * *

That evening, Amanda was sleeping on a cot in the flat when Blue came back from a mission shooting pictures at the Marne. He had bad news.

She heard him on the steps of the flat—four flights down—heard his heavy coughing from cigarettes. On the bed in the bedroom Bullard was passed out drunk all day since their return from the aborted mission to the Hindenburg Line and Amanda, recovered but weary, lay on her back. The ancient tabby on her belly licked its paws. She had been looking through her photographs.

"You're not bad, Dane," Major Palmer had said to her. "You take pictures of character which won't pass the censors of course, but once I see one of yours, I never forget it."

She had taken one of Lincoln just after the battle. He was sitting on a rock at the edge of the wood, his arms on his knees, leaning forward, the classic pose of the high school athlete in his team picture, but the eyes—and this she noticed particularly as she lay on the cot in the flat in Paris—were war-battered, fixed in place like the eyes of a dead man.

"Hey Sam," Blue said gently, sinking down on the cot. He still had his helmet and gas mask, his gun locked under his arm. "I didn't think you'd be here."

"I got sick," Amanda said.

"You look sick," Blue said.

"I'm better now. But I was too sick to hang out of the airplane taking pictures."

Blue wiped his face with his sleeve.

"I've got bad news," he said.

Don't, she wanted to say. Don't say anything I already know.

But he had said it.

"Your cousin was killed last night at the Marne. I heard about it when I got there this morning."

He ruffled Amanda's short black hair.

"Sorry, buddy," he said.

"Right," Amanda said. "Thanks."

FIFTEEN

AT ELEVEN IN the morning of November 11, 1918, the Great War was over. In Paris, a submarine moored in the Seine opposite the Chamber of Deputies saluted and bells all over the city rang. People rushed into the street and as if by magic everybody in Paris knew everybody else. Parades formed instantaneously and on the rue Royale flags appeared in every window. The old veterans in battered helmets were singled out of the crowd and hoisted on shoulders. Marshal Foch's automobile was mobbed on his way to a meeting at the Council of Ministers and Amanda with Blue Bones crossed le pont Neuf over the Seine and marched with the others to la place de la Concorde. On the way, they picked up two pretty French factory girls and ran along with the girls locked between them, Blue kissing them. All day the streets were full of merriment and drink. At dusk, Amanda went back to the flat and by midnight Blue had returned with a bottle of champagne which they drank just the two of them since Bullard had found a woman at the celebration and was locked away in the bedroom with her.

Blue lay on the couch across from Amanda.

"So I guess you're going home," he said.

"I am. I don't know when."

"On a troop ship, I imagine. They'll start leaving soon."

Amanda closed her eyes. On the streets outside their window there was singing and dancing.

"Let's go, buddy," Blue said swaying toward the window to look out.

"Too much champagne," Amanda said. The baby spread across her belly, cresting her pelvis, but because she was tall she looked as if she'd simply put on a little weight, although she was certainly four months pregnant. Sometimes she thought of telling Blue, especially now, lightheaded with champagne, the war over, a spirit of the confessional in the room. But Blue was soon sleeping, snoring that way until morning, half off the couch.

The week after the armistice, Major Palmer called with arrangements for Amanda and several other civilian photographers to go home. Only the bonded war correspondents could stay in France.

"Good luck, Dane," Major Palmer said. "I'll look for your pictures."

Blue was solicitous, almost maternal, with Amanda.

"You've gotten so quiet, buddy," he said.

She found herself lonely without the war, almost despairing, and Blue responded to this new dark countenance with uncommon sweetness. Sometimes she was afraid he would make her weep when he brought her offerings, a pack of cigarettes, a beer, when he ruffled her hair.

She was pleased to be pregnant. Already she felt the presence of this young life as company. She would go back to Wisconsin with the child, she thought, live at Bad River. Certainly her grandparents wouldn't wish to have her in Washington, full-bellied and unmarried. Her mother's daughter, after all.

She had not grieved for Lincoln. It struck her as coldhearted and strange the way she thought about him. Their love affair moved her as if she'd read about it in a book. But not the loss of Lincoln Draper, although when she thought about him the picture she had was of a splendid-looking man and brave. What actually made her unbearably sad, what she wept for, was the loss of his love for her.

"Blue?" She walked into the kitchen the last night of her life in Paris; Blue had bought a chicken, was roasting it in herbs. She had rehearsed many scenes of this kind in her mind. She would tell Blue the truth. Somehow she had lost interest in Sam Dane since Lincoln had been killed.

"I'm not a bad cook," Blue said taking the skinny wartime chicken out of the oven. "We'd have a good time if you stuck around."

"We would," she said.

"I wish you could."

And she knew then by the genuine sadness in his face that she couldn't tell him the truth. He would be betrayed by it. Although what she urgently wanted was to drop Sam Dane's clothes on the floor of the bedroom and fall into bed with Blue Bones for this last night.

A quiet overtook them during the meal. Even too much wine did not make a difference. The closeness between them had been instinctual, unearned by the little time they had spent together. She felt closer to him than to anyone but Flat Mouth and the memory of her mother and he didn't even know who she was.

That night she could tell he watched her sleeping although she was not sleeping; she lay with her eyes closed, conscious of a sense of longing like dampness filling the corners of the room.

Blue had left by the time Amanda woke up in the morning to take a train to a ship which was scheduled to leave Calais in the evening.

Dear Sam, he wrote.

> *Call if you ever get back to Paris, buddy. I doubt I'm coming home.*
> *Send me your pictures of the war.*

Blue

SIXTEEN

BACK IN WASHINGTON, awash in victory, Amanda went to bed. Every day, late November into December, she sat in her old room propped up with hills of pillows and read the letters from her mother and Flat Mouth, recipes from Louisa's cookbooks, and looked at the pictures in the large illustrated books from her childhood, loving especially the dangerous innocence of Arthur Rackham's water babies.

She had been welcomed home in late November as if she'd been on a holiday in Paris. There was no mention of the war at all—they had asked her nothing about the baby except whether the father was living and she told them he was not. Then one night, her grandfather knocked, came into her bedroom, stood at the end of her canopy bed, and told her the news that would alter her life as if he were giving news of the daily life of close relations.

"We have said nothing about your shenanigans as a photographer in Europe," he said. "And of course we won't."

"What about the baby?"

"About the baby, your grandmother and aunt and I have spoken tonight."

"I am planning to go to Wisconsin," Amanda said. "As soon as I'm stronger."

She had been too tired to go to Bad River, too mind-weary with the last few months, but she planned to go soon after Christmas before she was too pregnant to travel.

"We have been fortunate to find a young widower with two grown sons, a physician with whom I work who remembers you from your first year here and is willing, actually delighted, to marry you."

"To marry me?" Amanda said in astonishment.

"He is Jonathan Abbott and he's quite well-off, agreeable, and youthful for forty-five. And handsome, your aunt says."

"I am not going to marry him, of course," Amanda said. "I'm not going to marry anyone at all."

Dr. Jonathan Abbott was handsome, as her aunt had said, tall and elegant with a long forehead, narrow water-blue eyes, a fine nose, and slender lips. Amanda was pleased to look at him and actually pleased to talk with him, remote from human intercourse as her life had become in her recovery from the war. There was something awkward and touching about him—the formal way in which he spoke to her, his careful solicitation, even the way he looked at her with obvious admiration. He could not take his eyes off her short black hair, struck by the danger of it on a woman.

"I like your hair quite a lot," he finally said one afternoon at tea, for that is when he came to see her in the back parlor, darkness having already settled around the house and her grandmother having arranged that they be left alone.

His proposal to her was charming in its self-effacement. It came in late December, just after the Christmas parties at which Amanda had not appeared to preserve her honor, as her grandmother had advised.

"I have no sense of dishonor," Amanda had said. "But I'm just as glad to miss the parties."

She had called Lincoln's parents to tell them how sorry she had been to hear about his death. What surprised her was the terrible rush of emotion when she spoke to them—how long it had taken her to make the call, how long to repair after she had made it. She began to wonder if her nerves were shattered. Perhaps, she thought later, she should have told the Drapers about the baby. They would have taken her in certainly, given her a room with special service, dinner in the company of people with whom she had no familial history. But she didn't tell them. She knew absolutely that she wanted the baby to be her own, undivided.

Jonathan Abbott told her she was under no obligation. He would be very happy to marry her if she'd consent. He had quite a large house on P Street and entertained. His sons were almost grown, off to college, now the war was ended. His wife had been dead of tuberculosis for five years and he'd be pleased to have her young life lightening his house. And the baby, he added.

It was the first mention he had made of the baby.

"I'd be pleased to have you see the house if you'd like to," he said.

She laughed. "Honestly, Jonathan," she said. "This is 1918. We don't marry houses any longer." She was actually comforted by his offer, although she knew she had no business marrying, especially this kind man, fragile and thin-skinned as she was, undependable. She could leave him tomorrow.

"And what do you mean by obligation?" She knew very

well what he meant but she made him say it in his labored
nineteenth-century prose.

"A responsibility to the marriage bed," he called it.

"Oh sex." She laughed and ran her bare toes across the
tops of his polished shoes.

They married quietly in the parlor of her grandmother's
house two days after her nineteenth birthday. They agreed
at the Stewards' request to say that the marriage had taken
place in May but had been kept secret because of
Amanda's desire to volunteer as a nurse for the war effort,
another decision the Stewards made, and that Amanda had
continued to live on N Street where she could get proper
care from Louisa and her grandmother because she had returned from France unwell.

"I can't move to P Street now," Amanda said after the
ceremony, although the plans had been for them to move
that evening. "Not tonight."

She was out of breath with anxiety. She had not understood the depth of her accumulated terrors. She wanted to
place her life in a small lined box, without risk, without
danger of alteration to the predictability of days. She
stayed in her bedroom, venturing no farther than the garden, and Dr. Abbott accommodated her. He became a regular visitor in her life and although she did not love him
in any romantic sense, she began to trust the hour of his
stated arrival, the nature of his conversation, the truth of
his promise that her life with him would be without obligation.

Sara was born on the fourth of March, 1919, in the bedroom of the Stewards' house—a particularly small, downy
baby girl, agreeable from birth.

AMANDA
AND
SARA

ONE

AMANDA FELL IN love with Sara, a kind of paralysis of love, adhering as if to sustain a permanent condition of pregnancy. The power of her feelings was entirely unexpected, called out of a cavern of her own childhood like a high fever which left her susceptible to nightmares.

She dreamed of dead babies. In her dreams, they floated facedown in Lake Superior, their tiny arms spread like tipped sails on the water, and she, near the shore, knee-deep in the water, reached out toward them with a long stick, but the current was taking them downstream.

"It's not ordinary," Jonathan Abbott said after the first few months of Sara's life made it clear that Amanda actually believed Sara's life was in peril.

"You mean unnatural," Amanda said crossly.

"Uncommon," Jonathan said. "We could easily afford a nurse."

"I would hate to have a nurse," Amanda said.

"You'll be ill."

"I don't get ill," Amanda said. "Besides, I have never been this happy in my life."

And she was, although it was a strange kind of happiness plagued by a sense of doom.

"I'm perfectly fine," she said to her grandfather, to whom Jonathan had spoken about her unusual behavior.

"She is unnaturally attached to this baby," Jonathan had said. "Even when Sara is sleeping, she stays in the room, lying on the bed beside her, sitting in the dark."

"She could die," Amanda said.

"It's not likely that a healthy child would simply die."

"It happens. I've read about it in the news."

She carried Sara with her everywhere like a mother kangaroo, in a sack which Louisa had made her from old damask curtains in the parlor of the Stewards' house. Even at dinner, the baby was either in her sack on Amanda's lap or lying in her carriage close by.

"If anything happened," Jonathan said, "which is entirely unlikely, there would be nothing you could do."

"But *you* could do something," Amanda said. "Couldn't you?"

He ran his fingers through her short black hair. "You were the spunkiest little girl I ever knew," he said. "I remember once at dinner with your grandfather—you sitting across from me full of suspicions, pretending, of course, not to be able to speak. Remember? That was the year you came to live with your grandparents right before your father died."

"I couldn't speak," Amanda said. She took Jonathan's arm. "Answer me," she said. "If something untoward happened to her, could you do something?"

"I'm sure I could," Jonathan said.

But at the hospital the following day, he told Dr. Steward that Amanda's mind was showing real signs of unraveling. Perhaps they should take measures.

"If someone, a child for example, drowns," Amanda asked Jonathan one night after one of her drowned-baby dreams, "would he float on the surface or sink?"

"Both," Jonathan replied.

He pulled her chair closer to his and took her hand. "Please don't allow yourself such awful imaginings." He kissed her forehead.

She hated it when Jonathan was kind to her, indulgent, even patronizing, as if he thought she was so insubstantial that the losses of her life could simply be rubbed away.

"There is nothing the matter with my mind if that is what you're thinking," she said. "I know you've been talking to my grandfather about it, wondering if I've inherited my father's damaged mind. Which I have not."

"You misunderstand," Jonathan said.

"No," Amanda said. "You misunderstand. And my grandfather does as well."

"I do understand, darling. I have been a doctor dealing with ladies for many years. Some ladies are extremely sensitive about their children," he said. "I'm not criticizing you."

"Some ladies," Amanda tried to get up from the dinner table but Jonathan held her arm.

"Everybody died," she said quietly. "My parents. Sara's father." She rocked the carriage with her foot. "My brother died when he was a child. Of course I worry about children dying."

She took Sara out of her carriage, wrapped her in a blanket, and started upstairs. Jonathan followed her to the bedroom, down the corridor from his, a simple white box of a room with a single bed covered with a blanket Grandmother Yellow Flower had sent for her wedding. The baby's cradle was alongside. There was a rocker, a small oriental rug, and Amanda's photographs from the war propped against the wall.

"I don't like anything on the wall," Amanda had told Jonathan shortly after she moved into his house. "Certainly not pictures of flowers."

At first she had tried his bedroom, lying night after night wide awake beside him in the huge four-poster, hoping he would not reach for her.

"Right now I need things to be very simple," she said when she finally decided to move to a single room. "I would like an undecorated room, alone, just with the baby for a while, and then I'll move back to your room."

He was not insistent.

"It simply pleases me to have you here," he said with great kindness.

He had seemed pleased. They moved into his house after Sara was born in March and Amanda took an interest. She had the walls painted white, took down the heavy damask curtains, and left the long windows bare, even those facing the street. She filled the attic with furniture so the rooms were half empty and there was in the bleak museum of a house a new sense of air and space. She learned to cook, although she was quite bad at it; the meats came to the table dark and hard, the vegetables limp, the custards separated. Nevertheless she loved the kitchen, the rich smells of food cooking, the warmth of it, especially

since she had lived without a kitchen at the hospital in
Ashland. It was agreeable to live with Dr. Abbott. He was
formal and sweet, a man who had not been called to do
any battles but the ordinary ones of birth and death; so he
lived with the general expectation of goodwill. Although
distant, he was of a cheerful disposition. Amanda was not
bored by him nor was she particularly engaged. She was,
rather, more comfortable than she had been for years—
since before she had left Wisconsin and Flat Mouth.

In fact, if he had not shown such extreme concern about
her feelings for Sara, there would have been no reason for
trouble to develop.

Jonathan mentioned the dead brother to Dr. Steward, who
spoke to Amanda.

"Your brother died before you were even born," her
grandfather said to her one afternoon in the park. "You
never knew him."

"What has Jonathan told you now?" Amanda asked.

"That your extreme fear for Sara has something to do
with the death of your brother." He linked his arm through
hers.

"I didn't need to know him," she said. "His death was
bred into me."

That night at dinner, she told Jonathan she would leave
if he continued to talk to Dr. Steward about her.

"You can ask my grandfather," she said. "I have left before."

TWO

THE SUMMER OF 1919 was breezy, rare for Washington,
with a light wind in the bright afternoons, blowing the curtains so they floated like angels around the bed where
Amanda sat while Sara was sleeping.

At night with Sara sometimes in the bed beside her,

sometimes in the cradle, she imagined Flat Mouth next to her, his hand across her belly, on her breast.

Dear Flat Mouth, she wrote in early July.

> The weather here is like Wisconsin this summer and I am sick for home. I had intended to come to you in November after I returned from the war but my grandfather arranged a marriage to avoid the humiliation of my pregnancy to this very nice doctor I have mentioned to you who, until lately, when he decided I am mentally ill, pleased me to be with. All of my life I have looked out for myself and this Dr. Abbott is the sort of man who truly looks after others which has been very nice and not like my father who I now believe had only a slim hold on reality all the years I knew him and certainly no wherewithal for looking after a daughter.
>
> Sara looks like my mother. Or at least she looks like my memory of her, with olive skin and eyes like mine but of course mine are like hers were—and small, not so sharp featured as I am or at least perhaps not. But her temperament is sweet which I am assured mine was not—I was altogether too agitated for sweetness, I suppose. It is lovely to be a mother except—and this is the present difficulty—I am afraid she will die.
>
> Sometimes I wake four or five times a night to check her for breathing. Which is the reason Dr. Abbott and my grandfather are concerned that I have gone crazy—my words, not theirs.
>
> They ought to pay attention to my grandmother who has done exactly that. Gone crazy, I mean. She sits in the window overlooking the back garden in a dress she claims is her wedding dress. Since I am nursing Sara, she tells me it is unbecoming for a lady to nurse in these modern times and there are ladies she knows about personally whose breasts fell off as a result.
>
> I would like to come to you before the weather gets cold. I am kept a kind of prisoner here with these physicians examining my every move under their microscopes.

*I send my love to Day and to Grandmother Yellow
Flower and to you. I hope you are not thinking of marrying just yet.*

Love forever,
A Man

On Sunday mornings during church, Amanda visited her
grandmother in the sitting room where Mrs. Steward spent
the days and nights. She would no longer share the bed
with Dr. Steward or for that matter sleep at all except
propped up on the French love seat, in case of an intruder.
She did not change to nightclothes.

Mostly during these visits, her grandmother made no
sense. She spoke of hallucinations as fact—large-headed
birds who lived in the bathroom, an intruder whose head had
been surgically removed who came to her room at night, a
soft-bodied colored woman who bathed and dressed her every morning, although in truth she did not bathe for weeks
at a time, refusing the assistance of Louisa.

But occasionally during these visits, she spoke of personal matters with such lucidity and rage that Amanda believed her absolutely. It was on one of these occasions that
Amanda learned in some measure the range of her father's
sickness.

"William was obsessed," her grandmother told her.
They were having tea in the sitting room, small lemon
cakes made by a bad-tempered Louisa.

"Be careful of the lemon cakes, Amanda. Smell them
for cyanide." Mrs. Steward picked up a lemon cake and
smelled. "Like nutmeg," she said.

"Even as a little boy, your father was obsessed," Mrs.
Steward said. "We had pigeons living under the eaves and
William objected to their cooing. You know about the
sound of pigeons?" She took another lemon cake. "He was
six, I suppose, and one afternoon I went in his room and
there he was standing on a chair twisting the neck of a pi-
geon with his sweet plump hands. It was unbearable. 'Ex-
tremes,' Dr. Steward said. 'Given to occasional paranoia.' "
She poured tea for Amanda. "I don't like men very well.
Do you?"

"Well, I think I do," Amanda said. "I never quite thought of it that way. Men as a group, I mean."

"I think of them as a group. And I don't care for them. Except there was one—much younger, a medical student of your grandfather's, a very gentle man. He never forced himself on me," she said. "And then your grandfather found out and he was never invited to our house again of course."

An odd looked crossed her face.

"Your grandfather punished me for that," she said. She broke a lemon cake in half and gave half to Amanda. "He put his thing in my mouth and it went right down my throat. He made me do that once or twice a week for a long time. I thought I would die of it." She called to Louisa to take away the tea and when Louisa had come and left, her gray eyes were thick as cream soup again.

"Sometimes if I was angry at my children when they were small—I had problems keeping help because your father was so difficult—I had fantasies of cooking them in a pot on the kitchen stove." She looked over at Amanda. "I can't believe I had such thoughts," she said and then in a voice entirely different, she went on. "Your grandfather thinks you have your father's illness. I heard him talking to Jonathan."

"Well, I don't," Amanda said. "My grandfather doesn't know everything." She picked Sara up and held her on her shoulder.

"No, he doesn't," Mrs. Steward said sadly. "Sometimes I think he knows very little."

At noon, on the dot, when church was letting out, Amanda leaned over and kissed her grandmother's soft cotton hair. She put Sara in the small buggy and went down the back stairs to say good-bye to Louisa.

"I may stop by on Wednesday," she called.

Just then perhaps—certainly, according to Louisa, before Amanda left with Sara by the front door—Mrs. Steward climbed out on the windowsill from the third-story sitting room. She must have stood on the narrow ledge, balancing herself by holding on to the shutters. And then she jumped.

Dr. Steward, entering the garden entrance after church, found her.

"Died instantly," Dr. Steward said to Dr. Abbott, who told Amanda.

That night Amanda searched the box of her mother's letters for one she remembered about her father and found it in the envelope with the newspaper clipping of her father's death.

Dear Mama, her mother had written.

> *Tonight at supper William asked me if I had ever considered taking my own life and I said no. Of course not. And then later, feeling bad about what I had said, although of course insulted because here I was a new bride with a young man contemplating suicide—but later I asked him was he deeply unhappy. In waves, he said, like drowning. I thought it was the Welsh who had a dark humor and the Americans were the ones lighthearted and full of expectations.*

> *Today I tasted whiskey for the first time. It was homemade and bitter.*

> > *Yr. loving daughter,*
> > *Anna*

That night in bed listening to the soft breathing of her daughter, Amanda wrote to Blue.

Dear Blue, she wrote.

> *Here I am back in the U S of A almost a year gone since I left Paris—and I wondered how you are and what is going on in Paris. What kind of life do you have without the war?*

> *I had a bad time for a while. No work, no girlfriends, no cash, no good times. But that was my fault and things are swell now—back to taking pictures of high-hipped ladies with bow-lipped smiles.*

> *You can write me in Wash. D.C. in care of the Georgetown P.O. I'll stay in touch. Who knows? I may be back.*

> *Be in touch,*
> *Yrs.,*
> *Sam (Dane. Remember?)*

P.S. My grandmother died this afternoon. I didn't even like her particularly but I've been in a blue funk since it happened. She jumped out of her bedroom window.

She addressed the letter, turned off the light, and lay in her bed unable to sleep. Mrs. Steward's death had undone her. She had learned more than she wished to know about her grandmother. That night she had violent dreams of distorted men, hundreds of small-backed naked men beating soft fleshy girls with a weapon of indescribable size. It was as if the whole dimensions of her grandmother's life had been contained in the last half hour of it, as if Amanda as a witness had a responsibility.

In the morning, however, she woke with a certain lightness of spirit just at the chance of being Sam Dane once again. She dressed, dressed Sara, fed her, put her in her carriage, and set off to Georgetown to post the letter to Paris.

THREE

ON THE ANNIVERSARY of Lincoln's death, Amanda went to call on the Drapers, whom she had phoned sometime after she returned from France but had made no effort to see.

She had planned the visit for weeks.

"Hello," she'd say, taking a seat in the formal living room. "I have come in particular for you to meet your granddaughter Sara," she'd say.

Or else she'd say, "I have wanted you to meet my daughter whose father was killed in France. Yes, I was in France as a photographer, not a nurse in spite of what my grandfather has told you."

She wanted the Drapers to know that Sara was the child

of a great romantic love affair, not the fanciful remnant of
Dr. Abbott's middle age. She wanted them to claim her.

The Drapers' house was dark with heavy furniture, ma-
roons and deep blue velvet, drapes drawn across the late
afternoon, the smell of flowers funereal. Congressman
Draper was not at home, kept late at the House, Mrs.
Draper said, for a vote on a bill.

"He works all day and night since Lincoln died."

Mrs. Draper was a solid midwestern woman, handsome,
self-contained, not given to expressions of sentiment.

"Did you ever see Lincoln while you were in France?"
she asked.

"Once," Amanda said. She was good at lying, of course,
lied easily and without confusion, falling into the invented
story without a hitch. "We had dinner with his battalion
outside of Château-Thierry when I was traveling to the
south. He seemed very well but thin," she said. "Handsome. I have a picture I will send to you."

"I was told he behaved extremely well," she said. "I
have a letter from a photographer who happened to be
there on the morning Lincoln was killed. He wrote to say
that Lincoln was extremely brave. He gave me small details which were helpful, like the fact that he had died
quickly and they had had breakfast together with the rest
of the soldiers."

"I could tell when I was there that he was very well
thought of."

"I am glad of that," Mrs. Draper said.

Just before Amanda left, Mrs. Draper picked Sara up
and looked at her with real interest.

"She doesn't look too much like you, does she,
Amanda?" she said.

"I think not."

"Like her father? Jonathan is actually fairer than you
are with quite thin features, isn't he? I've always been interested in genetics, the way things fall out, you know."
She ran her finger across Sara's small face. "She's a darling girl."

Amanda caught her breath. She was going to tell. She

could feel the words flying out before she had a chance to reconsider.

"She's not Jonathan's daughter," Amanda said.

Mrs. Draper looked perplexed. "Oh, I didn't know," she said. Then quickly, sweetly, her face took on a gentle demeanor. She did not question.

"She's the daughter of a soldier in the war who died," Amanda said.

"Well, he must have been a very handsome man."

There was a moment when Amanda could have said more. Or Mrs. Draper could have asked the inevitable questions. But the moment, which belonged to Mrs. Draper, passed.

"He was handsome," Amanda said.

Later, at her grandfather's house copying the last picture of Lincoln for his parents, she knew that Mrs. Draper had made a conscious choice. Perhaps she'd thought the child was Lincoln's. Perhaps not. Either way, she chose not to know.

At the door, Mrs. Draper kissed Amanda awkwardly.

"You know," she began, "your husband is my doctor and a friend. I was his first wife's schoolmate."

"I didn't know."

"We have always been very close."

"I'm glad to know that."

"And I haven't had you over because of Lincoln, of course, because of you and Lincoln. Not to be rude."

"I certainly understand. It would be awkward for me too."

"But I did want you to know that he has confided in me his concern for you." They walked together down the path to the front gate.

"About Sara and me."

"That you're too close. He is worried it is unnatural."

"He and my grandfather have told me as much."

Mrs. Draper opened the front gate.

"He asked me whether I thought he should take extreme measures."

"What did he mean by that?"

"I told him that women from Illinois were against extreme measures of any kind," she said. "I probably should not have mentioned this but since we're both women . . ." She looked away, shyly, uncomfortable with confessions. "Sometimes when I can't sleep at night, I think about ways I could have saved Lincoln from dying."

Amanda touched her cheek, not unlike Lincoln's. The high cheekbones, the strong chin with a cleft, high color.

"Thank you for tea," she said and pushed the buggy up N Street and home.

FOUR

IN LATE NOVEMBER when darkness settled early and the days were cold and deep, Dr. Abbott engaged the services of P. Melvina Jones, a tall woman, pale chocolate, with a temperament which, whatever its character—and she could be bad-tempered—expanded to fill a room.

"You'll just feel better with Melvina around," Jonathan said to Amanda.

"I feel perfectly fine without her," Amanda said. She had given up her room at the back of the house for Melvina and had moved to the third floor to the room next to the attic under the eaves, with small windows which opened onto the tops of the trees.

"You'll feel safer with Melvina here," Jonathan said.

Amanda did not respond. Since the anniversary of Lincoln's death, she had developed specific fears. Someone was following her, she told Jonathan finally—at the park where she went, at the market, when she met her friends for tea in Georgetown, on her walk between her grandfather's house and Jonathan's. He had in mind to kidnap Sara.

"I would like to move to the country," she told Jonathan.

"Describe the person," Jonathan said.

"I can't describe him," Amanda said, aware of the foolishness of her fears but unable to help herself. "I haven't exactly seen him. To describe that is."

"You must let me know the particulars the next time you see him," Jonathan said. He seemed to take her seriously.

In early November, she had fixed on leukemia. Jonathan had a patient who had leukemia.

"I wonder if you could describe the symptoms of leukemia to me," she asked him one night at supper.

"No," Jonathan said crisply. "I couldn't."

She tried to appear nonchalant.

"I was simply wondering," she said.

"If you want to check Sara out for leukemia, read the medical books yourself."

Amanda did. There were signs, she decided. Bruises—or they could be bruises—at the very least, discoloration on her arm—a certain passivity, Amanda noticed, which could be attributed to a gradual and debilitating weakness.

"I'd be interested to have some blood work done on Sara," Amanda said. "Just to check. There's nothing to be concerned about."

"I'm not concerned," Jonathan said. "Not a bit. Sara is absolutely fine and if she's lethargic, it might be as a result of smothering."

Amanda folded her napkin, pushed back her chair, stood up, and took Sara from her carriage parked beside the dining room table.

"I think I would like a divorce," she said.

The following morning, Jonathan hired P. Melvina from the cleaning staff of Georgetown Hospital. He had known Melvina Jones at the hospital for several years—she'd been a cleaning lady with a capacity for dealing personally with patients, particularly the young.

"I need help with my wife," he said.

And so, just after Thanksgiving, P. Melvina moved into the Abbotts' house on P Street. She had instructions.

* * *

Between Thanksgiving and Christmas, Amanda stopped sleeping. She sat up at night, usually in the dark, and watched Sara sleeping. She tried to read but could not concentrate. Occasionally, she wrote a letter to Flat Mouth but she never sent it. He had not written back to her since her last letter and she worried that something had happened to him or that their friendship was gone as it had left that summer at Bad River. She had no energy for Christmas, she told Jonathan, no interest in decorating the house or baking.

"You can do everything except take care of the baby," she told P. Melvina.

"I believe Dr. Abbott engaged me specifically to assist you with Sara," P. Melvina said. "He told me you had gotten overtired and to be strict with you about it."

"The baby," Amanda said patiently, trying to be sweet, "is mine."

"Of course," Melvina said.

"She is only mine," Amanda said.

At Christmastime, Jonathan brought up the subject of another baby.

"I would like to have another child."

Amanda was quiet.

"And it would be good for Sara to have a sibling."

She shook her head. "I don't know," she said. "Of course another baby would be lovely. But right now, I can't imagine."

He brushed her hair off her face.

"Is it that you'd rather not have a romantic life with me at all?"

She pulled away. "I don't know, Jonathan. I simply don't know anything any longer."

Jonathan came that night late. She was awake as usual in her small bed under the eaves, and he came up the steps, opened the door to her room so the light slid across her gown, and then closed it, coming down on her, not gently, impatient, urgent with desire.

"I can't stand this," he said to her afterward. "It's not a normal way to live."

"I can't seem to help it," Amanda said.

When he left, she turned on the light beside her bed. She was shaking and took a sweater out of the cupboard and then a cloak to keep warm. The lovemaking had stirred her—that was certainly true—and there was still the dull ache of wanting in her groin, but the smell of Jonathan, the way he had come to her at night while she lay virginal, girlish in her single bed, was like her father.

That night she took Sara into her bed with her and the soft heat of her child breathing beside her almost brought on sleep.

FIVE

P. MELVINA JONES was a tall, heavyset woman, flat-chested with flesh on her belly and soft pockets under her chin. She wore pink makeup on her cheeks and her hair short in the shape of a black cap. She refused to wear a uniform to work and made no effort to be convivial.

Something about her struck Amanda as unsettling. Some general impatience with daily matters of living—the washing of sheets and ironing of Dr. Abbott's shirts, cutting up vegetables for supper. The large house, empty of everyone except Amanda and Sara, vibrated with Melvina's temper, which was not bad, not even irritated, but in the air like the smell of smoke.

Amanda was drawn to her. She liked to be with Sara in the room where Melvina was working, liked to watch the efficient movements of her body, her hands especially, the way she ironed a long-tailed white shirt to perfection, the way her chin jutted just so, the tilt combative.

"I take pictures. I took them in the war," Amanda said one afternoon in the kitchen nursing Sara while Melvina cooked.

She wanted to establish a friendship. It had occurred to her that in the year since she returned from the war, she

had made no women friends. She had spent her last year
in high school with Lincoln and then she went to war. But
even in the years with Flat Mouth and until the invented
Sam Dane, she had lived a life with men—in the hospital,
at the reservation except with Grandmother Yellow Flower
with whom she was not confessional. At Sidwell Friends
School, she had held herself apart, elusive, as a mute and,
later, after her father died, as an amateur photographer hidden behind a lens. She was suspicious of women—their
secrets with one another, their indirection. Until Sara was
born and her longing for her own mother exploded,
Amanda had not been conscious of how her mother's
death had altered her trust in women.

"I'd like to take your photograph," Amanda said.

Melvina raised her eyebrows.

"I'd like to take your photograph just there where you
are, the light falling like it is."

Amanda sensed an old excitement. It was the first time
since the war that she had been moved to take
photographs—that the world had widened as it used to do
from the small detail to a frame.

"No," Melvina said.

"No, M'am," Jonathan would correct Melvina, and she
seemed to listen, attentive, but she never said "M'am" to
Amanda. Although it was a small thing, Amanda was admiring of it.

"I have taken a great many photographs but always in
action," Amanda said. "Here," she said as she handed Sara
to Melvina dusty with flour. "Let me show you."

She brought down a stack of mounted pictures and a
few taken before she went to Europe of the slums behind
the Capitol, spread them out on the table for Melvina to
see. She had not looked at the pictures from the war since
she returned, and seeing them now she was struck by her
absence of feeling as if they were photographs she was
seeing for the first time. Her life had no reality except the
present moment, no progression. She could remember the
girl who had gone to war as Sammy Dane only in a dream
from a deep sleep recollected fitfully.

"You were there?" Melvina asked.

"I was," Amanda said. "I went as a boy." She had told no one except her grandparents. Even Jonathan thought she had been in France as a nurse and now without a question she had told this woman, this stranger, whose admiration she deeply wanted, for reasons she did not entirely understand, as if some former sense of herself could be rekindled through P. Melvina Jones.

"You were that close to the fighting?" Melvina shook her head. She was looking at the picture of the soldiers crawling across the field under fire.

"Here," Amanda said. "There are two of them." She picked up the other. "One taken while the men were alive crawling across an open field from the Allied woods to the enemy side and the other taken just after." She showed Melvina. "They are all dead."

"I would not have thought of you as a woman who could take these pictures," Melvina said.

Amanda shrugged. She stood back and looked at Melvina. "I could take your picture there on the rocker with the light."

"I want to comb my hair," Melvina said. She ran her hands over the tight cap of hair. "And put some color on my lips." She took a tube of magenta out of the pocket of her coat and outlined her lips, put two red dots high on her cheeks and rubbed them in. "Why do you want a picture of an old colored woman anyway?" she said.

"Sit down there." Amanda pointed to the rocker. "You're not old. You're just a little mean."

"And I should smile?" Melvina laughed low in her throat. "I don't think I've smiled once since I was ten years old. Not even on Christmas Day."

"Then don't smile now," Amanda said.

She stood with the light from the window behind her and the light from the morning sun fell across Melvina's lap, a shaft with color across her breasts, and cast her face in shadow so the eyes were even blacker and the skullcap seemed painted on her head. Except for Lincoln in France, it was the first portrait Amanda had done, and what pleased her was not the picture itself or even taking up the camera once again. But the sense of herself as objective.

* * *

She developed the pictures at her grandfather's that afternoon in the darkroom she had made when she was in high school. Louisa was there, not in the kitchen but in the parlor actually sitting down in the small rocker by the piano doing needlepoint. Since Mrs. Steward's death, Louisa had filled the space as if Amanda's grandmother had never been, dressing up now as the lady of the house, her hair shiny, her eyes with a certain brightness. She had grown bold with confidence.

"I suppose you've heard about the Spanish flu," she said with a wicked intention.

"Spanish flu?"

"That's what I hear from your grandfather, who keeps up with the doctors at Georgetown who are attending people with this terrible flu."

"I didn't know."

"I thought you read the paper," Louisa said. "And certainly Jonathan has been at the hospital as well."

"He didn't mention anything to me," Amanda said, shaken by the news. "He has been working late."

"Well, it was in the paper this morning."

"I haven't read the paper." She put on Sara's coat and hat, wrapped her in a blanket. "And I suppose it's not surprising that Jonathan didn't mention it. He knows I'd be upset."

"I never saw your mother again after the epidemic that killed your brother. She didn't come to Washington."

"No," Amanda said. "I imagine she didn't." She stopped at the front door. "Can you tell me about this flu? What my brother died of was diphtheria. The treatment was available even then and my father ordered it from New York, but it didn't arrive in Ashland in time to save people. So you wouldn't die of diphtheria today."

"No, this is another form of influenza. A virus. People have been dying all over Europe and now it's traveled the Atlantic and they're dying here."

"Actually dying of the flu?"

"One hundred and seventy in this morning's paper."

On the walk home—surely the cold crisp air would kill

the lingering virus—Sara, seated in her carriage, burst with babbling, cocked her small head coquettishly.

"Mama smile," she said. "Sara smile. Bye-bye. Mama. Bye-bye." *Smile* had been her first word after *Mama*. "Speaking so early," everyone said when they met Sara. "Of course," Jonathan would reply. "All day long her mother is talking to her, carrying on a conversation as if she's been verbal since birth."

"Mama smile," Sara said again, but with a certain perplexed expression for in fact Amanda was weeping. She thought of her mother—her lovely mother repeated like an angel in Sara's face—the unimaginable loss of her boy, still a child, and then she thought what it must have been for her mother to lie in that bed where Amanda remembered her, to know, as she must have known, that she was going to die. How she must have held on to her life to last as long as possible for her daughter.

Once at home, Amanda spread the photographs out on the dining room table for Melvina to see.

"What do you think?" she asked.

Melvina wiped her hands on her apron and put them on her hips.

"I think what I thought before. That's the ugliest woman ever was reproduced so many times."

"But you should have a picture, whatever you think. Maybe your husband would like to have it."

"I haven't got a husband," Melvina said. "I used to and I say I'm married because I am but I don't have him around anymore." She examined the pictures with great care. "At least this one doesn't look like I have horses' teeth," she said. She picked up another one. "And here. This picture is a falsehood. The woman here looks nice enough to say good morning to."

"So you like this one?" Amanda picked it up.

"I didn't say I liked it," Melvina said. "I said this woman isn't as ugly as the same woman in these other pictures."

Amanda took her pen and wrote "P. Melvina Jones on a winter afternoon. Amanda Steward."

"I don't need the news of who this woman is, you know. I can recognize her," Melvina said, lifting Sara out of her carriage to the floor where she was beginning to pull herself up holding on to the chairs. "My husband, aforementioned, left."

"I'm so sorry," Amanda said.

"You had nothing to do with it." She picked up the picture and held it out. "He walked out when my baby daughter died. So I know about you and babies dying. And don't say you're so sorry. There's no 'I'm so sorry' for that."

She had the picture under her arm, her back straight, her face fixed. "She got pneumonia on a Tuesday. We didn't have any heat in the house and how was I to know she had pneumonia? She died on Friday night in the bed with me. Pauline. I called her Pauline and after she died I took on the name Pauline Melvina. P. Melvina so she'd have a life with me." She looked directly at Amanda in a kind of challenge. "Joseph left for parts unknown the following Monday and he's kept his parts unknown because he knows very well I'd shoot him in the heart if I found him."

"Does Jonathan know about this?" Amanda asked.

"What would a man like Dr. Abbott do with that news?" Melvina asked. "Besides, that was ten years ago when I was twenty-one, and ten years is a long time." She headed into the kitchen but Amanda heard her mutter under her breath, "not long enough."

And that was that. Melvina fell back to her routine, laconic, sharp-tongued, impersonal. The subject of dead babies did not come up again and when Amanda asked Melvina did she know about the Spanish flu, Melvina said everybody knew but Dr. Abbott meant to keep it a secret from Amanda.

"It's in the paper," Amanda said.

"That's why it's not a secret anymore."

"And he must be coming back from work exposed."

"We're all exposed," Melvina said. "You're going to go crazy worrying about ways to die."

That night at supper, Amanda put Sara in the corner of the living room away from Jonathan.

"As long as this flu is around, I think it's best you stay away from Sara," Amanda said.

"Of course," Jonathan said. "And away from you as well, although I will hardly be able to tell the difference."

SIX

Dr. Abbott came home from the hospital ill on New Year's Eve.

Melvina told Amanda at breakfast that he had awakened in the middle of the night burning with fever and that she, Melvina, at his request, was to tend to him.

"He says you aren't to go to his room," Melvina said, boiling water for tea, squeezing oranges. "Young women are particularly susceptible, he tells me."

Amanda sat down at the kitchen table, restraining Sara who was no longer willing to be still, taking the salt and pepper shaker, the tiny jar of preserves, stuffing them in her mouth.

"He says you ought to go to your grandfather's," Melvina said.

"I won't do that," Amanda said.

Melvina shrugged. "Suit yourself," she said.

"He's certain it's the Spanish flu?"

Melvina covered a tray with a linen napkin, set the juice and teapot on it.

"He ought to know," Melvina said. She sliced the bread in thin pieces.

Amanda walked to the window overlooking the back garden. It was wet, even lush for winter. The temperatures had been unseasonably warm, too warm for coats. The rhododendron and broom and azaleas had early buds.

"If the temperature would fall to freezing, we might have a chance to stop this flu," Jonathan had said. "Don't go into shops," he had warned Amanda. "Not even out for tea."

* * *

All morning New Year's Day there were calls.

Mrs. O'Brien had died. Mrs. Baxter showed signs of improvement. Peggy Nonan had a turn for the worse. Mr. Childs had lost consciousness.

"Dr. Abbott is himself too ill to come to the phone," Amanda said.

She did not know what to do. Certainly, she could not stay in the house with Spanish flu. Upstairs in the small scrubbed bedroom, she could hear the sounds from Jonathan's bedroom, the deep cough, the struggle for air. Her grandfather called to say perhaps it was not a good idea for her to come over as he, though not yet ill, was not well either.

Outside, P Street was empty. Occasionally a woman hurried down the brick walk leading a small dog or carrying packages, but for a warm sunny New Year's Day there was no sign of conviviality on the streets, little sign of life.

"It must be bad," Amanda said standing in the kitchen while Melvina prepared lunch for Jonathan.

"It's not good. Dr. Abbott says it's the worst he's seen in his lifetime."

Amanda crossed her arms, leaned her head against the door frame. Upstairs the baby was sleeping. The house had darkened almost overnight. There was the rancid smell of sickness about it.

"How is he?" Amanda asked.

Melvina shook her head.

All morning Amanda had had a rush of feeling for Jonathan Abbott. He was a good and unselfish man, innocent for a man of his age and worldliness, generous in his affection for her. And she, pragmatic, deeply protective, perhaps even ruthless, was probably going to leave him.

She was glad to have had a daughter and not a son. Men, she thought—young men, old men, even boys—were unbearably fragile.

Melvina put water in a large pot and set the fire.

"We're going to be boiling everything, Dr. Abbott says."

"Is he worse?" Amanda asked.

"He's not better."

"His breathing does not sound right," Amanda said. "He should be in the hospital."

"He won't go," Melvina said. "They're short on beds." She looked up at Amanda, her expression critical.

"You could look in the room without catching the influenza, you know."

"I could, I suppose," Amanda said, feeling the blood slide out of her, leaving her weak.

She walked up the back steps, down the short hallway to Jonathan's room. The door was ajar. He lay in bed on his back, propped up, his head in profile against the pillow, his eyes half open. His breathing was labored and his arms fell, as if there were no life, was disturbing.

"Jonathan?"

He did not turn his head to look at her.

"I am so sorry," she said.

He raised his hand to silence her.

"I shouldn't come in, I suppose."

"No," he replied.

"Would you like a light?" she asked, wishing to do something generous and quickly before the germs fled his room to greet her at the doorway.

"Please no light," he said.

Upstairs, Amanda washed her hands and face, let the hot water run over her hands until it burned them, changed her clothes, and threw the ones she had been wearing down the laundry chute. Then she took down her valise.

When she called the lumberyard in Ashland, Wisconsin, a young woman called Star who knew Amanda from childhood answered the phone.

"Star?" Amanda asked.

"I was called also Lighting Star. Remember?"

Amanda did not remember.

"I remember you very well," the woman called Star said. "You were like electricity. Whenever you came to Bad River, the trees lit up."

"You must be younger than Flat Mouth and I am," Amanda said.

"Sixteen," Star said. "And I have one baby."

When Flat Mouth came to the phone, his voice was strange.

"Amanda?" he asked as if the name had no meaning for him.

"A Man."

"Of course I know," he said. "I just didn't expect you to call on the telephone."

"But you never wrote me back," Amanda said.

"No," Flat Mouth said carefully. "I did not write."

"So I had to call."

"You spoke to Star?" he asked.

"Yes."

"You remember her from Bad River?"

"I don't think so."

"She was quite small but we used to play with her when you skipped school," Flat Mouth said. "Now she is my wife."

There was a pause.

"So that's why you didn't write," Amanda said softly.

"I didn't want you to know," he said. "In your letter, it sounded as if you wanted to be my wife."

"No, Flåt Mouth. That was a tease. I'm married. I told you that."

"Yes. But you are a strange girl. You're the only girl I know who went to war and so I thought maybe you would like to have two husbands as well. Who knows? I haven't seen you for a long time."

"Well, you are going to see me now," Amanda said.

There was a low grunt.

"At least if you want to."

"I want to," Flat Mouth said gruffly.

"There is an epidemic of influenza here in Washington and now even my husband is ill so I am coming to Ashland with Sara."

"I will be glad to see you," Flat Mouth said without expression.

"You don't have the epidemic there, do you?"

"Not yet," Flat Mouth said.

"Then I will take the train tomorrow morning and be there in two days."

"I should tell you," Flat Mouth said. "Star and I have moved to my father's since he died."

"Day is dead?"

"In June," Flat Mouth said. "On the twelfth of June at four in the afternoon. It was raining," he said.

In the morning, Jonathan was worse. Melvina knocked on Amanda's door just after seven.

"They have a bed for him in the hospital," she said. She looked around the room. "You're leaving?"

Amanda nodded.

"Dr. Abbott thought Sara and I should leave the house," Amanda said. "Young women are particularly susceptible, he said."

"So I hear," Melvina said. She picked up the valise.

"I'm going to Wisconsin," Amanda said. "To the town where I was born. I'm going home," she said, as if that would excuse her betrayal of Jonathan Abbott.

"Suit yourself," Melvina said.

An ambulance took Jonathan to the hospital just after nine.

"It's fine," he said when Amanda told him she was leaving. "It's the right thing to do."

There was a chill in the air when Amanda and Sara left the house on P Street, a sharp wind and a gray sky, but she sailed toward Wisconsin Avenue and a taxi to the train station, lightheaded, wings on her heart.

SEVEN

FLAT MOUTH: AN *Ordinary Life in Photographs* was published as a book in 1926 and established Amanda as a photographer, particularly in New York where the strong and powerful black-and-white photographs were first exhibited at the Broome Street Gallery. The pictures themselves, one hundred and fifty of them, were taken over the course of the winter that Sara and Amanda lived in a cabin on the Bad River Reservation.

In the morning, Amanda would leave with Flat Mouth, carrying Sara in a pack on her back, and spend the day with him at the lumberyard outside of Ashland.

"What are you looking for in these pictures, A Man? What are you trying to find?" he asked, gradually pleased over the months by the scrutiny of Amanda's eye.

"Who knows?" Amanda said. "Myself, I suppose."

"Well, you're not going to find yourself in pictures of me," Flat Mouth said. "You'll not even find me."

But she did find Flat Mouth. And herself as well, a familiar sense of energy, a warm sweet taste in her mouth.

In the time they spent together, a mysterious connection rose up like veins on the back of a hand, blue with blood. They seldom talked at length and never personally—Flat Mouth would not permit personal conversation although he did remark on letters he had found from Anna to his father and wondered if there had been a love affair between them.

"I would like to stay here forever," Amanda said to him one early twilight wandering beyond the forest of the reservation, along the lake. Sara was walking, tentative at first on her short round legs—not looking back to check her distance from her mother as children inevitably do, too certain of Amanda to doubt a proximity.

"But you will leave, won't you?" Flat Mouth said, his feeling ambiguous, for certainly Amanda's presence disturbed him as much as her steady interest affirmed his life. "You'll go home of course."

She shook her head. "This is home," she said. "You don't understand because you've never left."

Jonathan Abbott recovered. He was back at work in early February after the influenza epidemic had subsided, and there were frequent and predictable letters, formal, affectionate, without implication.

* * *

Dearest Amanda, he wrote.

I am quite well but tired and the daily routine at the hospital is wearing. The residue in heart and lung problems fills the hospital to overflowing every day.

The house is dark without the light sounds of you and Sara babbling back and forth. Only bad-tempered Melvina who has joined the Roman Catholic Church.

Your grandfather is keeping company with Louisa but only in private. When I had dinner there the other evening, Louisa was at table and a new cook had been hired.

I hope the photography is going well and that you and Flat Mouth have resumed your friendship without discomfort.

> *With my love to you and Sara,*
> *Jonathan*

He never asked her when she planned to come home or if she did. He never criticized her for leaving although she had written him a letter of self-reproach.

Dear Amanda, he wrote.

You left Washington out of a sense of protection for Sara.

It is not necessary for you to apologize or explain. Anyone who has seen one of nature's animal mothers protect her young from danger knows that instinct is ferocious and appropriate.

> *With love,*
> *Jonathan*

At night, when the cabin at Bad River was dark and the only sound at all was the wind weaving through the trees, Amanda thought about Jonathan—warmly, as a father, as a good predictable father who never left the carefully drawn limits of the role he had taken, never insinuated himself. But for Flat Mouth, she felt desire.

Flat Mouth had a broad commanding handsome face, a strong, lean body, an easy gait, and he wore his straight black straw hair long. He was almost conventional in his good looks, the shape of his face, the cast of his expression, the way he held himself, squared off against adversity. But there was, as well, something unpredictable in his familiarity. That was the clue Amanda captured in her photographs which gave them power and made Flat Mouth both himself and representative of his people.

Sometime in early March, the ground still frozen solid, Flat Mouth and Amanda realized that what they were doing together was in some small way remarkable. Amanda had set up a darkroom in the back of the cabin—what should have been the kitchen. She and Flat Mouth were looking at the day's developed shots. Amanda leaned against Flat Mouth's shoulder.

"So, A Man—you've played a trick with my face," Flat Mouth said, uneasy with the pictures.

"No trick," Amanda said. "There it is. Your face."

"But not as it is in a mirror."

"Your face inexactly."

And in a gesture too quick for consideration, she put her finger between his lips. He grabbed her wrist.

"No, A Man," he said gently.

"You did once."

"I am married now." He held on to her hand, which had dropped by her side. "Now you are grown up and too much woman. Then you were like a boy."

In August, a cool breezy month, the air sweet with summer, Amanda and Sara boarded the train in Ashland for Chicago and home. The last she saw of Flat Mouth was on the platform where he stood, his face fixed, his arm linked through Star's.

"Wave good-bye to Flat Mouth," she said to Sara who was sitting beside her, her bottom lip out.

"No," Sara said. She covered her eyes with her fingers so as not to see Flat Mouth.

"Good-bye, Flat Mouth," Amanda said quietly.

"No good-bye Flat Mouth," Sara said.

Amanda had not spoken of anyone as Sara's father. She called Jonathan by his Christian name and Lincoln's name had never come up. She had put off the question of who was to be Sara's father until Sara was old enough to understand the real circumstances of her birth. In fact, she had not thought a father was necessary for Sara at all.

"Flat Mouth is my father," Sara said, her eyes still covered with her fingers. "Bye-bye," she called to the window filled now with the landscape beyond Ashland. "Bye-bye, Flat Mouth."

Amanda and Sara took a room at Mrs. Plummer's house in Greenwich Village and Amanda began working on the exhibit of photographs of Flat Mouth and writing the text for *Flat Mouth: An Ordinary Life in Photographs.* Over the next few years, they spent weeks at a time away from the house on P Street where Amanda and Jonathan had established a quiet and agreeable life together, almost satisfactory.

Sara was a mysterious child, a private collector of secrets, earnest and serious, stubborn, literal-minded as Amanda was not, graced with a settling temperament. She moved back and forth with Amanda between Washington and New York, packing her small valise with her books, her one party dress and everyday dress, whenever her mother said it was time to change locations. She did not complain and until late August 1926, just before Labor Day, Amanda was of the opinion that Sara was blissfully happy in a life of adventure with a mother in whose eyes she was everything.

On the 30th of August, a Monday—Amanda remembered exactly the day and the time and the place as if the scene had been photographed—Sara announced that she wanted to go home.

They were at Schrafft's sharing a chocolate soda. Always they shared.

"You order and I'll take a bite," Amanda would say. It was a thick and golden honey day. No breeze. Sara was dressed in her everyday dress, a gray jumper and white starched blouse, her yellow hair loose around a sweet face, round with high color and wide-set eyes.

"I would like to go home to my father," Sara said, quiet and serious as she was almost always. "I'd like to live there all the time."

Amanda's heart fell. "But we must live also in New York, darling. For my work."

Sara licked the chocolate from the back of the spoon.

"You can come to New York without me," Sara said. "You'll be fine without me. But I would like to live all the time in Washington with my father."

"You know I married Jonathan after I was pregnant with you." Amanda's voice was thin. She had suddenly lost her sense of judgment.

"Besides," Sara said, not wishing to hear bad news, "I need to go to school. I need to be in first grade."

"Of course," Amanda said. "I had thought I'd teach you at home for a while."

On the walk home to the room on 9th Street, Amanda was weak and out of breath, as if at twenty-six her heart had failed and she was slipping out of the world.

She lay that night on the narrow single bed across from Sara's and listened to her child's soft breathing.

"You can call me Amanda," she said to Sara the next morning at breakfast, too profoundly hurt to consider the impact of her words. She tore her toast in small bits. Her face was flushed and her heart pounded against her breastbone. "Amanda. Just like everybody else does."

EIGHT

SARA RAN AWAY—as Amanda described it, although Sara insisted she had just gone home—on a warm rainy Wednesday in early September. It was the first time Amanda had ever left her alone and this time only because Sara had a summer cold.

Amanda had a meeting arranged with Edward Steichen, the war photographer who wanted to include the photographs of Sam Dane in an exhibit on photography of World War I opening at the Library of Congress in Washington. Sam Dane, according to Steichen, could not be located.

"As it happens," Amanda said, "I have a large number of his unpublished photographs."

"You know him then," Steichen had said to her.

"I knew him," Amanda said, suggesting a failed love affair, indicating by her tone that there would be no further discussion about Sam Dane.

On this particular Wednesday, Mrs. Plummer was home for her bridge club so it seemed entirely safe to allow Sara to stay in the house with her.

"I'm sure I'll be fine, Mama," Sara said. "I can't be stolen from inside the house."

Amanda had warned Sara about the stealing of children.

"Especially in New York," she had said. "I have read about stolen children in the *New York Times*. Even in Ashland, a boy was stolen from his carriage outside the post office."

"I'm not the kind of little girl people want to steal," Sara said.

"You are exactly that kind of girl," Amanda said.

In New York, Amanda dressed like a man. Sometimes if the weather was cool enough she wore a morning coat of her father's, black trousers, and a white lace blouse gone slightly yellow which had belonged to her mother. This morning, she tied a bright purple scarf around her waist.

"I like it best living in Washington where you wear dresses," Sara said plaintively, turning on the radio. "I like your blue dress with flowers on the skirt and white collar. That's my favorite."

"Then I'll start to wear dresses more often here," Amanda said. She put on a black cloth hat.

Just before she left the room, the announcer came on the air to say that Harry Houdini had died suddenly of an accidental punch in the stomach. Amanda turned off the radio.

"Who is Harry Houdini?" Sara asked. "I want to know why he died."

"He was a magician," Amanda said kissing her goodbye. "He got out of impossible situations."

"But the radio said he died," Sara insisted. She turned the radio back on.

"Mr. Houdini was struck a fatal blow to the stomach by a college student in a prearranged punch."

Amanda started toward the radio and changed her mind.

"I'll be back by three, love. No later. And you can ask Mrs. Plummer for anything you need."

Sara was sitting in a worn maroon rocking chair beside the radio listening to the news about Houdini.

"You never tell me the truth if it's bad," she said to Amanda. "But I can feel things in the air."

On the bus up Fifth Avenue, Amanda thought about what Sara had said, about the way she had managed every detail to make a perfect life without dead mothers or mentally unbalanced fathers, but Sara was right, of course. The truth was in Amanda's blood, and whatever life she invented, she could not protect Sara from the real terrors of her own life.

As soon as Amanda left and the story of Harry Houdini's life and death was over, Sara packed her blue valise, wrote a note to Amanda, took $42.50 from the envelope in the bottom drawer of the dresser, walked down the steps past Mrs. Plummer's living room, out the front door, and down 9th Street to Fifth Avenue where she hailed a taxicab.

She climbed in the back seat.

"Penn Station," she said to the driver. She and her mother had taken this trip so often that she knew the details exactly.

Amanda had been so protective that Sara never thought to be afraid. She was like a domesticated animal without a scent for danger. And now, weaving through the streets of New York City, she could barely contain her excitement.

"How old are you going on a trip by yourself?" the taxi driver asked.

"Eight and a half," Sara said, lying about her age.

"I would have thought you five or six," the driver said.

"No," Sara said. "I am eight and a half and I take trips alone quite a lot."

She could not remember such exhilaration, even at Christmas or on her sixth birthday when Amanda took her to Broadway to see *The Desert Song*.

In the coach of the eleven o'clock train to Washington, D.C., she sat next to an elderly man filling the bowl of his pipe with tobacco and across from a pretty young woman inspecting her lips in the mirror of her compact, putting on bright red lipstick.

She wanted to tell someone what she had done, perhaps the conductor when he collected the tickets, but then, she thought, they might ask her to get off the train. They might call Amanda or Jonathan or the police.

At one, just after the train stopped at 30th Street, Philadelphia, Sara went to the dining car. The lady with bright red lipstick followed her and sat down at the table, unfolding her linen napkin in a graceful gesture which Sara imitated.

"I hope you don't mind if I join you," she said in a soft voice.

"I am very pleased to have you," Sara said in the manner of Jonathan's speech, which she admired.

The lady in raspberry lipstick ordered fruit cocktail without a maraschino cherry and a cup of Manhattan clam chowder.

Sara looked at the long menu, confused by the variety of choices; not wishing to call attention to herself or to order something the woman might find a foolish selection, she ordered a fruit cocktail with the maraschino cherry and a cup of clam chowder.

The lady in lipstick—Amanda never wore lipstick or makeup of any kind—was dressed beautifully, out of a magazine, in a navy blue skirt, very short, and a soft red print blouse open at the neck with long white pearls. Her yellow springy curls peered out of a navy blue cap and her fingernails were long and painted with a clear nail polish. On her right hand, she wore a large ring with a pale blue stone.

Sara loved to look at costumes, especially in New York where there were so many and varied and people were very rich, so Amanda had told her, and could afford to wear quite elegant clothes.

"I find it odd that you are interested in clothes," Amanda had said to her once.

"I love pretty things," Sara said. "Houses too. I love our living room in Washington and to sit on the red couches at

Saks Fifth Avenue when we shop for Christmas and smell the perfume and watch the ladies in their very high heels."

"You astonish me," Amanda had said. "I thought when I had a child she would be just like me, only smaller. It's as if you came from Jupiter."

"Well I didn't," Sara had said in her literal way. "I came from you."

Now, free from her mother's strong mind, her unhidden opinions, an escaped prisoner, Sara was falling in love with the beautiful stranger.

"I am surprised to see a girl your age traveling alone," the woman said.

"I travel alone all the time," Sara said. She considered lying once again about her age but changed her mind. This lady might actually know about the ages of children as the taxicab driver had not. "My father lives in Washington."

"They're divorced?"

Sara hesitated. Although she did not know anyone but Mrs. Plummer who had been divorced, it sounded daring to have divorced parents, she thought, very grown-up. "Yes," she said. "They are."

"I understand." The woman bowed her head, lowered her eyes confessionally. "I am divorced as well."

Sara was pleased to have found a common ground.

"My father is a doctor in Washington and Amanda—I call my mother Amanda—is a photographer in New York."

The fruit cocktails were brought and Sara put her maraschino cherry on the side plate. Perhaps, she thought, it was in bad taste, as her grandfather Steward would say, always worrying as he did about good and bad taste—but perhaps it was in bad taste for a young lady to eat a maraschino cherry since the beautiful stranger had refused to do it.

"By any chance, is your mother Amanda Steward?"

Sara's heart fell. "Yes," she said thinly. "She is Amanda Steward. How do you know her?"

"I don't exactly know her," the lady said, clearly excited by the news. "I saw her Indian show in New York. A lot of people know about her. She is one of a very few women photographers."

"Well." Sara shrugged. "She wears trousers, you know. She's rather like a man."

The beautiful stranger shook her head. "I've actually seen your mother in her trousers and she is lovely." She reached over and touched Sara's cheek. "Unusual looking. You are very lovely as well."

"I don't look like my mother at all."

"Perhaps your father."

"I'm too young to look like anyone old," Sara said, glad to change the conversation from her mother but also heartened that her mother had such force as to be known by strangers.

The beautiful lady got off the train in Baltimore to visit her aunt and as she left she slipped the small compact which Sara had so admired in her lap.

"For you, as a memento," she said.

All the way from Baltimore, Sara was lightheaded with happiness. She had made her own friend, independent of her mother. And even though the stranger knew her mother, her mother did not know the stranger. What is more, she had discovered that she was safe anywhere in the world because she was Amanda Steward's daughter.

She was thinking about the lady and her costume when she got off the train at Washington, D.C., and did not look down to see if the steps had been pushed up to the coach.

The last Sara remembered when the train arrived at Union Station was a very tall lady in a red hat who seemed to be screaming, but in actual fact it was Sara screaming as she fell between the platform and the train to the tracks.

Mrs. Plummer announced the bad news.

"I thought she was with you, Miss Steward," she said offering Amanda a cup of tea. "Cake?"

"No. No," Amanda said. "She was not with me. I told you I was leaving her here and to listen out for her."

"I did. I did listen. My bridge club was here for lunch and we all listened. But when Maria got around to doing the rooms upstairs, Sara was no longer there. I went up and checked and assumed of course that you had come and taken Sara with you and not mentioned it to me, not wishing to bother me perhaps."

Amanda ran upstairs. The door to her room was ajar and when she went in, she saw exactly what she had most feared. The closet was empty of Sara's clothes. Her books were gone and her little blue valise, and on the bed was a note.

> *Dear Amanda,*
>   *I have gone home to my father so I can go to school.*
>   *Your loving daughter,*
>   *Sara*
>   *p.s. I don't like to call you Amanda.*

Amanda could not reach Jonathan. He was in the hospital, the nurse said when she called at three. He should be back at any time.

"Tell him I am coming home," Amanda said. She packed her clothes, packed everything, paid Mrs. Plummer, and told her it was unlikely she would be back.

Jonathan was in the emergency room of Georgetown Hospital when Sara regained consciousness, standing over her in his white coat.

"What happened?" she asked.

"You bumped your head," he said. "You bumped it quite hard."

"Mama is going to be sick with worry," she said sadly. "She knew something like this would happen."

He brushed the hair out of her face and kissed her forehead.

"Are you angry at me?" she asked. "Will I die of this?"

"Of course not," Jonathan said. "It was an accident. You were lucky. You could have been hurt badly and you weren't."

He pushed the stretcher up to the room on the third floor and lifted Sara into the bed.

The nurse in his office gave Jonathan the message from Amanda and he met her at the train. She saw him at the gate when she disembarked and her heart leapt up, in fear that he was there to report bad news, in relief that he was there at all.

"She's here, isn't she?" she asked, her voice shaking.

"She is here." Jonathan took her arm.

"And something's happened, hasn't it?"

"She'll be fine, Amanda," he said. "She fell." And he told her the story.

They walked out in front of Union Station into a late twilight, the dome of the Capitol suspended, a silver moon behind it, a light rain falling.

"You remember when she was tiny and I was crazy that something awful would happen to her?" Amanda asked.

"Of course I remember." He hailed a taxi to take them to the hospital. "How could I forget?"

"And something did," she said and she was weeping. She seldom cried, never in front of Jonathan, but she couldn't stop herself. "And you were there." She lifted his hand and kissed the palm of it.

On the third day after the accident, Sara was released from the hospital. She had a concussion from a blow to the back of her head and a broken ankle, little to pay for her large victory.

"I met a very beautiful lady on the train who was wearing bright red lipstick," Sara had said on the evening after the accident. "I will certainly wear lipstick when I'm older."

That morning Amanda went to the hospital to pick her up wearing the blue dress with flowers on the skirt, which was Sara's favorite, and makeup, even lipstick.

On the way home from the hospital, Sara asked how long this time they would be in Washington.

"We live in Washington now," Amanda said. "We will not be going back to New York to stay."

"For how long?" Sara asked.

"For as long as this time lasts," Amanda replied.

That evening, Sara settled quietly in her own room, Amanda knocked on Jonathan's door. He was sitting up in bed, his legs crossed on top of the covers, reading the morning paper as he did at night, his hair tousled, a light gray shadow of beard on his chin, and he smiled to see her there, a boyish smile. He seemed handsome to her for the first time and strong, entirely reliable. She liked the smell of him.

"I was wondering if you'd mind if I spent the night in here with you?" she asked.

"I'd be very pleased to have you," he said.

"Just tonight," she said. "Not necessarily always."

"Of course," he said.

She sat down on the bed next to him, slipped her hand into his, and gradually let her body fall against him until the weight of it transferred, and in a small safe moment she felt weightless, as close as she had ever known to a love story.

SARA

ONE

SARA ABBOTT WAS fourteen on the fourth of March, 1933, the day that Franklin D. Roosevelt was inaugurated as the thirty-second President of the United States and Jonathan Abbott died of a massive heart attack in the operating room at Georgetown University Hospital as he scrubbed for surgery.

Sara was dressing for the inauguration, to which she had been invited personally because of Amanda's professional association with the President-elect. The President, who knew of her book *Flat Mouth: An Ordinary Life,* had contacted Amanda shortly after the election in November to take some family portraits. In fact, when the call from Georgetown Hospital came, Amanda was at Blair House photographing the First Family and Melvina answered the phone.

Sara, in her mother's room trying out the makeup which her mother kept but did not use—brown eye shadow on her heavy lids, loose beige powder on her forehead, across the bridge of her nose, pale peach on her cheeks—did not hear the telephone ring, lost as she was in the drama of dressing up. The dress for the inauguration was Jonathan's choice, lavender silk with a high-collared blouse. She had developed early with full breasts and broad hips, a tiny waist, the appropriate body for a young woman at the turn of the century but too fleshy, too rounded and feminine to suit the boyish style of the thirties. She had an oval face, complete at twelve, like the paintings of Renaissance Italian women whose faces last unchanged to middle age. Older men were taken with her.

Sara's life, unlike the downward slide of the country, had taken on a tranquil sense of sweet invulnerability. She struggled to be ordinary against the huge force of her mother but that was her only serious struggle. She had many friends and made them easily, requiring little of other people, expecting goodwill. What was rare about her had to do with a quality of spirit developed early like her face.

"That call was for your mother," Melvina said in her crisp unbroken voice although her face had lost its color. "Your father is dead."

Sara turned from the mirror where she was putting on peach lipstick. "Dead?"

"They called from the hospital to say he'd had a heart attack in the operating room," Melvina said.

"He can't be dead," Sara said. "We had breakfast just a little while ago. You know that. We had pancakes."

Melvina went into the bathroom and took a washcloth from the towel rack, wetting it with warm water. When she came back into the room, Sara was sitting at the end of the bed, ashen, the color on her cheeks stark against her bloodless face.

"We'll wash that color off that face of yours right away, baby, before people start coming to the house and you dressed up like thirty years old." She scrubbed Sara's face.

"I'm fourteen," Sara said. "Today I'm fourteen. I can wear makeup, high-heeled shoes, anything I want. Amanda says I can."

"Well, your mama's not here and someone's got to take charge." Melvina scrubbed hard, especially on the eyelids, and then in an uncharacteristic gesture she kissed the top of Sara's head.

"What do we do first?" Sara asked, too stunned to actually react. "Do we go to the hospital?"

The telephone was ringing.

Melvina shook her head. She picked up the telephone and laid the receiver back on the cradle without saying hello.

"Everybody's going to be calling any minute soon as they hear, so we've got to keep our wits."

"I've got my wits," Sara said.

"We go to the White House and get your mother," Melvina said.

"Or call," Sara said. "I will call." She picked up the receiver, dialed 0 and the operator connected her to Blair House, where the man who answered said it would not be possible to reach Miss Steward, who was photographing Mr. Roosevelt.

"It's an emergency," Sara said.

"What sort of an emergency?" the man on the other end of the phone said.

"A real emergency," Sara said in a voice of surprising authority. "Her husband is dead."

The speaking of it had made fact of her father's death.

It was Melvina's job to protect Amanda from the well-wishers who by noon had filled the house.

Just after ten Amanda had arrived by limousine accompanied by a member of the President's family, a pleasant woman, a cousin, who brought her to the door, kissed her lightly on the cheek, and left.

Amanda stood in the foyer as if she were a stranger.

"Mama," Sara said and hugged her mother's slender shoulders.

Sara picked up her mother's hand, which was cold, and kissed it. "People have been calling and calling," Sara said.

Amanda stood entirely straight and still. The expression on her face was peculiar, a look Sara had never seen before. Not grieved or even frightened but stunned, as if a photographer had captured her expression in passage between the moment of impact on the body and the message of pain to the brain.

"So Mama, there's a lot to do, isn't there?"

But Amanda didn't move.

"Mama?" Sara said.

Amanda seemed to be asleep on her feet, her eyes fixed beyond the room.

Melvina was in the kitchen safely hidden behind the details that needed her attention, the kitchen floor, soup for supper, bread rising in the south window.

Sara appeared in the kitchen door. "Something terrible is the matter with Mama."

"Of course something's the matter with her," Melvina said brusquely.

"You have to help," Sara said. "Now. Quickly."

So Melvina took Amanda upstairs, settled her in the

room on the third floor where she had lived when Sara was a baby—not the room she had shared with Jonathan. She shook her head when they passed that room. "I can't go in there," she said holding Melvina's hand.

Melvina wrapped her legs in a blanket, sat her in a chair, took off her coat, her hat and gloves, her shoes. "Soup?" she asked.

Amanda leaned her head against the soft flesh of Melvina's belly and shook her head.

"Then tea," Melvina said. "And brandy. When the trouble came to me and Pauline died, I had whiskey and stayed drunk for weeks."

Quickly the house filled with people weaving through the downstairs rooms, speaking to Sara and Dr. Steward and Louisa. The minister of Grace Church came and the President of Georgetown University and Jonathan's sons. The dining room table became crowded with food as the day progressed, baked ham and turkey, rolls and platters of vegetables, sweets, cakes and pies, glazed tarts. Flowers arrived all afternoon so the room downstairs took on a certain stiffness of arrangements, the sweet sick smell of death.

"Melvina," Sara said catching her in the kitchen late in the afternoon, in the pantry pretending to look for dishes. "Mama isn't speaking. She won't say a word, not even to me."

Melvina shook her head, dipped a slice of turkey in a jar of mustard. "Why should she speak?" Melvina said putting her arm around Sara's waist. "What she got to say?"

Sara sat down on Melvina's lap.

"I don't even cry. Have you noticed?" she said. "What do you think is the matter with me?"

She had felt nothing except a loss of blood like the onslaught of the flu. When people began to arrive she was pleased to talk to them, pleased to stand in for her mother, and secretly extremely pleased to be surviving a terrible event to which her mother had succumbed.

Grandfather Steward, dry and cranky with age, leaning on his cane, was in a temper when he came down the back stairs from Amanda's room.

"She won't speak," he said to Melvina. "Did you know that?"

"She can't speak," Sara said defensively.

"She can speak. She can say hello at least and the house is full of people, associates of mine and Jonathan's dear friends, waiting to express their sympathy."

"Maybe she's got nothing to say," Melvina said.

"What she doesn't have is manners from growing up with Indians and a mother who was a servant." He cut a slice of pecan pie and ate it. "My servant."

Later as the day darkened, the light sinking from the window, Sara sat with her mother. The room unlit was charcoal gray.

For most of the day Amanda had sat in the overstuffed chair, sat very still as if too fragile to move, her legs wrapped in the blanket, her hands folded.

It was after eight when she finally spoke. "Downstairs," she said, "in the bottom drawer of my dresser, you'll find a box of letters marked ANNA."

"I know," Sara said. "I've seen them before."

"I'd like you to read them to me."

Sara went downstairs, passed the bed where Amanda and Jonathan had slept. The bed was made up, the sheets straightened from his last impression. She did not want to look at the place where he had lain, not out of sadness, still elusive to her, but out of fear of death. She opened the drawer, got the letters, and ran upstairs.

Upstairs, she sat in the chair across from her mother, turned on the small lamp, the only light in the room, so her mother was shadowed in darkness.

Dear Mama, Sara read.

> *It's November in Wisconsin and cold and damp but I am not unhappy. I find, quite to my pleasure, that my mind can be full of a whole life other than the one I am leading and when the days are dark as they have been I am glad for this new life.*

> *Yr. loving daughter,*
> *Anna*

Dear Mama,

I am going to have a daughter, I'm certain. There is something entirely different about this pregnancy. This child, unlike my son, is not complacent.

                                     Yr. loving daughter,
                                      Anna

Dear Mama,

I had a dream about you last night—a perfectly ordinary dream. We were crossing the road in Rhyl to see Grandmama in her cottage and you were telling me about a rabbit you had hidden in the coal bin for a pet when you were small. The dream was so real that it was not until after breakfast doing up the dishes that I realized you are dead.

                                       Yr. loving daughter,
                                      Anna

Melvina brought up bowls of soup and cheese for supper. "People are still coming. Twenty of them or more right now," Melvina said. "Mrs. Barnes and Dr. Friedman and Mary James."

"I'll be down tomorrow, Melvina," she said. "Tell people that tomorrow I'll see them."

Amanda pulled the covers down on her bed and climbed in. Sara lay down at the bottom.

"Someday when this is all over," Sara said, "I'd like you to tell me about my real father."

Amanda brushed her hand absently across Sara's face. "Jonathan was your real father," she said.

TWO

THE TRAIN LEFT Jackson, Mississippi, on the morning of the tenth of August, 1934, headed for Nashville with several stops in between, too many for Sara Abbott, anxious to get home.

Sara sat in the colored section beside Amanda, whose darkly tanned face was shadowed by a broad-brimmed cowboy hat, her camera around her neck. Across from Sara, P. Melvina Jones cut up an apple. There was also a two-year-old Mexican girl called Bonita whom Amanda had picked up in the Panhandle and planned to keep. Bonita sat on Sara's lap dressed in a navy blue sailor's dress and patent leather shoes and holding a Shirley Temple doll dressed as a cowboy. They had been on the road for ten months, since the eighth of October, 1933, just after the beginning of Sara's sophomore year at the Sidwell Friends School.

It was hot and dusty. The windows on the train were open and dust flew in, gathering like a veil between them, but the group of travelers was too tired to speak until the conductor came through collecting tickets and told Amanda she was in the colored section and should move forward to the next car.

"This is the section where I sit," Amanda said taking off her cowboy hat and running her fingers through her short damp hair.

"It's not allowed," the conductor said.

"It's allowed," Amanda said. "I've been from one end of this country to the other and this is how I travel."

"I'll check."

"Check," Amanda said. "I'm white. I can sit where I like." She had grown snappish since Jonathan's death, sometimes bad-tempered, not with her family but with strangers, with anyone who stood in the way of her plan. People, especially in the South, were unaccustomed to such forthright temper in a woman and left her alone.

Sara was admiring of her mother in spite of every instinct to be cross since, out of the blue, or so it had seemed, Amanda decided to take Sara out of school and head across the country to California, going out the northern route, returning by the southern, taking photographs of poverty.

The trip was inspired by President Roosevelt's New Deal programs to help the nation recover from the effects of the Depression.

"Before and after is what the President wants," Melvina said. "You take the before pictures so all the country can see how bad it was before his miracles."

"What miracles?" Sara asked. "I haven't seen any miracles."

But there had been miracles in the first months of the new President's administration. For Amanda, the chance to leave the place where she had been happy with Jonathan, to do something as a photographer, to feel useful once again, was a small miracle in itself.

Sara understood the importance of the trip. She knew her mother's grief for Jonathan and with her customary generosity she did not object to leaving school, although the thought of rolling across the country on a train with Amanda and Melvina, sitting hour after hour on the hard seats of the colored coach, sleeping in the tents they carried, living with the poor, had been the very last thing she would have chosen for her fifteenth year.

Amanda carried a large map of the United States, two tents, two outfits, and her camera equipment. In addition, Sara brought books. It was her plan to read a book a day, and she had made an extensive reading list at Sidwell Friends, where she was an excellent student, so that she could complete her sophomore year without attending classes.

Mostly, she did read a book a day unless there was an emergency in the place where they were staying. Most of the emergencies, and there were many, had to do with children dying or a labor argument which led to bloodshed or a fight between people whose patience with hunger and deprivation had been exhausted.

Always Amanda got involved.

In Pittsburgh, Amanda planned to photograph the Jones and Laughlin Steel Mill, whose equipment was so out of date that thousands of people died or were injured every year.

The foreman, a brawly, large-headed, suspicious man who introduced himself to Amanda as Mr. Lakman and insisted on accompanying her, said he didn't want pictures taken too close to the equipment since the disturbance might cause an accident.

Amanda had just walked into the large equipment area of the factory where there was a catwalk wide enough for two people. From there, she could look down on the workers on the floor. She was standing on the catwalk, her camera focused on the workers and machinery below her, when a piece of rotating machinery held by a tall, lanky, dark-haired man in overalls broke off. The equipment was in motion when the piece, the size of a boy, broke off in the young man's hands.

The accident happened with such speed that Mr. Lakman was not able to stop her photographing the accident. But he grabbed her camera just as the large piece of moving equipment went through the young man's belly and cut him quite literally in half.

"You'll have to leave," Mr. Lakman said to Amanda.

Amanda picked up her camera and was able to get a picture of the dying workman convulsing on the factory floor before Mr. Lakman pushed her ahead of him.

"You've got to leave," Mr. Lakman said, shouting over the sound of machinery still running. "I'm needed on the floor."

"Your equipment is out of date," Amanda said. "Hundreds of people have been injured or died here."

"Your information is incorrect."

"Even the President of the United States knows about the condition of your factory," Amanda said.

He had her out of the building in a matter of seconds, had a driver take her back to the YWCA where Sara and Melvina waited, but Amanda had seen enough to write a story with her photograph of the young man, whose name was John Trainer and whose death left a young widow ill of tuberculosis and three small children living on wages of $369 a year.

They were on the next train to New Philadelphia, Ohio, and then to Cleveland, where Amanda developed the photograph of John Trainer which showed exactly the moment that the piece of machinery had broken off and was on its way through his belly.

* * *

In South Dakota, riding horses through the farm country, they stopped at a house just before nightfall to ask for shelter. The mother of the house came to the front door carrying a dead baby boy already stiff in her arms.

"Take my picture," the woman said, worn and aged by circumstances, although young. "Take my picture with this poor dead boy and send it to the President of the United States."

Most nights, if the weather allowed, they set up the tents, went to the market, built a fire, cooked supper, and went to bed.

"I don't know why I agreed to do such a thing as this," Melvina would say reading her Bible or her catechism by kerosene lantern night after night. "I must have been crazy."

On the train rides, especially if the coach was too bumpy to read, Sara imagined her life, as if her mind were a canvas to which she added a little every day she had the time for reverie. She would marry a tall and slender man with black hair, older of course, with a way about him she'd seen in the movies, and they'd live in Washington, D.C., not Georgetown, but a part of Washington where the lawns were broad and the trees thick and heavy, a place for animals, dogs certainly, maybe even a pony for the children, of which there would be six. She even named them—James, Franklin, Alexandra, Eleanora, Peter, and Pamela, born two years apart. The house would be decorated in broad chintzes, flowers, and color—not the sleek monochromatic look of contemporary houses. She even filled her closet with dresses which she designed, silk, mid-calf, sleek over her hips, across her stomach, provocative. Perhaps she'd call her husband Hal. Hal Blakemore. She liked that. Sara Abbott Blakemore. That was a lovely name. In her daydreams, she kissed Hal Blakemore on the lips.

"What are you thinking now?" Amanda would ask from time to time, catching the swift changes in Sara's expression.

"Oh nothing," Sara would say, her mind fixed on a red

silk evening gown that slithered when she walked. "Just Jane Eyre, I suppose. I was wondering why she heard the voices."

Amanda didn't read books at all. She read only the newspaper and that with little interest, although one would not guess to talk to her. She compensated with sight. Her eyes were fixed on the world as she saw it, which provided sufficient drama to engage her. It occurred to Amanda on the trip from Jackson, Mississippi, that she would be glad not to settle ever, to move from place to place, from scene to scene, her life a moving picture, not a single narrative but frame to frame, with many stories isolated from one another, and she would be at the center.

Already her life had been as if she had taken a box of candid photographs of the years since 1900, tossed them in the air, and let them fall at random—herself at three with Anna, at five at Bad River, at twelve with her father in Ashland, at sixteen mute at the Sidwell Friends School, the war and Lincoln Draper, Sam Dane and Blue Bones in Paris, Sara, Sara and Jonathan, Jonathan, and Flat Mouth once again.

Time had changed its disposition. In a real sense, there was no longer the sequential time of a specific place, day after repeated day, lived out in a single story of birth and marriage perhaps, or work perhaps, or both or neither. And death. Real time was in the mind, always available. And if the scenes of people's lives were to change daily in this century with airplanes and radio and telephone, if there were no longer a place to live, then time and place belonged within. And so Amanda's thoughts went from train station to train station across the country. She began to imagine herself a new kind of photographer, not a realist exactly, because realism diminished the object it reproduced, but one who captured in the faces of people the time and place of their individual lives.

In California, they followed the migratory workers, stopping for some time in Fresno with the Blakes, a young proud family who had made a life in a tiny shack they built for themselves on sand just off the land of a cattle farmer. They built a front porch and a play yard for their babies, a big sandbox walled off and filled with toys made from things of the land, twigs that were people for playing house or church—Mary, Joseph, and the baby Jesus—sticks that were trucks and buses. Smaller sticks were cars, coconut beds for the twig people, palm leaf trees shading the tiny tents made of palm leaves. They made a ceremony of dinner at the Blakes. There was always the luxury of fruit and though there was no running water, Anna Blake washed her children and herself head to toe, their clothes as well, every day in the river half a mile down the road and insisted the children have shoes.

They were in Dallas just after Prohibition was repealed and celebrated at the B-Gun Canteena, where Amanda saw Blue Bones. Actually Blue Bones saw Amanda just across the bar, slid off his bar stool, and came over.

"I know you from somewhere," he said to her.

"I recognize you too," she said. "I don't know from where." He had grown swiftly old and somehow frail. He moved with a sense of caution and although he was familiar, she had seen so many people in her trip across America that everyone had begun to seem familiar.

He sat down next to her.

"My name is Amanda Steward," she said. "Is that a name you know?"

"I'm Blue Bones," he replied.

She was too startled to reply at first. She had written him years before when Sara was born and he had never written back. She had even lost sight of him in her memory. She took a deep breath, extended her hand.

"Were you a photographer in the war living in Paris?"

"I was," he said.

"And stayed?"

"I stayed until twenty-six and then I met a pretty woman from Texas and married her and followed her here and had a baby boy and then she left last year with a man who's got some money."

"I'm sorry," Amanda said. "People are leading terrible lives in this country now."

"I know. I'm headed back to Paris as soon as I can get money."

"Do you remember a man named Sam Dane in Paris during the war? A photographer who lived with you?" Amanda asked. She had hesitated at first, thinking she would forget it, have a drink with him, say thanks and maybe they'd meet again and sorry I didn't turn out to be someone you knew. But something was stirred in her, not for Blue Bones but for herself lost in the First World War.

"I'm his cousin," she said. "He told me about your work. I'm a photographer too."

"He had another cousin who died in the war," Blue Bones said.

"I know," Amanda said. "My cousin too."

"I liked Sam Dane," Blue Bones said. "I liked him very much."

"He liked you too," Amanda said. "He told me so."

The Texas Panhandle was the worst. There was a kind of speechless poverty, families stunned by want and the endless heat. They sat outside their houses waiting. Even the arrival of Amanda and her troupe did not stir them, except one Mexican mother married to a Texas farmer and with a pile of children, eight at least, brightened when Amanda arrived to take photographs.

The Busbys—that was their name—lived in a shack which caught Amanda's eye for the spunk and courage of the place. All over the outside of the house Mrs. Busby had hung material, a piece of bright red cloth outside one window, some calico over the door, a bright green rectangular piece of felt on a stick in the front yard like a flag. The house, sprinkled with brown-skinned children, had a certain sense of triumph about it. Mrs. Busby, a fleshy, round-faced Mexican woman with an appealing smile, was extremely pleased to have her picture taken, although Mr. Busby, growling from the roof which he was patching, was not.

"Why would you take a picture of poor folks unless to poke fun?" he said, adding to his wife, "Goes to show that it takes a stupid woman to want her picture took when she doesn't have the kind of clothes for dressing up, like it takes a stupid woman to keep having babies when there isn't food enough for what we already got."

Mrs. Busby, smiling all the while, spoke back to him in Spanish.

"I can't understand you unless you speak English," he said.

Mrs. Busby shook her head. Her face took on an expression of great sadness. "Too many babies," she said. "One, two, three, four, five, six, seven, eight. And . . ." She raised her hands in despair. "My little Bonita, there is no food for Bonita since yesterday."

Amanda took two bananas out of the pack she carried. "For Bonita."

"No, no, bananas are for you. We will not take from you." A broad smile crossed her face. "We will give to you. We will give you Bonita and then she is yours and you give her a banana and it is okay." She rushed inside and came out carrying a little girl with a mass of black curls, enormous black eyes, and a diaper.

"For you," she smiled and gave a little bow. "Bonita."

And that was how Bonita joined Amanda and Sara and Melvina on their trip.

"Say good-bye to Bonita," Mrs. Busby called out to her other children.

"Good-bye, good-bye," a few of them said. Mr. Busby did not look up from the roof where he was hammering a piece of tin over a large hole.

"Good-bye, good-bye," Mrs. Busby said, happily kissing Sara and Amanda and avoiding Melvina, who gave the clear message that she did not want to be kissed.

Bonita seemed perfectly happy to go along with Sara and Amanda although she did not speak a word that could be understood.

"She probably has the scurvy," Melvina said crossly that evening after they had purchased sunsuits and diapers and a Shirley Temple cowboy doll. "So they give her to us. Why not?"

"Not the scurvy, Melvina," Amanda said.

"Then head lice or leeches or diarrhea. Something's the matter with her."

But in the days to follow, nothing seemed to be wrong with Bonita. She had a golden sweet temperament, an instinctive sense of adventure, and she settled easily into her new life, adopting Melvina as her mother, sleeping in the tent with her, scrambling on her lap as they traveled town to town in Texas by bus.

They arrived in Nashville, Tennessee, on the 15th of August, 1934, and stayed outside the town at Melvina's sister's house.

"You'll be the only white people in the place," Melvina had said disgruntled.

"That's no problem," Amanda said. "I'm getting accustomed."

"And she's not a good-tempered woman, my sister Jess," Melvina said.

"Nor are you, Melvina," Amanda said. "Besides, I'm looking forward to sleeping on a bed."

"Who said there was a bed?"

But there was a bed in the shantytown outside of Nashville and a kitchen sweet with baking and evenings full of song with Melvina's sister and nephews and cousins and brother and all number of friends knocked out to see white folk living in the house with the colored as if it was the most natural thing in the world. And so they stayed on into a second week, especially after Bonita got the flu and had to be iced down in the tub outside to break her fever—until the 23rd of August, when a telegram came from Melvina's older sister Grace in Washington, D.C.

DEAR MELVINA, it said.

JOSEPH JONES ARRIVED THIS AM SICK AS A DOG STOP HE WANTS YOU BACK STOP IF HE WAS MINE ID SAY SCRAM STOP SUIT YOURSELF STOP NOTIFY IMMEDIATELY

GRACE

"So?" Amanda asked sharply.

"I'm going home."

"He walked out twenty-five years ago and you're going home?"

"That's what I'm doing," Melvina said rocking Bonita. "He is my husband."

"It took him a long time to remember," Amanda said crossly.

"Well, he has remembered now."

Amanda packed her things.

"You don't have to come with me. You stay here and get your pictures," Melvina said. "I'm tired of poor folk myself."

"We're coming," Sara said, thrilled by the news of Joseph Jones's reappearance, saved by him, home at last.

The last train ride in the hottest week of the summer went on and on.

"We'll go home?"

"I suppose," Amanda said. She had not thought of what else to do but certainly the thought of returning to Georgetown to the house where she lived with Jonathan filled her with a sense of her own death.

"Perhaps we should move to New York?" she said.

"I want to finish high school," Sara said firmly.

"Of course you do, darling. Maybe when you leave, I'll go to New York." It occurred to her as she watched the landscape of Virginia snap by the window that when she returned to the house on P Street, she could fill it with people and diffuse the accumulated losses of her life.

They arrived at Union Station, Washington, D.C., on August 30 in the morning, a damp hot summer day.

"First off," Sara said, "I'd like to see my friends. Pamela and Jane and Susanna especially."

Bonita, in her new pink dress from Nashville, clutching her Shirley Temple doll and a sugar cookie, trotted along beside Melvina, holding her hand.

Amanda and Sara sat in the backseat of the taxicab.

"I'd like to have stayed on the train for good," Amanda said. "All of us locked in that coach, moving across the country." She reached over and took Sara's hand.

"I don't like memory," Amanda said as the taxicab pulled up at the house on P Street. She leaned forward to pay the taxi driver.

"Then why did you become a photographer?" Sara asked.

"Bad luck, I suppose," Amanda said. "A lack of judgment."

The bright sun filtered through the trees and cast a lace pattern of light across Amanda's hair like a wedding veil, her face in shadow, her eyes preternaturally sad, obscured; for a brief moment, before they got out of the taxicab and went into the house, Sara saw her mother as she might have looked in childhood, unguarded, credulous, almost vulnerable.

THREE

It was nearly three years before the exhibit of Amanda's *Poverty, U.S.A.* opened at the Broome Street Gallery on a mild February afternoon in 1937. Sara, in her freshman year at Barnard College, went downtown to meet her mother for the opening, where Amanda's photographs of their year traveling across the United States were included among ten photographers, all men with the exception of Amanda, who had taken photographs of America during the Depression.

By the time Sara walked in the front door of the gallery shortly after two, a little later than she had been expected, Amanda had already been discovered by Hendrik March.

"Poverty in America" was the first thing he had said to Amanda in his heavy Viennese accent. "Here in the land of milk and honey. Such a tragedy." He kissed her hand. "I am Hendrik March," he said. "Only one week from Austria but my English is good."

He was a small man, Sara's height, shorter than Amanda—intense and darkly handsome with black eyes, a mass of black curly hair, and a broad head which made him seem taller than he was. He had strong bones, a commanding mobile face, an easy, mischievous smile, an incurable optimism. He had come to America with his brother, Albert, who was older than he, by Hendrik's definition a gloomy journalist. "He sees the world as black," Hendrik said, "and I see it as color. We have therefore a good marriage." They intended to start a newspaper, he said, a political newspaper of ideas to bring to the attention of Americans what was really going on in Europe with Germany under Hitler, especially what was happening to the Jews.

"I am a Jew," he said at lunch in the small cafeteria across the street from the gallery to which he had insisted on taking Amanda and Sara.

"I buy lunch," he said magnanimously. "In a year, two years, I will be dead if I stay in Europe and so I come here and tell the Americans the bad news. I hear in America anything is possible. So I make a newspaper, maybe in New York."

They sat in hard booths at a table which overlooked Broome Street, an odd group even for New York. Hendrik was poorly dressed in old clothes too large for him. Amanda, her grandmother's cape around her shoulders, was in black trousers, her hair long, unstylish, straight and loose around her shoulders. And Sara, like a magazine model, was lovely in a teal blue crepe suit with suede pumps she had bought with her second-semester book money, thinking that if she had to stay at Barnard, if Amanda insisted, she would borrow the books from someone else in her classes. She still had some money left over for a dress she had seen in the window at B. Altman's just that afternoon.

"So what do you think?" Hendrik asked. "New York for a newspaper?"

"Perhaps," Amanda said. "I don't know very much about newspapers. I would imagine they are very expensive to start."

Hendrik ordered more coffee. "More coffee for everyone," he said to the waitress.

"But I work and get money. Right?" he said. "Not so hard."

He picked up Sara's hand. "Porcelain. Like china, this hand. So beautiful."

Sara smiled. She had actually never met a European man and she was, in spite of herself, charmed by his foreignness.

So was Amanda, she noticed. At lunch, she saw her mother as she had never seen her—a certain cock of her head, the way she pushed her hair back off her face and spoke softly, melodically.

"You were flirting," she said to Amanda later that afternoon in the room at Grace Hotel where her mother was staying.

"Of course I wasn't," Amanda said crossly. "I don't flirt." She took off her trousers and stiff white blouse, opened her small valise. "I wish I'd brought a dress for tonight," she said pensively.

"We could go shopping," Sara said lying down on the twin bed. "I saw a dress at B. Altman's."

"No," Amanda said. "I hate shopping." She looked at herself in the mirror over her dresser, brushed her hair back. "I think my hair's too long. It makes my face thin." She put on another pair of trousers. "I'm going to have it cut right now. There's a place on Fifth Avenue."

Sara laughed. "I have never in my life seen you pay attention to the way you look. What's gotten into you?"

"Absolutely nothing," Amanda said swinging her cape over her shoulders.

"Hendrik whatever his name," Sara said.

"His name is Hendrik March," Amanda said. "He liked you. He liked your porcelain hands. Don't you remember?"

"Now I remember," Sara smiled. "How did you meet him?"

"He wandered into the exhibit and came right up to me when he found out I had taken some of the photographs."

"Because you're a woman," Sara said. "Mr. March prefers women photographers, don't you think?"

Amanda linked arms with Sara. "Come with me," she

said and they walked down the corridor to the elevator, down and out the door of the lobby to 10th Street.

"I've been meaning to tell you," Sara began, glad for the noise of the traffic, the activity of the street, her mother's distraction. "I'm not at all sure that I'm suited to college."

"You're just homesick," Amanda said. "I've been homesick all of my life." She moved Sara in and out of the parade of people walking toward them.

"For what have you been homesick?"

"For home," Amanda said breezily. "For my mother, I suppose. You'll be fine, darling."

"Maybe," Sara said, disgruntled, thinking of the dress at B. Altman's and whether she might persuade her mother to go uptown.

"I wish I had had a chance to go to college." They crossed at Fifth Avenue and turned left. "The place is in the middle of this block, I think," Amanda said.

"But you're famous. What difference would it have made?"

"I don't know things. Only what I see. Besides, I was very bad at school and you're not."

"Perhaps I could go to school in Washington," Sara said.

"Stay the year," Amanda said. "Then we'll decide."

They went into a small shop decorated in black and white: HAIRCUTS WHILE YOU WAIT.

"If you didn't have Bonita, you'd be too lonely to allow me to come to New York," Sara said.

"That's not true. The only reason I tolerate your leaving is for your own sake." She leaned over the counter. "I'd like a haircut," she said.

"What if I'm unhappy?" Sara followed Amanda to the back of the shop where a shop girl waited to wash her hair. "What if I'm absolutely miserable?"

"Happiness doesn't just happen," Amanda said. "And certainly you're not miserable in that new and expensive suit."

"What if I were to tell you I'd met someone?" Sara said, ignoring the comment about her clothes. She pulled a chair up next to Amanda's. "That I'm going to marry him and leave school."

"Have you?" Amanda asked, sitting up from the sink while the shop girl wrapped a terry cloth towel around her head.

"I said 'what if.' You couldn't keep me from leaving school then."

She followed Amanda to the chair where the woman stood who was to cut her hair.

"I can't keep you now," Amanda said. "I was too young when I started a life. I was awkward on the East Coast, never at home. And also uneducated. So I'd like for you to be educated and to feel completely at home."

The hairdresser cut Amanda's hair just below her ears.

"Curls?" she asked.

"No curls." Amanda followed the hairdresser to the dryers.

"You haven't met anyone, have you?" Amanda asked.

"Only Hendrik March, who has asked me to marry him for my porcelain hands."

Amanda pulled the dryer over her head.

"You were never a smart aleck until you went to college," she said.

"See the danger?" Sara said.

By the time Amanda's hair was dry, it was five o'clock and they had to rush back to the hotel to get ready for the party honoring the ten photographers, to which Amanda had invited Hendrik March.

"Why in the world would you invite a stranger?" Sara asked. "He could be involved in criminal activities."

"Just to be kind," Amanda said checking her new haircut in the mirror above her dresser.

FOUR

SARA PUT HERSELF to sleep at night dreaming of Hendrik March. It was as if she had been to a movie and fallen in love with the romantic hero, for the time of a movie was all the time she had spent with him—two hours at the party for the exhibit, maybe a little more. She daydreamed of her imagined wedding to Hendrik March, perhaps in the spring of 1939 just after she was twenty, at St. John's Episcopal Church, Lafayette Square, across the street from the White House. Or else she'd marry in the winter because she'd like to wear velvet, cut on the bias to make her seem more slender. She would carry long-stem roses tied with a peach satin ribbon.

Dear Amanda, she wrote to her mother from Barnard in early spring of her freshman year.

> *I have given my college education a great deal of thought. Although certainly I value the opportunity, I could take advantage of it just as well in Washington, perhaps George Washington University. Please consider.*
> > *Your loving daughter,*
> > *Sara*

Dear Sara,
> *No.*
> *Please reread your letters before you send them.*
> *I am your mother. Not your legal advisor or the clerk at a department store.*
> *Don't call me Amanda or send me impersonal documents.*
>
> > *Your Mother*

Dear Mama,
> *Calling you Amanda was your idea. Not mine.*
> *Do you happen to have Mr. Hendrik March's address*

*in New York? I thought I might invite him to a tea one
Saturday at Barnard. He might be in need of a friend.*

> *Yr. loving daughter,*
> *Sara*

Darling,

Hendrik March
c/o Rubble, 7 West 10th

*But I believe he is moving to Washington, D.C. In
fact, this week on Thursday, he is coming down by train
with his tiresome brother Albert and staying here while
he gets a footing to start his newspapers.*

*I have started to do portraits of people, not exact por-
traits but slightly obsured to alter the face in specific ways
by this process of developing I discovered by accident.*

*I was invited for dinner at the White House. I wore a
long dress, actually one I found in the attic which must
have belonged to Jonathan's first wife who was very
tall. The dress was too long and I tripped going down
the stairs to dinner and broke my wrist.*

*Hendrik March tells me you are the most beautiful
young woman he has seen in America. I have told him
he is too old for you.*

> *Love,*
> *M.*

Hendrik March had told Sara himself that she was
beautiful—"enchanting" was his word—walking uptown
to Barnard the day after she had met him at the gallery.

"I will take Sara back to her university," he had said at
the party the night before, "and then I get to know New
York."

"I'll come with you," Amanda had said. "And then I'll
catch a train back to Washington."

They had walked all the way uptown from the Grace
Hotel, Hendrik between them, with a kind of boyish excitement and curiosity, so Sara saw New York City as if
for the first time—the towering buildings, the way light
slid from the sky onto the street where they were walking.
The people were in such a hurry, he said, so lighthearted.
He talked about communism and how it would work in

America, how there were so many poor in the world and nothing for them, and after all Amanda had found plenty of poor in America, about Hitler and his mother and sister who would not come to America and did not believe as he and Albert did that trouble lay ahead, about how he loved to dance and to sing. He sang in German and then in French and then in broken English a song he made up: "Sara—you are an enchanting child, merry and sweet and beautiful, with hair of gold and eyes of stars, lalala."

He asked Amanda all about herself. Sara was astonished that her private-minded mother actually told him about her time in the war, her father, her husband.

"So much trouble you have had," he said. "You must be a Jew by accident." He asked Sara about college and whether she was smart in school and was reading philosophy, which he had read, or literature. By the time they arrived at Barnard and Sara had kissed her mother good-bye and Hendrik had kissed her hand, both hands, her cheeks, he knew more about them than their friends did.

He ran his hand softly across her face.

"I take a picture of your beautiful face with my hand so when I am alone in my room, there you are on my hand, lovely as life. You see?"

After Hendrik, college was tedious. Her roommate was giddy about this boy and that boy—should she kiss Samuel even though it was Ralph she loved but Ralph had an interest in Mary Baker in the next dorm so perhaps she ought to kiss Samuel just to keep him interested in case Ralph went off with Mary Baker.

Sara loved school. She loved the process of learning, of reading and lectures and taking notes, of organizing her time and her notes, underlining with red and green and yellow pencils so her Philosophy I notebook looked like the notebook for a course in design. But she did not by nature cast herself into an imagined future in which her college education was a part of a grand plan. Her friends at Barnard—and there were many who sought her company because there was comfort in it, a certain ease—were set on an intense and serious course. They were going to be lawyers and physicians. They were going to do something for the poor or travel to India—although their conversation was all of boys and sex and whether one had dropped out of school to have a baby or another who had a reputation for frigidity was in fact a lesbian. There were seldom high-minded conversations late at night, with cigarettes, occasionally Scotch, the girls sitting cross-legged on the floor of someone's room. The talk was could I borrow your straight skirt with the tight black sweater for a date or do you want children and how many and a real wedding with a gown?

Dear Amanda, Sara wrote after she had received her mother's letter regarding Hendrik March's residence.

> *I didn't know you had stayed in touch with Mr. March and his brother.*
> *How old is Mr. March? You mention the difference in our ages. Surely he is closer to my age than to yours.*
> *S*

Darling,
> *Mr. March is 30. Seven years younger than I am. Twelve years older than you.*
> *He had a wife in Austria and a baby daughter. The wife was killed in an automobile crash four years ago when the car in which she was driving hit a tree and the baby daughter is being raised by her parents. The only other personal information that I know is that he is allergic to fish.*
> *Did you ask me for personal information?*
> *Love,*
M

Darling,
> *I haven't heard from you for a week. Is everything all right? Have you the flu like everyone in Washington? I placed a call to the college and left you a message. Please call.*
> *Love,*
M

Sara,

I have called Barnard four times this week. They tell me you are appearing in class and attending meals and seem to be quite well. I will be in New York on Friday if I haven't heard from you.

Love,
M

On Friday, March 19, there was a telegram.

SARA ABBOTT STOP AM COMING NEW YORK TOMORROW STOP BE IN TOUCH IMMEDIATELY STOP MOTHER.

"What is going on?" Amanda asked when Sara finally called late that night.

"I've been busy," Sara said coolly. "I have a lot of work."

"I've called the college four times."

"I got your messages," Sara said. "They were put in my mailbox."

"Are you angry?" There was a note of desperation in Amanda's voice.

"In what room are you going to have Mr. March sleeping?" Sara asked.

"Upstairs. He and his brother are on the third floor next to Melvina's room and I'm in my room and Bonnie is in her room and your room is waiting for you to come home."

"I see," Sara said. "The house seems too small for all of us."

"Oh no, there's plenty of room." Amanda hesitated. "Are you angry that Mr. March is living with us? He's very nice and lively and funny. I thought you liked him, Sara."

"I do like him," Sara said. "I like him very much."

Sara's room at Barnard overlooked the quad and it was quiet. Her roommate, who had joined the Communist Party on campus, was either at party meetings or out with a man at Columbia. Sara had the room to herself and spent the spring semester studying. She was known at Barnard for her intelligence and gentleness, qualities rare in the hard-edged young women around her.

Men fell easily in love with her. She was soft, affirming in her sensuality.

She had dates to dances and the theater and lectures, fraternity parties at Columbia, and she had kissed a few boys good night under the glaring light in the vestibule of her dormitory. But they were like puppies, these high-spirited Columbia boys, clumsy, grappling after her breasts, kissing her so hard her neck could break, tripping along beside her on long gangly legs.

She was not interested. She was interested only in Hendrik March.

According to Amanda's letters through the spring, Hendrik had printed the first copy of *The Honest Truth* out of the basement of their house in Georgetown.

> *Dear Sara,*
> *Hendrik has set up a small office next to my dark-room in the basement and I am working with him to raise money which we have done. Joseph Jones died March 31 finally, so Melvina is back in her old room, pleased to be with Bonnie who has taken a terrible dis-like for Albert. It will be good to have you come home for the summer especially with Bonnie whose Mexican blood runs hotter as she gets older.*
> *Hendrik attracts people like fly paper. Already he knows more people in Washington than I have ever known. They crawl out of the woodwork. There are never fewer than six extra for meals. Melvina, of course, doesn't trust him because he has a foreign accent.*
> *Have you thought of cutting your hair?*
>
> > *Love,*
> > *M*

"I think Sara has fallen in love with Hendrik March," she told Melvina once. "What do you think?"

"I keep my nose clean," Melvina said. "And you should too. Especially about people who don't speak the English language. Right."

In June, after exams, Sara packed her steamer trunk, her books, the poster over her bed, her chenille spread, told her friends good-bye and that she would write and see them in September, although she knew certainly that she was not returning to Barnard.

FIVE

AMANDA ASSUMED FROM the start that Hendrik March and Sara would marry, after college, after Sara had the beginnings of a career. She had even imagined the wedding, which would be small and civil in the parlor of the house on P Street with Bonita as a flower girl and only a few guests—Flat Mouth would be there, of course, and Louisa who had finally married Dr. Steward just before his death. She'd ask the Drapers, with whom she had kept in touch. Surely Mrs. Draper had noticed the resemblance to Lincoln, not in Sara's face exactly—her face was Anna's—but there was the memory of Lincoln about her. Melvina would come and her sister Grace; perhaps Blue Bones would be in the country, although his letters from Paris confirmed Hendrik's conviction that there was going to be another war and he would remain for it.

Sara and Hendrik could have the house, Amanda thought. Already Hendrik had filled the basement with *The Honest Truth,* which was published in magazine format once a month. The readership was left-wing, intellectual, mostly Jewish, and young. The purpose of the publication was to tell the true stories, insofar as they could be known, of what was happening politically in Europe under Hitler and Mussolini with observations of a critical nature in America as well. Many of the young writers Hendrik used for the journal were members of the Communist Party which, he told Amanda, he would be if he liked groups, which he did not.

Amanda had no interest in politics at all, no ideology, although she did believe in good and evil with a child's sense of injustice. But she liked having the March brothers in the house, happy for their company, even though she found their work generally dull.

If she gave Sara and Hendrik the house, Amanda thought, then Bonita would stay with Melvina, and Amanda would travel, back to Wisconsin, maybe to Paris. Bonita was really Melvina's child anyway.

"We got her in Texas for you," Amanda had said.

"I would have done with a church dress instead or a hundred dollars if you were in the mood for gifts," Melvina said. "What do I need a baby for?"

But Melvina clearly needed a baby and Bonita filled her life. Chattering away in Spanish and English, settling easily into her new life, she showed no sign of missing her family in Texas.

When Sara and Hendrik married, presuming they would, Amanda would keep her room on the top floor where she slept now. She had opened up the attic so the room was large, whitewashed, with eaves and dormer windows at both ends, so she lived at the top of the trees and the room filled with the cool northern light in the afternoon and the light from the south in the morning as well. The room was simple, even bare. There were photographs on the wall, the one of Flat Mouth when he was small, the jacket photograph from *Flat Mouth: An Ordinary Life,* which was an unforgiving close-up showing the irregularities of Flat Mouth's handsome face, the way his eyes did not exactly match, the picture of Lincoln at Château-Thierry the last time she saw him, a photograph of Jonathan when she first began to take portraits which captured the generosity in his slender face. Her bed was on the floor with pillows piled against the wall, an old oriental rug from her grandfather's house with a black background and a faded rose pattern softened the starkness of the room. She stacked the books she was reading on the floor, mostly art books. She didn't like to read, not even fiction, but she loved to lie in the mountain of pillows on her bed and put herself to sleep looking at pictures.

In the mornings, she got up early. Already the house was buzzing with the telephone and Hendrik dashing up and down the stairs between his study and the layout table

in the basement or Albert banging out stories on the upright Remington or Bonita singing "God Bless America"
with the radio. It was like her romantic memory of life in
Ashland before her mother died when she had lived with
the warm security that life could blow around her like a
spring wind and she could be in the room on the top floor
in splendid isolation without the cost of loneliness.

Sara had enrolled for classes at George Washington University and by late fall 1937 had a whole new group of
friends from college who came for tea and Coca-Colas and
sat around the kitchen smoking cigarettes, telling secrets.
Late afternoons while the days were still long enough for
light, Amanda and Sara often took a walk to Dumbarton
Oaks, through the gardens, and on those walks Sara would
tell her mother small secrets, enough to still her curiosity,
nothing about boys although there was one in particular,
older, a figure painter, who took Sara to coffee and had
kissed her. Sara said nothing about Hendrik March except
to remark on his funny-looking shoes and the odd odor of
European tobacco in the house. Certainly Amanda never
mentioned her plans for Sara's marriage.

"I had thought you might have a crush on Hendrik
March," Amanda said, hoping for information.

Sara shook her head. "No, not at all," she said. "He is
a very nice man with an unpleasant brother who I wish
didn't spend the day in our study."

However, by Christmas 1937 there were unaccountable
tensions. Sara was quiet and sullen, Amanda had developed a temper, and even Hendrik had taken on his brother's dark demeanor.

"What do you expect?" Melvina said to Amanda. "We
have a house full of women and one man and one rat. It's
lucky we're speaking."

"I don't understand, Melvina. I honestly don't. Things
were fine until Sara came home. I had imagined that
Hendrik would take an interest in her."

Melvina hammered a chicken breast flat, lifted Bonita to
the counter, and gave her a cookie hot from the oven.

"He did take an interest. What else? He took an interest

in you too. Soon, if we keep up this hothouse in George-town, he's going to have an interest in me and we'll have a Jew boy and a nigger girl. There'll be no end to that trouble." Melvina laughed heartily, very pleased with herself.

"I think he's worried about Europe. About Hitler. And that's the reason for his black humor."

"He's worried about whether he likes the young girl or the old girl best," Melvina said. "Hitler can take care of himself."

There were tensions at dinner. Albert no longer came to meals but Hendrik was often gloomy, uninterested in food, uninterested in conversation.

"Maybe he's ill or homesick," Amanda said to Melvina.

"Lovesick," Melvina said. "This is his home."

"I haven't seen you in trousers for months," Sara said to her mother one afternoon making Christmas cookies with Bonita, cutting out pine trees and bells and Santa Claus. Her voice had an edge. "You have all these new clothes. Are you making a lot of money?"

"I don't really have many new clothes," Amanda said. But it was true. She had been conscious of the way she looked since Hendrik moved in. She dressed carefully in the morning before she came downstairs, something she had never done with Jonathan. She was growing her hair again.

"I actually need to dress for the kind of work I'm doing now. Going into people's homes for portraits," Amanda said.

Sara shrugged. "I assumed you had met someone." She was irritated at her mother, sometimes irrationally angry.

"Of course I'd tell you if I had met someone." Amanda took a Christmas bell cookie, licked the sugar off the top. "I doubt I'll ever meet someone after your father."

"My father?" Sara asked.

"Jonathan," Amanda said, trying for patience.

Although Sara knew very well about her real father, they never discussed him.

Sara lifted Bonita on a chair and washed her hands.

"Why don't you ever talk about my father?"

"You have never asked," Amanda said. "I've told you everything when you asked me." She sat down in the kitchen chair next to Sara.

Sara rolled out the cookie dough.

"And you weren't married to him."

"No I wasn't."

"You didn't need to tell me, you know. You could have pretended Jonathan was my real father and saved me this humiliation," Sara said looking her mother straight in the eye.

"Humiliation?" Amanda said.

"The humiliation of a mother who sleeps around," Sara said crossly. It was not a term she ever used but for the moment it suited the occasion.

Amanda's throat filled with tears. She went up the back stairs to her room and shut the door.

Melvina was right, she thought, lying down on the bed, covering her eyes with her arm. There were too many women in the house.

SIX

JUST AFTER MIDNIGHT on Christmas Eve, a light snow falling with large weighted flakes sticking to the trees and bushes, Sara was in her bed, not sleeping but lying on top of the covers in the dark watching the shimmering of silver flakes outside her window.

Melvina, in the room next to hers, was reading her missal, mumbling the words aloud. Bonita was sleeping and even Amanda, who never went to bed, often working in the darkroom until one or two in the morning, had had too much champagne at the Drapers' Christmas Eve party and had fallen asleep on top of her bed in her clothes. Hendrik and Albert had gone for a walk to the White House to see the Christmas tree on the Roosevelts' front lawn. They had been gone for a long time when Sara heard footsteps on the back stairs, along the corridor, past Bonita's room and Melvina's to the front of the house where Sara was half-sleeping. There was a knock on her door and Hendrik walked in.

"I come to take you for a walk," he whispered, coming across the room.

Sara sat up. She was in her nightgown, her feet bare, and she tucked them under her gown.

"I didn't hear you coming," she said. "I was asleep."

"I come in secret," Hendrik said, walking awkwardly like a duck across the room on his toes. He kissed her hand. "Remember?" he said. "I put your hand to my face imprinted."

"It's so late," she said. Her face was flushed.

"But beautiful outside. Like magic and not cold." He lay his hand against her hair and she shivered. "You put on your clothes and I'll wait for you in the kitchen. We must see the snow."

He tiptoed across the room and she watched him in the pale silver light open the door, which creaked, and slide into the corridor.

"Shhh," he whispered across the room to her and she heard his footsteps down the corridor to the back steps.

She dressed quickly in a skirt and sweater, stockings but no shoes so she would not be heard especially by Melvina's sharp suspicious ears, brushed her hair loose around her face. In the mirror over her dresser she looked lovely, expectant.

Hendrik was downstairs by the back door, the collar of his coat up, a cup of coffee in his hand. He shook Sara's coat off the hook and held it for her.

"There you are," he said. He turned her around as if she were a child, buttoned up the front of the coat, pulled the collar up around her neck.

"So the snow won't go down your back," he said.

He opened the back door, linked his arm through hers, and they went into the weather soft with thick flakes which fell like cold cotton on Sara's cheek, on her tongue, which she stuck out to catch them. In the streetlights, the snow sailed in a long shimmering streamer and Sara stood

under the light in front of their house and let the snow
streamer coat her cloth jacket with white.

"You look like an angel," Hendrik said swinging around
the lamppost.

"I am," Sara said.

He leaned toward her as if he were going to kiss her.

"You can't," she said cocking her head.

Amanda had heard the sounds of footsteps downstairs, had
sensed a flurry of activity, and in spite of the champagne
had gotten up to check on what transpired. She opened the
door to her bedroom and heard Sara padding in stocking
feet down the corridor and when she looked out the dormer window facing P Street, there they were, Sara lit by
the streetlight, her head tilted back, the snow falling on her
face, and Hendrik swinging around the lamppost, around
Sara, brushing the snow off her long hair.

Amanda turned on the light. It was late, after two, her
head was heavy with champagne—and the snow was falling wet and thick as it did on Christmas Eve in northern
Wisconsin.

Dear Flat Mouth, she wrote.

   *It's Christmas Eve and snowing like Wisconsin and I
write to you to say I'll be coming after the winter for
more photographs—this group will be about Bad River
itself. Not you.*

   *Besides I'm almost forty. Too old for trouble. I re-
member when Grandmother Yellow Flower was forty
and she seemed aged.*

   *Remember how in summer, especially the summer of
the big heat, we'd watch the mother birds push their babies out of the nest and I said: Not me. My birds will stay.*

   Now I know definitely that birds fly or die.

   I think of you.

                                              Love,
                                              A Man

Hendrik put his arm around Sara's waist, pulled her
strongly toward him.

"So what do you think?" he asked. "We will walk to Paris?"

"Why not?" Sara said softly, her wet cheek resting against his. "In Paris, they stay up all night, I hear."

SEVEN

THE HONEST TRUTH was a journal of serious political essays about contemporary affairs and to the surprise of everyone—Amanda, the investors, Albert March, everyone that is except Hendrik, whose optimism was unshakable—it was an extraordinary success.

In 1938, Hitler had appointed himself War Minister and marched into Austria. There were pogroms in Germany and although news of the slaughters was slow to reach North America, even Europe, the August 1938 issue of *The Honest Truth* had a black cover with POGROMS written in red across the front and a long essay by Albert, the principal writer of the brothers, including what information he could find about the troubles in Germany.

In England, Anthony Eden resigned in protest against Lord Chamberlain's policy of appeasement and Winston Churchill moved into the leadership and the news. In the United States, Congressman Martin Dies became chairman of the newly formed House Un-American Activities Committee.

The October issue of *The Honest Truth* had an essay by Hendrik which was largely hidden in the issue and created little interest among the readership. The essay, which would later alter the life of Hendrik March and his family, was entitled "Hitler, Chairman of Un-German Activities" and compared the Nazi state of the fallen Weimar Republic with the United States of America, suggesting that the House Un-American Activities Committee portended a similar danger to democracy as Hitler had to Germany.

The Munich Conference took place in September 1938.

Germany moved in to occupy Sudetenland and finally before the turn of the year Roosevelt broke diplomatic relations with Germany and recalled the American ambassador. There was going to be a war.

By 1938 the March brothers occupied not just the basement and the study of the house at the corner of P and 31st Streets, but the dining room, Sara's bedroom, the upstairs sitting room, and the sun porch off the back of the living room. There were six regular employees—university students, recent graduates—and a daily string of young men, some women, some members of the Communist Party, mainly socialists in the post-Depression spirit, in and out of the house with essays or ideas for essays or just a chance to sit around the kitchen table and smoke cigarettes and talk about the state of the world.

For Amanda, the people wandering through the house, strangers mostly but people with a reason to be there, gave her a sense of many friendships, of conviviality, which she had never had—tending by temperament to isolation. Except for Sara and Flat Mouth, in a lesser way Melvina and Bonita, Amanda had no investments of the heart. Now the house was always full and Amanda had the illusion of family.

But Hendrik was taking over.

"What I don't understand," Amanda said to Sara in the fall of 1938, "is why you gave up your room to Hendrik."

Sara shrugged.

"He needed the room," she said. "Albert had to have a study."

They were sitting in Amanda's room, next door to the room where Sara had moved when she gave up her own room to *The Honest Truth*. On the bed, Bonita was cutting out paper dolls of the Dionne quintuplets and dressing them in matching outfits.

"I am a mommy with five babies," she said happily. "Five here and five at home."

"Pack up your five babies and we're going to Alexandria to take pictures of the Baker children, Bonnie,"

Amanda said, packing her camera bag with film and zoom lens and flashes.

"I don't like to take pictures," Bonita said. "I am going to stay with Melvina and eat cookies and on Saturday I'm going to the zoo with Albert."

"Perhaps you should leave him in the elephant house," Amanda said.

Bonita cocked her head. "Leave Albert?"

"Exactly," Amanda said.

"He isn't an elephant," Bonita said earnestly.

Sara brushed Bonita's black curly hair.

"It was your idea, Mama. You brought the March brothers in here and then things developed. You could ask them to leave."

Amanda sat down on the rocking chair beside her daughter.

"What other things have developed?" she asked. "You're very secretive, Sara."

"What has developed is a friendship between me and Hendrik."

"What do you mean?" Amanda asked.

"You know what I mean," Sara said.

Amanda put her feet up on her bed.

"Not on my baby quintuplets," Bonita said moving Amanda's feet.

"I assume a personal relationship. But who is to say? You are always off at school and Hendrik works twenty-two hours a day. Tell me what is going on?" she asked, suddenly expecting the worst. "Are you married?"

"Not yet," Sara said.

She was unaccountably nervous to tell her mother anything about Hendrik, as if she and Amanda were in a silent competition to win his favor. To her shame, she had won the match. "If it is agreeable to you, we are going to get married. Not soon. Sometime."

"Of course it's agreeable," Amanda said too quickly, getting up, pretending to look in her closet for a sweater. "I have always hoped that you would."

Of course she had hoped they would marry. Planned for it. But for reasons she didn't understand, it wasn't fine now. She didn't think it was wonderful at all. She felt as if she had been in a competition with Hendrik for Sara's affections. And Hendrik, for whom she had done everything a person could do for another, had given him a home and a business and friends, had stolen Sara from her. She wanted to kill him.

"You will be pleased, Mama," Sara said warmly. "In time you will be. We all are very fond of each other."

Amanda felt tears. "Of course," she said briskly, lifting Bonita off the bed, putting the Dionne quintuplets and their clothes in a shoe box with the rest of the paper dolls. "You might consider reclaiming your room when you get married. Or suggest to Hendrik that he rent a larger space."

Bonita put her arms around Amanda's shoulder. "I will marry Albert," she said. "On my birthday."

"Lucky you," Amanda said. She swung her camera bag over her shoulder. "You can get married in the parlor. I've thought we could have the wedding there and a supper afterward if Hendrik would clean up the first floor."

"Actually," Sara said straightening the corner of Amanda's coverlet, "I had thought of a wedding in church."

"In church?"

"At St. John's. I would like to have a dress and attendants and flowers. Even a minister. A real wedding. Didn't you have a minister with Jonathan?"

"Yes, I suppose I did. But it was at home," Amanda said. "And I don't know any ministers." They'd talk later about the wedding, Amanda said, and she carried Bonita down the front steps, meeting Hendrik on the way.

At first she thought to say "Congratulations." She had even thought that that was what she was going to say, but instead she asked him to please move out of Sara's room and the dining room as well.

"I feel as if I've sacrificed my house to communism," she said, "and I'm not a believer."

"I am not a believer in communism either. I am a believer in the truth," Hendrik said. "You misunderstood."

Amanda buried her face in Bonita's shoulder. "No," she

said. "I understood very well. You want to marry my daughter."

Outside the sun was bright and hot, a late summer sun, too bright—the out-of-doors shimmered, glazed with silver. Amanda pulled a straw hat square on her head, the brim a shade from the weather.

Sara met Hendrik on the stairs. He grabbed her hand, kissed the inside of her wrist. They waited for the front door to shut.

"She's gone," Sara said. She put her hand on Hendrik's arm. "She knows," she said. "I told her."

"The news did not seem to please her," Hendrik said.

"It will, I promise. By tomorrow."

EIGHT

SARA, STILL IN her nightgown although it was almost noon, lay in her bed with a pillow over her face to keep out the light from the late summer sun. In the next room, Amanda and Hendrik were fighting. Their voices were as clear as if they had been fighting in Sara's room, on her bed, fighting over her, which was in fact exactly what they were doing. Fighting over Sara, fighting for her as if she were a doll pulled back and forth by children—"Mine," "Mine," "Mine." And that's how Sara felt—"Theirs"—exhausted by the struggle, too tired to get out of bed and marry Hendrik March, which was what she was supposed to do, had arranged to do at six o'clock that evening of September 1, 1939, at St. John's Episcopal Church, Lafayette Square.

"It is, after all, my house, Hendrik," Amanda said. "And it's so full of papers and posters and notes and books and pamphlets as if we're providing a warehouse for the left wing. I could not possibly have had the wedding dinner here."

"You didn't tell me you wanted to give the wedding dinner," Hendrik said.

"I asked you to move your junk out."

"Then I will move my business and I will move Sara to Silver Spring where I can afford to live."

"I just said move your junk," Amanda said. "Not Sara. You and Sara are living here. That's been arranged. I'll be mostly in New York or somewhere."

"Sara will be my wife and I will live with her where I want."

"You'll live with her here. She'd hate Silver Spring."

"Shut up. Shut up." The voice was Albert's. "Today is supposed to be a happy day and not a funeral. Besides, today Danzig is annexed. Germany has taken Poland and tomorrow there will be war."

Sara pressed the pillow over her ears.

"I'd like to run away," she said when Melvina came into her bedroom.

"Who could blame you?" Melvina said. The fighting had been going on for weeks. "They should marry each other."

"They may as well. I'm too tired to get married today."

Melvina brushed Sara's hair off her face. "Get up and take a long bath. Keep the water running so you don't hear them," she said. "They fight because they love you, after all."

"Great," Sara said. "I am dying of love."

"You are your mother's heart and soul," Melvina said. "She cannot stand to lose you."

Sara sat up. She was dizzy and leaned her head down over her knees.

"It's not she who is losing me," Sara said getting out of bed. "It is I who am losing myself."

She turned on the bath, sat on the toilet, and watched the tub fill, the words of Amanda and Hendrik muffled by the water. And when the tub was up over the nozzle so the sound was gone, she sank her body into the warm water, lying in the tub, the water over her ears so the sounds she heard were hollow oceanic sounds, and her mother and Hendrik were drowned.

Sara had four attendants, whose rich peach silk dresses, long, cut on the bias with cap sleeves and a lift to the shoulders, hung in her room where they would be dressing that afternoon.

Sara had designed the dresses and the broad-brimmed crownless hats with seed pearls, and she had made her own ecru silk dress, extremely simple with a high waist, a long train gathered in the back. She was wearing a veil of Italian lace which had belonged to Pamela's mother.

Pamela was her closest friend from high school—tall, lanky, fiercely masculine, she wore her hair cropped short, her broad heavy-boned face without makeup. She had made plans to be a physician unless, as she told Sara with enthusiasm, there was a war and then she'd prefer to be a spy.

Pamela arrived while Sara was still in her bath and then Susanna, already married to a young man from Yale who had gotten her pregnant in her freshman year, and Jane, who was extremely bright and actually quite beautiful behind the large glasses she wore, the loose-fitting sweaters and skirts, the hair pulled straight off her face. By one o'clock, they were all there, sitting around the kitchen with cups of lemon tea and tuna fish sandwiches, Bonita sitting on Pamela's lap and then Susanna's and even Jane's before she rushed out to the garden to pick flowers.

These were the women of Sara's childhood—the girls she had played field hockey with and talked with during lunch and recess or after school at Jane's house, which was the largest, where they used to dress up in Jane's mother's formal gowns and dance together. They knew each other without the need for conversation.

"I have never understood why you don't have women friends," Sara had said once to her mother. "It's different with men. There's no real sympathy in those friendships."

Amanda shrugged. "There were no women friends to have when I was a girl. Only Flat Mouth," she said. "And now you."

At the kitchen table they talked of sex until Melvina said she couldn't listen to such talk on a day of marriage blessed by the Lord. And then they lowered their voices and whispered about sex.

They were interested in Hendrik. He was older and a Jew. He had been married.

He made no pretense of interest in them except Pamela, whom he found smart. Like Amanda, he simply tolerated Sara's life.

"Of course Hendrik knows everything since he's been married and on his own for so long," Jane said.

"I wouldn't know," Sara said. She had a quality of confession in her demeanor although she seldom revealed anything specific. There was just a general sense of revelation about her, perhaps in the softness of her voice, the way she looked directly at the person to whom she spoke.

"You've done nothing?" Pamela asked. She lit a cigarette.

"Kissed," Jane said. "Right? Just kissed and a little more."

"And you're probably going to get your period tonight. It always happens. That's what my sister says," Pamela said.

"You could wait. Do it later, not tonight. There's no fixed rule," Susanna said. "It's not been the most wonderful experience in my life. I had a better time at my second birthday party."

And they all laughed.

"I should tell you, although probably this is exactly the wrong time, but my parents had a dinner party last night," Jane was saying. "And Hendrik's newspaper was the subject of conversation."

"My father mentioned it last night too," Pamela said. "You know my father. 'It's not that he's a Jew,' he said. 'But are you sure your friend Sara knows she is marrying a Communist?' "

"Hendrik's actually not a Communist," Sara said.

She was surprised at the strength of her reaction. "He's interested in the truth—not a particular ideology."

"I think it's wonderful to do what he's doing," Pamela said. "But the truth is not actual, of course."

"It's actual that there are pogroms in Germany, that Hitler is killing the Jews and we don't hear about it." Sara got up and poured more tea.

"I think it's interesting to be marrying a Jew who's a foreigner and older," Susanna said. "It would be exciting if he is a Communist— a great deal more exciting than the undergraduates at Yale."

"And it's supposed to be a happy day so we shouldn't talk about communism," Jane said.

"Communism is happy. At least, some people think it's the road to happiness," Pamela said.

"Are you happy?" Susanna asked, touching Sara on the arm.

"Of course," Sara said. "Of course I am."

"I hope you are. I was so unhappy on my wedding day, so deeply miserable, I could not get out of bed."

"But you were pregnant," Sara said.

"I would not have been happy anyway," Susanna said. "I hope you are."

"I really am," Sara said, her voice just below the water level, breaking with tears.

They walked down the long aisle of St. John's Episcopal Church, past the pews painted white with bunches of wildflowers tied with ribbons at the end. Amanda was the last to go in before the wedding party, after Albert and Melvina.

Flat Mouth had not come.

"I can't," he had said to Amanda on the phone. He mentioned difficulties with his wife. But she knew very well that he had heard the longing in her voice and did not want to be involved.

The Drapers were there. That pleased Amanda. They had come back early from Illinois before Congress was in session just to be at Sara's wedding. Surely Mrs. Draper sensed the importance of the event.

Amanda felt alternately old and young—older than thirty-nine, awkward, mannish in her beige silk dress, her hair curled for the occasion, and young as she had as a girl with legs too long and arms set too far out on her shoulders, dangling as if from a yoke. She missed Lincoln. She never thought of him at all although his picture, the one she took of him, the last one, age nineteen and eleven months, hung in her bedroom. But she thought of him now, wanting him, wanting him back.

> He loves me,
> He loves me not,
> He loves me,
> He loves me not.

Bonita plucked the petals off the roses she carried, standing just in front of Sara at the back of the church.

"See, Sara, he loves me. I did it for you." She kissed Sara's hand. "Hendrik loves you."

"I certainly hope he does," Sara said.

And then the wedding march began to play and it was Sara's turn to walk down the aisle toward the altar, alone, just behind Bonita scattering rose petals.

Amanda and Hendrik had turned their heads back to look at her—and there seemed to be from where she was walking just barely enough space between them for her to fit.

NINE

AMANDA LEFT IN a snowstorm in late January 1940. Her plan was to go to Ashland for a month to take a series of pictures, portraits really, of the faces of an American midwestern town. But the plan had been invented on the spot when she got a birthday card from Flat Mouth.

She had not heard from him at all since the wedding although she had written as she always did once or twice a month. The card, which came December 30, two days before her birthday, was oversize with a bouquet of yellow roses printed on the front. Inside he had crossed out the sentimental message. "Dear A Man," he wrote. He had not called her that for years. "Happy Birthday. It is not possible to believe you are forty. Love always or forever as you would say, Flat Mouth."

It was a message of love and so she packed her few possessions, two pairs of trousers, two loose-fitting shirts of Jonathan's, a heavy sweater, her photographs, her mother's letters. Her intention was to return to Washington by the first of March but the date was arbitrary.

Since the announcement in late December of Sara's coming baby, she had begun to feel a stranger in her own house. There were still dinners with Sara and Hendrik and Albert, sometimes Melvina and Bonita, but after the news of the baby, Sara and Hendrik were locked together with a secret. Their bedroom, formerly Jonathan and Amanda's, was closed off to the rest of the house. Melvina and Bonita had each other and Albert was too unpleasant for personal associations. More and more, Amanda had the empty feeling of estrangement among company.

She had not done serious work since the trip across the country in 1934 and although she continued to do portraits and was sought after and handsomely paid for her work as a portrait photographer, her heart had never been in it. There was no chance to tell the truth as the war had given her or the book on Flat Mouth or the Depression. People whose photographs she took were paying her to make them look better than they did in life. The Roosevelts had introduced her work to many of their associates and between 1936 and 1940 she had become a sort of court photographer for political Washington. Her photographs of the children and wives of men in power were on the round tables and grand pianos of many of the houses in the city. But the work was not satisfactory. Besides, she had a creeping sense that Sara was beginning to look at her as a responsibility. She could imagine conversations Sara had with Hendrik behind the bedroom door: "We ought to have coffee with Mama after dinner, Hendrik." Or "We ought to invite her on our walks," she'd say. "Perhaps she could take pictures for the journal." And Hendrik would shake his head and say he did not wish to be involved with Amanda professionally. She was too difficult. Sara would reply, "I worry about her."

"I don't like for you and Hendrik to talk about me," Amanda said to Sara.

"We don't, Mama," Sara insisted.

"You have no reason to worry about me," Amanda said. "I'm fine alone."

"I know you are," Sara said, wary of her mother in these humors. "You always have been."

But after the baby started, Amanda could not bear to be in Sara and Hendrik's company. The furtive glances at the dinner table, the secret kisses in the hall, the looks.

So Flat Mouth's birthday message came at just the right moment.

She traveled by train, with a small valise, her photographic equipment, a raccoon coat Louisa had given her when the styles changed. Sara took her to the station.

"I feel as if you're leaving in protest," Sara said walking with her mother across the marble floor of Union Station.

"Don't be silly. I'm doing an assignment," Amanda said.

"But you've seemed angry at me—since the wedding really. Maybe just since the baby. I feel as if I've failed you when all I've done is to get married to the man you said you wanted me to marry and have a baby."

"Maybe I'm growing ill-tempered with age."

They stood at the gate in silence and waited for the boarding call unable to think of what to say to one another. The moment had the quality of a final parting or the danger of change.

"If you need to do something major with the house, do it," Amanda said.

"I'll take good care of the house," Sara said.

"Make it your own," Amanda said. "Do what you want to do. I'll only need one room."

The train to Chicago was called and Amanda hugged

Sara quickly. "I'll be back in March unless there are developments."

"Good-bye, Mama," Sara said, her eyes full of tears. Please don't be mad at me, she wanted to say, but instead she kissed Amanda's cheek. "Good-bye. Good-bye."

As it turned out, there were developments and Amanda did not come back for eighteen months until the end of 1941 after the Japanese had bombed Pearl Harbor.

That morning after the train for Chicago left, Sara drove home, parked the car, went in the front door of the house, and within an hour of her mother's departure was planning the redecoration of the house where she had grown up.

Dear Mama, Sara wrote in February.

> *I have done some painting in the downstairs. I hope you like it when you return. The house has always seemed a little white to me so I've painted the living room a pale yellow and the dining room a rich peach with yellow pigment in the paint, sort of the color of the roses in the back garden. I made slipcovers in the living room, flowers all over, a lot of color. I hope you won't mind.*
>
> *We have separated* The Honest Truth *from the rest of the house and Melvina has moved to the second floor. I think you'll like it better.*
>
> *Yr. loving daughter,*
Sara

Amanda sent a postcard by return mail.

> *Darling,*
> *I suppose because I take pictures, I like white backgrounds, but I'm sure the house looks lovely and it's fine about the yellow and peach and flowers.*
>
> *When I was small Grandmother Yellow Flower told me a legend which I did not understand. In the legend, the daughters of a particular Indian tribe, not Chippewe, another tribe, swallow their mothers whole,*

*move into the tent with their fathers, and take up house-
keeping. Such a strange story.*

I hope you are feeling well—and the baby is growing.
Love,
A

TEN

SARA'S LETTERS TO Amanda were brief and informative.

Dear Mama,

*We need a new roof so I have arranged that it be
done in the spring. Unfortunately there was a leak in
your room and one of the photographs from the war is
spotted.*

I am enormous. Much bigger than Susanna was.

*Hendrik has taken out papers for citizenship. Not Al-
bert, who says he doesn't like America. I say he should
go home. "I can't," he says, which of course I know. So
I suggest he go to Australia. At dinner he complained so
much about America that Hendrik has asked him to take
his meals alone. Hendrik says that if we join the war, he
will go. I tell him he is too old to be a soldier but he in-
sists he will find a way.*

Sooner or later, I suppose we will go to war.

*Susanna comes frequently to lunch with Sammy and
complains about her marriage but otherwise it is very
nice to have a friend in my condition. I doubt Pamela
will ever marry.*

*I have designed maternity clothes which are very sim-
ple, and I think elegant. I plan to make them in good
wools. Did you wear maternity clothes or Jonathan's
shirts? Did you show when you were Sam Dane?*

*I had a letter from one of my professors in philosophy
at Barnard returning a paper which he had never returned and suggesting that I consider an academic life.*

I can't imagine anything more dull but I was glad, especially at this moment, to think he found me worthy of such a letter.

Yr. loving daughter,
Sara

Darling,
You remember my mother had twin boys, who died before I was born. Perhaps you are enormous because you are carrying twins.

How are you and Hendrik? I hope things are going well but I sense something disquieting in your letters.

I am working on a new process of developing to make my photographs more varied in texture. Particularly the faces of people.

I did not show when I was in France and I can't for the life of me remember what I wore when I was pregnant with you. Or at any other time. Except my grandmother's cape and I remember that for the sheer weight of it.

You should think of a career. Sometimes I worry about you.

Love,
M

Dear Mama,
In haste. No doubt, there are twins. Running this hotel is my career. Sufficient for me. Things are quite lovely—even serene.

Love,
S

Sara's pregnancy moved Hendrik to romance—her growing belly, the softness of her breasts, the color in her cheeks. He fell in love with her over and over again, lying in bed at night, his hand on her stomach, in the parlor reading a mock-up for *The Honest Truth*. At the dining room table late in the evening after Bonita had gone to bed, Melvina to her Bible, Sara could feel his lust. It pleased her, this power she had, pleased her that just the sight of her stirred him from his obligations.

* * *

"I find it lonely to be married," Susanna told Sara over tea in Georgetown. "I don't even think I love John any longer, just the baby. I can't understand it," she said. "My parents seemed perfectly happy together for years."

Sara was pensive. "I am actually not lonely," she said.

"Of course not. Hendrik's always in the house."

"But busy," Sara said. "I could be furniture."

"I am left alone day after day, even at supper, sometimes until ten o'clock," Susanna said. "But I would hate it if he were at home all the time." She leaned across the table. "Are you happy?"

Sara did not wish to confess to happiness—it seemed too ordinary, too agreeable, too frivolous and unthoughtful. But she was happy, peacefully happy, safe as a child with Hendrik closeted from the world in her flower-strewn peach and yellow house as if she were a young girl in a fairy tale in which the frogs are princes from the start.

There were things she knew about her life, even at twenty-one. She knew she was a woman for Hendrik, not Sara Abbott, not herself, but a woman whose look pleased him to watch across the room, whose temperament was accommodating and sweet, on whom he was coming to depend for a certain spirit in the house, distilled in the air. But he didn't know her. He was too occupied to take specific interest, too involved in his work, too energetic. He had, and Sara knew this, a specific interest in Amanda because she fit into a compartment of his life and he considered her opinions. She was forthright and had answers and goals, familiar to Hendrik, familiar to men. And she was by nature unaccommodating.

"Sometimes your mother is like a man with her long legs and her big black camera," Hendrik said. "I do not know how you can turn out so soft."

Sara smiled. "In self-defense," she said.

In late May, Pamela finished college and came home to start Georgetown University Law School. On afternoons after classes, she and Sara met for lunch.

"You see where you're headed, don't you, Sara?" Pamela said. "Straight into domestic warfare."

"What is domestic warfare?" Sara asked.

"In a matter of a few years, you'll be chained to the house with babies and meals to prepare and dishes and laundry and Hendrik will be begging you to be his secretary and bookkeeper and shoe polisher. You had the best grades in our senior class," she said. "You should be the one going to law school."

"I don't want to go to law school," Sara said. "I think I'm suited to a domestic life. I like running houses."

Pamela reached down and patted Sara's belly. "An elephant?"

"No," Sara said. "Twins. I'm certain."

"Well, that's a start. I suppose if you have them two at a time, you could have eight or twelve."

"I'm hoping," Sara said, unwilling to give in to Pamela's dark message, disbelieving the implications.

Sara had in mind the household she had dreamed about on the long train trip across America—a warm house with the sweet smell of baking, vaguely untidy with children and dogs, perhaps a few cats, with Hendrik's staff at lunch at the long table in the dining room, the children and Bonita and Melvina at dinner. She would be the mother of them all—her children and the animals and Hendrik and Albert and the staff of *The Honest Truth* and the visiting students. Even her own mother when Amanda returned from Wisconsin. That pleased her particularly. She would run the house like a benevolent orphanage, or a hotel, providing and providing—a place of safety, the home her mother had not made for her.

She didn't miss Amanda in the months she was pregnant, only later after her sons, called Jonathan for her father and Frederick for Hendrik's father, were born. After the babies, Sara had days when she longed for Amanda's voice, her clearheaded opinions, her familiar oddness.

But she was glad that the house was hers in Amanda's absence. She wandered each room of it, cluttering the surfaces of tables and bureaus, painting the walls, hanging prints, making curtains and dust ruffles, laying claim.

ELEVEN

By early autumn 1941, the house at 3106 P street, a tall three-story clapboard end house painted sunny yellow, was known around Washington, certainly political Washington and among students and the small intellectual community which had developed under the New Deal, as "the Yellow House." In fact, in September the neighbors in the other houses between 31st and 32nd streets had complained so much of the number of people who had come to their door by mistake that Hendrik put a sign on the front door which said THE YELLOW HOUSE and the door was left unlocked.

Sara had rearranged the first floor so that a visitor came into a large sunny hall, to the left of which were the offices of *The Honest Truth* and to the right the home of Sara and Hendrik, Bonita, Melvina, Jonathan and Frederick, and most recently Albert, who had moved into Amanda's former bedroom with the understanding that he would move out immediately if he heard she was returning.

By late 1941, *The Honest Truth* had a circulation of more than thirty thousand. In the summer alone, there had been fourteen essays in the paper, some by Albert, a few by Hendrik, others by contributing writers, covering such subjects as religion subsequent to the blitzing of Coventry Cathedral in England, the infiltration of Europe by the Germans with the invasion of Crete, the arrival in Scotland of Hitler's deputy Rudolf Hess, and the warning to President Roosevelt from Joseph Grew, the American ambassador to Japan, of the possibility of Japanese attack.

The story about the warning, which appeared in the November issue of *The Honest Truth*, created a flurry in the Office of Wartime Censorship and Hendrik was called to reveal his source, which happened to be indirectly the President of the United States. Mrs. Roosevelt, who took an interest, among other things, in entrepreneurial humanistic ventures, often read *The Honest Truth* and brought several articles to the attention of the President. Hendrik had been invited to meet with the President briefly in early September and Sara, Hendrik, and Albert were invited to a small private dinner at the White House the week before Thanksgiving, to which Albert refused to go because he did not believe that journalists should accept the dinner invitations of national leaders. There was an article in the *Washington Post* about Hendrik and Albert, an enthusiastic feature suggesting, however, that at least one of the brothers, probably Albert, was involved with the Communist Party. After the article appeared, which described as well Hendrik's life with Sara as idyllic and included pictures in the garden with Sara and the twins, the Marches became minor celebrities in Washington.

The house was always full of life, people in and out, students especially. And at the center was Sara.

"It's as if you're running a major business," her friend Susanna said one afternoon when she had come for lunch with her son, Rufus. They were in the kitchen, the twins on the counter eating cream cheese sandwiches, and Sara was slicing a baked turkey for lunch, which might this afternoon include anywhere from ten to twenty people, students from Georgetown University, an alcoholic newspaper writer of Austrian descent whom Hendrik was allowing to sleep in the room in the basement, two editors from New York visiting the offices of *The Honest Truth* hoping to have Hendrik and Albert collaborate on a book, Melvina and her sister Rose who had taken a fall and was spending a few weeks, and Bonita drawing on the kitchen table.

"This isn't the sort of life I imagined for you," Susanna said. "Mother of the Western World. You used to be so dreamy."

"I'm still dreamy," Sara said lifting the twins down to the floor. "It's the best place for dreaming, this kind of life."

It was a cold, damp, gray December day in Washington and Sara built a fire, brought the sandwiches into the living room, and sat on the floor with the twins and Rufus.

The Victrola played "Peter and the Wolf," and Sara and Susanna were comfortable in easy conversation about babies and food and the way to keep weight off and whether it was appropriate to dress in low-cut dresses after you were married. Outside the day was darkening with a kind of quickness that sets the nerves on edge.

They did not even hear Hendrik come into the living room until he was beside the couch. He picked up Frederick and held him close.

"The Japanese have bombed Pearl Harbor," he said quietly. "Tomorrow we will go to war."

Susanna picked up Sammy, put on his leggings and coat and hat, put on her own coat. "It's getting dark," she said as if she expected the worst. "I should hurry."

"That darkness is weather," Sara said, "not war."

But there was a sense of war out-of-doors. Sara picked up Jonathan, the smaller of the twins, the more fragile, and walked over to the window to watch Susanna hurry home pushing Rufus in his carriage. Standing there, stilled by the news of war, abstracted, she was suddenly aware of an odd catch to Jonathan's breathing as if there were a metal clip in his chest that snapped. She put her head against his chest and heard it clearly—a little *thump, thump* like the hollow sound of piano hammers and then a click. She would have mentioned it to Hendrik if the telephone had not rung at that moment with Amanda calling from Ashland to say that she was coming home.

TWELVE

At forty, Amanda was striking with thick black hair turned gray around her face, entirely gray but only around her face as if she had met with a sudden surprise. She had the clear-eyed, occasionally severe look of a woman who had a quarrel. And she did have.

Except for the few years with Jonathan, she had lived independent for too long. Although she would have considered the word *lonely* to be self-indulgent, she was often at silent battle with a sense of emptiness. If someone were to ask her to name her friends, she would have named five, two dead—her mother and Jonathan, Sara, Melvina, and Flat Mouth.

At the time she left for Ashland, Wisconsin, in the winter of 1940, she was restless, uncertain of a future and put out of her own house. Not specifically of course. She wasn't given to sentimentality. But emotionally, she had been left behind.

She went to Ashland because people knew her, she told herself, although that wasn't actually true. Very few people remembered Dr. Steward and if they did it was as a man who had slipped from prominence and died in shame. Or his difficult daughter who refused to go to school. Only on the Bad River Reservation was Amanda remembered.

She moved into the second story of a clapboard house on Arch Street, a spare white living room and bedroom, entirely to her liking. She put up her photographs of Sara and Melvina, a picture of her with Jonathan, a picture of Sara and Bonita, the high school picture of Lincoln Draper which she had cut out of her yearbook, and the first picture she had taken of Flat Mouth when she left Bad River to move to Washington, D.C.

In February, she did not see Flat Mouth at all except the first day of her arrival after she had found a place to live. They met for a beer at Clive's on Arch Street and it was awkward. He looked the same as he had looked when she had seen him in 1933, his eyes darkening with age, sinking deeper into his head, the skin on his face toughening.

"You look the same except for your gray hair," he said. "But the fire is out."

They had two beers. Flat Mouth was in a hurry to get home and conversation was difficult. But just before he left, she sensed him looking at her, actually looking at her directly as he had not done perhaps since they were children. Her hand was resting on the counter of the bar and he laid his hand on top of hers.

"Call me if you need me," he said solicitously.

She bristled. "For what would I need you?" she replied.

He smiled, just barely, at the corner of his mouth. "Good girl," he said.

He was right of course, she thought, lying on the double bed next to the window overlooking Arch Street, walking the streets of Ashland, the markets, the diners and bars, the playground of the elementary school, the athletic fields of the high school, taking photographs of faces darkened by the brief light of winter. The fire had gone out of her. Some mornings she was too tired to get out of bed. Life seemed endlessly long. She would lie on top of the covers, not sleeping, looking at the decorated tin ceiling of her apartment, battling nostalgia.

By late February, she had lost interest in photographs of people, bored by the faces which began to seem repetitive. Perhaps, she thought, she should go home to her house turned by Sara into a pastel flower garden. She had made no friends in Ashland, made no effort at friendships. She began to wonder if, roused by the familiar smells of her childhood, her father's mental illness was surfacing in her.

But she didn't go home. March came. The days were longer and although it was very cold, there was the feeling of spring off the lake. One sunny blustery afternoon in early March, she wandered into the cemetery where she thought her mother might be buried, although she could not remember being there before. It was a large cemetery with mausoleums and tiny gravestones, decorated statuary, competitive in death as small midwestern cemeteries can be. At first it was her intention to find the grave of her mother, but as she wandered the small wooded paths between the Ashland family grave sites, over the hills back toward the lake, across from which was the house where her parents had first lived, she fell into the life of the cemetery, caught up by the narrative of the tombstones themselves, the record of lives locked permanently on the Wisconsin hills. MARY, BELOVED WIFE OF EZRA PEDERSEN. BORN JUNE 12, 1798. NEW YORK. DIED MAY 5, 1853. ASHLAND, WISCONSIN. Ezra died May 6, 1853. Because of

Mary, he died, Amanda thought. The sun fell just behind the tombstone, casting a shadow, but the writing on the marble was clear. Amanda took out her camera.

JAMES PEDERSEN. BORN 1873. DIED 1873.

SARA CONROY PEDERSEN HOPKINS, BORN MARCH 1, 1874. DIED MAY 23, 1935.

THOMAS A. PEDERSEN. BORN JUNE 11, 1875. DIED JUNE 11, 1917.

WILLIAM O. PEDERSEN. BORN AUGUST 17, 1879. DIED JULY 4, 1932.

JOHN STANLEY HOPKINS. BORN JULY 30, 1870. DIED JULY 30, 1930.

Someone had placed a dried wreath on the grave of Sara and there was a pot of frozen geraniums.

Amanda went to the cemetery again the following day and the next, taking rolls of film in different light. She didn't find her mother's grave until late March and then by accident. It was an unseasonably warm day when she was wandering along the shoreline of the lake and came upon a single grave between the family plot of Linton and Hall. There was a simple marker, thin marble, slightly tilted toward the sea.

ANNA JERMYN STEWARD, BORN MARCH 31, 1874, RHYL, NORTH WALES. DIED APRIL 11, 1903, ASHLAND, WISCONSIN.

She wondered had there been a funeral and had she gone to it. She did not recall her father ever mentioning a grave. She didn't remember ever seeing this marker before. She was struck by its simplicity, and struck as well by the sweetness of her father to include her mother's birth in Wales. Somehow it dignified her life to record that she had crossed the ocean to America, that she had died in a place where she was a stranger.

For days, Amanda wept. In bed at night, she read her mother's letters and sobbed deep, wrenching, internal sobs. Occasionally her landlady would knock or call out, "Are you all right?"

"Fine," Amanda would reply. "I'm fine."

And gradually as the collected record of death accumulated in black-and-white photographs on her desk, she began to be fine again.

At the end of March, just before Easter, Flat Mouth called her on her landlady's phone.

"I'm coming over," he said.

They walked down through the town and beyond to the lake where her parents had lived and where now an actual community had grown up, through the cemetery and into the town again, talking easily as if they had never stopped talking, the whole of a gray cool Saturday, their shoulders brushing, their fingers occasionally touching.

"I didn't call because I didn't know what to make of you, A Man," Flat Mouth said.

He followed her upstairs to her room on the second floor, took off his coat and hat and gloves.

"You fly in and out of my life like a storm, blowing off the tree branches," he said.

Her back was to him, hanging up her coat, when he came up behind her, put his arm around her waist, pulled her to him and kissed her on her lips, her neck, the heavy sweater concealing her breasts. And he pulled her with him to the bed.

That was March of 1940. In the months between that afternoon and the bombing of Pearl Harbor on December 7, 1941, Amanda and Flat Mouth made a life together. He came on Saturdays when Star was with her mother for the night; every morning before work, they met for coffee and other days depending on circumstances in his life. Amanda took photographs of people once again and by the autumn of 1941 she had a collection different in style from the photographs she had done before, a narrative called "A Story of a Middle Western Town," stark, evocative, and strange photographs of faces, close up, of lives lived parallel, of graves.

She had used a particular method of developing which gave the photographs the still quality of Dutch painters in domestic scenes, people trapped in time and place, highly detailed, almost luminous.

"You are the way I knew you when we were children," Flat Mouth said to her. "It is good you came to Ashland."

It had been good. She knew she wouldn't stay, that she couldn't live a life peripheral to Flat Mouth's real life or even live a life with Flat Mouth at Bad River if he were free to make it.

So when the news came that Japan had bombed Pearl Harbor, when America's entry into the war was inevitable, she was ready to go.

"I'm going home," she said to Flat Mouth that afternoon. "I'll be back."

"And love me forever."

"Of course." She laughed.

For once he was the one deeply sad, as she had always been with him, and she was pleased to have caused it.

She packed her book, her few things, spent one last sweet night with Flat Mouth, and got on the train from Ashland to Chicago and home.

This time she would go to war, could go to war, as a woman.

THIRTEEN

THE WINTER OF 1942 was long and icy. There were intermittent heavy snows which melted in deep puddles on the lawns, on the brick sidewalks, along the curbs. Before the fickle sun had a chance to dry the surface of the earth, a ferocious cold would blow in from the Middle West and freeze the ground. The weather suited the temper of the times. People walked out of their front doors and slid down the steps. On the streets, they walked with their arms extended to keep their balance. Everyone knew someone with a broken leg or arm or a concussion or else had one himself. It would snow and melt and freeze. By day the citizens covered the sidewalks with salt and sand and by night the snow would be back as if the gods of weather were preparing the people of Washington, D.C., once again a city of soldiers, for an unpredictable future.

At the Yellow House, decorated in the winter of 1942 with a banner which hung from the second-story window, sewn rather poorly by an earnest young writer in yellow on a white background—YELLOW HOUSE: WELCOME—there was new excitement every day, almost every hour.

Hendrik was going to the war as a correspondent. He was too old for war at thirty-five, but he had persuaded the *Chicago Tribune* to send him nevertheless.

In late February, with a broken left arm and a broken right wrist, from a fall facedown on the front steps, he was preparing to leave.

The United States and Britain had declared war on Japan on December 8, 1941, the day after Pearl Harbor. Germany and Italy declared war on the United States and it was becoming clear all over the world that the Nazis had begun the gas chamber murder of millions of Jews. Hendrik wrote a piece about the transfer of ten thousand Japanese-Americans from the West Coast to inland camps, about the Japanese invasion of the Dutch East Indies. But his heart was in Europe, not the Pacific, and he could not wait to leave.

At night, Sara lay in the dark beside him, unable to sleep—too agitated by his conversation about the camps, the bombing of Lübeck and Cologne. About how Sara would run *The Honest Truth* and keep Albert in check. He would miss her day and night, he said. It was difficult for Sara to believe that a man so excited for war would give much thought to his wife at home as he flew east over the Atlantic. Night after night, he talked about the day's events, the prospect for tomorrow, the war, and then he'd fall instantly asleep leaving Sara stiff with longing beside him.

He was sweet to her, solicitous about the boys, but his concern seemed perfunctory, as if his sons were cousins once removed and Sara a romantic heroine whom he had seen in a motion picture.

"It's not the fact of your going to war although of

course I will miss you and be worried," Sara said. "It's that you've fallen in love with it."

Amanda was no better than Hendrik. She had come home for Christmas in 1941, looking vibrant, younger by years than Sara felt. She took over her old room and set about immediately to be assigned as a photographer in Europe. She spent time with Sara and the twins and Bonita but she was not engaged by their lives. Rather, like Hendrik, she dipped in and out of daily conversations as if her family were a part of a large sprawling English novel whose predictable characters can be counted on to remain the same.

So at twenty-three, with a large house and two young sons and meals and laundry and arrangements and doctors' appointments and details, Sara was alone. She had been at war's center for a long time, with Hendrik and her mother fighting to possess her. Although that had been unsatisfactory, although she had felt as if she could die of suffocation, she had gained stature in her own eyes by their attentions. Now she felt tethered not by their affections, which seemed superficial—after all, they showed no interest in Sara specifically, asked no questions about her daily life and thoughts—but by their present need for her.

In the months after Pearl Harbor, while Hendrik prepared for war, Sara began to feel that her existence, the actual physical presence of flesh and blood, was locked in place. She was needed for their sustenance. Robbed of the role of provider after they left for war, she would not exist at all. If she reached up to touch her own face, her hand would sail through thin air as if there was no head attached to her shoulders.

"I feel insubstantial," she said to Susanna at tea one afternoon shortly after Susanna's husband had left for France as a captain in the army. "It's as if I'm invisible. I am what I cook for dinner or sew or do for the twins. That is the only proof of me."

"You've gained weight." Susanna shrugged. "Like me."

"So my mother says. 'You're gaining weight, Sara. It's a sign.' 'Of what?' I asked her. 'Of losing interest in yourself,' she said. 'It's a sign of eating too much,' I said to her, which is true, and she drives me crazy since she got back from Wisconsin."

"Do you think you are losing interest in yourself?" Susanna asked.

"I don't know. I don't have time to think," Sara said. "Perhaps."

"I have. I actually think I have. I don't even bother to look in the mirror when I brush my teeth."

Sara ran her fingers through her long hair. She had not washed it for days, not since Jonathan had stomach flu on Tuesday; afterward she'd been too busy, and then she'd forgotten.

"They have lost interest in me," Sara said. "Hendrik and even my mother."

"Don't be crazy," Susanna said, ordering more cakes for tea—carrot cake and a slice of chocolate cream pie. "I have never known a woman to be loved like you are. We used to say at school that your mother was going to sew you to her trousers. And Hendrik worships you."

"As an abstraction," Sara said. "Not as a person."

"What about Amanda?" Susanna asked.

"My mother wishes I were more like her. In fact, like her exactly," Sara said.

"You mean she wishes she had had a son."

"No. She's perfectly glad I'm a daughter, in fact happier. She just wishes I were a daughter more like a man, like she is, than a woman."

"I suppose you're right," Susanna said, dipping her finger in the cake icing. "We all loved your mother because she wasn't like our mothers."

"My mother is of the opinion that you need to be a man to survive," Sara said, actually realizing as she spoke something new about Amanda. "She didn't have an example of survival in her own mother, who died when she was three."

Amanda had told Sara only the romantic stories of her childhood, about leaving school at thirteen, and racing on ponies through the woods with Flat Mouth, about life at the hospital as the only child on the grounds, about Bad

River and Grandmother Yellow Flower and the credible god of her growing up called Hole-in-the-Day. Sara sensed a dark and unpleasant secret about Amanda's father. She even sensed that he may have committed suicide although Amanda never directly spoke of the way he died, only a suggestion that it was sudden and violent. But somehow Sara understood that Anna Steward was the force in her mother's childhood, although she had been dead for most of it, that the imprint on the heart like the fossilized remains of bones was a permanent record.

Hendrik left on a Thursday by train to New York and then to France. Sara had been ill for days.

"With sadness," Susanna had told her. "Even I was ill when John left and I'm not particularly fond of him."

"You think it's a tragedy," Albert said to Sara. "But wait. By Saturday, you'll be glad he's gone. He takes up too much room."

The night before Hendrik left, Sara lay in bed in a new gown, her hair washed, her cheeks rouged, waiting for him. It had been weeks since they made love. He had been too excited to settle, blaming the broken wrist and arm at first and then forgetting entirely until the last night when he came to bed after two in the morning, subdued, abstracted, slipped into the bed next to her, under the sheets. He lay there quietly for a long time, his breathing uneven, his eyes open when she glanced at him, and then he took her hand and put it over his erection. They made love quickly, uneasily, as if he was certain it would last, and Sara lay awake all night until dawn began to light the sky and then she slept fitfully until morning.

At Union Station, Hendrik could not concentrate his attention. He carried both boys, Jonathan fretful, almost agitated, with an odd blueness around his lips.

"Could he be cold?" Sara asked.

"Thin-skinned," Hendrik said.

"I suppose you're right," Sara said.

When the train was announced and Hendrik told her

good-bye, he was briefly hers again. He took her hand and kissed the palm and lay it on his cheek.

"To hold forever," he said to her. "Your life on my face."

FOURTEEN

ON THE DAY that Hendrik left for the war, Amanda woke up with a bad cold and did not go to the station with them as she had planned to do. She and Hendrik had spent a great deal of time together in the months since she had returned, long lunches at the kitchen table talking about the war, hours after dinner discussing the annihilation of the Jews, walks in which Hendrik confessed to her that since the war began he had become deeply homesick. He could not properly attach to his children and to his life at home. He was restless and had lost patience with Sara.

Amanda found herself stirred by his confessions, by the old attraction she had had for him. After months in the small room of the Victorian house in Ashland, lying with Flat Mouth, she had become accustomed to romance.

The head cold was no surprise. Two nights before Hendrik was due to leave, he had come very late, after midnight, to Amanda's room, opened the door without knocking.

"We must talk," he whispered across the dark spaces.

"Here?" Amanda asked.

"No, no," he said. "Outside. We can't talk in the house."

They walked across Georgetown in a steady rain, bitter cold, with a wind that blew through them, down M Street to Pennsylvania Avenue, past the White House dark on the early March morning, his arm through hers, his hand gripping her arm, his hot breath on her cheek. On the walk, he told her about his mother, that she had been beautiful when she was young, but too gentle as a mother for boys—Albert had inherited the dark countenance, the tendency to bitterness of his father—that his mother was like Sara in her innocence, that he had been sometimes cruel to her as a child, annoyed at her gentleness as if it were a sign of vulnerability, annoyed that she was easily hurt and that he was responsible. What he had needed when he was small and now, perhaps even more than then, was a certain toughness in a woman, someone as strong as he was.

Amanda could feel his desire in the air. She pulled away, turned up the collar of her coat.

She had come close, she thought later, under the covers, her hair still wet from the rain, the muscles in her back quivering with cold. She had asked for trouble, courted it, irritated at Sara for taking over the house, for her ease with people, jealous of their affections for her for which Amanda had no gift. Amanda had the respect of others, perhaps admiration, even awe, but no affection. She was angry at Sara for gaining weight. Something in the comely plumpness of her daughter disturbed her. She had thought she was disappointed that Sara had let herself go but as she tried to fall asleep after the long wet walk with Hendrik, a picture from the hospital where she had grown up in Ashland surfaced in her vision. She was small, lying on the white sheets of her mother's bed, her head on her mother's soft broad belly. It was a hot, still morning, barely any air. Her mother lay against pillows stacked against the wall and when Amanda in her mind's eye looked up to see if her mother was sleeping, the face against the pillow was Sara's face, her long honey-colored hair against the pillow, her eyes closed, the lashes pencil lines against her white cheeks.

Amanda was in bed looking at pictures, with a pot of tea and a heavy sweater over her pajamas, when Sara returned from Union Station seeing Hendrik off. She did not hear the car door close or the front door open but she certainly heard the desperate cry of Sara's voice from the first floor.

"Mama," Sara called. "Something is the matter with Jonathan."

FIFTEEN

ON THE DRIVE home from Union Station in a light sleet, the boys squabbled. When Sara sat up very straight and looked in the rear-vision mirror, she could just barely see the tops of their heads in the backseat. They were not actually fighting. Jonathan was whimpering in a tiny voice and Frederick was saying, "No. No. No. Mine." At the stoplight before Dupont Circle, she turned around to see Frederick with his arms wrapped around a red metal fire engine, his face wrinkled in frustration, and Jonathan leaning away from him, his head on the armrest under the back window.

"What happened?" Sara asked in the even voice she managed to maintain in difficulty. "Jonathan?"

"Frederick hit me."

"Mine," Frederick said holding tight to the fire engine.

"Did you hit Jon with the fire engine?"

"No," Frederick said.

"Yes," Jonathan said.

"Then give the fire engine to me."

"Mine," Frederick said.

Sara pulled on the emergency brake and reached in the backseat.

"Please give me the fire engine," she said to Frederick.

She put the fire engine on the seat beside her and drove around Dupont Circle to P Street, listening for more trouble but there did not seem to be any. She parked the car two doors down from the Yellow House, turned off the engine, pulled on the brake, got out, and leaned over the front seat to lift the boys out.

"Jonny's sleeping," Frederick said, his hands folded in a tight fist in his lap.

She was not initially alarmed. She lifted Frederick over the seat and set him on the sidewalk.

"Wait for me to get Jonathan," she said pulling his wool cap over his ears.

"Jonny's sleeping," Frederick said again and there was a strange void in his voice as if he suspected with his child's sense of reality that this was not an ordinary sleep.

At Georgetown Hospital emergency room, Amanda sat next to Sara on a sunken leather couch and waited for news. It was noon when they got to the hospital and by three there was still no news. A young man who introduced himself as Dr. Granger, although he appeared too young to have finished high school, had come to the waiting room about 12:45 with a pad and pencil, his face becalmed, without clues.

"How old is the child and what illnesses has he had and have you noticed anything unusual except that he is smaller and more frail than his twin brother?"

Sara told him about the metal click she had heard in his chest on the day of the bombing of Pearl Harbor, and she had also noticed a certain startled or pained expression on his face when he was walking, especially upstairs. He often whimpered.

"What about today?" the doctor asked.

She told him about Hendrik's leaving, about the bickering in the car, about the fire engine and her concern that Frederick could have hit Jonathan in the head with it.

Dr. Granger thanked her for her help and left. He made no remarks about the fire engine.

"I hate that they fight," Sara said to Amanda.

"Children just do," Amanda replied, hearing the forced sincerity in her voice.

"Frederick is actually mean to him. And how can you be mean when you're only eighteen months old?" Sara leaned her head against the wall. "It's because Jonathan is small. Already as a baby, Frederick hates that his brother is so little," Sara said, picking at the thread of the hem of her skirt which was unraveling. "I know you think I'm too fat."

Amanda didn't reply. She didn't know what to say.

"And I should have known about the click. I heard it. I

knew then that something was the matter. A heart doesn't click like that," Sara said. "And he's always been so blue-skinned. I told Hendrik and he said it was nothing. That it was perfectly normal for one twin to be bigger than another, that his skin was simply fairer than Frederick's, more like mine. I wanted to believe him and he was in such a hurry to go to war." She got up, ran her fingers through her long hair, rearranged her skirt. "I despise this stupid war."

It was 3:15 by the clock over the admissions desk where a very small dark-skinned woman sat making an effort not to look at Amanda and Sara although they were directly in her line of vision.

"I will lose weight," Sara said quietly. "I'll start tomorrow." She went over to the desk and asked the woman if she could call to find out if the doctors would come out to let her know what they had determined was the matter with her son Jonathan March.

"They'll come out and tell you when they know something," the woman said.

"I want to talk to them now," Sara said.

The woman shook her head.

"Policy," she replied.

Sara turned away from the desk. "Mama?"

To Amanda she looked as she had as a child, the age of the twins, plump and rosy-cheeked, with a certain softness in her manner, an instinctive gentility. Amanda could not bear to see the accumulated sadness. It was too soon in life for the blood to drain out. She got up, walked over to the nurses' desk.

"Get Dr. Granger please," she said to the woman.

"I told her," the woman said.

"I heard what you told her," Amanda said.

The woman picked up the phone.

"This is against policy," she said grudgingly.

Amanda took Sara's hand and led her to the bathroom, sat her on the closed toilet seat, and washed her face with a wet cloth, brushed her hair off her face, kissed her on the temple, on the nose, on the chilly tips of her fingers.

"I will stay with you," she said.

"And not go to Europe."

"Of course I won't go to Europe," Amanda said.

Sara rubbed her face against her mother's woolen jacket.

"It used to be you wouldn't leave me at all," she said. "I couldn't even go to the bathroom without your fearing I'd fall and hit my head on the porcelain bowl. Remember?"

"I remember," Amanda said.

SIXTEEN

SARA SETTLED EASILY into the life of nursemother, vitalized by the daily responsibility for a child whose life depended on her attention to detail, by his mysterious fragility.

The doctors at Georgetown Hospital had not been certain of their diagnosis. It appeared that Jonathan had a weak valve leaking oxygen and an irregular heartbeat. The irregular heartbeat had caused him to lose consciousness in the backseat of the car. The doctors were concerned not only about his heart, which was a condition they did not know how to correct, but as well about the possibility of brain damage from the loss of oxygen to his brain.

Amanda stayed through the spring until Jonathan had gained weight and could walk to the corner of P and 30th without losing his breath. She had an arrangement with Sara. Sara cared for Jonathan and Amanda took care of Frederick, took him on walks in Dumbarton Gardens, to the park, helped Melvina with the daily chores, occasionally cooking dinner if Melvina's knees and ankles were bothering her. She didn't think about the war except for the morning report from Albert delivered like a speech from the kitchen door just after eight while they sat at the breakfast table over coffee, feeding the children. She didn't think about photographs or even Flat Mouth, whose correspondence was more frequent and sweeter than it had ever been.

In the morning, Sara got up before dawn, dressed, checked Jonathan's color which had a permanent cast as if his cheeks had been painted pale, pale blue and glazed, put her hand up to his lips to feel the heat of his breath, watched the rise and fall of his chest as she had every hour through the night, rising to an alarm clock under her pillow. In the kitchen, she made him breakfast, a demitasse cup of Cream of Wheat with brown sugar, an egg milk shake in a tiny glass, a piece of toast cut with an inverted juice glass in the shape of a circle, half an orange. She woke him always before Frederick, had to wake him since he never seemed to wake on his own. They had breakfast together and took a walk just as the day was beginning, without Frederick because Jonathan hadn't the strength to run and Sara wanted to conceal his weakness especially from Frederick. Hour after hour she read to him sitting in the large wing chair in the living room.

She was satisfied by small victories—the days when Jonny walked a block without losing his breath, the meals he finished, each fraction of a pound. In the afternoons while the twins were napping, she called cardiologists all over America. What new was being done and who was good and was there any particular research in pediatric cardiology on heart valves and arrhythmia. She read medical books before dinner, publications for physicians, scientific journals. She developed a friendship with Dr. Nathan Brady, a pediatric cardiologist at the Cleveland Clinic. He called her sometimes once a week with information and in late May she and Jonathan went by train to Cleveland where Jon was examined by Dr. Brady and his team of pediatricians.

"At the moment there is nothing we can do," Dr. Brady said. "But hold on, take good care of him as you have been doing, and perhaps by the end of the year a surgery will have been perfected to replace a child's valve." He walked with her to the hospital entrance and in kindness—she knew it was simply in kindness—he kissed her goodbye. Just on the cheek but she held the kiss on the long train ride overnight to Washington. He had said that she had been taking good care of Jonathan. He as much as told her she was a good mother and she was exhilarated by his approval.

In the evenings, Amanda and Sara would talk into the night, Sara lying on the long couch in the living room, her former elegant costumes replaced by large wide-legged blue jeans, spotted with milk and cereal, Jonathan's old striped shirts, her hair tied back with a rubber band. Their conversation was incidental but deeply personal, as if each were talking to the other half of her own self. All that spring, they completed one another in the way that women of different temperaments will do with their capacious accommodation.

In the first months of America's entry in the war, the Yellow House became its own kind of front for domestic warfare. There was *The Honest Truth* itself under Albert, which was less risk-taking than it had been when Hendrik set the tone, but the news was increasingly censored so information was difficult to come by. As Sara's confidence in Jonathan's health increased, she and Amanda took in soldiers on their way through Washington. They turned the top floor into a dormitory and Amanda moved downstairs to the room next to Melvina's, a frivolous room done by Sara in tiny rosebuds and matching curtains and spread and flowery dressing table, ill suited as a backdrop for Amanda's black-and-white photographs, especially of the war. There was always a turkey baking and the milkman came every day, filling two boxes on the front porch, the bread man saved the leftover bread at half price and Mean's Market delivered staples. Their lives took on the rhythms of regular chaos. There were always soldiers for dinner, sometimes drunk, frightened, and cocky in their last weeks or days or hours before shipping out. There was the daily monitoring of Jonathan and Melvina's high blood pressure, which caused her ankles to swell so large that she could not walk on them and sat instead in the rocker in the kitchen, her feet on the radiator. There were the students about to be soldiers hanging in the kitchen for conversation and sympathy and not least Albert who, in Hendrik's absence, had become more convivial, even garrulous. It was clear to everyone, even the visiting soldiers, that he had fallen in love with Sara.

"It's driving me crazy," Sara said to Amanda. "Every time I turn around, there he is as if he hasn't a thing to do all day."

"It's sweet," Amanda said.

They were in the kitchen with Melvina slicing apples for pies.

"There are too many men in this house any way you look at it," Melvina said. "Always eating and crybabying about this or that and he's the worst of the ones I've seen."

"He has an unfortunate manner," Sara said.

"And to my way of thinking, he doesn't look so good either," Melvina said.

"If he cut his mustache," Amanda said.

"He'd have to cut a lot more than his mustache," Melvina said.

But the fact was that Albert March had turned from a sharp-edged, sometimes unpleasant man with an acerbic wit and the strong odor of European tobacco to a warm, tentative middle-aged man full of longing.

"Waterlogged is what he is," Melvina said. "I liked him better mean."

"The paper is going to fold if he continues like this," Sara said.

"If he continues like this, I'm moving in with my sister," Melvina said. "I can get soap opera on the radio."

He asked Sara's advice about *The Honest Truth*. Should they do a piece on Jimmy Doolittle's bombing of Tokyo or the Czechs' assassination of Gestapo leader Heydrich? Should Professor Gerald Morgan of Georgetown University be asked to do the piece on the air raids of London or was he too much of an academic? Would she like to hear Bartók's Violin Concerto with him? Could he help her with Jonathan, read to him perhaps? Perhaps he'd like to be read to in German? Would she care to take a walk after supper? The answer was no. Always no. She was tired or busy or helping Amanda or cooking with Melvina or taking care of the babies or helping Bonita with her math or writing a letter to Hendrik, letters of domestic detail and general expressions of affection, almost impersonal.

Albert was not to be put off. Every day there were the same requests, the same interest expressed in her opinions about the paper as if she were a professional, and gradually she actually became involved in the daily workings of *The Honest Truth*, meeting with the staff writers after breakfast.

"Just to hear what's going on in the world today," Albert said. "In case."

"In case what?" Sara asked.

"In case I drop dead and you have to be the editor. What else?" This possibility seemed to please him enormously.

"Maybe he will get the scurvy," Melvina said. "That thought brightens my day."

"It's not really a bad idea for you to know everything about the paper," Amanda said.

Sara was actually glad to be involved. She felt like a general with a large command directly under her—*The Honest Truth* and Albert, the children, the kitchen, the house, even Melvina and her mother. It was as if the war in Europe and Japan were being fought as a model front on P Street.

By late spring, everything was beginning to seem possible. Even Jonathan's survival. By her careful attention to the details of his life, she had saved him.

What was more—and this she had told no one—not even Amanda, she was pregnant again.

SEVENTEEN

NICHOLAS MARCH was born on Christmas Day 1942 at Columbia Hospital for Women. Pamela was with Sara when her labor began, lived with her in fact since Amanda had

left for Europe in June, and it was Pamela who took Sara
to the hospital, stayed in the room with her until the doctor
arrived, and then waited in the waiting room. The hospital
waiting room was full of friends or parents or siblings of
the women in labor, wives of soldiers. Only one actual father waited. He was apologetic not to be a soldier and felt
he owed the people in the waiting room the explanation
that he had a weak heart and could not fight.

It was Sara's choice to name the baby Nicholas since in
letters back and forth Hendrik had mentioned only the
name Margaret and said he hoped it would be a girl. She
had sensed from the beginning it was a boy and certainly
when she got so big that she had to make the living room
couch her bed for the last month, she was sure the baby
was an enormous boy. Which he was—ten pounds with
chicken feathers on his head and dots of red on his cheeks
and blue-black eyes. By afternoon, the tenants of the Yellow House had moved to the hospital for Christmas, except the twins who stayed at home with Melvina—so
Susanna was there and Pamela and Bonita, even Albert
came for a short time.

In the months since Amanda had left, the Yellow House
had turned into a small hotel. Pamela moved into the sun
porch on the second floor. She had been fighting with her
parents, she said, and could not afford her own place until
she graduated from law school so it was agreed that for
the duration of the war or law school, whichever came
first, she would live with the company on P Street. The
third floor was always full of soldiers, at least three
camped out on their way between home and the front. In
October, word came from the Pentagon that Susanna's
husband had been killed by a land mine explosion in an attack on the German border. To the surprise of everyone,
especially Susanna, who had imagined that her marriage to
John was over long before his death, she was devastated.
First she moved in with her mother-in-law but her son,
Rufus, broke a vase of Waterford crystal and threw up on
the champagne velvet settee in the parlor so she moved in
with her own mother and father. By the first of December,
she was not speaking to her mother. Rufus had been bitten

by her mother's Persian cat. Her father had suggested a psychiatrist or at the very least a regular physician to determine why she was so nervous all the time. She was frightened to live by herself, unable to bring herself to cook, sleepless at night, too tired in the day to look after Rufus.

"Move in," Sara said one day in the first week of December and by late that afternoon Susanna and Rufus were settled in the rosebud room. "Stay as long as you like," Sara said.

Once Susanna and Pamela had moved in, Jane came by often for dinner and sometimes on the weekends.

After Sara and Nicholas came home from the hospital, they all settled easily into a life together. Even Melvina was in high spirits. Evenings, the children ate in the kitchen, sometimes with Bonita. Jonathan, although not well, was better. He had more endurance and could play for a short time with Rufus and Frederick without losing his breath but he still preferred to sit on the bed next to his mother and look at books.

After the baby, Sara worked on *The Honest Truth* from her bedroom for a while. She and Albert would discuss the plans for the day every morning at breakfast. They'd go over the proposals which had been submitted for stories, go over any stories which had been turned in, and then it was Sara's job, because of Albert's abrasive personality, to call the writers with editorial suggestions. She'd spend the day with the children, Melvina taking Nicholas and sometimes Jonathan if he was unwell, while she and Susanna took Rufus and Frederick to the park.

They put the kitchen table at one end of the dining room table for dinner since there were so many of them every night—Melvina and Bonita, Susanna and Pamela, sometimes Jane, Albert depending on his stomach problems which had developed as soon as he discovered Sara was pregnant with another baby. There were always soldiers. After dinner, after Albert had left, the children in bed and Melvina as well, Bonita to her homework, they would dance with the soldiers to music on the Victrola or sit around the living room with bourbon and Coke, smoking cigarettes and talking. They didn't talk about the war at all.

"I love the way we live," Susanna said one evening. "All of us girls together and children. And soldiers for as long as we want them. I don't ever want to marry again."

"It is peculiar how pleasant it is," Sara agreed. "Almost as if marriage is a romantic illusion even while you're living it some of the time."

"I will certainly never get married," Pamela said. "I'd rather the man I'm with be married to someone else."

"It feels right to be married to me—to have a husband and to think of myself as a wife," Sara said. "But I do love the way we're living now and I don't have the same easy love for being married." She picked up Nicholas sleeping on the couch and carried him upstairs. "Of course this is crazy conversation," she said apologetically. "Hendrik is my life."

But the fact was, Hendrik had slipped so quickly out of her life that she was worried, as she had been once on the afternoon her father died. Perhaps she had only an imagined capacity for deep feelings except those she had for her children and usually Amanda.

For all of 1943, the Yellow House continued as a dormitory. The women were entirely satisfied to spend an evening dancing in the living room with young men who would be gone by morning. Two or three times, there was more than dancing. Susanna spent the night with a young man from Kansas and another time with an older officer, but the next day there was no confessional conversation about what went on and the soldiers were seldom in Washington for more than a week.

One young man, actually a boy no more than nineteen from a small town in Minnesota, came into Sara's bedroom one night, crawled into the bed with her, and took her by the shoulders.

"I've never done it," he whispered to her. "And now I could die without ever . . .." He hesitated. It was the spring after Nicholas's birth, a light spring night, the windows open, the breeze across the sheets, and Sara held him, considering whether she should. But as it turned out, the young man was entirely happy to press his face between her breasts and fall asleep.

"You watch yourself," Melvina said to Sara the next morning.

"Oh I do, Melvina," Sara said. "I watch myself almost as carefully as you watch me."

She kissed a few of the soldiers and there was one she liked a great deal, a particularly handsome and urbane young man from Atlanta, but nothing happened. He went to bed after the dancing and left before breakfast.

As the year went on, the war seemed more remote. Sara worried, especially about her mother, and she kept up with the news but she was not engaged by the war unless the news came from the south of France where Hendrik was.

Churchill and Roosevelt met at the Casablanca Conference in January. The Japanese were driven from Guadalcanal. The Russians destroyed the German army southwest of Stalingrad. The Allied armies in North Africa were placed under the command of General Dwight D. Eisenhower. The United States captured the Aleutians. Mussolini was dismissed. Romanian Ploesti oil fields were bombed by the United States. General and Mme. Chiang Kai-Shek met with Roosevelt and Churchill in Cairo and agreed to liberate Korea after the Japanese defeat. The Allied round-the-clock bombing of Germany began.

These stories of 1943 were certainly known by the women at the Yellow House but their real conversations had to do with Albert's vicarious love affair with Sara or Pamela's new boyfriend who was a law professor at Georgetown with three grown children and a wife. Or Rufus's difficult personality, his tendency to violence. Or the occasional handsome soldier passing through the Yellow House attracted to one or another of them. Or Jonathan's precarious health.

By May, everyone had noticed that Jonathan was not growing. Even his hands and feet were blue and at night, when he was sleeping, Sara could hear the click in his heart without putting her ear to his chest.

"What do you think about Jonathan?" Sara asked

Melvina one morning in the kitchen where she was feeding Nicholas.

"Same as you think," Melvina said. "I think he isn't good."

"Children are cruel to him because he's sick," Sara said. "It kills me."

It was not simply children but mothers on the playground, in the park—women on the street looked at Jonathan and shook their heads sadly as if Sara were responsible for this shadow of a child. Sara was ashamed at her failure to make him well.

"You can count on human beings to be mean if they've got a chance," Melvina said, "especially to the weak."

The doctors at Georgetown Hospital were pessimistic. Jonathan's heart was enlarged, they said, and overworked. An old, tired heart in the body of a little boy and they could not make promises.

She didn't write to Hendrik about him. He didn't want to hear that he had a weak son with an oversize heart, and besides there was nothing he could do. But she did write to her mother. Although there were weeks between the question asked in a letter and the answer by return mail, Amanda always responded.

Dear Sara, she wrote in early June 1943.

> *Please tell me if you need me to come home. Of course you are doing everything you can for Jonathan.*
> *We grow up believing in solutions, especially in America—maybe only in America. Sometimes there are no solutions except the act of looking for them.*
> *The war is terrible. Have you seen any of my photographs in the magazines or press? One at the German border taken late in the day shows an orderly line of dead soldiers, neatly arranged for attack, cut down in surprise, and across their bodies, because of the way I caught the light, is my own shadow. It is the best photograph I have taken. The St. Louis Post-Dispatch printed it a while ago but I had hoped it might be picked up elsewhere.*

I don't know how my mother stood it—the lost son—ox blood in her veins perhaps or else she was a saint. Genetically these things skip a generation, I understand. The ox blood, I mean.

Hugs,
M

Jonathan did not die. At the end of a hot and wet July, too hot for children playing in the gardens of Georgetown houses, Dr. Brady from the Cleveland Clinic called to say he had that summer performed two heart valve replacements on children, one six years old, one four. If Sara was willing to take the risk, he was willing to try the operation on Jonathan. The risk, he said, was a big one, however. Any small thing could go wrong.

Sara went. She did not tell anyone except Melvina. And Bonita, who slept beside her on the top sheet the night before she left and gave her a small bouquet of buttercups for the trip.

"By great good luck," Dr. Brady said after the operation, which was successful. "And you."

She stayed three weeks in Cleveland and when she left Jonathan had gained weight, his hands and feet were warm and pink, his eyes were bright, and Sara had fallen in love with Dr. Brady.

"It is difficult to leave," she said to him in the examining room of his office at the Cleveland Clinic. "I will miss you."

"You needed someone to watch after you for a while," Dr. Brady said, laying his hand on her cheek.

He was right of course, she thought on the train going home. It was not a romance—not Dr. Brady that she had fallen in love with, but the way he had been with her, taking on the chore of Jonathan's life so, for just a moment, she could walk on air.

"What women need are doctors," Sara said to Susanna one evening after she got home. "Personal doctors on a regular basis, ill or not."

"I'm perfectly happy with soldiers," Susanna said.

"That's because you haven't tried the other," Sara said.

Sometimes during the fall of 1943, Sara would wake suddenly in the middle of the night with a terrible fear. She'd see scenes of Hendrik injured in France or blown to smithereens by a land mine or her mother dropped by helicopter into enemy territory. And then she'd go into the room next to her own, stand by Jonathan's bed, and watch triumphantly the even breathing of her healthy child.

EIGHTEEN

IN APRIL OF 1945, the day after the death of President Roosevelt, Hendrik March landed at Andrews Air Force Base. Sara was there to meet him as he disembarked—thin, weathered, intense as she remembered, even in his gait.

She had not seen him for three years and in the past year his letters had been short and infrequent. No doubt, like her, he had forgotten who she was exactly—the smell and feel of her beside him were mixed with distant memories of other women. What she knew of him, really since just after the birth of Nicholas, when, with the strain of distance, his letters became impersonal, was the person in the pieces he sent back for *The Honest Truth.* Always in his reports of the war, he found a real story to tell—a young German soldier who in dying said to him: "Speak German? Find my wife and say I love her." Or a very old Frenchman who stopped him on the streets of Normandy after D Day in 1944: "If you please," he said, "I seem to have misplaced my mother."

Sara fell in love with the writer of these stories although she could not actually remember the presence of him in her house.

The Yellow House had emptied at the end of 1944. Pamela moved to an apartment on Q Street by the Buffalo

Bridge where it was easy for the married law professor to spend the night if his wife was out of town. Susanna had remarried, in spite of her protestations, just after Christmas, a widower in his late thirties with two children whom she had met on the street when she was out walking with Rufus.

"After all," she said defensively to Sara, "the war won't go on forever. Hendrik will be home and then what for me but life alone again."

There were no longer soldiers passing through on their way to war, and the staff of *The Honest Truth* had been cut considerably. The circulation had dropped since Hendrik left, not, according to Albert, because of an absence of interest but rather because the war had cost them their readership, which was primarily young and male.

Hendrik was different. Even Albert said so on one of the occasions when he walked with Sara and her children to the park.

"He is too quiet," Albert said. "You think so?"

"He's very quiet," Sara agreed.

"He used to be hot-tempered and his temper has died," Albert said pensively. "Yes?"

Sara nodded. "I think he's very tired," she said.

"You find him like a man still? Like before?"

Sara was unwilling to continue the conversation. She understood the implication.

There had been no sex between them. The first night home, Hendrik had taken the top blanket and slept on the floor, and the second and the third, until he decided to make a bed on the floor with the pillows from the love seat. He had not reengaged with *The Honest Truth* and didn't wish to speak with the other writers, sometimes locking himself in the bathroom to avoid conversation. For the rest of the spring, he sat in a large blue flowered chair pulled up to the south window in the study which overlooked the back garden, his eyes wide open, seldom slipping into sleep. There was no telling what he saw. He talked infrequently and with some difficulty.

One afternoon in early June, shortly after noon, he was

sitting in the blue chair with a tuna fish sandwich and a Coke when a young student from Georgetown University who was assisting Albert burst into the study with the news that the whole front of the Yellow House had been desecrated.

" 'Commies' is written all over the front of the house."

Red paint was splashed all across the yellow clapboard house, and on the front door someone had written in dripping red to imitate blood:

COMMIES LIVE HERE

"I'll wash it off," the young man said.

"No," Hendrik said. He dipped his finger in the fresh red paint. "It's oil. It won't wash off." Above the word COMMIES, with the red paint on his finger, he wrote DANGEROUS JEWISH.

"I want to get it off today," Sara said. "It makes me feel peculiar, as if we're marked."

"Leave it," Hendrik said.

"Leave it?" Melvina said. "We'll be shot. The police will hide out in those bushes across the street and shoot us when we come out the front door."

"For being Communists?" Hendrik asked.

"For being marked people," Melvina said. "I'm moving back to my sister's and taking Bonita until this gets cleared up."

Sara was sitting in the kitchen with Hendrik.

"Who could have done it?" she asked.

"A lot of people," Hendrik replied.

"A lot of people hate us?"

"A lot of people hate *The Honest Truth*," he said. "And they should."

By the energy in his voice, the combative way he stood, Sara could tell that Hendrik was surfacing again in the vacant shell of the man who had returned from war.

He took a beer from the icebox, sat down at the kitchen table, lit a cigarette, and wrote a piece called "Communists Live Here," the first piece he'd written since his return from the war.

By the middle of a hot dry June, the city of Washington

alive with soldiers returning from the front, stirring with optimism and victory, Hendrik was himself. He woke before the sun, woke Sara with his plans for the day—a story he was doing about Roosevelt, the new United Nations charter signed on the 26th of June, Hitler's suicide on April 30th and the ensuing controversy over whether he was actually dead or only hidden. At least with Mussolini, they knew the Italian partisans had killed him. And Mussolini was, after all, not the same as Hitler, not entirely despicable. He wrote a piece about the division of Germany, the three-party occupation of Berlin.

The house was full of people once again, ex-soldiers on their way home sitting around the table late at night, young writers fresh from the war exploding with passion. Hendrik would not allow the front of the house to be scraped and painted although the neighbors complained that the graffiti gave P Street the feel of a ghetto.

"Not yet," Hendrik said when Sara insisted on repainting.

"I don't mind being called dangerous," Albert said. "Or Communist for that matter. But Jewish is too personal to have painted across your front door."

Hendrik accused Albert of anti-Semitism and Albert argued that his pride in being Jewish was affronted. They fought for nights and on the first of July Albert packed his bags and moved out, taking his clothes, a coffee cup he had purchased at the drugstore, and a pack of Hendrik's European cigarettes. Where he went was Jane's house at Dupont Circle and to the astonishment of everyone, especially Sara, he married her.

"I simply had no idea you were good friends," Sara said when Jane and Albert returned from a wedding trip to New York City, where they had eloped.

"Actually," Jane confessed, "I didn't know we were good friends either. I answered the door the night he left your house and there he was with a dozen roses. He said he thought I was the most beautiful woman he had met and smart for an American girl." She laughed.

"He's an anti-Semite so he needed a shiksa wife for

cover," Hendrik said crossly to Sara. "And he was too chicken to go to war."

All summer, the brothers fought—Albert silent or sullen and Hendrik volatile and combative, argumentative with Jane and Sara and Melvina while they made lunches or talked over coffee or folded the laundry in the kitchen.

"Albert says Hendrik is angry because he didn't fight in the war," Jane said.

"Hendrik didn't say that," Sara said.

"He says Albert is anti-Semitic," Jane said, "which is absolutely untrue, or I think it's untrue."

"It's a fight of sorrow, not disagreement," Sara said. "I think they're fighting because their mother died in the war."

"Albert doesn't talk about his mother."

"But you knew she died."

"Hendrik told me," Jane said. "Albert doesn't like personal conversation."

"Nor does Hendrik really," Sara said. "Mostly his conversation is political."

"Actually," Jane said sadly, "Albert doesn't like any conversation."

And they both laughed.

After Jane and Albert were married, Jane came over most days after work, sometimes for lunch. She and Sara talked, sometimes about themselves but usually about their husbands. They talked about their husbands' ideas, their thoughts, retold their stories.

"We're talking for them," Sara said.

"We may as well," Jane said. "They won't talk for themselves."

And then abruptly on the sixth of August, 1945, when the United States bombed Hiroshima, the arguments between the brothers stopped.

Hendrik and Sara and Jane and Melvina were in the kitchen having coffee at the counter when Albert came into the kitchen white-faced.

"Do you know what has happened?" he said out of

breath with emotion. "Did anybody hear? Is the radio on anyplace but my study? We have bombed the city of Hiroshima." He leaned against the counter. "Ordinary people, children, eating lunch were killed."

He poured a glass of bourbon. He poured a second one for Hendrik and they sat at the kitchen table, wordless, listening to the news on the radio, drinking another bourbon and then another until they were both very drunk, too drunk to get up from their chairs until night. They did not fight again for a very long time.

Three days later, on the ninth of August, 1945, the day the United States bombed Nagasaki, Eleanor Steward March was conceived. Sara was certain of this information although she did not ever tell Eleanor—the news of her beginnings was too dark to tell a child.

Hendrik had come upstairs early that night. Sara was resting, the twins were sleeping, Nicholas just in his crib. Hendrik closed the door, turned off the light, and fell on Sara with a sense of desperation and yearning she had never seen in him.

The girl—Sara had believed it would be a girl, had been certain of it—a tiny black-haired doll baby of a child with a birthmark in the shape of a peanut on her cheek—was born earlier than expected on the first of May, 1946, in Sara's own bed with only Amanda and Melvina at home on a clear sunny afternoon smelling of lilacs and early perfumed spring.

SARA
AND
ELEANOR

ONE

Flat Mouth was coming.

"I don't like Indians," Eleanor said sitting on the kitchen floor taking off her snow boots and snow pants. "They kill people like us. I saw it on television."

"We killed them first," Jonathan said from his usual place at the kitchen table, where he sat with a cup of hot chocolate making up crossword puzzles of which he had already sold three to the *Washington Post* and he was not even ten. "Why shouldn't they kill us?"

"I don't like them," Elly said.

She pulled her chair up next to Jonathan and sat down.

"Tell me a question," she said looking at his crossword puzzle. "An easy one."

Eleanor March was small with dark skin, black eyes, a thick cap of black curly hair, almost Spanish in appearance. Not at all like her long, leggy, fair-skinned brothers. Already at four, she was outspoken.

"Whose baby is she?" Hendrik had asked when she was born.

"Bonita's sister," Melvina said.

And she did resemble a Mexican baby—even in her temperament, which was explosive.

"She never sleeps," Hendrik said. "We will have to put her out in the garden or the rest of us will die of no sleep."

Sometimes in the middle of the night, Sara would find Eleanor sitting up in her crib instructing her stuffed pandas and rabbits and pigs.

"I don't know what will become of her," Hendrik said. "Such a formidable girl with such a gruff voice in the body of a baby doll."

Sara was fascinated by Eleanor. Some days she simply followed her from one project to the next one. She couldn't take her eyes off her daughter.

"Born trouble," Melvina said of her. "She should have been born colored."

"Just ask me one question," Eleanor said leaning her head down on the table next to where Jonathan was working so her mass of curly hair was in the way of his pencil.

"What's Hebrew for *dog*?" Jonathan asked.

"That's easy. That's too easy," Eleanor said. *"Kokosh."*

"That's not even a word," Nich-o said in disgust. He was a tall beautiful boy with straight-cut blond hair and perfect features, on a face that would become handsome when he grew up, all planes and angles—the kind of looks and sweet predictable disposition of which Melvina was fond of saying, "Made the flowers open without the sun."

"You make things up, Elly," Nich-o said.

"I don't. I tell the truth."

"Flat Mouth is a real Indian. Did you know that, Elly?" Frederick said cleaning the mud off his snow boots. "A real Indian with feathers."

"Amanda said no feathers," Elly said earnestly.

"Well," Frederick said, "Amanda hasn't seen him for a long time. She may have forgotten the feathers." He sat down next to Jonathan and pulled over the paper on which he was working so he could read it. "There, I knew it," he said. *"Calib.* That's Hebrew for *dog*."

Frederick was good-looking and energetic, evenly proportioned like his father, but he was complicated in unexpected ways as the twin brother of a smaller, meeker boy who had had their mother's complete attention. Sara understood that what seemed to be aggressive in Frederick was actually defensive. But instinctively in every situation, she could not help herself. Her heart went out to Jonathan.

Upstairs, Amanda was resting. She had had pneumonia in France during her first year there and then again when she fell in love with a British captain and followed him to London. She felt susceptible, especially in January 1950 after the flu over Christmas and her fiftieth birthday.

For her birthday, Flat Mouth had sent her a beaded band which had belonged to Grandmother Yellow Flower.

* * *

Dear A Man, he had written.

> *This is my grandmother's and when she died, the women gave it to me for my wife but I could not give it to Star because she does not seem so much my wife as you do.*
>
> *I am free to come to Washington as soon as I hear from you that it is agreeable.*
>
> Love forever,
> Flat Mouth

"It is agreeable," Amanda wrote back.

In the eight years since she had left Bad River for the war, she had seen Flat Mouth only once, when he met her in Chicago for an exhibition of her "Middle Western Town" photographs. But they wrote regularly at least once a week except during the time she was in France. There was never a mention of Star's presence but neither was there an indication of her absence, so the freedom he mentioned in his birthday letter was perplexing to her. Perhaps Star had gone to live with her own family as Chippewe women used to do.

Elly knocked on the door and walked in without waiting for Amanda to answer.

"Does he have feathers? Frederick says he has feathers."

She climbed onto the bed with Amanda, sitting exactly like Amanda was sitting, her legs out, her back straight, even assuming her grandmother's severe expression. Amanda felt a strong affinity for Eleanor.

"She's just like you," Sara said happily to her mother, pleased to have produced a miniature replica of Amanda. She could spend hours with her mother in genetic conversations, sometimes even arguments, especially when Sara felt that Amanda was criticizing her slow, reflective temperament in favor of Eleanor's colorful, combative one. But generally the conversations were the warm and satisfying self-congratulations of a family in love with itself.

"No feathers," Amanda said.

"So he's not a real Indian."

"He's a very real Indian. If he wanted to wear feathers, he could."

"And you love him, Mama says."

"I love him," Amanda agreed.

"And maybe you'll marry him, Frederick says."

"No. I won't marry him. Already he's married to Star." Eleanor was pensive. "And anyway you're too old."

"Who says?" Amanda asked.

"You're a grandmother," Eleanor said. "That's too old."

Later, Amanda checked her face for age, which showed if she put a mirror on her bed and leaned toward it so the loose skin on her face fell away from the bones.

"You look wonderful, Mama," Sara had said to her. "Why should you worry about fifty?"

"It's not worry," Amanda said. "It's fact. I feel exactly the way I felt when I was a child, but inside where I can't see it things are changing. All of a sudden one day, I'm going to be old."

"Maybe you could take my picture as a soldier," Elly said.

"I didn't know you were a soldier." Amanda picked up her camera from the bedside table and focused on Eleanor.

"I am," Elly said. "Frederick says you were a soldier in the war."

"I was a photographer in the war."

"Me too," Eleanor said. She crossed her legs and put her hands on her hips. "Now do I look like a photographer in the war?"

"Exactly," Amanda said.

"Good." Elly jumped down from Amanda's bed.

"What does the Indian eat?" she asked.

"His name is Flat Mouth, darling."

"I know. I call him 'the Indian' so I'll know what he is. Frederick says he only eats buffalo meat and corn and Nich-o says the Safeway doesn't have buffalo meat—only corn."

"He eats what we eat."

"Ice cream?"

"I'm sure."

"If you like, he can sleep in my room because Melvina says she doesn't sleep on the same floor with Indians."

"Don't worry about Melvina. There's always something she's not doing."

"She says she's going to move in with her sister, especially if he smells bad."

"Well, he doesn't smell bad."

"Thank goodness," Elly said happily and ran downstairs to tell Frederick about the feathers.

"The children have planned a wedding," Sara said to her mother early on the morning that Flat Mouth was due to arrive from Milwaukee. They were in Amanda's room and Amanda was dressing. Usually she wore trousers and lace-up boots, heavy sweaters in the winter, but this morning she was trying on Sara's clothes, long wool skirts which were short and loose on her, but she had been feeling aged lately and the romance with Flat Mouth, just below consciousness, had surfaced once again. She wanted to look pretty.

"What kind of a wedding?" Amanda asked, tightening one of Sara's skirts with a safety pin.

"One between you and Flat Mouth tonight before dinner," Sara said watching her mother try on clothes. "Nich-o says it's a way to make him feel at home."

"They do understand that Flat Mouth is already married?" Amanda asked. She decided on a long sweater of Sara's and her brown leather flat shoes, which were slightly tight. She even wore makeup.

"Of course," Sara laughed.

Downstairs, Elly was putting orange juice glasses on the table for flower vases, filled with holly and evergreens which Melvina had clipped from the garden. Frederick, who was going to be the minister, had on the black cape which had belonged to Anna's mother and had wrapped toilet paper around his neck to serve as the priest's collar, and Nicholas had borrowed his friend Jay's father's tuxedo on the premise that his father, Hendrik, didn't have a tuxedo and was going to a wedding.

Jonathan, always a literalist, wasn't playing.

"Flat Mouth is already married so it doesn't make sense," he said.

"At least you could play the piano," Nicholas said to him. "We have to have music and you're the only one."

Jonathan didn't move from his crossword puzzles.

" 'Rudolph the Red-Nosed Reindeer,' " Elly said. "It's my favorite song."

"Not for a wedding," Frederick said. "I love those dear hearts and gentle people," he began singing, "who live in my home town."

"That's really dumb," Elly said. "You play what you like, Jonny."

Jonathan was tempted. "It should be romantic." He sat down at the piano and played "I'm in Love with a Wonderful Guy."

"I'm as corny as Kansas in summer," Elly sang.

"I hate that song," Bonita said from the sofa in the living room where she lay, sullen since the first day of her eighteenth year, her leg over the back of the couch. "I like 'Some Enchanted Evening.' "

"So what're you going to be at the wedding, Bon?" Elly asked. "I'm going to be a flower girl and Nich-o is an usher and Jonathan's playing the piano. Maybe you can be a maiden of honor."

"I'm not coming to the wedding." Bonita threw her arm over her eyes.

"It's at dinner," Elly said. "You have to come to dinner."

"I don't have to do anything," Bonita said. "I don't have to eat."

"You could wear a dress of mine," Sara said. "My red wool dress would look beautiful with your black hair."

Bonita uncovered her eyes.

"And maybe some of my red lipstick."

"Do you have any lipstick to match your red dress exactly?" Bonita asked.

"I do," Sara said. "And I've always thought you should try mascara, which would make your eyes seem enormous."

"They are already enormous without mascara," Bonita said crossly.

The plane was late and Amanda had two cups of coffee while she waited in the lobby at National Airport. By the time Flat Mouth did arrive from Chicago, she was nervous from caffeine as well—and Flat Mouth too was agitated as he always was when he was uncomfortable. The ride to Georgetown through Rock Creek Park was long with awkward pauses. Flat Mouth didn't belong in Washington, Amanda thought. It had been a crazy idea for him to come. She wished she could put him right back on the plane to Milwaukee. She couldn't imagine how they would survive even a few days together. And then what? Would a bad visit be the end of their friendship? Could they have a love affair here? And how was it possible on the third floor of the P Street house with Melvina listening and all of the children and Hendrik? What in the world would Hendrik and Flat Mouth have to say to each other?

"Where are we going?" Flat Mouth asked when they turned off the parkway.

"My house," Amanda said. "We're almost there."

"I am going back to Milwaukee," he said. "Turn the car around and take me to the airport."

"No," Amanda said. "You came all the way here and you have to try it."

"I don't even know you in Washington," Flat Mouth said.

"Don't be stupid. Of course you know me."

"In Wisconsin, yes." He folded his arms across his chest. "Here you are a stranger. I want to drive the car."

"Now?"

"Now."

"You want me to stop now and let you drive this car."

"Yes."

Amanda hesitated. "I bet you don't even have a license."

"I don't have a license of course," Flat Mouth said, "but you know I can drive a car."

Amanda stopped. She got out of the driver's seat and

walked around to the passenger side of the car, got in, turned on the radio, pulled out one ashtray, and lit a cigarette.

Flat Mouth drove down Pennsylvania Avenue past the White House to Constitution Avenue, past the museums and the government buildings to the Capitol and around to Union Station, behind the station into the slums, driving for a long time before he finally stopped the car at a small bistro on Capitol Hill.

"Lunch," he said solemnly.

When they sat down at the small wooden booth, he grabbed her legs with his legs and pulled her toward him underneath the table.

"So, A Man," he said smiling broadly, "now I am here in Washington and for what?"

"That's exactly what I wondered when I got your letter. For what?" Amanda said.

"There I am in Ashland, fifty-four years old with not the best liver and I wonder to myself why don't I marry A Man, which is what I want to do."

"And you answer yourself. Because I already am married to Star."

"Not exactly." He took her hand and kissed her fingers. "That is not exactly what I say to myself."

"Well, Flat Mouth, you're lucky you came to Washington today, because we are getting married tonight before dinner," Amanda said putting her fingers across her lips. "It's already arranged."

The dining room and living room were candlelit, the best silver on the table, crystal goblets, linen napkins, the smell of pine, of fire burning in the fireplace.

"Shall we do it in Indian or American?" Frederick asked.

"Indian," Flat Mouth said.

"The trouble is I only know American," Frederick said.

"Then we'll do it in American now and Indian later," Amanda said. She was wearing black trousers and a heavy sweater for her wedding, but Elly had insisted she wear a lace handkerchief on her head and carry a branch of holly.

Jonathan played "Some Enchanted Evening" while the guests took their seats on the couches in the living room— Hendrik and Albert and Jane, Bonita in Sara's red dress, Sara, Melvina in a bad humor.

"I don't like weddings anyway," she said, "but certainly I don't like made-up weddings. What's the point, Amanda? I think you've lost your senses since fifty."

When the guests were seated, Jonathan played Mendelssohn's Wedding March. Frederick walked to the fireplace holding the Book of Common Prayer and Elly walked behind him in a full pink slip and a long chiffon scarf pinned to the top of her head, carrying a large bunch of unrelated cloth flowers.

Flat Mouth, with a five-and-ten-cent-store feather headdress, walked across the living room and stood in front of Frederick.

"Dearly beloved, . . ." Frederick began. "We are gathered together in the company of God."

"HOORAH," Flat Mouth shouted a war call. "HOORAH. HOORAH."

Later in Amanda's narrow bed, the lights out, whispering together, they heard Eleanor's knock at the door.

"Amanda?"

"Don't answer," Flat Mouth said in her ear.

"Amanda?" Elly called again. "It's me, Eleanor."

"Good night, Elly," Amanda said. "I'm sound asleep."

"Good night, Amanda," she called. "Tell the Indian good night if you see him."

And they listened to her bare feet slap the wood floor as she padded down the hall, down the steps, and back to her room.

TWO

IN LATE MARCH 1952, when the news came that life at the Yellow House was going to change, Eleanor was at home alone with chicken pox. Melvina, in a black temper since Bonita had gone to El Paso to meet her real mother, was at the market buying supper. Sara was volunteering at the library of the boys' school and Amanda had moved into a first-floor apartment in Greenwich Village where she lived weekdays and taught photography at New York University. Weekends she was back in Washington in her stark white room with war photographs on the walls and a Flat Mouth Shrine, as Sara called it—photographs of Flat Mouth and the beads from Grandmother Yellow Flower and the red, blue, and green feathers from the headdress which Flat Mouth had worn at his wedding to Amanda.

The wedding had not worked. At least not in the way that the March children had imagined it would work. Flat Mouth's wife returned from her mother's shortly after the wedding and Flat Mouth went home to Ashland. But since then, Amanda had spent the month of August in Wisconsin in the same room she had had before the war and so, as Sara told the children, there was a kind of marriage, just not the ordinary kind.

Eleanor was in the kitchen when the doorbell rang. A man with a pasty white face said he had come with a letter for Mr. Hendrik March, editor and publisher of *The Honest Truth*. Very important.

"He is at his office," Eleanor said. "There isn't any *The Honest Truth* any longer."

The man looked perplexed.

"*The Honest Truth* closed," Eleanor said.

In fact, *The Honest Truth* had slipped away in increments after the war, slowly at first from a weekly newspaper to a biweekly to a monthly and finally, in the spring of 1951, the last issue was published without fanfare, only a small notation of its demise in the *Washington Post*. There was a final sentimental editorial by Hendrik along with an article by Albert with a fierce attack on complacency in postwar America.

No longer was there a place, particularly among the young, for a left-wing newspaper. By 1950, Communists were the enemy and prosperity had a much greater attraction than political change. That year Congress passed the McCarran Act calling for severe restriction of Communists in sensitive positions and for registration of all Communist organizations, and in 1951 Julius and Ethel Rosenberg were sentenced to death for espionage against the United States. Ordinary citizens were building bomb shelters underground and there were frequent bomb drills in the public schools. But life in America, superficially at least, was prosperous and essentially uneventful.

The man who came to the Yellow House with a message for Hendrik was a bearer of bad news.

He said it was a matter of serious consequence, an emergency, and he asked Eleanor to sign her name on a sheet to say she had received the letter. Then he took the sheet with her signature and warned her of danger if the letter did not get to her father immediately.

Eleanor watched the man walk down the front steps, across the sidewalk, and climb into a black car. Then she called her mother at Key Elementary School and told the secretary who answered that it was an emergency.

"He had a gun," Elly told Nich-o when he came home from school that afternoon. "And his face was the color of snow."

"How do you know he had a gun?" Nich-o asked, following Eleanor into the kitchen.

"It bulged in his pocket," Eleanor said.

"Eleanor is making things up again," Nich-o said to his mother, pouring himself a glass of lemonade.

But Sara wasn't listening. It was late afternoon and the sun in the west fell across her lap where she was sitting in the rocking chair reading the letter delivered by the white-faced man that afternoon. She was not interested in talking to children.

Since January 1950, Hendrik March had had a column in *Democracy*, a political journal which had started up after the war. It was well thought of as a serious journal by old Democrats and not considered a threat to the rising spirit of caution and conservatism. Hendrik was, as Sara said to Jane, concerned with justice and not revolution. And so his educated European point of view was not out of place in the fifties in America. His column was human and emotional and moral. By 1952, he had gained the affection of a new readership.

Albert, on the other hand, had struggled to find a place for his bitter, acerbic voice. Although he was a better writer, he could find no American publication interested in his point of view. So after *The Honest Truth* folded, Albert stayed home while Jane worked at CBS, and as a diversion from the tedium of domestic life he wrote the first of what would eventually become a salvation for the March families.

Behind Closed Doors was a spy novel about the Second World War espionage of a British ex-convict called Billy Tudor who lived a life of sufficient danger and sexual adventure to be entirely satisfactory to the readers of the fifties in America and Britain. The novel came out in early 1951, sailed to the top of the best-seller list and made Albert and Jane rich by any standards.

In March 1952, when the bad news came, Albert had just completed the second Billy Tudor novel and Hendrik was in the process of writing an extensive article which he hoped he could develop into a book about the repercussions in the Soviet Union of the dictatorship of Stalin and who would succeed him as Secretary of the Central Committee of the Communist Party.

In the evenings after supper, the brothers would often meet at Hendrik's and walk through the streets of Georgetown inventing stories for Billy Tudor from real-life stories Hendrik took off the wires, while Jane and Sara talked about them in the kitchen of the Yellow House. Their lives had taken on the somnambulant quality of a permanent holiday, a daily sense of possibility and ease, of time extended over the lazy afternoons. But there was as well a growing emptiness subtle as cancer spreading through the glands, especially with the women.

The night the letter came, Hendrik was late for supper.

Sara had called him with the news but he was not in his office at *Democracy*. Then Jonathan came home from school with chicken pox and Frederick found a dead kitten under the back steps of a neighbor's house. Melvina had to lie down because of her heart and Bonita called long distance collect from El Paso, Texas, to say she was going to stay a little longer with her real family.

"She won't come back," Melvina said crossly when Sara told her.

"She will. You *are* her mother, Melvina."

"I know what the world's like," Melvina said going up the back stairs to her bed. "That child won't be back until my funeral."

When Hendrik did arrive shortly before eight, the kitten was being buried in a shoe box in a formal ceremony in the backyard with Frederick in his role as minister and Nich-o singing "Jesus Loves Me," which was the only Christian song he knew.

"I've been with Albert at a bar," he said to Sara who sat in the rocking chair in the kitchen smoking a cigarette. "He got a letter from the House Un-American Committee today."

"So did you." Sara took the letter out of her pocket and handed it to him.

"A-*ha*," Hendrik said, full of energy. "I knew it. The Gestapo in America," he said and poured himself a bourbon. "Heil McCarthy. You should have a drink, darling. Relax. One small drink to relax."

"No drinks," she said solemnly.

It was a game with Hendrik. "Just one drink," he would tease her. "To relax. You need to relax at night before bed so you can sleep. Right?"

"Wrong," Sara said. "I don't need a drink to relax."

"You are so serious," Hendrik laughed, kissing the top of her head. "So serious about so little a thing."

At supper, Hendrik was full of excitement.

"I want to tell the children," he said. "It is important that they know."

Sara set the dishes of mashed potatoes and broccoli and roast pork in front of him, poured the milk. "You could go to jail," she said. "This is not a celebration."

"To go to jail for nothing, that is fine. I can get some writing done."

He sat down at the table, pushed the dishes away from him, folded his hands.

He told the children about the House Un-American Activities Committee and Senator Joseph McCarthy. He showed them the article he had written in *The Honest Truth* in 1938 about the Gestapo and how they were no different from the committee.

"I want you to listen carefully. Jonathan, sit up," Hendrik said. "Now," he said, "they think I am a Communist. Do you know about a Communist?"

"Jay Burger's father says you are a Communist," Frederick said. "I said you are an Austrian."

"I am neither, Frederick," Hendrik said. "I am an American." And he told them about the letter.

From the first sign of trouble, Hendrik's spirits were high.

"Nothing will happen," he said one evening when the March brothers and their families were in the kitchen on P Street. "Nothing can possibly happen. This is America," he said.

"Things happen in America," Sara said. "Look at what is happening to other people accused of communism."

"They are in jail," Jane said. "Their careers are ruined."

"So?" Hendrik said. "Wait and see."

Albert was not optimistic. He sat in the kitchen with his forehead resting in his palm, filling the room with smoke, drinking beer.

"What can they do to you?" Hendrik asked. "You don't even use your own name. What can they do to a made-up spy called Billy Tudor?"

"Jail. That is what they can do to me," Albert said. "They know what my name is."

"Who is 'they'?" Frederick asked.

"The Gestapo. The American Gestapo," Albert replied.

"Jay's father said you should not use the word 'Gestapo' in America. It's a profanity," Frederick said.

"So how does Jay's father hear what we say at the dinner table unless you tell him, Frederick?" Hendrik said.

"I don't like Jay anyway," Eleanor said. "He's too mean."

After the subpoenas, Jane and Albert came to dinner most nights and there were arguments at the table, high-spirited arguments without animosity, generated by Hendrik, who honestly believed that his subpoena to appear before the House committee had given him an opportunity to set things right in the country, to tell the truth as he saw it, to stop the dangerous campaign of Senator McCarthy once and for all.

The children were revolutionized. Eleanor had a plan to poison Senator McCarthy with roach poison and Nich-o, patriotic and uncomplicated, said he would write a letter to President Truman. Frederick defended his father in spite of the efforts of Jay and his other friends at Key Elementary School, who were hard on the March twins, especially Jonathan, an easy target, since it was written up in the *Washington Post* that their father was probably a Communist.

"Nothing can happen to us," Frederick insisted. "We've done nothing wrong."

Only Jonathan, whose sensibilities were much more in tune with those of Sara than of his father, could not sleep at night for fear that something dreadful was about to happen.

"What do you think, Mama?" he asked his mother one afternoon while she was making dinner. "You think Father could go to jail?"

"Of course he could go to jail."

"And you think he will?"

"Others have." She tried to be calm but Hendrik's innocent optimism frightened her. She expected the worst. "People who have done less have gone to jail."

"You mean you think he is a Communist?"

"No. I don't think he is or was," she said. "I don't think it matters. If they decide he is a Communist, he is."

"That doesn't make sense," Jonathan said quietly.

"No," Sara said, "but it's true nevertheless."

Sara did not sleep at all. She watched the car headlights fly across the ceiling, down the wall, and when they stopped, when it was too late for cars to be traveling on P Street, the panic of insomnia set in.

Amanda wasn't helpful.

Like Hendrik, she didn't believe anything substantial could possibly happen.

"It's not life-threatening," Amanda said when she called from New York where she was assembling a retrospective of her work for the Broome Street Gallery.

"You only believe in the danger of death," Sara said to her mother. "Germs and accidents. You have no sense of the danger of life, like reversals or misfortunes."

"That I suppose is true," Amanda said.

And it was. Amanda had not eroded by the accumulation of years. Rather she gathered the daily experience of her life like artillery, a tall slender arsenal moving about with her camera slung over her shoulder.

But by Wednesday, April 23, 1952, when Hendrik March was due to testify before the House committee, Amanda had come home.

Eleanor knocked on her bedroom door early that morning and walked in without waiting.

"I threw up," she said.

"Did you?" Amanda took her on her lap.

"Just now. I didn't tell Mama."

"Are you ill?"

"I threw up because I know Father is going to jail," Eleanor said.

"None of us knows that, darling," Amanda said. "Things may turn out well."

"Frederick knows. He told me. His friend Jay told him

Father is going to jail. Everyone in the world knows he's a Communist. That's what Jay says and so do other people."

"Well, they're wrong," Amanda said. "We know they're wrong."

"Anyway," Eleanor said combing her long hair with her grandmother's brush, "Mama says I have to wear nice clothes today and not blue jeans and I have to braid my hair." She lay down at the bottom of Amanda's bed. "Mama is wearing a navy blue suit with a white bow so she'll look like a choirboy. That's what she told me. And no lipstick. Just rouge. What are you wearing?"

Amanda raised her eyebrows. "Trousers, I guess."

"Mama wishes you'd wear a dress," Eleanor said.

"She said so?"

"Yes. She said she wished you'd wear her black linen suit and white blouse."

"Then I will," Amanda said. "Of course I will. You go downstairs and bring it up to me. And stockings too and a garter belt. Tell Sara I only have trousers and no good shoes."

Amanda had come home on Monday late afternoon just after the opening reception for her show, which had included selections of her work since the First World War. The Sunday *Times* had a story about Sam Dane—the first time the real story had been told, but so many years had passed, so much had happened in the world, that the story created only the mildest interest and one telephone call from a woman novelist who sounded quite drunk and asked Amanda whether she could fictionalize her Sam Dane story for a novel.

The review of the show, "Amanda Steward: An Adventurer in Black and White," in the same issue of the Times was favorable: "What is original and striking about her photographs is the search for new subjects, new forms, new methods for discovering reality. She is a contradiction in photography and uses the camera more as an abstract painter who alters form to find the essence of a subject." Amanda read only the beginning of the review, perplexed as she always was by reviews of her work, unable to con-

nect her work with language. It was simple. The world as
she saw it was framed by the camera lens.

She had been at home very little in the spring of 1952
and was surprised when she arrived on the afternoon of the
21st of April to find Hendrik as high-spirited as he was
and Sara as unhappy. In Amanda's separations from home,
particularly from Sara, she imagined her daughter more
like herself. More inventive and resolved, less sensitive
than Sara really was, less tentative or dogged in her slow
determined way to maintain a life of careful definition,
without surprises.

The subpoena from the House Un-American Activities
Committee had actually been a complete surprise. In the
spring of 1947, the Attorney General's List, a checklist of
organizations and people with Communist or fascist views
was compiled to be used secretly to screen federal employees. But in fact the list was published. At the time, *The
Honest Truth* was included, but not the names of Albert
and Hendrik March, although Albert did write an amusing
piece which appeared in the May 14, 1947, issue of *The
Honest Truth* called "Bye-Bye Freedom, Good-Bye."

By 1952, the mood in the country was grim. Senator
McCarthy's Senate committee and the House Un-
American Activities Committee had run through the black-
list. Many people had been jailed, their professional lives
ruined. Charges of Communist affiliation became wilder
and more unlikely. In the period of paranoia, even the
United States Army was charged by Senator McCarthy
with disloyalty. The House, concerned primarily with indi-
viduals hostile to the state, increased their list by twenty-
five or thirty citizens declared dangerous, and that list
included Hendrik and Albert March.

On the morning of April 23rd, Hendrik was up and
dressed before the sun. He actually was nervous, almost
apologetic. At the hearing, he sat next to his lawyer, a liberal
Washington lawyer well known for his representation of cli-
ents who appeared before the committee, and pressed his
fingers together, bit his bottom lip. The Marches were all
there, including Jane. Melvina, who had insisted that she

would never go to a courtroom, sat straight and without moving, between Sara and Amanda.

Eleanor's memory of the events of that morning were imperfect. She recalled a congressman who was large, bearish, and unkempt with an unpleasant friendliness about him. There were several other unsmiling men around a table. But what she remembered in particular was the size of the assembled men. They were taller than her father. Her father seemed to take on the diminished shape of a man gone quickly frail with illness or bad luck. He was uncomfortable. She could feel his discomfort from the chair where she sat next to Nich-o and she was afraid, as she told Nich-o, that she might throw up again.

"Don't," Nich-o said. "If you do, I'll kill you."

What she did remember clearly was her father handcuffed, put in a car to go to jail, attached to the wrist of another man. She didn't know whether that happened after the hearing or later at another time and she never asked. The subject of what happened on the 23rd of April was not brought up until years later when the March children were grown up and asked Amanda to tell them everything she remembered about that day.

Albert did not go to jail. Although he was the one who had been a member of the Communist Party, had become a citizen of the United States reluctantly, and was not an enthusiastic American, it was Hendrik with his boyish enthusiasm who in the eyes of the committee was a danger to the state.

The night after the hearing, Eleanor moved into Sara's room, climbed into the double bed, sleeping where her father had slept. Her parents' bedroom was next to her father's study and their bathroom was quite small and had the usual facilities—a stall shower, a linen closet, and a doctor's scale on which Sara kept track of her weight. Often at night after Eleanor moved into her parents' room, her mother, always restless, would leave the bed in darkness, go to the bathroom, and lock the door.

"I'm reading," she'd say if Eleanor called her. "I'll be back in just a moment."

When she did come back to bed, Eleanor was always asleep.

One morning early in May, before school, Sara still asleep, Eleanor went into her parents' bathroom, which she seldom used, sharing instead a bathroom down the hall with Melvina, to find toilet paper in her mother's linen closet. When she opened the door of the linen closet, the towels were all pushed to the back and mixed in among the packages of toilet paper and cardboard boxes of Colgate toothpaste and Prell shampoo were bottle after bottle of empty liquor, mostly Bellow's Bourbon, some Gilby's Gin, hundreds of them in her memory.

Quickly she shut the door of the linen closet, tiptoed through her father's study in order not to wake her mother, went down the hall, up the stairs to Amanda's room, and climbed into Amanda's empty bed. She would tell her mother she had the stomach flu and could not go to school.

On the bedside table, next to the Flat Mouth Shrine, there was a stack of old letters. She opened the one on top.

Dear Mama, she read.

> *I woke up this morning missing you terribly. Such stupidity, I thought at my age. Such childish feelings. Tomorrow I will be twenty-nine years old.*
>
> Yr. loving daughter,
Anna

ELEANOR

ONE

ELEANOR MARCH WAS under the large-skirted table in the living room while an argument between her mother and father went on just beyond where she was hiding. It was not an ordinary argument or Eleanor might have given notice that she was there.

In fact, she was not expected to be in the house at all, which was no doubt why her parents were at liberty to fight as they did, in such a way that years later Eleanor was still able to recall exactly the dialogue of that hot August afternoon in 1953.

She was supposed to be with her brothers in the shed at the back of the garden, which had been turned into a playhouse and where on this particular afternoon the March children and several friends were having a party. The friends were boys, mainly friends of Frederick, since Jonathan had very few friends and Nich-o was on a camping trip. Under Frederick's leadership, the friends had decided to upend Eleanor March, who had at seven a reputation for provocation, take off her underpants, and check for pubic hairs, now in secret abundance on the older girls for whom these eighth grade boys lusted.

It was not Frederick's idea, he insisted later, and besides, as he pointed out, nothing had actually happened. Which was perfectly true. Somehow when Sammy Lendering got hold of her shorts, she twisted away from him with such force as to break the button and zipper of the shorts and break away as well. She flew through the garden, up the back steps to the kitchen, through the dining room, and, certain that one of them, probably Frederick, was after her, she dove under the stripe-skirted table in the living room just as her parents walked in the front door from Jane and Albert's house.

* * *

During the fifteen months that Hendrik had been in prison, Amanda had moved back home to help Sara, made suddenly weary by the reversals in her life.

Melvina was not around. She had quite literally almost died of a broken heart. When the letter from Bonita, visiting her real family in El Paso, came, addressed to Amanda, not Melvina, saying that she "felt right out here," Melvina had a massive heart attack.

"Daughters can kill you," she said to Amanda, who spent all the days and nights sleeping on the couch in the waiting room of intensive care until Melvina was out of danger. "They'll eat you alive."

So with Hendrik and Melvina gone, Amanda had taken over. Sara handled the details of the house, unless she was too tired, and Amanda handled the details of the world, primarily money, which since Hendrik's imprisonment the Marches no longer had.

"We have no money," Sara said sitting on the couch next to the table where Eleanor was hiding. "In June, we took four hundred dollars from Jane and Albert, five hundred in July, and this month because of Jonathan's doctor bill, I have had to ask Jane for a thousand dollars to run this house and pay the bills."

"So?" Hendrik said. "They have plenty of money and he is my brother."

Because of his prison sentence Hendrik no longer could be in the newspaper business, so he was working on his book about the Soviet Union and postwar Germany. There was no contract on the book—no promise of money in the future—but Hendrik was optimistic.

"They have plenty of money, yes, but it's their money," Sara said. "I am ashamed to ask for more."

"Well, I am not, so I will do the asking."

"I'd like to have a job," Sara said. "I'd like to begin in September as soon as the children are back in school."

"What can you do?" Hendrik asked, snappy with Sara. "You're a mother."

"I can do a great many things," Sara said. "I'm a good cook. I could teach. I used to love design."

"Clothes design?" Hendrik asked with a note of contempt.

"I like clothes," Sara said quietly.

"I'm trying to write a book and this isn't the time for you to try something. Albert is glad to help us. He is rich by accident," Hendrik said. "It is—how would you say it—no skin off his back."

There was a long silence. Eleanor tried to hold her breath so they would not hear her in the silence.

"It is skin off my back, Hendrik," Sara said finally. "What I would like to do is turn this house into a small hotel. We could make an apartment on the top floor large enough for all of us and then the rest of the house could be a hotel with a dining room.

"A hotel?"

"A small hotel."

Hendrik laughed.

"What a very strange idea," he said. "A small hotel with a dining room," he said with an edge of sarcasm. "And then perhaps you can drink with company and not alone, Sara."

Later in the afternoon just before the hour of supper, Eleanor found her mother in bed under the covers fully dressed, propped up with pillows. She sat down as close as possible, pressing her body against her, putting her head on Sara's shoulder.

"Jonathan tells me that Frederick was quite unpleasant with you this afternoon." Sara's voice was tired.

"Mean," Eleanor said. "Frederick is mean. You know that."

"What exactly did he do?"

Eleanor hesitated. She hadn't come to Sara's room to ask anything of her mother, who seemed at this moment to be beyond giving, but as a comfort. She didn't wish to be a bearer of bad news.

"What did Jonathan tell you?" Eleanor hedged.

"He said that Sammy tried to pull down your pants." Sara closed her eyes in exhaustion as if the secret troubles of the day were accumulating too fast to accommodate. "But Jonathan indicated it was worse."

"I guess it was a little worse," Eleanor said.

"Will you tell me?"

Eleanor considered. "I don't want to," she said.

"Then I should ask Frederick?"

"No," Eleanor said. "Maybe ask Jonathan."

"I'd like for you to tell me."

"I can't," Eleanor said. "He'd kill me."

Sara was actually happier not to hear. She didn't really wish to know. There was evidence enough that Frederick was unkind, perhaps even troubled. But he did well in school, was handsome to look at, and was not disruptive in obvious ways. She couldn't bear to pay too much attention.

Something was the matter with Sara most of the time. She felt afloat on a fast-moving stream spinning down through a low-hanging forest into a river which would swallow her up.

"I wonder, darling, if you could look in the fridge," Sara said to Eleanor. "I think we have leftover chicken from Thursday and vegetables."

"You want me to put dinner on the table?" Eleanor asked.

"Please," Sara said. "That would be lovely. Nich-o won't be home tonight but Amanda will be so that's six of us—Melvina won't be back until tomorrow."

Sara waited until Eleanor had closed her door and then she got up. She wanted a drink. That was all she could think of. She went to her bathroom, shut and locked the door, sat on the closed toilet seat, and had two capfuls of bourbon. For a few moments while the alcohol sprinted through her bloodstream, she felt a swift surge of electricity, a lightness of being. Then she brushed her teeth, swished mouthwash through her mouth, washed her face with cold water. She had in mind to put on makeup for dinner, just a little color on her cheeks and lips, but when she looked in the mirror over the sink, her face was blurred as if it had been painted in impressionist repetition on the glass. She went back to bed.

Downstairs, Eleanor set the table on the back porch. She picked flowers from the annual garden, cut up broccoli and cold potatoes for potato salad. Jonathan was working on his crossword puzzles in the kitchen. He told her that he was sorry about what had happened in the shed and that he had been the one to tell their mother.

"I know," Eleanor said. "Mama said."

"I didn't tell her everything," Jonathan said, "but you should."

"She's too tired," Eleanor said cutting carrots in small strips. "She doesn't want to know."

Frederick came in with Sammy, his eyes blazing.

"So," he said to Eleanor, "did you tell?"

"Tell what?" Eleanor asked.

"You know what."

She didn't reply. She picked up the bowl of cold chicken and carrots and took them to the table on the porch. She could feel Sammy behind her.

"I'm coming for dinner?" he said.

"No," Eleanor said.

"Why?" he asked. "Frederick said it was okay."

And her rage at the morning in the shed exploded. She picked up a glass of water on the table, drank a little and spit it at Sammy Lendering's face.

"I'm going to tell," Sammy said.

"Tell," Eleanor said. "Go right ahead."

Upstairs, when Eleanor went to get her mother for supper, Sara was sleeping, an abandoned sleep, her head fallen against the pillow, her mouth open.

"Mama's not feeling well," she said when they were all at the table.

"I'm sure she's not," Hendrik said with an edge.

"What do you mean?" Jonathan asked, always alert to criticism of his mother.

But Amanda interrupted. "This is a much better dinner than I could ever make, Elly," Amanda said. "You're going to be a wonderful mother."

"I'm not going to be a mother," Eleanor said flatly. "I don't even want to be married."

That night after the dishes were done and Amanda had gone with Eleanor to Weaver's for ice cream, there was another argument between her parents. Eleanor could hear it from her room. So she went upstairs to Nich-o's empty room where the only sounds were the birds in the high branches, an occasional car on P Street, and there she finally fell asleep.

TWO

THE SPRING OF 1954 was cold and rainy, day after gray day of a steady rain, the ground soft and wet underfoot. The back lawns of the Georgetown houses were muddy ponds. The colors of the season, deep roses and purples of rhododendron, pure linen whites of the dogwood and azaleas, the lavender of lilacs, had a particular poignant brilliance in the pale charcoal afternoons, painted colors, unnatural.

Tempers were short. Dampness clung to the inside walls, the drapes, the clothes hanging in closets. There was the smell of mildew, of basement rooms, even out-of-doors.

Eleanor sat behind the shed smoking a cigarette from the pack Frederick had given her in secret for her eighth birthday. She did not inhale. Even so, the smoke in her mouth, in her nose, made her sick and so, alone, without Frederick in attendance, she was practicing for the ceremony which would make her a member of the March Club—the only girl and the youngest next to Nich-o, who was a provisional member since at the time of his ceremony he had thrown up on the sofa in the shed when he smoked a cigarette.

The rites of initiation required smoking two cigarettes, holding a live goldfish in your mouth until it lost consciousness or died, and, for Eleanor, kissing Sammy Lendering, which she planned to forgo, if in fact she decided she wanted to be a member of the club at all.

It was a cool Saturday afternoon and Eleanor had taken advantage of a rare break in the spring rains to leave the house, which was full of workmen preparing for the September opening of the Small Hotel. Albert had bought the house next door on 31st Street. The workmen had demolished the common wall between the houses, so the Yellow House was going to have the space at least to be a small hotel. The rest of the plans, including the displacement of Amanda and Melvina to New York, had been Hendrik's idea. As a result, all winter long with the March children and the workmen and Amanda's unhappiness with moving, the Yellow House had been full of tension.

Eleanor knew too much. Perhaps if she hadn't heard the first argument between her parents about the hotel or opened the linen closet in her parent's bathroom, she wouldn't have been waiting for disaster. But as it was, she had been shot out of childhood while the imaginary walls of her family's life collapsed with the demolition of the Yellow House.

When Amanda and Melvina had moved to New York in early March, Eleanor took over. She got up early, made breakfast for the boys and Hendrik, made the lunches, since all winter Sara faded into the bed sheets, without the energy for keeping house. When she came home from school, seldom with friends because there was such a lot of work to do, Eleanor helped Sara with dinner and the cleaning up and the laundry as well as the plans for the Yellow House as a small hotel. She never talked to her mother about important things, what was on her mind or what had happened in school that day. Sara was too fragile for significant conversations. But Eleanor stayed close to her all afternoon, taking her homework into the room where Sara was reading or talking to workmen, as if Eleanor's physical presence was a kind of back brace to her mother.

She didn't tell Sara the bad news. And there was plenty. Frederick had put his penis into Amy Shell one afternoon in the shed—that news from Nich-o—and although it was something Amy Shell let him do, he had hurt her and she said she was going to tell her mother although, so far, there had been no call from Mrs. Shell. Jonathan was ridiculed at Gordon Junior High for being a "girl" and Frederick, protective of his own reputation, did not come to Jonathan's defense. Eleanor was in terrible trouble in second grade. On her last report card of the year, she had been told she was going to flunk cooperation and responsibility, everything but initiative, and she got poor grades in academic subjects. "Eleanor is difficult and headstrong," the second grade teacher said. Only Nich-o, golden Nich-o, went about his daily life as an angel although certainly he, as well, knew there was trouble afoot and braced for it.

The March Club was in a real sense the brave attempt of the children to put their lives back together in some fashion.

Hendrik worked night and day in the basement writing his book, appearing only for meals, and then he was snappish with Sara, unpleasant with the children. Sara slept late. Some days she spent entirely in her room alone and gradually the March children became parents to themselves.

THREE

ALL OF THE winter of 1954, Amanda and Hendrik had been at odds. Since prison, since "the failure of America" as he referred to it, Hendrik's effervescent optimism had given way to a different kind of energy, still an emotional force in the house but combustible. The children learned to stay out of his way. Sara, accustomed to the particular fury of his morning temper, pretended to be sleeping until he had dressed and gone downstairs to work. But Amanda took him on. She attacked him for Sara's drinking, fighting him in corners of the house, in the kitchen, following him into the basement study, railing at him for the slow erosion of her family.

"You take up all the room," Amanda said. "There's nothing for Sara's life but details."

"You Americans need too much," Hendrik said. "She has

a good home and children, and whatever you might say in your malice, she has a good husband who loves her."

"If it's European love to center your life around yourself, without regard, then you're quite correct," Amanda said. "We Americans need too much."

The fights, too intimate for honest conversation, fell into generalized attacks on America versus Europe. Their sense of failure was profound. They blamed each other.

Meanwhile, Sara slept through the winter, through the reconstruction of the Yellow House as a small hotel.

"If she has to get up every morning for a job," Amanda said to Melvina, "if she has responsibility . . ."

"It won't make a difference," Melvina said darkly. "She could get up now. She's got responsibility. She's got children to tend to."

"Not babies," Amanda said. "They don't need her every day."

"They need her every day," Melvina said in her ice cool voice. "She's just not available."

Amanda couldn't sleep at night. She tried everything to change the state of affairs. She didn't work. Instead she got up early to help Sara with the hotel, doing things that held no interest for her at all—material and reupholstering, lamps, carpets, bedspreads and sheets, the design of rooms. Things that Sara had always loved. It was as if her daughter, still lovely as a girl but fleshy, unnaturally flushed, was a small obstinate child. And Amanda was trying to divert her bad temper with treats.

She begged her to stop drinking.

"Please," she said one afternoon in Adams-Morgan looking for furniture in used-furniture stores, a cache of Albert's money in Sara's pocket. "You are killing yourself."

"I don't know what you're talking about, Amanda," Sara said.

She never confessed to drinking. "I drink occasionally," she'd say. "Never socially."

And that was true. She never drank in public or before dinner with Hendrik, only occasionally, as she said, that anyone could see.

What was peculiar, given the great effort she made to

conceal the evidence of her shame, was the accumulation of empty bottles in the linen cabinet.

"Of course you drink," Amanda said. "You drink in the bathroom by yourself and lock the door."

"I lock the door to the bathroom because I'm a private person living in a houseful of people," Sara said evenly.

"And you drink." Amanda wanted to pull out her hair in frustration.

"Occasionally at night when I have insomnia, I have something to drink."

"You are drunk from five in the evening on," Amanda said.

"Don't shout, Mama," Sara said. "I'm thinking of getting vitamin B-twelve shots. Jane has them and she says they're very good for exhaustion."

"You're not exhausted," Amanda said.

Amanda couldn't help herself. That afternoon she brought up the subject of drinking in the kitchen in front of Melvina.

"Tonight for once don't go upstairs and have a drink in secret before dinner," she said. "Please."

Melvina, cutting the fat off the pork chops, shook her head.

"Sara, please," Amanda said.

Sara looked up at her mother from Melvina's rocking chair where she was balancing her checkbook. There was a vacant look in her eyes, a looseness about her lips.

"What did you say, Mama?" she asked.

"Oh damn," Amanda said quietly.

Sara shook her head, a small smile on her face.

"Mama," she said very sweetly. "You have such an odd idea about me."

Amanda lost her temper. She picked up the stack of plates on the counter for dinner and smashed them on the floor just as Eleanor came in the kitchen door from sledding. She ran up the back steps to her room on the third floor, turned on the light, took the photographs framed and matted off the wall and slammed them to the floor where the glass shattered—the picture of the American soldiers on their bellies crawling across the open field to Belleau

Wood, the picture at Château-Thierry of Lincoln Draper, the photograph from World War II, the jacket of *Flat Mouth: An Ordinary Life*, the picture from the Depression of Bonita's family, her father on the roof, the pictures from the Midwest. She smashed them all. They lay around the floor of her room covered in splintered glass. Then she lifted the haunted picture of Sara's father out of the rubble.

What a stupid thing to think, to actually believe she could have raised a child alone. She shook the glass off the handsome face of Lincoln Draper, ripped the picture in pieces, and dropped them in the wastebasket. She wanted to shake Sara, shake her and shake her, until the bile of growing up was shaken out and she was a perfect little girl again.

She heard Eleanor running up the steps, heard her cautious knock.

"What happened?" Eleanor asked when Amanda opened the bedroom door.

"What happened is I lost my temper." Amanda picked up the photographs from the floor, shook off the glass into the wastebasket.

"What's going to happen now?" Eleanor asked out of breath.

"Now," Amanda said, her voice even, "I'm going to clean up the glass, shake out my rug, go downstairs, and sweep up the glass in the kitchen. Then," Amanda ran her fingers through Eleanor's hair, "we're going to have dinner. Pork chops and mashed potatoes."

"Melvina's already cleaned up the broken glass in the kitchen," Eleanor said.

Amanda took a broom from the upstairs closet, picked up the photographs, laid them on her bed and swept the floor.

"Father came upstairs from his study after the dishes got broken and said you are going to move to New York."

"He did?" Amanda asked.

"Are you?" Eleanor asked. "He said tomorrow."

"Not tomorrow, darling," Amanda said.

"If you move, I'll be sick," Eleanor said helping Amanda with a dustpan.

"Whatever I do," Amanda said, a certain familiar lightness in her voice, "I will try not to make you sick."

Later, after supper, almost an ordinary evening, Hendrik asked Amanda to take a walk while Sara put the children to bed.

It was early March, very cold and clear, and they walked a long time before either of them spoke.

"I hear from Eleanor you are asking me to leave," Amanda said finally.

"Once we have this hotel, we will be too crowded."

"You might remember, it's my house," Amanda said.

"I had thought you wanted to live in New York."

"Sometimes," Amanda wrapped her scarf around her neck. "Sometimes I want to live here."

"It would be better for Sara, Amanda," Hendrik said. His voice was genuinely concerned. "We are, the two of us, too much for her. She needs not to be between us." He laid his hand on her cheek. Before she was even aware of what he was about, he had pulled her face toward him.

He didn't actually kiss her. She slapped him before he had a chance.

"You haven't turned out as well as I had hoped," she said and, to her astonishment, she was weeping. "You've turned out terribly."

They had walked a long way, all the way up the hill from Georgetown to the Washington Cathedral. The night was starless with only a slender moon, very dark, and they walked home, shoulder to shoulder, their hands deep in their pockets, Amanda's anger subsiding in the cold.

"I'm sorry," Hendrik said.

She understood it was about Sara that he was sorry. Not about trying to kiss her.

"Never mind," Amanda said softly. "We both failed."

"Not forever," Hendrik said with his old familiar optimism.

"God, I hope not forever."

The lights were on in the house when Amanda and Hendrik came back after midnight and Sara was sitting on the steps, still dressed, entirely sober.

"I hate it when the two of you go off together—as if I'm a child whose life must be discussed in private."

"You weren't the subject of our discussion," Hendrik said. "We were discussing Amanda's leaving."

"Good," Sara said fiercely. "It's way past time. I'm too old to have a mother hovering over my shoulder, full of disappointment."

"I'm not full of disappointment," Amanda said. "I'm—" but she didn't know what to say. Disappointment was not a word with sufficient strength for what she felt about her daughter's disillusion. The word was more like heartbroken.

She walked up the steps, climbing over the one where Sara was sitting, up the second set of stairs to the third floor, her heart beating hard in her throat.

The light was on in her room, the door open, and Eleanor was sitting on her bed.

"May I spend the night?"

"No," Amanda said with more irritation than she had intended. "It's after midnight."

"Mama's furious at me."

Amanda took off her coat and hat, her boots, unbuttoned her heavy cardigan.

"I'm tired," she said. "We'll talk about this tomorrow."

"She said I love you better than her." Elly was unwilling to give up.

Amanda put on her flannel pajamas, took down her hair which she wore sometimes in a long braid wrapped around her head, sometimes in a bun.

"I don't," Eleanor said. "I love you equal."

"Of course you don't," Amanda said. "Now go back to bed."

"I'm small," Eleanor said moving over to the far side of the bed. "I'll sleep on the inside. Besides, I threw up on my bed."

Amanda climbed underneath the covers, turned off the bedside light. "It's very difficult to be a mother," she said. "You have no idea."

"It's very difficult to be a daughter too," Eleanor said, situating herself next to Amanda.

"I was a daughter for only three years," Amanda said.

"I've been a mother for thirty-five so I know much less about being a daughter."

"Mama told me your mother died of your being born," Eleanor said.

"I suppose that is how it seems," Amanda said.

It had occurred to her that one way or another daughters kill their mothers, eventually, unintentionally—and in her case it had been too early.

FOUR

THE SMALL HOTEL opened on the first of September, 1954, with six bedrooms defined by Sara's gift for intimacy, her sense of personal detail. The Marches didn't advertise except by word of mouth and by the middle of September they were already booked up through October.

What Sara had wanted was to recapture the years of the war with soldiers passing through. She wanted the excitement of *The Honest Truth* when the house was full of students and young writers and people looking for conversation. She wanted energy around her like wind, the sense of being needed, even the satisfaction of serving.

"I don't want you to be in the kitchen," Hendrik said. "It should be as if you are giving a party."

And for quite a long time, it was exactly like a party every night.

* * *

We are all well and happy, Eleanor wrote on December 25, 1954, in the five-year diary Jonathan had given her for Christmas of her ninth year.

> *We live in a hotel on the third floor which has been made into an apartment. At night we have dinner with guests at a round table next to a window so we can see the garden and the shed. But we of course don't have to pay to eat here because it's our hotel. Actually Mama's*

hotel. Daddy writes his book about the Russians and Germans and only eats here and spends the night.

Nothing bad has happened since September when the hotel opened except Mr. Barter from New York City died of a heart attack in the room Mama calls the lily of the valley room because of the wallpaper and he had to be taken out during breakfast, so of course I couldn't eat. We have had only one mean person named Mrs. Shneider and she argued that the bill was too much and Mama said okay and Daddy said the bill was what the bill was. Later Mama cried and said she wanted to close the hotel. But by morning she was fine.

Mama is not as tired as she used to be. Actually she only gets tired at night after the boys have gone to bed—only me awake listening for things. Good-bye for now. I'll talk to you tomorrow.

Your friend, Eleanor Steward March.

At night, after the dinner dishes were done, the children in bed, the house locked, Sara could not sleep.

"If you'd come to bed earlier," she said to Hendrik when he complained that she was always locked in the bathroom when he came to bed. "It's after midnight when you finally stop working."

"I don't need sleep," Hendrik said, kissing her forehead.

"Kiss my lips," she said petulantly. She pulled his head toward her. "I hate to be kissed as if I'm a little girl."

He laughed. He always laughed if she took exception.

"So I will come to bed earlier, all right, my treasure," he said.

But his mind was on his book, she supposed, or some idea he had for an article. When they made love, he was either intense with need or else abstracted.

Most nights, Sara was too agitated to sleep when Hendrik finally did come to bed full of conversation about the Germans and the Russians, about President Eisenhower and the end of Senator McCarthy. She would wait until Hendrik turned off the light, wait for his sleep to deepen, and then she'd creep down the hall to the bathroom right across from Eleanor's room where Eleanor lay wide awake under the blankets waiting for the soft pad of her mother's bare feet down the hall.

"Why?" Hendrik asked, awake one night when Sara came back to bed.

"I can't sleep," Sara replied. "Sometimes I'm awake until dawn."

What she felt was hunger, but unspecific. She wanted something. Was it something warm to drink or ice cream or chocolate or a light lemon cake? Something sweet, certainly. Or her mother inexactly—Amanda but softer, less obtrusive than her mother was. She knew she wanted to make love but not the swift coming together she was accustomed to—and then sleep. She wanted to make love endlessly, in and out of sleep, half awake, half dead.

"Drink keeps you awake," Hendrik said.

"I have a cavity inside of me," Sara said, turning off her light. "That's what keeps me awake."

She waited until his breathing deepened and then she slid quietly out of bed and tiptoed down the hall past Eleanor's room.

FIVE

INITIALLY, ELEANOR WAS very pleased that her uncle Albert was spending such a lot of time at the Small Hotel. She liked him. He was tentative with the children, which gave them a sense of their importance to him. His sharp sometimes bitter wit, which had always made people angry, expanded to a genuine warm humor with children. Besides, his presence made Sara happy.

Since the beginning of the summer of 1955, Sara had been different. For one, she had stopped slipping into the bathroom for extended periods before she went to bed. Eleanor no longer even bothered to stay awake to check on her.

The success of Billy Tudor had made a difference in Albert's character. Unlike Hendrik, he had not expected good fortune in his life, so when it came he was grateful and turned from dark distrust to a surprising ease. It was that man who came in the afternoon after a morning of writing Billy Tudor—Jane at work, sometimes until late at night—to visit Sara and check up on the Small Hotel, which was largely his investment.

Eleanor liked coming home from school and seeing them in the kitchen with a cup of tea, her mother flushed and talkative, her voice pitched a little higher than usual.

"Sit down and tell me everything that happened today," Sara would say.

Albert always took an interest in her studies. He had a specific question to ask and advice to give on what she should read. He seemed to have all the free time in the world, as Frederick remarked one evening at dinner.

"Doesn't Uncle Albert have a real job?" he asked. "He's never working."

"He has a real job," Sara said. "But like your father, he can work at his own pace."

"It's not like me at all," Hendrik said quickly. "He's writing light, entertaining books about spies and I'm writing a history." There was in the tone of his voice the whine of a defensive position. "He can invent his book and I have to work long hours because of the research."

"Of course," Sara said softly, touching Hendrik on the arm. "It really takes Albert no time at all to write his Billy Tudor books."

"And why is he so rich?" Nich-o asked since it was well known among the March children that Albert was in part responsible for the Small Hotel, which was, until Hendrik finished his history of the Germans and Russians during the Second World War, responsible for their support. "Will we be rich when you've finished your book?"

Hendrik shrugged. "People like spy books," Hendrik said. "They are an escape from the real world."

"What your father is writing is a book people will go back to read again and again for information and intelligence," Sara said kindly.

Her relationship with Hendrik had changed in the last

few months. There was a note of artificiality, an unintentional subtle condescension since he had lost his optimism, really since America, from which Albert never expected a thing, had let him down.

"People read Uncle Albert's books only once for entertainment."

"Doesn't it make him angry that he's simple and you're not?" Frederick asked. Even Eleanor could tell that Frederick was searching for a secret which he sensed—which they all sensed—but could not name.

"Why should he be angry?" Hendrik asked. "He's very rich."

"Well, he has enough free time to spend every afternoon at the hotel," Frederick said, measuring his words. "No matter what time I come home from school, he's here."

"Not every afternoon, darling," Sara said.

"He wasn't here yesterday," Jonathan said, jumping in as he always did when his mother was in some kind of danger.

Hendrik looked up from his dinner.

"I didn't know Albert was here so frequently," he said. "I knew he stopped by to check on the hotel from time to time."

"More milk?" Eleanor said quickly. "Anyone want more milk?"

No one replied.

"Nich-o?"

"No."

"No thank you, darling," Sara said and for the moment the conversation slipped away.

But that night, Eleanor overhead an argument in her parents' room and later Sara came out of her bedroom and spent the night on the couch in the living room.

"What were you trying to do last night?" Jonathan asked Frederick on the way to school. "Uncle Albert makes Mama happy. He pays attention to her."

Frederick shrugged. "He pays too much attention."

"So?"

"So I don't like it," Frederick said.

But for a time, a long time, almost a year until just before Eleanor's tenth birthday, the subject of Albert did not come up in a serious way again.

SIX

IN THE FALL of 1955, Amanda and Melvina moved into a larger apartment two doors down on West 13th Street from Amanda's old apartment because it had a bedroom for Melvina, who had been sleeping on a couch in the living room. Melvina went to Macy's and got some blue printed chintz for curtains, recovered an armchair, and made a coverlet. She was very pleased with the results. On the walls, she had pictures of Bonita and one of her late husband, two colored prints of spring bouquets with tulips and daffodils and lilacs, a framed picture of Jesus as well as a crucifix over her bed. Amanda was glad to see her take an interest. When the possibility of New York had come up in the first place, Melvina had said no, not on her life. Why would she want to live in a place as dirty as New York City when she could live with her sister who had a garden out front of her house on U Street?

"My apartment has a garden out back," Amanda said. "And there's a Catholic church on the corner so you could meet people."

"I don't go to the Catholic church for a social life," Melvina said. "I go for God as you certainly know. For a social life I go to the Baptist church and there are no Baptists in New York."

But Amanda found a Baptist church in Greenwich Village, so by the end of the first year in the city, Melvina had begun to adjust.

When Hendrik had said there would be no room on the third floor of the Small Hotel for Amanda, he included Melvina as well.

"The work that needs to be done in the hotel will be too

strenuous for Melvina," he said. "Besides, there is the problem of space."

"I don't know what she can do," Amanda said. "She's lived in this house for thirty-five years. She must be almost seventy."

"Take her to New York," Hendrik said.

"Maybe I will," Amanda said. As soon as Hendrik had suggested that Melvina move with her, it struck her as the right thing to do. She was glad to have Melvina's sharp-edged temper to combat her old age.

"What am I going to do in a place like New York?" Melvina asked.

"Help me," Amanda said.

"I'm done cleaning houses," Melvina said. "Done with that for life."

"Help me with my work," Amanda said. "With photographs."

"I don't even like those photographs you take. They're too gloomy. I like colored pictures."

"You don't have to like them to help me."

So Melvina agreed to try New York City. "But if I don't like it, I'm coming home to my sister's on U Street."

At first Melvina was disgruntled, even after she met some women at the Baptist church who invited her over for suppers on Sunday nights and to watch "Mama" on Fridays.

She said the city smelled bad and she'd seen a rat in the garden and there were no good markets to buy a chicken and none of the right vegetables—no greens. But gradually she and Amanda settled into a life together, eating supper when Amanda got home from teaching at New York University, talking sometimes late into the night, living in a small space comfortably and out of one another's way.

Amanda had in mind a new book of photographs about women, all ages of women in the twentieth century—men too of course, but men as seen through the eyes of women, like her pictures of a doomed Lincoln Draper at Château-Thierry. She had begun to imagine the book just after the move to the new apartment. And then one morning in the fall of 1955, she woke up early as usual, a hot morning, very foggy, and she noticed that her vision had altered since the night before. Or had it been in the process of changing? Her pupils were not dilating in the dim light. She could not see well.

She went into Melvina's bedroom and sat down on the end of her bed.

"It's lucky you moved to New York with me," she said. "If I go blind, I'll need your help taking pictures."

"If you go blind, I figure you won't be taking pictures," Melvina said.

"I'll always take pictures," Amanda said.

She lay down on the twin bed across from Melvina.

"I've been thinking of a new book just this week," she said. "Mainly women."

"Given the choice, I'd leave men out myself," Melvina said. "They get in my way."

"I don't mean leave them out, of course," Amanda said, preoccupied with her own imaginings.

"Well, if you go blind and I end up taking the pictures for this book, they won't be in black and white and there won't be any men," Melvina said. "Only I do like Mr. Jackson who comes to the Baptist suppers. I'd include a picture of him. And my late husband I suppose, especially since he's dead."

"I never really understood why you took Joseph Jones back after he deserted you," Amanda said.

"He was my husband for better or for worse," Melvina said climbing out of bed. "No one promised me there'd be more better than worse. And they were right not to bother." She sat down beside Amanda. "Now let me check your eyes in the light and see what's happening to the black circles in the center."

"Don't worry. I'm not going blind," Amanda said. "My eyes just have a veil over them."

And by the time she had finished breakfast, the day had lightened and she could see without difficulty.

Nevertheless, she worried. Her mind was seldom free after that, from the memory of temporary blindness. She would have to get to work quickly on the new book, just in case.

SEVEN

ELEANOR'S TENTH BIRTHDAY was to be a very big event, a surprise. But she could sense the secret in the air and was prepared. She was not, however, at all prepared for what happened with her mother and Uncle Albert on the day before her birthday.

It was late April and unseasonably warm—already the azaleas and dogwood and lilac were gone, the rhododendron in full bloom, and Eleanor was spending the afternoons in the shed to be out of the way of the business of the Small Hotel.

As of the spring of 1956, the shed was off limits to everyone except members of the March Club, which now included friends of Frederick, friends of Nich-o, Posy Franklin, Jonathan's one friend, and Eleanor, who had passed the initiation except that she had by accident swallowed the goldfish before it died.

This particular morning, the day before her birthday, she was spending all day in the shed. She had sent Nich-o to school with a note she had written imitating Sara's handwriting, claiming she was ill with strep throat. Fourth grade had been another difficult year. She was restless, uninterested in her studies. She had difficulty sitting still in class and was often in trouble for disturbing the instructions from teachers.

But the real change which perplexed Eleanor more than it pleased her was that she had suddenly turned into the leader of the fourth grade. It was not a role she wanted but she had no choice. The students wanted her. She was elected president of the class in September and captain of the patrols in the spring. People looked to her for opinions, copied the way she dressed, the lower register of her voice, her slow, deliberate way of speaking. At one point, just after Christmas vacation, several of the girls came to school with a birthmark in the shape of a peanut painted on their cheeks.

"I don't understand what the appeal is, Eleanor," the fourth grade teacher had said in early April. "You never get a grade higher than a C and you do extremely poorly in cooperation."

"You don't fit in," the gym teacher said. And she was right. But the fact was that people were drawn to her precisely for that reason. She didn't seem to need the girlish associations, the whispered secrets vital to her peers.

"I don't actually get it," she said to Nicholas who was in his last year of Key Elementary and familiar with the rising leaders of the younger classes. "Last year I was considered difficult and rebellious and stupid and this year everyone wants to be exactly like me."

"Probably not exactly," Nicholas said. "I don't think they want to be stupid."

"I'm not stupid," Eleanor said. "I just don't study my life away like you do."

"You boss people around," Frederick said from his desk as president of the March Club. "Even us."

"It's not bossy," Jonathan said. "Elly's just one of those people like Papa."

"Like Papa used to be," Frederick corrected. "Before jail."

"She's like Amanda," Nich-o said. "General Amanda Steward of the U.S. Standing Army."

"Anyway," Jonathan said, "I, for one, think it's very nice that you're president of everything, Elly."

"And it compensates for the D's in academics and poor minus in deportment," Frederick said.

It was for the poor minus that Eleanor had sent Nicholas to school with a note about her absence. She had received a letter from the principal which said, "A poor minus in cooperation is not satisfactory for the president of the fourth grade. Please see me tomorrow at 9." On the way home, tossing the note in the trash can outside of Little Hamburgers, she decided to take the day off.

Eleanor was not rebellious in a conventional sense at all. She simply had her own sense of order. She was like her father in many ways—determined as he was, single-minded. She was of all the children most troubled by what had happened to Hendrik—the way he had grown rigid, even bitter, since jail.

"He's not so funny anymore, is he?" she asked her mother once.

"Not so funny," Sara agreed.

"How come?" Eleanor asked. "Because of prison?"

"Because he believed in America and was let down," Sara said. "He believes too much."

"I suppose that's true of me too," Eleanor said, intending by her defense to protect her father against what Sara said critically of Hendrik.

"Yes," Sara agreed, "you believe too much as well."

On the morning before her birthday, Eleanor lay on the floor of the shed reading Nancy Drew. She didn't want to be seen since she was skipping school and often the guests at the Small Hotel came into the back garden after breakfast and her mother might come out to cut the daffodils to fill the vases in the dining room. But no one came out. By noon, the beds were usually made, the tables set for dinner, the dinner half-prepared in the kitchen. Her father would be at the Library of Congress to which he had moved in order to use their extensive resources. Her mother would be at the market, perhaps the hairdresser's, since lately she was taking good care of herself. She had lost weight, cut her hair shoulder length, and wore makeup, even on her eyes. The cook, who prepared the evening meal for the guests, would be free from noon to three. So the house was certainly empty and Eleanor was starving.

She opened the door to the shed, checked the garden, and went up the back steps to the kitchen, thinking about a tuna fish sandwich and chocolate chip cookies. She peered quickly into the kitchen which she thought was empty. Then she leaned down to get the key to the back door kept under the mat and when she looked up, there was Albert, his side to her, standing next to the entrance to the dining room. And pressed against him, in a picture she would not forget for the rest of her life, her head tilted back, her lips on his lips, was Sara, her mother. Sara March. Mrs. Hendrik March.

Eleanor slid down to the ground so they wouldn't see her through the kitchen window.

Later, she remembered everything—the dress her mother had been wearing, pale rose, and high-heeled black patent leather shoes, her golden hair full and wavy, her hand on the back of his head and his hand, his right hand, against her cheek. Eleanor lay on the couch in the shed with the picture of her mother shimmering across her eyelids, over and over again, like a newsreel repeated in Technicolor.

That night when Sara came in to kiss her good night, even the familiar smell of her, the light sweet scent, seemed to have mingled with the sour odor of Albert's European cigarettes. She lay very still with her eyes closed.

"Tomorrow when you wake up, you'll be ten years old," Sara said.

"If you're planning a party," Eleanor said, hoping her voice wouldn't catch in her throat, "please cancel it."

"Of course, darling," Sara said smiling, misunderstanding entirely. "I'll cancel it first thing tomorrow."

There was a party of course with puppeteers and games and twenty friends, but Eleanor didn't remember it, even as it was happening.

EIGHT

ELEANOR WAS SIXTEEN before Hendrik, or anyone else for that matter, discovered the secret she had witnessed the day before her tenth birthday.

It was the Christmas of 1962, and the country, in love with itself, in love with its young king and the glittering assemblage of his court in Washington, his beautiful wife, lay on a precipice like a giant rock shaken loose from its foundations. There was no sense of the danger to come among Americans, only great optimism and excitement at the beginning of a new age.

At the Small Hotel, daily life for the Marches had been sweet, almost carefree, for several years. In the winter of 1962, Frederick was in college at the University of Michigan where he was editor of the school newspaper, outspoken in his editorials, considered courageous and talented, taking out his personal anger at his father's misfortunes in liberal ideology. The times had swung around to Hendrik's point of view again. Jonathan had developed a mild heart problem when he left home for the Rhode Island School of Design to study graphics and had returned in his first semester to make a career as a writer of crossword puzzles. And Nicholas was a freshman at Yale, uncomplicated, solid, at home with conventional ambitions.

At fifteen, Eleanor had started Sidwell Friends School. Sara insisted after Eleanor fell desperately in love with Jack Richardson, who attended Gordon Junior High from the boys' reformatory on Wisconsin Avenue where he was incarcerated for stealing a Cadillac from the parking lot at K Street and 14th and assaulting the cashier at G. C. Murphy's.

What had caught Eleanor's attention about Jack Richardson in the first place had occurred after a basketball game between Gordon Junior High and Alice Deal, when Jack lost his temper and smashed his fist through the enormous glass window in the gym. He was taken by ambulance to the Georgetown Hospital, blood covering the front of his white basketball jersey.

"I don't understand what is courageous about slamming your hand through a window," Nich-o said.

"You didn't see it," Eleanor said. "He was so controlled he didn't even look like anything bad had happened and his hand was spurting blood."

"Good news," Nicholas said at dinner. "Eleanor has fallen in love with a criminal."

"I hope he's a successful criminal," Hendrik said.

"He isn't a criminal," Eleanor said. "He's had a hard life and today, when he got injured, he was extremely brave."

But Sara took Eleanor's love affair seriously.

"I'm afraid Elly has the temperament for trouble," she said to Hendrik that night.

Hendrik shrugged. "Women like violence," he said. "They are fond of soldiers and guns, especially when they're young. I wouldn't worry," he said. "She's a passionate girl."

"That's exactly why I am worried," Sara said. "She's too passionate."

"You're worried about this juvenile delinquent?"

"About this kind of attraction," Sara said with an instinct for her daughter's vulnerabilities.

In general, however, life at the Marches was easy and pleasant. The Small Hotel was almost always full. Hendrik's book on the Russians and Germans was published by Alfred A. Knopf in 1960 to serious reviews and modest sales, and Albert continued to spend the afternoons with Sara at the Small Hotel, coming occasionally for dinner with Jane if she wasn't working late.

Eleanor seldom thought about her mother and Albert together and when she did, it was as if she had remembered a growth in her throat, unobtrusive unless she thought about it.

Nothing prepared her, however, or any of the March children for what happened on Christmas afternoon 1962.

The Small Hotel was closed for the holidays. Hendrik
had taken a week off from his new book *The German
Character*. Amanda was visiting and the boys were home
from school. There was no sign in the air to suggest trouble. Sara was at ease with her mother for the first time
since Amanda had moved to New York. She was not
drinking at all. Frederick was in particularly high spirits
since he had been hired by the *St. Louis Post-Dispatch* to
begin work as soon as he graduated and Jonathan had a
girlfriend, quite a pretty maternal sort of girl named Molly
Saucer who worked as a waitress at the Small Hotel.
Nich-o was Nich-o, steady, predictable, slightly acerbic,
but only with Eleanor.

It was a mild gray December day with the forecast of
rain, and Frederick had bought a case of champagne for
the occasion. The March family was gathered in the main
parlor of the hotel, a large, cheerful room with fireplaces
at either end. Eleanor was sitting on a velvet settee, her
feet on Amanda's lap, Melvina was at Mass, Jane was re-
covering from the flu and coming later. But everyone else
was in the parlor, the boys merry with drink. Frederick
opened the champagne, filled the glasses, and gave the
first toast to Albert, whose fourth Billy Tudor book had
been published in time for Christmas.

"Billy Tudor rises again," Frederick said.

"To Uncle Albert," Nicholas said and there was a mur-
mur of voices as everyone raised his glass.

"To Uncle Albert."

No one noticed Hendrik standing by the fireplace, his
hand resting on the mantel and around the stem of his
glass. Just as people were lifting their glasses to drink,
Hendrik stepped toward Albert, swung his arm back, and
hit his brother directly in the mouth. Albert stumbled, put
his hand to his bleeding mouth, and slid down between the
couch where Amanda sat with Eleanor and the chair where
Sara was sitting.

It happened too quickly, too unexpectedly for the cele-
brating March family to react.

In a voice of surprising steadiness, Hendrik said he was
going for a walk and would be back for Christmas dinner.

In German, which no one in the family understood, he said something to Albert about Sara. "Be out of here when I come back," he said in English. "And don't come back."

Sara was not deeply sorry to have Albert leave. She hadn't actually loved him. The interest he took in her felt like love. Somehow she did not have, as Amanda seemed to, the resources to feel clearly about herself without the affirmation of someone else. He made her feel beautiful and desired.

On Christmas night, with the children and Amanda in the kitchen munching on the Christmas dinner which never got served, Sara went upstairs to change to nightclothes. She looked at herself in the mirror over the dresser to see if the effect of the scene before dinner was visible in her face, and she was astonished at what she saw—the high color in her cheeks, the brightness of her eyes, the life in her face. She looked beautiful. Later, the house quiet, Hendrik made love to her, and for the first time since the war Sara had a sense that he had claimed her.

That night Eleanor lay in bed and waited for her mother to come out of the bathroom. She was woozy from the champagne, of which she'd drunk a lot. No one got around to sitting down for Christmas dinner but picked instead at the turkey and had spoonfuls of potatoes and beans in the kitchen, wary with one another.

Very late, Nicholas came in and sat down on the bottom of Eleanor's bed.

"What are you thinking?" he asked.

"Not much."

"That's not true," Nich-o said. "You're thinking plenty. We all are."

"I suppose I'm thinking Papa seemed himself again today. Like he used to be when I was small," she said.

"You're not furious at him?" Nicholas asked, surprised.

"Albert must have done something to make him very angry," Eleanor said.

"Well, I'm furious and so are the rest of us," Nich-o said. "He ruined Christmas."

"Maybe," Eleanor said.

Nicholas shrugged. "Night, Elly," he said.

"Night, Nicholas," she said softly.

On the first of January, the Small Hotel was closed and shortly afterward workmen were back again separating the two houses so the one on 31st Street which Albert had bought could be put up for sale.

NINE

AMANDA AND MELVINA left New York City in late January 1963, just after Amanda's sixty-third birthday. Melvina was seventy-five, thin and stooped to five feet six with occasional angina. But her eyes were good. Excellent. She had never needed glasses and she could read with ease and did so every night the small print in her Catholic missal.

"I'll probably have a heart attack," Melvina said when they were packing up the New York apartment to sublet it for a year.

"You might," Amanda agreed.

"We'll be in one of those towns you like to go to without hospitals," Melvina said.

"You don't have to go," Amanda said.

"How're you going to see if I don't go?"

"I see fine," Amanda said. "I have no real difficulty."

"Tell the truth," Melvina said gruffly. "You're going blind and you need me to come along for your pictures."

"The edges are blurred in what I see. Otherwise, I see perfectly well."

The doctors had not been able to determine Amanda's condition. She wore bifocals, but both in reading and seeing long distance her peripheral vision was blurred. The objects around the edges of the frame were obscured and month to month she saw a little less clearly.

"So do you need me or not?" Melvina asked. "I'm not in the mood for a vacation."

"I need you," Amanda said reluctantly.

* * *

They traveled by train. Amanda had chosen towns, one or two a month—Richmond, Virginia; Dayton, Ohio; Chicago; St. Louis; Bismarck, North Dakota; Gary, Indiana; Poplar Bluff, Missouri; Oskaloosa, Iowa. August in Ashland with Flat Mouth as usual, and in August Melvina would fly home to spend the month in Nashville with her sister Grace.

Amanda was looking for women in particular who struck her fancy.

"What do you want to find?" Melvina asked.

"I don't know exactly," Amanda said. "I'll know when I see it."

She selected the towns they were visiting not only because they represented a broad geography of America but because she knew someone there, another photographer usually, or his family, someone professional—all of her friendships were professional—and that person put her in touch with families. It was slow work. She knew the look of the book she wanted to photograph but she couldn't give a name to it except that it would have something to do with mothers and daughters, one generation after the next.

They went first to Richmond and stayed in the house of Melvina's cousins since Melvina couldn't stay in a hotel in the South with Amanda—or even in the house which belonged to Blue Bones's sister, whom Amanda had met on the trip during the Depression and with whom she had kept in touch after Blue Bones died of heart failure in Paris after the war.

In the mornings, they walked the streets of a small, white, middle-class section of Richmond. They followed the schoolchildren to school, the fathers in the neighborhood to bus stops, the mothers, mostly housewives, shopping.

Almost immediately Amanda was taken with a family called Stark whom Blue Bones's sister knew from church—the daughter in particular who was overweight, with a striking face lost in too much flesh, restless for a southern girl.

"I don't know what you like about that girl," Melvina said.

"Watch her," Amanda said. "She pays attention to everything around."

"How do you know she's paying attention when you don't know her?" Melvina said. "And what use is paying attention anyway unless you're crossing the street?"

What interested Amanda about the Starks was their unease. It was what she felt in America. Still felt, grown-up, unsettled. There seemed to be a kind of truth to it.

Amanda worked in a hurry. It was not that her sight was bad but she sensed that she could wake on any given morning and it would be. She felt as if she should be in a hurry.

"Help me with the edges," Amanda would say to Melvina, and Melvina would lean over Amanda, look through the lens, and catch the subject in the landscape of trees or a room of furniture, any busy scene. Amanda could see the focus of her photographs but her vision faded as the scene in the lens spread out.

One afternoon photographing Kathy Stark, Amanda discovered a new perspective which seemed to her, once she had developed the pictures, to capture the fractured quality of lives in America in the twentieth century.

Kathy was in the bathroom on the second floor of her house getting ready to meet her friends at the mall. Unaware of Amanda's presence on the steps, she was putting on makeup—her small plump face pressed up against the mirror, kissing her own lips in the reflection, her eyes lowered—her bare feet were pointed in toward each other like a child's, her mother's tan stockings on the floor beside her. She wore gray gym shorts and the tops of flannel shorty pajamas. She was a picture of a young girl at the cusp, her baby flesh giving way to small breasts. The face in the mirror understood there was something in store but, misunderstanding sexuality, she beckoned herself.

There wasn't sufficient distance from the top of the stairs where Amanda was standing to capture the reflected image in the bathroom mirror. So she shot the photograph in three parts—the child's bare feet and the bottom of the gym shorts, the flannel top with her small breasts, and the vamping baby face.

"It's crazy if you ask me, which you didn't, taking pictures of somebody's feet or the middle of them," Melvina said. "What kind of sense does that make? I like people whole and not broke up."

"Most of the people in the book will be whole, but broken up is what Americans are now," Amanda said. "Time melts together," she said. "The lines have gone."

"My life used to be perfectly organized. I had good luck and bad luck but not complications until Bonita."

Always at the end of the day when Melvina was tired, she brought up Bonita.

Bonita had gone to live in El Paso with her brothers and sisters. She was married to a Mexican man and had two sons, or so the notes at Christmas said, impersonal except for the *x*'s for kisses at the signature.

"Bonita didn't work out as we had hoped," Amanda said.

"Nothing does," Melvina said. "Especially children."

Usually, however, Melvina was high-spirited and good company. They worked all day together, bickering only occasionally, and at night they sat in bed, Melvina reading her missal or the *Catholic Digest*, Amanda transcribing her mother's letters to a tape recorder in case she did lose her sight entirely and could no longer read.

Melvina paid no attention to the reading of the letters, but one night Amanda sensed that she was listening. In all the years she had known Melvina, more than forty, she had never seen a show of emotion except anger, and she stopped reading the letter aloud, turned off the tape recorder.

"Read it," Melvina said thickly. "Just read that letter to me."

"The whole thing?"

"From the beginning," Melvina said.

So Amanda read.

Dear Mama, Anna had written on January 1, 1902.

> *Today is Amanda's second birthday. Since I've been ill, she has been like a baby kangaroo in the pocket of my bed sheets and today she climbed out of my bed after lunch, marched out of the room, and when I called her, she didn't answer or come back. It plunged me into a despondent afternoon from which I'll have to recover because I very well know she has done with running to my call.*

> *Yr. loving daughter,*
> *Anna*

TEN

In early January 1963, the day before Frederick was leaving for his last semester at the University of Michigan, the membership of the diminishing March Club gathered to finish up the Christmas champagne which had not been drunk by Hendrik and Frederick after Uncle Albert was sent away.

Amanda and Melvina had left on their photographic journey around America, Albert had gone with Jane to the Virgin Islands for an extended vacation, and the Small Hotel was reassuming the look of a single-family house.

"So what do you think happened between Papa and Uncle Albert, El?" Frederick asked, lying on the desk Jonathan had set up, on a large crossword puzzle half-finished on butcher paper.

"You saw what happened," Eleanor said. "Papa hit Uncle Albert."

"Why is the question," Nich-o said. "I asked Amanda before she left. 'Families are very complicated,' she said. 'Great,' I said. 'Any more good news?' I think Amanda's getting old."

"No, she's not," Eleanor said. "She's protecting Mama."

"From what?"

"From what happened," Eleanor said.

Jonathan said he felt sick. He thought he was getting the flu, he said, but he stayed nevertheless on the couch resting against his girlfriend, the former waitress Molly Saucer.

"What are you talking about, Eleanor?" Nich-o asked. "Papa and Uncle Albert have had a long-standing argument from boyhood. They've always been on the edge of fighting. At least that's what Papa said."

"So?" Eleanor shrugged. "Then you know everything."

"What are you implying, El?" Frederick asked.

"I'm implying nothing," Eleanor said.

"She's implying that Mama and Uncle Albert had an affair," Jonathan said quietly.

"Are you kidding?" Frederick said.

"You thought so yourself, Frederick," Eleanor said. "You were always furious at their relationship."

"Not possible," Frederick said crossly. "Completely impossible."

"Do you think so, Elly?" Nicholas asked, his voice breaking.

"Get it together, Nich-o," Frederick said.

"I don't know anything about what went on between Mama and Albert," Eleanor said. "But the reason Papa hit Albert was that he thought Mama was having an affair."

"Jesus," Frederick said. "Does anybody else think that? Really think that?"

"Let's drop the subject," Nich-o said. "I don't want to talk about it."

"Then exit the building, Nich-o," Frederick said. "That's what we're talking about."

"I don't want you guys to talk about it either," Nicholas said. "It's disrespectful."

"Of whom?" Frederick asked.

"Of Mama, of course," Nicholas said and he did leave because he was weeping.

"So, Jonny. What do you think?" Frederick asked.

"I think Eleanor's right," Jonathan said.

"So it's only me and Nich-o in the dark while the March family is going merrily to hell," Frederick said.

"Jesus Christ." And he left the shed, not toward the house but toward the alley where the car was parked.

By that spring, life for Eleanor March had changed entirely. Her brothers were back at college. Jonathan, since Molly Saucer, no longer counted for company. The Small Hotel had closed and her parents had fallen in love again. Now when she came home from school, the house which had been full of guests and her mother and usually Uncle Albert was empty except for the workmen replacing the walls, repairing the house.

Dear Diary, she wrote on April 24, 1963.

> *Nothing is happening. Not even any trouble. Jonathan is in love with bossy Molly Saucer. Do this. Do that. Eat this. Eat that. Mama says it's lovely since otherwise Jonathan might have spent his life in the shed doing crosswords. Amanda has taken off with Melvina to do her book on happy American women if she can find any. And the worst news of all is that Mama is now Papa's research assistant for his new book so they go off together every morning to the library. I am completely alone.*
>
> *In history, we're studying the conditions present at the time of the American Revolution. I wish I'd been around then. I would have had a horse, a soldier, and a war to fight in.*
>
> *I need a revolution.*
>
> ESM

ELEVEN

IT WAS THE 13th of September, 1966, hot and airless in Philadelphia, and Eleanor, back at the University of Pennsylvania for her junior year, lay on the bare mattress surrounded by boxes and suitcases, rolled-up posters, a bag of school supplies. It was too hot to move.

She had come back to school three days early, before any of the rest of the students, because Tom Clay—whom she'd met once in August with Amanda—was coming to Philadelphia. He had telegrammed her in Washington. "ANY CHANCE YOU CAN MEET ME IN PHILLY SEPTEMBER 13? T.C."

The room, a single at the back of a grand old house at Thirty-ninth and Locust Streets was long and narrow with a window overlooking the parking lot and was the same room Eleanor had as a freshman when Rosie Kyle was murdered right under her window.

That was November 1964. In November, the one-year anniversary of the assassination of President Kennedy, there had been fights on Locust Street with fraternity men too drunk to hurt one another. But the riot squad of Philadelphia came in in their helmets, with tear gas and banging around their billy clubs, locking some of the slower boys who could not get away into the backs of paddy wagons, so by eleven o'clock the main streets of the University of Pennsylvania campus—Locust, Walnut, and Spruce—were silent and Eleanor was in bed reading a letter from Amanda.

She folded the letter, put it in the box of letters she kept under the bed. She turned out the light and was imagining a romance with a young man in Kappa Sig whose face she admired but whose name she didn't know when she heard laughter outside her window. At least it sounded very much like laughter and it didn't seem unnatural to hear voices as she drifted off to sleep. But the laughter continued, in a higher key. Just as Eleanor was falling into a real sleep, she knew it wasn't laughter at all she was hearing.

She actually saw Jim Barclay stab Rosie over and over with a knife from the kitchen of the Kappa Sig house, watched from the window for several seconds at least, riveted by what she saw, by the extraordinary scene, out of a movie or a dime-store novel or TV. By the time she had run to the telephone at the landing of the second floor to call the police, the rest of the house was up, the police had been called, the parking lot was filling with students, and Rosie Kyle lay on her side on the edge of the parking lot making strange little sounds, although Eleanor did not go out to witness. Jim Barclay was caught by members of his own fraternity as he ran toward Walnut Street. He was too drunk to run fast or to make sense when the police took a statement from him, but it did appear in the *Philadelphia Inquirer* that he said Rosie Kyle was cold and uppity for a southerner and he'd never done it to a colored girl.

By 1966, Jim Barclay, according to rumors, was out of jail, where he'd spent a short time, and back in southern Maryland tending bar, Rosie had been dead two years, and Eleanor had her revolution.

"I am not interested in movements or issues or politics any more than you or Mama," she wrote to Amanda in December 1964. "I'm not like Papa or Uncle Albert at all. But Rosie Kyle was a real person. I didn't know her personally, but lying in my bed in Philadelphia, I heard the last sounds she made on earth. I saw her die under the glare of the streetlight and somehow, because the picture of her dying is stuck in my brain forever, I feel a responsibility."

In the spring of her freshman year she started ROSIE.

TWELVE

ROSIE TOOK CHILDREN off the streets. They were children who lived in the slums of West Philadelphia, the crowded row houses into which the black families had been pushed as the University of Pennsylvania spread out. Their mothers worked. Often their fathers had left and the extended families which for a century had been the underpinning of black family life were victims of urban poverty.

It was started as a small group, friends of Elly's, ten or fifteen undergraduates who took a few children each afternoon and taught them art and dance and music, read stories with them, played sports. By September of 1966, ROSIE had a hundred volunteers, and a chapter had opened at Columbia in New York after a small piece about ROSIE was published in the magazine section of the *Philadelphia Inquirer*.

At twenty, Eleanor looked like a small Amanda, slender, angular, flat-chested, narrow-hipped, with a dark and striking face. Sometimes she was beautiful, especially on the rare occasions when her face was in repose. There was an arresting quality about her. She could fill a room.

Except for Jack Richardson in high school and imagined love affairs, Eleanor had never had boyfriends. Boys were interested in her in college, interested in what she had to say. They liked to take her on, but either she was so full of longing that she frightened them or else she was too restless in her manner.

That changed with ROSIE. She was no longer at odds. Men began to show a different interest.

"It's crazy," she said to Amanda one afternoon in her grandmother's apartment in Greenwich Village. "It's as if I've got a new smell about me—an aphrodisiac perfume. And no one even expressed an interest in kissing me before except Sammy Lendering."

It was August 1966, and they were making sandwiches for lunch in the small kitchen which opened to the back garden overgrown with weeds. "And rats and snakes," according to Melvina.

Eleanor had come to New York for the opening of a small exhibit of photographs by several photojournalists including Amanda—called "After Camelot"—candid portraits of some of the young leaders who had filled the vacuum after Kennedy's assassination. One of these was Tom Clay.

Tom Clay had been a third-year law student at the University of North Carolina at the time of the lunch counter sit-in of February 1960 by four black college students in Greensboro. As Tom told Eleanor later, it had never occurred to him until that afternoon that black people could not eat at the same table with white people. That they were not allowed. He had grown up with segregation for so long that he was ignorant of it. He left law school in April just short of graduation and joined the civil rights movement. In the summer of 1961, he was a freedom rider taking buses into Alabama and Georgia, trying to integrate lunch counters and public bathrooms and drinking fountains. He taught in a Freedom School in Mississippi established to help children pass the literacy test, and in the summer of 1964 he worked in the voting rights campaign in Mississippi along with hundreds of other black and white students. In July of that year, shortly after the killings of the three civil rights workers, he was clubbed by a white policeman and ended up back in Raleigh, North Carolina, with a bad concussion.

When he recovered, he joined Students for a Democratic Society and within a number of months he had become a national spokesman for SDS. He was a charismatic speaker with his low, rolling southern voice—tall and lanky with black hair, blue eyes, a kind of roving sexuality, an ease about his body unfamiliar to Eleanor in the men she'd known.

He had made a point of meeting Eleanor after the opening of "After Camelot" because he had heard of ROSIE.

"He read about ROSIE in *Newsweek*," Eleanor told Amanda. "He is interested in my work."

"He's interested in you, Elly," Amanda said, making a pot of hot tea. "And he's married."

"I didn't know he was married," Eleanor said. "He didn't mention that. All he did was ask me about ROSIE and say we should do something sometime."

"And say you were beautiful and that he'd like to see you immediately. Tomorrow," Amanda said. "This is a very small apartment. I heard everything he said."

Eleanor shrugged. "He's living with a black family in Newark and he wanted to know how I'd started ROSIE. I suppose you heard that too."

"I heard that too," Amanda sat down at the kitchen table with Eleanor.

"Do they have children?" Eleanor asked.

"Ask him," Amanda said.

"I won't see him again," Eleanor said.

* * *

The telegram from Tom Clay came to Eleanor's house in Washington the day after Labor Day. The excuse she gave to Sara for returning early to school was ROSIE.

"I don't believe you," Nich-o said, standing in her room as she packed to go back to college. He had finished Yale and was starting Georgetown Law School in the fall, living at home since there wasn't the money for him to have his own apartment. "The telegram was from Tom Clay. Right? He's coming to see you about ROSIE."

"Yes."

"I've heard about him."

"He's well known."

"I read a story about him and his wife and their little boy living in the slums of Newark."

Eleanor hesitated. "So?"

"Amanda thinks he's interested in you," Nicholas said.

"She called Mama, I bet. Right?"

"Right, Eleanor. What a thinker you are."

"This family has no sense of boundaries," Eleanor said. "I expect to look in the mirror one day and there will be Amanda. Stay out of my business."

"What Amanda told Mama is that he's handsome, smart, and married," Nicholas said. "She's worried, of course. In her strange way she doesn't think you should have boyfriends who are married."

"That's out of her control," Eleanor said. "And yours too and Mama's."

The doorbell rang and Eleanor jumped out of bed, dizzy with the heat and excitement. She checked herself in the mirror on the back of her closet door, brushing her short black curly hair with her fingers. The front door was glass and Tom Clay stood there dressed in a bright yellow T-shirt and blue jeans, his nose pressed flat against the window like a boy.

"Hiya, my beautiful sweet potato," he said when she opened the door. And he picked her up and kissed her as if they had known each other forever.

THIRTEEN

ELEANOR WAS OVERWHELMED. Her heart was beating so fast she had to sit down on the landing to catch her breath, blaming the heat. He sat down beside her, lifted the skirt of her sundress and licked her knee.

"Hurry, hurry, hurry," he breathed in her ear.

She opened the door to her bedroom.

"Such a little bed," he said and shut the bedroom door. He sat on the end of the bed and pulled her between his knees, unbuttoned her sundress, running his fingers lightly over her breasts.

"Are you afraid of me?" he asked.

She shook her head. It wasn't fear exactly, but she did feel as if she could die of this afternoon.

He pulled her sundress off her shoulders and ran his hands very gently along the sides of her breasts, between her legs.

Maybe the expression in her eyes betrayed her. Certainly she did not intend to let him know she had no history with men.

He lifted her on the bed, put his hand on her cheek.

"Eleanor?"

"Mmm?"

"You've never made love, have you?"

She shook her head. "I'm really sorry," she said, feeling as if it were a source of shame.

"Oh no," he whispered in her ear. "You darling girl. You darling, darling girl."

He stayed two days and nights. And when he left, Eleanor slept a sweet abandoned sleep, claiming flu when her friends began to arrive for the autumn semester.

"So," Nich-o said when he came to visit for a weekend in late September. "You're in love."

"Not necessarily."

"I just wish you could start with someone who isn't married," Nich-o said.

"Me too," Eleanor said. "But." She couldn't think of any reason. "I started with Tom."

"Maybe he'll get divorced," Nich-o said.

"No," Eleanor said. "Never. She has multiple sclerosis," she said. "And a little boy."

She—her name was Matty and Tom spoke of her with affection—was also black. There was never any question of his intentions. He couldn't leave an ill black wife and maintain his integrity, even if he fell in love with someone else. Which, he told Eleanor in daily notes he sent her from Newark, he had done.

So they went underground.

The excitement of her new life was almost equal to Eleanor's childhood dreams of heroism.

"Meet me at 6th and Market Tuesday November 1 at noon. T.C."

"I'll be at 30th Street Station on Saturday November 12 at 3:00 on my way to D.C. T.C."

"Come to NYC for a few hours on Sunday. I'll be at the ticket counter Penn Station at 2 p.m. T.C."

"I love you. Tedum Tedum, my petito, mou-cha-cha. T.C."

Eleanor loved the intrigue of subterfuge, the high romance. She felt like a child on a long, invisible string with vast spaces to explore uninhibited but with a safety net in Tom Clay to catch her if she fell. She had no interest whatsoever in anyone else.

"I'm really not safe, El," Tom said. "What we've got together now is it. For life."

"I don't want to be married," Eleanor said.

"You may change your mind," Tom said.

They were on one of their monthly visits to New York City, late March, too cold for eating out-of-doors but that's what they were doing, bundled up, sitting on a park bench next to which an old drunk lay sleeping away the winter. "You may want babies."

"I don't need to be married for that," Eleanor replied.

And they both laughed. They woke the drunk on the ground by the bench and gave him the rest of their chicken sandwich.

In April and May, they saw each other only twice, once for dinner in New York and another time he spent the night. And then in early June 1967, the clinic obstetrician at the University of Pennsylvania Hospital confirmed what Eleanor was already certain was true.

FOURTEEN

MELVINA DIED ON June 26, 1967, at her sister's house on U Street. She was seventy-nine and had been slowly slipping for a year. Not her mind. Not her eyes either. But her body had already lasted for a great deal longer than anyone guessed it would. She died in her sleep.

Amanda and Bonita were both in the dark row house on U Street, already heavy with summer heat, sleeping in the living room on couches.

The week before, a Tuesday morning, Melvina had not gotten out of bed in the apartment in Greenwich Village. Amanda took her tea and toast, sat down beside her.

"Today soon as I can I'm going home while the going's good," Melvina said, a little breathless. "And don't you call Bonita and tell her I'm sick either."

On the pretext of picking up milk, Amanda went to the market at the corner of 13th and Fifth and called Bonita in El Paso. Bonita had been back to visit twice in the last years, since Amanda and Melvina had started the book together—once with her sons at Easter time and once in the summer staying at the house on P Street with the Marches. She had made her accommodation with Melvina, which had been easier than Amanda thought it would be. Melvina expected very little of people, little of the world in general. Not that she was grateful. But she was pleased to see Bonita arrive Wednesday morning.

"So you've come because you hear I'm dying," Melvina said when Bonita came into her room at her sister's house on U Street.

"You used to say I wouldn't come until your funeral," Bonita said. "And you were wrong. Here I am in the flesh."

They laughed a lot those last five days. Sara came over for dinner, actually bringing dinner with her, and they sat around the table and told stories—Melvina propped up at the table, too weak to talk but sufficiently alert to listen.

"Tell about the Depression," Melvina said. "What you put me through." And Amanda would recount the story of finding Bonita and traveling across the South in the colored section of the train.

"That was the worst time in my life," Melvina said. "Drug across the country like you did."

Evenings, Amanda would sit in a chair beside her bed, her feet up next to Melvina's.

"If I die, are you going to be able to get around all right?" Melvina asked Amanda.

"I'll be fine," Amanda said.

"You better not be fine," Melvina said. "Otherwise what use was there for me to spend the last days of my life in New York City with rats in the backyard?"

"You're a saint, Melvina," Amanda said.

"And if I'm not around to fight for my rights, I don't want you to cheat me out of my name on that book I did."

"Your name will be there," Amanda said.

"Put Pauline Melvina Jones," Melvina said. "You remember Pauline, don't you?"

"I remember."

Amanda could hardly bear Melvina's last brave days struggling for air.

Dear Flat Mouth, she wrote while she was staying on the couch at Melvina's sister's.

> *I thought I was done for feelings. At sixty-seven, I've felt enough. But Melvina is dying and I can hardly get through a day without going into the bathroom of her*

sister's house, turning on the faucets full force so I can cry without her hearing me.

I'll be there the second week in August. My eyes are not great. The world is blurred as if I'm permanently drunk. Only if I close my eyes and imagine the objects of my memory can I see clearly.

Love forever,
A Man

p.s. June 26, 1967. I didn't mail this yesterday. This morning I woke up and Melvina was dead when I took her breakfast.

Sara had not seen her mother fragile since Jonathan Abbott's death. She had never thought of her as old. But she did seem old after Melvina—cautious, unsteady on her feet.

"My mother is ancient," she said to Hendrik the night of the funeral.

"Bereft," Hendrik said. "Not old."

It made Sara unaccountably angry.

"Is there something wrong with your vision?" she asked her mother. "You seem so tentative since Melvina died."

"I see perfectly well," Amanda said, unwilling to confess weakness to Sara.

"You should see a doctor," Sara said.

"I never see doctors." She was competitive with Sara for good health as if there were between them a need to triumph over the other. "I'll check the prescription on my glasses, but I'm fine."

"What do you think?" Sara asked Eleanor who had come home for Melvina's funeral. "Amanda has aged years. She acts as if she's losing her sight."

Eleanor lay across the bottom of her mother's bed and watched her slip out of the navy blue dress she had worn to Melvina's funeral.

She was sleepy. That is how she'd mostly felt since she found out she was pregnant. Wonderfully sleepy and relaxed. She hadn't told her mother. She hadn't told anyone, not even Tom Clay, and probably would not for a while, but at the moment it was difficult to concentrate on the subject of Amanda's sudden age.

"I think she's okay, Mama," Eleanor said. "She's good enough to be on her feet all day taking pictures or in the darkroom."

"Her eyesight doesn't seem good," Sara said putting on shorts and a blouse.

"It's not," Eleanor said. "You know it's not."

Sara sat down on the bed, brushed her long hair into a ponytail to get it off the back of her neck. "I didn't know. She's never really said any more to me than that her eyes are weaker."

"That's weird," Eleanor sat up and crossed her legs. "Maybe she didn't want you to know."

"Apparently not," Sara said coolly.

"It's because of her eyes that Melvina traveled around the country with her," Eleanor said. "I thought you knew that."

"She told me Melvina went for company," Sara said.

"She went for company too," Eleanor said. "What Amanda told me is that the edges are blurred when she looks at things. The picture is out of focus."

"Well, I wonder why she never told me any of this," Sara said defensively. "I am her daughter."

Eleanor shrugged. "I guess that's probably why."

Everyone was home. Frederick from St. Louis where he was city editor for the *Post-Dispatch*, Jonathan, Nich-o who was at Georgetown Law and lived at home on the third floor in Amanda's old room. Albert and Jane were at dinner after the funeral. They had moved back into the Marches lives easily as if they had never left; Albert was quieter than he had been. Jane had a heart easily satisfied by work. Bonita was there. She had fallen apart at the funeral and had to be held up in the aisle of the First Baptist Church. At dinner, there were toasts to Melvina. Eleanor spoke, and Sara. Jonathan remembered their childhoods, Melvina's sharp tongue. Amanda said nothing. She hardly touched her food.

After dinner, Sara sat in the chair in the parlor and watched her mother pull herself slowly up the stairs as if her legs were no longer willing to serve her.

"I can't stand to see her like this," she said to Hendrik.

"Go to her then," Hendrik said. "Help her up the stairs."

Sara shook her head. "I can't," she said. "I can't even bear to look."

But she did go upstairs later with a glass of ice tea. Amanda was sitting in a chair, her feet on the bed, reading letters from her mother into a tape recorder.

Sara sat down on the bed.

"So you're still able to read," she said.

"Of course I am able to read," Amanda said. "I'm not blind."

She didn't actually look old, Sara thought. Her face was unlined, the bones too good for the skin to hang loose, for the features to disappear. Her hair was still gray only in a halo around her face. So it wasn't the actual look of her which was old. Perhaps her carriage, Sara thought. Or attitude.

"Why didn't you tell me about your eyes, Mama?"

Amanda turned off the tape recorder.

"Because you drink too much," Amanda said without a moment's hesitation.

"That doesn't make sense," Sara said.

"You asked why and that's why," Amanda said. "Whether it makes sense to you or not."

And later, it did make sense. They could not tolerate weakness in one another. Perhaps that was implicit in the mysterious relationship between mothers and daughters, Sara thought. Between women. She could easily forgive weakness in men, in fathers. Expected it even. But with her and Amanda there was no forgiveness, as if they were extensions of each other, more personally related than blood.

Eleanor went up to Amanda's room after eleven. She had been with her brothers in the shed smoking marijuana, no different in the quality of daring than the cigarettes they had smoked when they were younger. The light was on in Amanda's room so Eleanor knocked and went in. Amanda was still taping letters.

"Do you want me to come back to New York with you for a while?" she asked her grandmother.

"I'm not going back to New York," Amanda said. "Why should I want to go back to the rat-filled apartment with Melvina's clothes in the closet?"

"So you're staying with Mama this summer?" Eleanor asked.

"It's my house," Amanda said.

"I know." Eleanor lay across the bed. "Even Papa knows that."

"I'm staying here until August when I go to Flat Mouth's."

"You should try to get along with Mama better then," Eleanor said.

"I love your mother," Amanda said. "But she makes me so ill-tempered moving like molasses as she does."

"Slow genes," Eleanor said. "Certainly not yours."

"Her father's," Amanda said. She put the letter of Anna's she had been reading back in the box and closed it. "I didn't actually know her father well. I was only seventeen and in love with myself."

"You never married him?"

"He died in the war."

"He's the man in the picture, right?" She lay down across Amanda's bed. "I remember that story."

"He was too young to have become who he would be," Amanda said. "And I was too young to understand a young man and too wild at heart to have clear vision."

She was going to tell Amanda. She could feel it coming.

"What was it like to be pregnant and unmarried?" Eleanor asked.

"Unacceptable," Amanda said. She leaned forward and took Eleanor's bare foot in her hand, lifted it, and kissed her dirty toes. "Are you pregnant, Elly?"

Eleanor nodded.

"And what does he say?" Amanda asked.

"He doesn't know," Eleanor said. "He would likely say abortion."

"Probably he would," Amanda said. She stood up, took the bows out of her hair, and brushed it. "I could help you with that, darling."

"No," Eleanor said. "I'm not having an abortion."

"What do you think Tom Clay will say to that?"

Eleanor shrugged. "He can't say very much, can he?"

"I suppose he can't," Amanda said.

Eleanor leaned back on her grandmother's pillow.

"You don't like men very well, do you, Amanda?" Eleanor said. "That's something you and Melvina had in common."

"What we had in common was an absence of trust. I love Flat Mouth and I loved Jonathan Abbott. I don't know how things would have turned out with Lincoln Draper, who was your real grandfather."

"What about Papa?"

"I admire your father, as you certainly know." Amanda sat down on the bed beside her. "But we have a complicated relationship. We both wanted your mother for our own," she said running her fingers through Eleanor's hair. "And he won."

"Poor Mama."

"It has been hardest for her."

"I don't want her to know about me until she has to know," Eleanor said. "She'll be disappointed. She had hoped I would do something with my life besides babies."

Amanda laughed. "Oh, you'll do something, Elly. Children don't stand in the way of that," she said. "Women stand in their own way. Now good night."

"Good night, Amanda." She kissed her grandmother's forehead.

She wanted to say something sweet and admiring to her, something to acknowledge the powerful feelings between them, but all she could think of to say was, "I wish we called you by a name more personal than Amanda."

"But Amanda is my personal name," she said kissing the palm of Eleanor's hand.

Eleanor turned out the overhead light and went down the stairs to the second floor where her parents were sleeping—or whispering together as they were doing when she passed the door. A sudden rush of jealousy overtook her at their new lives together, lived in secret like thieves fearful of a sudden capture of attention by their children.

She slipped under the sheets of her bed, held a pillow in her arms, her face buried in its soft feathers. If the baby was a girl she'd call her Lily for the sound of music in the name. Lily March. Lily Steward March.

ELEANOR
AND
LILY

ONE

ELEANOR WAS IN the offices of ROSIE at 15th and Market when she heard on the radio news of what had happened to Tom Clay. It was late August, hot, stormy, and she was three months pregnant.

"Oh Jesus," Tom had said when she told him just after the Fourth of July in New York where she had gone to meet him. As it turned out, they had only an hour because her train was late to arrive and he had a meeting with Eugene McCarthy's people to head the South for the Senator's presidential campaign.

"What are we going to do?" he asked Eleanor, his voice more southern, more lilting and aristocratic than it usually was.

"Nothing," Eleanor said. "I just wanted you to know."

"It's crazy," Tom said. "You're only twenty-one."

"I won't have an abortion," she said, not allowing him the opportunity to recommend one, not wanting the humiliation of an argument. She didn't know why she wanted a baby. She just wanted one.

"But you know about me. I can't be involved," he said trying to be breezy. He tweaked her swollen breast. "And what are you going to do with a baby, going to school and running ROSIE? It's not like a kitten, you know."

"I'll be fine. It'll be a smart, tough baby and I'll be glad to have it around."

"If I were free, Elly—you know," Tom started.

"I know. I know," Eleanor said. "I just hope you don't have a lot of me's running around the country with big bellies."

He kissed her, pulled her toward him, and kissed her again.

"I love you, Eleanor," he said. "You are the only woman I have ever loved."

She leaned her head against his chest. She wanted very much to believe him.

For the rest of the summer, he sent her flowers or balloons or funny notes with cartoons of them together.

"TC as jackrabbit. EM as bursting bunny rabbit." Notes like that.

Eleanor turned up the news.

"Tom Clay, leader of the SDS, was shot today, apparently by the police, during the early morning rioting and looting on Fourteenth Street in downtown Newark. He has been taken to Mastland Medical Center where a spokesman for SDS says he is in critical condition with a gunshot wound in his chest." The radio announcer paused. "Several other young men and women were arrested during the riots for looting and one unidentified black man was killed by police gunfire in the same vicinity of Fourteenth Street where Tom Clay was shot."

Eleanor called the hospital and was connected with intensive care.

"I'm a close personal friend," she said, "calling to find out the condition of Tom Clay."

"Mrs. Clay is here in the waiting room," the nurse said. "If you'd like to speak with her, I'll put her on."

She hung up the phone, lay down on the top of the desk, and listened intently to the radio announcer for comfort, to settle her nerves, as if they were friends and he was in the room.

There was no update on Tom Clay's condition all afternoon, only a repeat of the earlier report.

At five, a steamy August day without a breeze, she locked the office of ROSIE and walked home to the apartment at 36th and Spruce which she had rented for the summer with two other ROSIE volunteers. It was the kind of hot day in the summer in the city when the cars run the red lights and drivers shout at pedestrians, where the expressions on the faces of the passersby are drawn into a permanent bad temper.

She was suddenly lonely and uncertain of herself. Why in the world had she ever taken on ROSIE or stayed in

Philadelphia for the summer or fallen stupidly in love? She wanted to go home to her mother.

She called Nicholas first. He was at the library and Frederick, when she called, was out of the office. Only Jonathan was at home. And Sara.

"Mama's sleeping," Jonathan said.

"At five-thirty on a Tuesday afternoon? Why is she sleeping, for chrissake?"

"She's tired," Jonathan said. "Overtired. Listen. Is this too easy for the *New York Times?* Seven letters. Long sleek black cat?"

"Of course it's too easy," Eleanor said.

"What about this?"

"Jonathan," Eleanor said. "I'm calling in a terrible humor."

"I'm sorry, Elly," Jonathan said quickly. "I'm really sorry."

"Is Mama tired all the time again?"

"Almost never," Jonathan said. "I haven't seen her really tired in weeks. But Papa went to New York about his new book and Nich-o has been at the library all week and I was in the shed."

"I miss you guys," Elly said. "Maybe I'll come home this weekend."

She was lying on her bed in her nightgown in front of a fan, wondering about Tom Clay's wife, Matty, and how bad her multiple sclerosis was and whether she might die of it, when the telephone rang and it was Amanda.

"I just heard the news on the radio, darling," she said.

Trust Amanda. Elly was warmed all over.

"I don't know what to do," she said to her grandmother.

"Go to Newark, El."

"Go to Newark?"

"He's hurt. You should go."

"What about his wife?"

"Be pleasant to his wife," Amanda said impatiently. "You don't need to have a heart-to-heart talk."

Eleanor laughed in spite of herself.

"Doesn't he love you? Didn't you tell me that he loves you?" Amanda asked.

"I think he does," Eleanor said. "He told me so."

"Of course he loves you, darling. He'd be crazy not to."

"Sometimes you lose confidence," Eleanor said.

"Go," Amanda said. "I wouldn't think twice about it."

Eleanor was glad to have something to do; she didn't give herself time to reconsider. She dressed quickly, listening to the radio as she brushed her hair. There was the announcement about riots in Newark and the commentator's report that Tom Clay was undergoing emergency surgery for the removal of the bullet from his chest.

It was 8:30 in the evening, still light, when she got to the hospital. The woman at the visitors' desk directed her to the elevator to the fourth-floor intensive care.

The waiting room was full. There were no whites except one reporter who was talking to a man whose face she recognized from the newspapers as that of the writer LeRoi Jones and it pleased her that such a conventional-seeming white man as Tom Clay could rouse the sympathies of LeRoi Jones.

She stood in the doorway rehearsing the story she had made up on the train.

"Hello," she said finally, standing in the doorway to the waiting room. "I'm Eleanor March, head of ROSIE in Philadelphia."

Several people looked up—one in particular whom she guessed was Matty Clay, a slender, striking black woman in a sunflower yellow sundress.

"I came to check on Tom," she said.

The black woman smiled wanly, patted the seat beside her.

"I'm Matty Clay," she said. "I know about ROSIE. Tom went to Philadelphia to help you get started."

"He did," Eleanor said, relieved that her story seemed to hold.

"We're just waiting," Matty Clay said. "He's in surgery. You sit here and wait with us."

All of Matty's family was there—her aunts from Newark, her parents, her sister who lived in Manhattan, her brother from Philadelphia had all come when they heard the news on the radio. And Eleanor saw Tom as his life without her must be in the cushion of this family, drum tight in its unity.

She sat down next to one of the relatives on the plastic couch and talked to Matty. Matty was the only one who did talk to her, but the rest were interested in her arrival and talked through Matty.

"Ask her does she know Blooms Drugstore in Philadelphia which my uncle owns," Matty's mother said.

"And does she live anywhere near Twenty-ninth and Market."

"Ask her is there the same kind of trouble going on in Philly as here in Jersey."

But when the doctors came out to tell Matty how the surgery had gone, called her over and took her into the corridor outside the waiting room, Matty's mother leaned over to Eleanor and whispered.

"You know Matty has the MS disease, don't you?"

"I did know," Eleanor said. What she had noticed was that Matty, whom she had expected to find weak at least if not crippled, by Tom's description of her, was the picture of health and vibrant good looks. "She looks good," Eleanor said.

"Looks good, yes. Matty always looks good," her mother said shaking her head. "But she's not good."

The news from surgery was that Tom was fine. Going to be fine. They had removed the bullet, which was high, close to the shoulder, and although he had lost a lot of blood his condition had been upgraded to serious and he would be out of the hospital in a couple of days.

Eleanor left when the news came. After all, that's what she had come to Newark to hear, she thought to herself. She had no other place at the hospital with Matty and her family, no rights to him, and if the circumstances were reversed—if it were she in the hospital—he might not even risk his domestic life to visit her.

She lay on the top of the sheets in Melvina's old room on 13th Street and listened to Amanda in the next room preparing the bed.

"You were married when Mama was born, right?" she asked Amanda when her grandmother kissed her good night. "I'm wondering what to do when this baby is born."

"Tom won't be there?"

"No," Eleanor said. "Not possibly. I realized that tonight in Newark," she said. "Somehow until I saw it, I didn't actually believe that he has another life and I'm not a part of it at all."

Amanda wanted to tell Eleanor the truth, that it would be unbearably hard, that she shouldn't have even considered trying to have a baby alone. But she knew very well that if you understand a life before you lead it, you'll never have the courage to try to lead it at all.

"Then go home," Amanda said.

"Home to have the baby?" Eleanor asked. "With Mama?"

"Certainly," Amanda said crisply. "With your mother."

"That's a very strange idea, isn't it?" Eleanor said.

"It doesn't seem strange to me," Amanda said.

Amanda was right. When the time came in early September to tell Sara—it was for Sara to pass the news to Hendrik and the boys—the task was simple. There was no argument from Sara, no blame, no mention of foolishness or regrets or impossibilities. No show of disappointment. Just pleasure. Pure pleasure, as if the news that her only daughter was going to have a child out of wedlock was a gift from heaven.

"Either she's a very good actress or else she's not as upset as I thought she'd be," Eleanor told Amanda on the telephone.

"She's a terrible actress," Amanda said. "She has no capacity whatsoever for the decent lie."

"It's remarkable of her, isn't it?" Eleanor said. She had never thought of her mother's extraordinary tolerance as strength. But of course it was.

"In her quiet way, your mother is remarkable," Amanda said. "We forget that. I forget it."

* * *

On the 19th of February, 1968, the Marches crowded around Eleanor at Georgetown Hospital like a defensive army—to be there just after midnight when Lily Steward March was born.

TWO

IN THE BLOODY spring of 1968—Martin Luther King had been assassinated in April, Bobby Kennedy would die in June—Eleanor graduated from the University of Pennsylvania and moved with Lily to a house in North Philadelphia. It belonged to a philanthropic man, an acquaintance of Tom Clay, who owned a lot of houses in Philadelphia and gave the house to ROSIE free of rent. Mount Airy, just at the north end of the city, had the feel of an old suburb, thick with oak and maple trees. There were large stone houses with huge gardens put in during the twenties and thirties, tall azaleas and rhododendron, rows of perennials. The headquarters for ROSIE was a three-story stone house, grand in the years before Mount Airy had integrated, set in the center of an acre of land which backed onto the railroad tracks where the Chestnut Hill local ran back and forth from the city.

"You must get ROSIE out of the center of the city this summer," Tom had told her after Dr. King was killed. "There's going to be war on the streets."

Tom stayed with Eleanor at the end of May for several nights, sleeping on the mattress in the downstairs study with Lily's bassinet beside them.

"As if we're a family," Eleanor said burrowing her face in his shoulder. "I promise that's the last sentimental thing I'll say."

"We are family," Tom said. "Just a subterranean family."

That was at the end of May before Kennedy was shot in California.

When Tom left to go back to Newark, he was not likely to return to Philadelphia until after the Democratic convention in Chicago. Eleanor was weepy the last morning they lay together next to the French doors, a light breeze blowing across them. She could not bear to see him leave.

"I'll call every day," he promised. "I'll write notes."

"And send balloons."

"Always balloons," he said.

He left early in the morning and all that day Eleanor was restless or she would not have been susceptible to Emma Gaits.

Emma Gaits was a slender child with pale blond hair in a long braid and cheeks sprayed with beige freckles, too nondescript in appearance, vacant in temperament, to change the whole course of a life as she would do Eleanor's.

Eleanor had seen her early in the morning walking back and forth on the other side of Gowen Avenue, just after Tom left when she was in the front yard putting up the sign for ROSIE—a green sign painted in white letters, ROSIE Inc., with a pink rose in the corner. A little later while Lily was sleeping and Eleanor was fixing the bedrooms for the volunteers from Penn who would be living there during the summer, she saw Emma Gaits again. This time she was sitting on the front steps with her back to the house writing with her fingers on the brick steps.

But in the afternoon, Emma Gaits came up the front steps of the house where Eleanor and Lily were sitting on a wicker swing.

"What's ROSIE?" she asked.

"It's a group that works with children, especially poor children," Eleanor replied, taking Lily on her lap.

"Do the children live here?"

"No," Eleanor said. "They live at home. The people who teach them live here. Like me."

"Do you take in runaways?" Emma Gaits picked a blade of grass and put it in her mouth like a cigarette.

"What do you mean?"

"I mean—do you have room for kids in trouble—you know—runaways—to live here?"

Eleanor considered.

"We haven't done that yet," she said. But, of course, she thought, they could. ROSIE could be a place for runaways as well. It could be anything. After all, they had room for more in the huge house on Gowen Avenue.

"Maybe we will," Eleanor said. "Sometime."

"I'm a runaway," Emma Gaits said matter-of-factly. "Can you tell?"

"Not really," Eleanor said.

"I'm from pretty far away," Emma Gaits said.

"Are you in school?"

"There's a school I go to if I'm at home but I'm not home now and I can't go back today."

Emma Gaits peered up at Eleanor from under her heavy lids.

"What happened is too bad to tell," she said quietly. "Do you think I could spend the night?"

Eleanor was thoughtful.

"I won't eat your food," she said. "I carry my own food in here." She opened a small satchel where there was a box of Ritz crackers and an apple. "I'll sleep on the floor."

"I suppose," Eleanor said, curious about this girl. "Just tonight."

And at that moment, for no specific reason, just a sense of the way things might turn out, Eleanor knew she had made a decision for trouble. But the next thing she knew, she and Emma Gaits were in the kitchen chopping vegetables for a salad, making muffins for the ROSIE volunteers who would begin arriving at six.

THREE

DURING THE SUMMER of 1968, Emma Gaits was a guardian angel sailing over to the house on Gowen Avenue early just after Lily had been fed, doing the breakfast dishes and the grocery shopping, cleaning the linoleum floors, the bathroom, weeding the garden planted with zucchini, tomatoes, peppers, eggplant, tarragon and rosemary, yellow squash, muskmelons, marijuana, cutting up vegetables for supper.

"I can't pay you anything for what you do," Eleanor said. "We are all of us living on a shoestring."

"S'alright," Emma said. "I love it here."

And she seemed to be telling the truth. Her face had color and her eyes were clear. She had begun to look at Eleanor directly and not cover her mouth with her hand when she spoke. But she was reserved about her private life and what Eleanor learned about her was by accident.

She was the youngest of three children, the only girl. Her mother, who was dead and had been many years, had been a nurse and her father, about whom Emma spoke very little, was her reason for running away in the first place.

One morning, she arrived particularly early, before seven, and said she had to leave the house early before he got up.

"Why?" Eleanor asked.

She went into the bathroom without replying, turned on the faucet and did not reappear for some time.

"Are you all right?" Eleanor asked when she came into the kitchen.

"Who knows?" Emma said.

But she wouldn't talk.

Another time she asked Eleanor the particulars about pregnancy. How do you know? How long do you wait to see a doctor? How long can you wait to have an abortion? She was asking for a friend at school, she said.

And then in late July, she told Eleanor that her father had found out where she was during the day.

"I thought he knew where you were."

"He thought I was at school taking Algebra I."

"So what will happen now he knows you're here?"

"Who knows?" Emma said. "Something."

America was stunned the summer of 1968. It was a volatile time and everybody young knew that the gates were down and that nothing they did, nothing they could imagine doing, in nightmares or in daydreams, would be surprising.

For the moment, Eleanor was glad not to be married to Tom Clay. He was in the paper daily—*the New York Times* and the *Philadelphia Inquirer*—on the radio and television as a spokesman for the SDS, as a critic of the Weathermen, as an advocate for civil rights, against American involvement in Vietnam.

He filled the mailbox on Gowen Avenue with sweet notes from North Carolina where he was working on Senator McCarthy's campaign and then Chicago where he went to prepare for the Democratic convention. He wrote her from Chicago:

> It could be a bad scene here, Mayor Daley could bring on the police and a lot of people could be hurt.
>
> I don't think you should have ROSIE take in runaways. Then you'll get druggies, hangers-on, girls wanting mother replacements, and angry parents wanting their runaway kids back, blaming you for the whole situation. Too much aggravation.
>
> I've always known it's issues I like—not people. Most activists are like me. We fall for the general condition of mankind, not the individual tragedy. And you're in love all the way with the single human heart.
>
> So if you take in runaways, you'll get involved. Something bad always happens when you get involved.
>
> Love ya to death, Chicken soup
> Kiss Lily on the fat little nose
>
> > TC
>
> p.s. The protest here in this windy city could knock the socks off the country. A lot of the antiwar people believe that Johnson's de-escalation speech when he withdrew March 31 from the race for President was a foil. We're bombing in Vietnam no less than before but more concentrated.
>
> There's a lot of angry men around here. In fact I haven't met a single one who's not.
>
> I'll be in Philly the minute this shindig is over.

Hugs and kisses to you and the lilliputian

TC

Don't publish my letters if I die in Chicago. My uptight upright Episcopalian Pop would self-destruct.

Dear El,

I don't like the sound of this scene with your personal runaway and her father. Look into it. And if he's trouble, tell her to volunteer at Planned Parenthood.

Love ya,
TC

p.s. Your Grandmama is a trip. Did you read this in *Time* magazine? I'm sure she'd never tell you she made it in the Republican news rag.

He included a news clip from the People section of *Time* which showed Amanda in Ashland photographing Flat Mouth at Bad River. "Photographer Amanda Steward at Bad River Reservation where she grew up, photographing for a new book on the American family in the 20th Century."

By mid-July, the house on Gowen Avenue was full. There were eight volunteers living at ROSIE. In the morning, they'd drive the ROSIE VW vans, old vans painted fuchsia with a bright pink rose on the side, pick up thirty ghetto children from Germantown, and run a day camp, with swimming in plastic pools in the backyard and whiffle ball, painting and drawing and storytelling and music and a hot lunch which Emma Gaits cooked. The summer rolled along pleasantly with repeated days and long evenings of conversation, until the afternoon just before the Chicago convention was due to open—in fact, Eleanor was on the phone with Tom when Emma Gaits's father came into the kitchen on Gowen Avenue in a black rage demanding her return.

"Emma is supposed to be taking summer school," Mr. Gaits said. "She told me she had never missed a class."

"I didn't know that until the other day."

"I went to Girls High two days ago and they tell me not only has she missed one class, she's missed them all," he said.

"I'm very sorry," Eleanor looked over at Emma who sat at the kitchen table, her knees drawn up, her head buried.

"Get your things and come home with me," Mr. Gaits said. He walked to the front door.

He was a small, heavy man, bright-cheeked and veiny as if he were a drinker, with thin black hair which he combed to cover the baldness. He looked out the window while he waited for Emma and didn't speak but just before he left—in fact, Emma was already down the front steps—he looked back at Eleanor.

"I don't want her here again," he said.

"Of course not," Eleanor said.

"You have a power over her, you know. That's what I don't like about it. Women who use power over children."

"I don't think I do."

"As long as you understand she's not coming back." He looked darkly at Eleanor.

"I understand that."

Eleanor would have given more thought to Mr. Gaits— she would have worried and talked to Amanda about him, maybe her mother and Tom—but he and Emma disappeared from her life and that afternoon the Democratic convention in Chicago opened. As Tom said when he called from a pay phone, "All hell has broken loose."

FOUR

AMANDA SAT ON the side of her bed in the rooming house in Ashland. Sometime in the middle of the night, Flat Mouth had slipped out and gone home to Star.

The summer in Ashland had been particularly lovely, almost mysterious in its softness, in the quality of air, clear as running creek water. They had spent hours in the cool blue and white bedroom of the rooming house, the windows open on the south and east sides—the breeze lifting the curtains, stirring the room. They lay without their clothes. Amanda was astonished at the preservation of their bodies, almost the bodies of their thirties, outlasting by years their faces, which had succumbed early to the weather, especially Flat Mouth's.

They kissed like young lovers, long, deep, personal kisses. Occasionally Flat Mouth would stiffen beside her and they'd make love, but mostly what they did that summer was to lie side by side and kiss.

From where she sat on the side of the bed, facing Main Street, already full of morning traffic, Amanda could not see the writing on the bold REXALL DRUG sign across the street. What was more, she noticed as soon as she opened her eyes, her vision had altered as it had done once before when Melvina was still alive. She covered her right eye with her hand. There seemed to be no difference in what she saw with her right eye uncovered. All of the objects in the room, the curtains, the windows, the signs on the stores across the street were blurred but identifiable. She covered her left eye. The room was black. She sat on the edge of the bed repeating the procedure several times. And then she walked very slowly across the room to see herself in the mirror. With her left eye covered, she was no longer there.

Flat Mouth would be gone all day with Star at their daughter's in the next town. She dialed her ophthamologist in New York. The nurse said he was on vacation. His associate said he would read her chart and call her back.

She had known for a long time that eventually she would lose her sight. But eventually seemed years away and for months, actually since the spring after Melvina died, there had been no change in her eyes. The sense of urgency which had accompanied the years when she and Melvina had worked on the book about American women was gone. She had more pictures to take but she wasn't in a terrible hurry.

She was sitting on the end of the bed, her hands folded formally in her lap, when the doctor in New York called back. "This can happen with your condition," he said.

"So the blindness in this eye is permanent?" Amanda asked, unreasonably calm.

"It is possible," the doctor said.

"And what about the other eye?"

"How is the other eye?"

"Not strong," Amanda said. "So I suppose it could go too."

"That's very unlikely," the doctor said. "But you should come right away. I wouldn't wait until your holiday is over."

She was packed and had left by noon.

Dear Flat Mouth, she wrote.

> *I woke this morning after you had left and my right eye was gone. Not even any light. So I'm off to New York.*
>
> *I can't imagine life without my eyes. They are the only way I've ever known the world. I hope my memory will hold.*
>
> *I love you forever,*
> *A Man*

In the end, she called Sara. The doctor said that surgery was the only possible way to protect her sight, she said, if it could be protected at all. The surgery should be immediate. For several weeks the eye would have to be covered, unexposed to light, in order to heal. And since the other eye was gone, she'd have to have help if Sara could spare a few days in New York.

Sara scrubbed the apartment in Greenwich Village, even the walls, cleaning out the drawers, the closets. It was neat when she arrived but not clean, which surprised her about her mother. There was dirt in the corners of the kitchen, accumulated dust on the tops of tables, lamp shades, the rims around the pictures hanging on the wall. Nothing had been thrown out of the refrigerator for a long time. Old bottles of olives, capers with gray-black rims on the bottle, a brown apple, raspberry jam lying hard at the bottom of the jar.

It gave her great pleasure, the washing for her mother. She certainly didn't like to clean at home. She liked only to redecorate which she wanted to do at Amanda's as well.

Add color. Blue especially—Dutch blue mixed with a lot of yellow. Rose in the living room—or peach. Everything of Amanda's was black and white or colors of the earth—the rugs were Indian, geometric, brick and gray, the walls white, the blankets thrown over the couches moss green and brown-striped.

"There's no color," she said to Eleanor who was lying on the couch in the living room with Lily sleeping on her belly. "I can't understand how Mama has lived without color."

"We'll bring flowers," Elly said. "Those wonderful purple and pink summer flowers at the market."

"Now she can't see them," Sara said.

"So?" Eleanor said. "We can see them."

Sara sat down at the end of the couch where Eleanor was lying and played with her soft curly hair.

"Funny how we've skipped generations in our family," she said. "You remind me of Amanda, certainly in your face, and I'm supposed to be like Anna. And Lily—what do you think?"

"Like you," Eleanor said. It was a conversation they had had before. Always the same conversation and it satisfied them both.

"A little," Sara said. "A little in her looks, I think, don't you?" It pleased Sara to think that this soft smiley beige-haired baby, plump in the belly and the cheeks, was her again. It gave her a sense of fresh happiness, of possibility, she supposed—or hope, which had sailed out the bedroom window, out of reach years ago when she was in her twenties and now since the birth of Lily revisited with a lightness of spirit.

In spite of Hendrik's bad humor about Tom Clay, Sara was secretly glad Eleanor wasn't married—even glad for Eleanor, who seemed very happy to have Tom Clay occasionally, to run her own life, her own work, without compromise. But Sara was particularly glad because it made Lily hers—because she was Sara's alone, so to speak. Sara had rights she would not have if Tom Clay were there or his parents.

She picked Lily up from Eleanor's belly, sat her on the

chair, and opened a jar of applesauce. She loved babies, she thought. All babies as long as they were reasonably pretty to look at. Perhaps that's what she should have done instead of the Small Hotel. Something with babies. An orphanage in northeast Washington or a junior village where older children were sent. She would have liked Eleanor's work. She simply didn't have the energy Eleanor had and could not have invented such a life on her own.

She wasn't unhappy. When *The German Character* was published, she would be listed under credits, in fact the first, and she did like sitting in her carrel at the Library of Congress imagining that she was the chief research assistant for a great historian. Not Hendrik. Hendrik was not a great historian. What distinguished Hendrik was his energy. He was good at starting things as Eleanor was with ROSIE. This man she imagined who was a great historian was older than Hendrik, more grateful than he was. He made no demands.

Since Albert, Hendrik had closed Sara's life. Actually her life had always been at home—with soldiers or friends or children or guests at the Small Hotel. What Hendrik did was close their home. He didn't want her friends over, except Pamela who stayed only a short time when she came. He was slightly irritated when the children visited, especially Eleanor and her baby. They claimed Sara's attention.

Hendrik paid more attention to Sara then he had, than he ever had except at the beginning. But in darker moments, she always knew his fascination with her was really a fascination with himself.

When the telephone rang it was from Amanda's doctor at New York Hospital saying they would be taking her down to surgery shortly. Sara gave Lily back to Eleanor, changed her dress to a light blue linen, and left.

Flat Mouth was there. Sara saw him when she got off the elevator on the sixth floor. He was standing, his back to her, in front of the nurses' station in a blue suit, his black hair streaked with silver, slightly ill at ease.

"I came," he said when he saw her.

He was genuinely shaken.

"That's lovely of you." She kissed him; she had never kissed Flat Mouth before. "Does Mama know you're here?"

"I have just seen her," he said.

His whole body seemed to be quivering. Maybe he was getting old. She couldn't tell. Sara didn't know Flat Mouth well. She certainly didn't understand the nature of his relationship with her mother nor Amanda's attraction to this strange, distant, handsome man.

"She'll be all right," Sara said. "You know that."

Flat Mouth shrugged.

"Her heart will last, of course," he said. "But her eyes?"

"That's true," Sara said. "She could lose her sight."

"Her eyes are everything," Flat Mouth said.

Amanda was already on the stretcher ready to be taken to the operating room and her eyes were covered with a loose cloth when Sara walked in.

"Hello, Mama."

She looked frail, thinner than Sara had thought—the white sheets dipped into a ravine between her hips.

"Did you see Flat Mouth?" Amanda whipped off the cloth over her eyes.

"He's just outside."

"Funny man," she laughed, girlish, clearly happy with his presence. "What an odd man. I had no idea he'd come. And all the way from Wisconsin."

Sara leaned over her mother to kiss her.

"I like your hair that length," Amanda said reaching her hand up. "And it has not turned gray."

"I'm not even fifty yet, Mama."

Amanda touched her cheek. "You should have that mole on your cheek looked into. I think it's growing. Do it now, while I'm in surgery. Just walk downstairs to dermatology."

"The minute you leave." Sara laughed.

"Look here again," Amanda said softly, reaching for Sara. "I want to memorize you right now as you look today."

She took Sara's face in her hands. "There," she said and put the cloth back over her eyes. "I see you exactly."

FIVE

FLAT MOUTH LEFT just after the surgery but Sara stayed almost two months, into October. Eleanor came on weekends with Lily.

All day, Amanda sat in a chair in the living room with the door to the garden open so she could feel the air.

"Don't you want to take a walk, Mama?" Sara would ask. "Or come out with me to the market or sit in the garden?"

But the answer was no. She wanted to sit in the living room until her eye healed. The doctor was optimistic but he would not know until October when the bandages were removed and the eye could be exposed to light.

"Walking wouldn't hurt, Mama," Sara said.

"I don't want to walk," Amanda replied.

For the first month, she seldom talked and Sara told the doctor she thought her mother was depressed. She was not unpleasant. Quite the contrary. She was docile and quiet but agreeable unless asked if she'd like to do something, to which her response was invariably no.

"Would you like me to read to you?" Eleanor asked.

"No," Amanda said. "I'm thinking."

"Thinking of what?" Eleanor asked, always interested in the workings of her grandmother's mind.

"Of pictures," Amanda said.

"Amanda is thinking of pictures," Eleanor said to Sara one night as she was getting ready to go to bed. They were sleeping in Melvina's old room, kept as it had been with the pictures on the wall, the curtains Melvina had made. Lily slept in a makeshift bed on the floor. "What do you think she does? Imagine the pictures she has taken?"

"I've never really understood Amanda as a photographer. And I've spent months with her taking pictures, a whole year traveling across the country."

"Well, she says she doesn't want to be interrupted because she's thinking of pictures," Eleanor said.

"Yes, she told me," Sara said, slightly exasperated.

Amanda was doing her book on the American women. She had Rebecca Stark and her mother in Richmond and Stella Grayson and her four sisters in North Dakota. She had a family in California, unrelated by blood, Mary and Sara Stanton in Kansas, the Burdine sisters in Wyoming, and the Hansens in Seattle. The jacket would be Mrs. Peter Burger of East Sandwich, Massachusetts, standing in her apron at the white fence around her Cape Cod shingled house, her gray hair loosely up in pins, her eyes off in the middle distance as though looking for someone about to arrive. She called the picture *After the Burial of Mr. Peter Burger of East Sandwich* and what had struck her was Mrs. Peter Burger's fortitude in the face of loss.

Since Amanda wasn't interested in conversations, Eleanor spent hours with Sara. They shopped and cooked and talked, played with Lily, took long walks through Greenwich Village. For Sara, there were no surprises in Eleanor. But Eleanor had always assumed a fragile mother without the wherewithal to survive alone, and she was struck by her mother's quiet strength, by her ease and accommodation.

"You know," Sara said one afternoon in late September walking along Fifth Avenue, her shoulder rubbing Eleanor's affectionately. "I'm having a wonderful time."

"Me too," Eleanor said. "It's cozy."

And it was cozy. There was no significant conversation, nothing which needed to be discussed, no emergencies, no business to attend to, just daily life. And through the weeks the Steward women fell easily together, bending in unison.

"Have you ever considered what will happen if Amanda is blind?" Eleanor asked one evening after they had turned out the light in Melvina's bedroom.

"The doctor has assured me that it's unlikely," Sara said.

"Amanda thinks about it," Eleanor said. "All the time."

Eleanor was right. Amanda believed she was blind. When the bandages were removed she was certain her eye would be gone. She practiced for it, recalling everything she had seen, putting things in place in her mind—the rooms of her apartment, the shelves, the darkroom, the closet with her equipment, the rooming house in Ashland, the way she went down the escalator in Penn Station and across the waiting room to catch the train to Washington. The house on P Street, the walk down P Street to 31st, where the front steps were. There was nothing important she had done that she couldn't do without her eyes, she thought, except take pictures.

SIX

In September 1969, ROSIE opened as an alternative school for children chosen from the North Philadelphia ghetto. It was funded by a grant from the Rockefeller Foundation and Eleanor was the director.

The project was located in the house on Gowen Avenue where Eleanor had been living with the volunteers, but after the funding from Rockefeller the first two floors were converted to classrooms. The third floor was an apartment where Eleanor lived with Lily, who at eighteen months was the perfect child for a mother alone who worked day and night at a job without boundaries. Independent and easily entertained, she could spend hours on the floor of Eleanor's office reorganizing the books on the shelves, playing imaginary games. She was indiscriminate about people, especially children, and wandered in and out of classrooms during the day, climbing on one lap or another. Eleanor was unbothered as a mother, unambitious in her plans for Lily, without expectations for her behavior except sweetness, which Lily had in abundance.

"God, I wish I could live with you guys," Tom said on the occasions that he came to visit, less frequent than he had hoped since the civil rights movement had escalated after the Chicago convention. "I could eat you up—both of you."

ROSIE as a school had been Tom's idea—actually Matty's, who said to Tom and Tom told Eleanor, if only some gifted black children could be discovered and given a chance. They would be the ones to lift up the others. So ROSIE was a chance.

There were ten teachers, mainly recent graduates of the University of Pennsylvania or Haverford or Villanova, former volunteers, determined to stay out of Viet Nam. There were about a hundred students someplace in age between childhood and drugs and Eleanor did everything except the teaching. She wrote the grant proposals, hired the teachers, worked with the principals of the ghetto schools to select the children, painted the classrooms with some of the volunteers, got desks donated from a private school going out of business. She worked all the time. The spirit of the late sixties in America suited her spirit. She belonged in the world as she found it.

"You are the real heroine of the sixties," Tom told her. And she felt that way. She felt powerful.

"I want another baby," Eleanor said to Tom in late February when he had a rare weekend he could spend with her. It seemed easy. She could do anything.

"Are you crazy?" Tom said.

She put her finger to his lips. "I want you to listen," she said. "Just listen."

They were sitting in the living room after Lily had been put to bed, drinking wine, Joni Mitchell singing on the stereo.

"I'll listen," he said.

"I could simply have the baby, you know. Nothing could stop me," Eleanor said. "I don't need to ask you."

"Please," Tom said.

"Just listen for one minute." Eleanor had thought about it. She was extraordinarily happy, more than she'd ever imagined. She was happy being a mother and she was not unhappy to be alone. It seemed entirely simple. She loved

Tom Clay and no one else. No one else even interested her and there were plenty of single volunteers and teachers, plenty of easy liaisons for a pretty woman alone at the end of the sixties.

"People who are married make these decisions all the time. One more baby. It's not so odd."

"Not so odd if you're married," Tom said. "But it's crazy for us. One maybe. But two?"

"I could have someone else's baby," Eleanor said.

"I don't much like that idea either," Tom said.

"Just two," Eleanor said. "It's not fair to Lily to be an only child. Too much depends on Lily and me."

"I wish you hadn't told me," Tom said. "You could have lied. Just gone off the pill and gotten pregnant and I'd have been so pissed if the baby was someone else's, you'd have made my day to tell me it was mine," he said. "Ours."

"I wanted you to know," Eleanor said. "We are grown up, after all."

"In a manner of speaking."

"And this is a real love affair. A real and impossible love affair."

Tom leaned back on the couch and closed his eyes.

"It would be a crazy thing to do if I were miserable," Eleanor said. "But I'm not. I'm on top of the world. Never once have I complained about the fact that we're not married."

Tom pulled her onto the couch with him.

"Just tell me one thing. Be honest. Do you ever think that Matty might die, which of course she could, and then . . . ?" he asked.

"Never, shithead," Eleanor said. "You are such a dark-tempered man. I think this is the life I have. And I love you, so why should I look for someone else. Most people hate each other, you know," she said. "They just tolerate being together day after day until one of them dies."

Late that night, Eleanor got out the tape recorder which she had bought after Amanda lost her sight, put in a clean tape, and spoke into it. Once a week on Sunday evenings

Eleanor made a tape and sent it to New York where Amanda lived alone with Day, named for Hole-in-the-Day, a golden retriever Seeing Eye dog with whom she traveled around the city, to her classes at New York University, to the speeches she had been more and more asked to give about her life and her career, especially her years as a man.

February 22, 1970. To Amanda from Eleanor.

"It's Sunday again, cold, rainy, gloomy, and I have decided to have another baby. Just two. I'm not going to be wildly crazy. Lily just turned two and I simply want one more. Tom's of course. He thinks I'm stark raving mad and why would anyone have two when already they've had one mistake and so on.

So he left tonight in a huff. Actually it's more like he left tonight in terror and says he doesn't know whether he'll be back or not. After all, it's just an affair and why make a mountain out of a molehill. And besides, he says, no woman genuinely wants to have children without a husband so I am laying some kind of very subtle trap, pretending I'm a superwoman, different from my gender, on and on. But the truth is, and I told him so, plenty of women would be just as glad, gladder even, to have the baby without the trouble of the baby's father. Me for one. I love Tom. If he were free, I'd probably marry him if he'd learn to stand up straight and change his glasses frame to one less girly. But again and again, I'm struck by the fact that women are stronger than men, more reliable, more resilient. And here he is, Tom Clay, hero of the underground, skittering away like a rabbit because I want another baby.

Oh well.

I expect I'm pregnant anyhow.

"Are you on the pill still?" he asked.

"Sure," I said.

"Promise?"

"Cross my heart and hope to die," I said.

Really!

My question to you is this. Not a question actually. I need your help.

Mama cannot imagine not being married. Even to Papa, when he's at his bear-awful worst—better to be married under any circumstances than not. And Papa. Papa is going to explode when he hears I'm pregnant, if I am, which I'm pretty sure of. So will you help me out?

No one can believe another person's happiness. Mama simply cannot understand that the life I have—one she would simply despise—is wonderful. I love doing ROSIE. I don't care about living with Salvation Army furniture covered in Indian cloth and old vans and hand-me-down clothes from the junior league for Lily and me in jeans—when I could look "drop dead beautiful," Mama says. Sort of disappointed that I didn't turn out more like her.

One bad thing to tell you: I was standing yesterday holding Lily on the corner of Germantown Avenue and Gowen waiting for the light to change and a U-Haul rental truck ran over the curb and hit Lily and me. What it did was hit me on the side not holding Lily and threw me on my back. We weren't hurt. Lily not at all and I'm a little stiff and bruised. But the whole incident gave me such a start that all day and last night I had premonitions of my own death.

Tomorrow I'm going to a lawyer in Chestnut Hill who handles business for ROSIE and make a will leaving Lily and X to Mama and you as guardians should anything happen to me. It's the sort of thing you worry about if you're not married, I guess.

My life has taken on more importance since I've had children. It now seems possible to die.

Give fat Day a hug. I read about your Sam Dane speech at Columbia and it sounded very funny, especially about the wandering penis, which you put more delicately in the speech, but about the time you stuffed your pants with a piece of cloth which came unwound and fell down to the bottom of your pants leg.

Hugs and kisses. I'll be up in the next two weeks to

*help you put together your Women and Girls Show—
probably next Friday after school.*

That was winter. At Easter celebrated in Washington with
Nich-o home and Frederick with his new girlfriend from
Ireland whom he'd met at a bar in St. Louis and Jonathan,
back with Molly Saucer who was living with him on the
third floor of the house on P Street, Eleanor knew she was
pregnant. She had not seen Tom Clay but he wrote notes,
sweet funny notes, and he sent tapes and books and clippings from the newspaper about his activities. Occasionally flowers.

"He won't come see me," Eleanor said to Amanda that
Easter. "He's afraid I'll get pregnant."

"So?" Amanda asked.

"So it's too late for him to worry," Eleanor replied.

Anna Katrina March was born on November 8, 1970, a
year before Amanda's last photograph show and the reappearance of Emma Gaits as trouble.

ELEANOR
AND
LILY
AND
KAT

ONE

KAT WAS NOT Lily, as Eleanor remarked to Tom Clay in the first few weeks of Anna Katrina's life. And from the start, she was at odds with the world.

By the end of the suffocating summer of 1971, Eleanor, exhausted with two children and ROSIE, was susceptible to the reappearance of Emma Gaits, taller, thinner, imposing herself on Eleanor's life like a persistent virus.

It was late August and a hot night, so the doors and windows on Gowen Avenue were open and Emma simply walked in the front door of ROSIE, up two flights of stairs to Eleanor's apartment where Kat was screaming and Eleanor was walking back and forth across the floor of the living room with Kat on her shoulders.

"Hello," Emma said.

"Oh, hello." Eleanor reached down to take a piece of puzzle out of Lily's mouth. Her heart had taken a leap to see Emma Gaits again.

"I came back."

"I see you did."

"And you got a new baby since I left."

"Who's driving me crazy."

"Here," Emma reached out and took Kat. "I'll take her," she said.

In the kitchen, dinner was cooking, chicken in the oven.

"Come in the kitchen with me," Eleanor said. Poppy seed bread was rising on the counter and the colander was full of yellow squash and lettuce from the garden.

"Poor Lily's starved," Eleanor said lifting Lily into a high chair. "Do you mind if I give her supper while you hold Kat?"

Emma smiled an enigmatic smile.

"I love to hold Kat," she said kissing the top of Kat's head as she stopped crying.

"Was the front door open?" Eleanor asked, falling into

an old friendship with Emma Gaits, easily, without self-consciousness.

"I just walked in."

"That was stupid of me," Eleanor said. "There was a break-in down the street last week."

"You should keep the house locked," Emma said. "But you're probably so busy you can't possibly do everything." Her voice was sympathetic.

It happened as simply as that. They had dinner and cleaned up and put Lily to bed with a story and Kat finally to sleep. Then Eleanor went downstairs to straighten the classrooms for the next morning and lock up the house. A call came from Tom in New York to say he'd be able to come on Sunday afternoon depending on Matty, who had gotten worse in the past few days. By then it was eleven and Emma was folding the laundry on the kitchen table.

"It's eleven o'clock," Eleanor said. "You'd better go home."

"I thought I'd spend the night," Emma said.

"Remember. I promised your father."

"That was a long time ago and things are better between us. I'm older, first of all."

"Then call him."

"I'd like you to give me a chance to help you. Just this week," Emma said. "Try me out."

"If you spend the night, you'll have to call."

Emma Gaits hesitated. "I suppose I could come back early in the morning." And then she changed her mind. "Okay," she said. "I'll call him."

"She could have called anyone," Tom Clay said later to Eleanor. "She could have called the weather and said 'Hiya, Pop. C'n I sleep over at Elly March's t'night?'"

They were lying on Eleanor's bed overlooking the back garden where Lily was playing in the sandbox and Emma was riding Kat around on her shoulders.

"She's a mouse," Eleanor said.

"Rabid," Tom said, pulling Eleanor on top of him. "I have a good nose for trouble and she's it."

They lay together all morning until the heat of noon had

made them weary and then they got up, showered, and made lunch. When they came into the kitchen, Kat was sleeping on a mat on the kitchen floor, Lily had eaten, and Emma was putting her down for a nap.

Eleanor sliced tomatoes and cucumbers for sandwiches.

"See?" she said. "I need her."

"You need someone," Tom said reluctantly.

Eleanor slid down at the table next to him.

"Will I see you next week?"

"Maybe," he said. "Probably."

"You seem tired all the time. Is it Matty?"

"I've been exhausted," Tom said. "I can do absolutely nothing and still be exhausted. But I don't think it's Matty. It's the times."

There was a spirit of exhaustion at the end of the sixties. In 1969, the Chicago Seven, indicted for violating the antiriot clause of the Civil Rights Act in connection with demonstrations during the 1968 Democratic convention, were found not guilty at the conclusion of a boisterous trial. Tom Clay was there in Chicago with Tom Hayden and Abbie Hoffman and Bobby Seale but in the end he was not happy at the outcome, not particularly interested. He seemed restless to Eleanor, a young man with half a law degree, a sick wife, a life which had been on the front lines of a war that was fizzling.

"Sometimes I don't know what to do when I get up in the morning," he said to Eleanor.

When four students protesting the expansion of the war into Cambodia were killed by National Guardsmen at Kent State in Ohio in May 1970, he spent two days in bed in the grip of a terrible headache.

"Finally," he said, making himself another sandwich, "I've had enough violence. At the heart of it I'm a southern white boy from a conventional family in North Carolina who went crazy."

That afternoon, they decided that in September he would go to work as a teacher at ROSIE.

During the fall, Emma Gaits became a regular feature of ROSIE. She came afternoons after school and stayed through dinner, through the washing up and stories and putting Kat to bed. In time, she did the grocery shopping and secretarial work for Eleanor, coming on Saturdays and Sundays. Subtly she insinuated herself in Eleanor's life until she was indispensable. Eleanor's energy, always capacious, had doubled in size, and if, on an occasional afternoon, Emma wasn't able to come, Eleanor was bereft.

"All of your worry about trouble with Emma," she said to Tom, "and nothing's happened."

"It will," Tom said.

Sometimes Eleanor lay in bed at night, Tom stretched out beside her, and thought with a kind of wonder about her life. The feeling wasn't one of self-congratulation or conceit but actual wonder. She had become a woman unlike any she had imagined—larger than her dreams for herself—in a way heroic like the games she made up when she was a child. That's how she felt. Heroic.

TWO

AMANDA WALKED TO the Broome Street Gallery with Flat Mouth and Day, who was a gentle and protective golden retriever, a little like Melvina without the bite, Amanda said to Flat Mouth, who was sullen at the naming of a dog for his beloved father.

"It's an honor," Amanda insisted. "I never had a son."

They walked slowly; Amanda was still uncertain on the street and Flat Mouth, thrown from his old pony, walked with a cane, chattering, a rarity for a man who was laconic by nature, grown silent with age.

Amanda had been excited that Flat Mouth was coming, an almost lighthearted girlish sense of excitement. He could still make her heart pound and it amused her to think that the heart remains susceptible even when the face dries up and falls away from the bone.

It was odd not knowing how she looked in the morning.

She had always paid attention to her face when she brushed her teeth, not out of vanity so much as interest, although she did like the sharp angles and considered her face distinguished, though not pretty.

"How do I look?" she asked.

"You look good. Fine," Flat Mouth said. "Brown as an Indian."

"I've been in the garden all summer," Amanda said. "Learning to do sculpture. That's why I have color."

It was a perfect day in early October, the few trees turning, the sun bright and warm and the air a rare clear cool New England air.

Amanda had spent the summer doing a life-size reclining nude in clay. She had never done sculpture, but with her eyes gone she was astonished at the range of her hands. Initially when she decided to try sculpture after the semester at NYU was over, she knew she wanted to work on the human form so she could feel her own body as reference. But once she started, the work was so sensual, especially working in the morning sun, that the figure she made was not at all like her body but a large fleshy Rubens woman, thick below the waist with great thighs, small rounded shoulders, and small breasts perfectly shaped as pears. She felt as if she could see the figure, especially when she was doing the toes, using her own toes as an example. She actually felt as if she could see everything when she was working, so strong was her visual imagination. It was only when she left the apartment with Day and had to make her way through the streets of the Village that she was conscious of being blind.

The exhibit was called "Some Families in Twentieth-Century America" but the narrative in the photographs belonged to the women in the families and to the girls. There were a lot of men and boys pictured, not as shadows, but always they were photographed in relationship to the women.

"When will you have a book of the pictures?" Flat Mouth asked.

"There are not enough pictures for a book," Amanda said. "So when a book is put together, maybe Eleanor and

Sara will do it for me—but then, I'm going to include photographs from my own life—you and Sara and Jonathan
and the children. They'll be filler," she said. "And it will
be my last book, so why not?"

Her family was already at the gallery when she arrived for
the opening. Everyone—Frederick and his new wife,
Beatrice from Ireland, Jonathan and Molly Saucer, Nicholas who had just moved to Rutland, Vermont, to practice
law and live on an organic farm with a young woman he
had met in law school. Sara and Hendrik had come with
Albert, Eleanor was there with the babies and Emma
Gaits, who had come along to help. The gallery was
crowded. People had gathered outside lining up as they did
for new movies. It was an event.

Amanda Steward had become a romantic figure, even a
legend. Her story of the young girl whose mother died
when she was three, growing up in a hospital at the edge
of an Indian reservation, her friendship with Flat Mouth,
her life as Sam Dane, her long career, the originality and
daring of her work—and then her loss of sight—suited
people captured by stories of hardship and romance, by
unlikely success. Amanda had become a celebrity although
she had no gift for the role, no patience with it, and report-
ers found her sharp-tongued and not forthcoming.

"I just take pictures," she said when asked about the
metaphors in her work. "Or I used to when I could see."

There was a moment early in the event when Amanda was
asked to speak. She had not come prepared, had in fact
said that she didn't wish to speak, but so many people had
come hoping to hear her that in the end she walked across
the long wood floor and stood half-facing the crowd. She
was dressed as she used to dress when she lived in New
York and Sara was a little girl: her mother's lace blouse
and black trousers, her hair pulled back off her face, a
man's morning coat, and, since the surgery, sunglasses.

"I have spent my life taking pictures," she said in her
low, steady voice. "And I won't be taking any more of

them, so in conclusion, I'll tell you two things about the pictures I have taken.

"In the beginning, I liked to look at things. Especially, I liked the way people fit a landscape and I liked their faces. I have always been interested in faces. But the real reason I began to take pictures was that my mother died when I was three. I learned at an early age that things change quickly and forever. There is no visible record of my mother's life. I don't even remember the look of her. And so I decided to take pictures, especially of faces. That's all. I'm not a very complicated person."

The crowd was silent and for a moment, a very long moment, Amanda, standing in darkness, thought she must have misspoken. And then there was the sound of people weeping.

Amanda and Flat Mouth walked back together after the opening, behind the Marches and the rest of the family to the restaurant where they were to have dinner. Flat Mouth slipped his arm through hers.

"I liked your speech," he said to her. "It was a good speech. Maybe after all you are a great woman, A Man."

"And not any kind of man?" She laughed.

"That's right," Flat Mouth said wryly and he took her hand. "It's not so bad."

THREE

ELEANOR AND LILY sat across from each other on the four o'clock train from Union Station to 30th Street Philadelphia. It was late July, the summer of 1972. Lily at four was a quiet, self-contained child with a lovely open face, thick dark-blond hair which she wore long and brushed, tied with a satin ribbon as if she were a child from the turn of the century. She preferred dresses, pastel pinafores with pastel plastic sandals, which were new that year. She had the kind of demeanor to which people, strangers on the street, responded with a sense of trust and she was company for her mother, easy and affirming, almost maternal in her manner.

This afternoon, after a long and unsuccessful day in Washington trying to get funding for ROSIE, whose grant from the Rockefeller Foundation was finished, Eleanor took off her shoes, tucked her bare feet under Lily's lavender pinafore, and opened the *Washington Post* to a story about terrorists in Israel who had killed a mother and her young child, blowing up the car in which they were riding out of Jerusalem. For reasons she didn't understand because she seldom responded personally to the bad news of strangers, she was overcome with emotion, teary even, and put down the paper without reading.

Lily, attuned like mercury to her mother's temperature changes, looked up. "Is there sadness in the paper, Mama?" she asked.

"There's always sadness in the paper," Eleanor said.

"That's too bad," Lily said pulling her coloring book and crayons out of her book bag, opening the coloring book on her lap. "I only like happy endings," she said matter-of-factly.

Eleanor folded the newspaper and took out her notebook of plans for ROSIE, taking down notes of her meetings at the endowment. It would take $300,000 to run ROSIE for another year. So far she had raised $50,000 from a private individual, $10,000 from Citizens for Action, and had been turned down by the University of Pennsylvania and the City of Philadelphia. She had submitted applications to fourteen foundations from which she had not heard.

"I only like the beginnings of things," she had said to Tom Clay.

And ROSIE was in the middle of its life.

"I especially hate the middle."

"What was the bad news?" Lily asked, coloring the outfits for Barbie.

Eleanor told her about the terrorists in Israel, about the antagonism between the Arabs and the Israelis.

"They are each fighting for what they think belongs to

them," Eleanor said. "Most wars are like that. And the mother and child were victims of the war."

"Like Emma's father wants Emma back from you," Lily said out of the blue.

"Emma's father?" Eleanor asked.

Since Emma Gaits had come back into her life a year ago, Eleanor almost never heard a mention of Emma's father. Although she knew that he was probably unhappy to have Emma back at ROSIE working with Eleanor, she assumed that his interest in Emma's life had subsided. After all, Emma was eighteen and in the last year had been well paid at ROSIE, so Eleanor imagined that if there were trouble she would have heard.

"What about Emma's father?" Eleanor asked.

"Sometimes while you're working in your office and Emma's taking care of me and Kat, he calls and says he will do something to you if Emma keeps working for ROSIE."

"To you he says this?" Eleanor asked.

"To Emma. But I listen in on the kitchen phone." She finished coloring Barbie's bathing suit purple and green and took out her book of fill-in-the-dots.

"Tell me exactly what he said," Eleanor asked.

Lily looked up. "He calls all the time, Mama. Last week he said to Emma, 'If you're not home in an hour, I'm coming to get you and you know what that means.' "

"Does Emma know you listen in?"

"She tells me to."

"And it doesn't make you upset to hear what he says?"

"Not so much," Lily said. "Emma makes a joke. She says he's an old buffalo, a crazy old baboon and anyway he can't do anything but talk because he hasn't got any legs." She finished a blackbird coming out of a pie in her book. "I'd like to see *Cabaret* with Liza Minelli. Emma says Kat's too little of course but she'll take me."

Eleanor put her things away and leaned back against the seat.

"We'll see," she said pensively.

She didn't bring up Emma Gait's father again because

she didn't want to make an issue, but she was going to talk to Emma as soon as she got home.

Emma Gaits was a strange girl. There was something "out of whack" about her, as Tom said.

"I've spent the last ten years with people running along the edge," he said to Eleanor. "And she's one of those. I'm sure of it."

Sometimes, especially when she was working in the kitchen and Emma was there or in the offices of ROSIE, Eleanor could feel Emma's eyes boring into the back of her. She'd turn around quickly and catch her staring.

"What are you looking at?" she'd say crossly, because it did make her uneasy.

"Nothing," Emma would reply. "I was just thinking."

Once she said, "I was just thinking about my mother," but Eleanor didn't pursue the conversation.

Every time Eleanor opened an opportunity for personal conversation, Emma leapt in and filled the vacuum. Already, she occupied every corner of Eleanor's life and although Eleanor needed her, could not in fact imagine raising her daughters and running ROSIE without her, there was a price to pay.

Tom was at ROSIE when Eleanor and Lily arrived a little after seven and opened the front door. Eleanor heard him in the kitchen arguing.

"I don't want him here, you understand?" Tom said.

"I work for her," Emma said. "Not you."

"I don't care who you work for," Tom said. "You won't be working for anyone if this happens again."

"Hello," Eleanor called from the hall, hoping to stop the argument before Lily heard any more. "I'm back."

"Hello, pussycats." Tom came into the hall, lifted Lily into the air. "Hello, Lily Stew—how's with you?"

Kat, in her diapers, slid down the stairs on her belly, toddled over to Eleanor, and hit her in her knee with her tiny fist.

"Hello, Kitty Kat March, sweet as ever," Tom said tousling her head. "Why did she hit you?" he asked Eleanor.

"She's politically against my taking trips, especially with Lily. Right, Kat?"

"No," Kat said.

Eleanor picked her up and took her upstairs to bed. "Come up," she said. "We'll have supper. Maybe pancakes."

"Yum," Lily said. "And ice cream."

"With chocolate sauce."

"God, what a mother!" Tom said.

"So what was that about?" Eleanor asked Tom when the children were in bed.

He sat down on the couch with his leg over the upholstered arm. "That crazy woman's crazy father came over to take her home with him."

"When?"

"He was here when I came in at six," Tom said. "She had put Kat to bed. He was sitting in the office and Psycho Path was coming downstairs with a piranha expression on her lips."

"Did you talk to him?"

"I'll quote you what I said." He imitated, extending his hand to Emma Gait's father. " 'Hello. I'm Tom Clay,' I said. He's a small, fat, plate-faced man with eyes he exchanged with the devil for his soul."

"I know," Eleanor said. "I've met him." She cut up a pear and gave half to Tom. "Did he say anything?"

"Of course," Tom said. "He's not a man at a loss for words and he spoke without ceremony." He imitated the lugubrious voice. " 'Do you fuck my daughter,' he asked, 'or is she the only one who fucks her?' "

"And what did you say?"

"I said, 'Get out.' "

"And did he?"

"I added, 'I'm calling the police.' "

"And he left?"

"Don't worry. You'll have the opportunity to see him again. He said he'd be back."

"Did he walk out?" Eleanor asked.

"Are you thinking he might have crawled?"

"No," Eleanor said with an odd expression on her face. "Emma told Lily that her father was harmless because he didn't have any legs. Has he lost his legs since I met him?"

"He has legs," Tom said. "He walked out on them and he'll walk back too."

FOUR

ELEANOR LAY IN her bed that night on top of the sheets, a fan billowing her nightgown. She could not sleep.

Tom had left late after dinner. Matty Clay was worse. He made light of it. One thing one day, one thing another, he said breezily. "This morning at breakfast, her mind was kaput."

He actually said very little about Matty. Nothing critical. He considered that the real adultery in his life was not his love affair with Eleanor but his complaints about Matty. And beyond the mercurial nature of the illness itself, he had none. There were weeks when it looked as if Matty would die, even a period when she was in the hospital with pneumonia, but then she'd rebound and could be almost well for a long time.

"By tomorrow, get rid of Emma Gaits or I'll send the Philadelphia riot squad," Tom said before he left.

"I will," Eleanor said. "I promise."

But just as he was walking out the door, he took hold of her shoulders.

"I've got to trust you about this, El," he said.

"Trust me."

He shook his head. "I can't," he said. "You don't have the right amount of fear. Too much adrenaline and an undersupply of fear. Anything could happen with Emma Gaits."

"Like what?"

Tom hesitated.

"Kidnapping. Murder. Name it," Tom said. "Her father is so fucked up. He thinks you're sleeping with his daughter. Or I am. Or both. And that's probably because he is." He kissed her hard. "Don't get me started."

It was after midnight and Eleanor was wide awake. She got up, went into the kitchen, and lit a cigarette. She seldom smoked, but Tom had left a pack of Kents so she sat in the dark, her feet up on the kitchen table, smoking.

Tom was wrong about fear. She knew about fear. She had simply developed a capacity to disguise it at an early age. She was, in a way, afraid of Emma Gaits. She knew that Emma had fallen in love with her. Knew that the reason Emma would do anything she asked had to do with a kind of wrongheaded devotion she felt for Eleanor. Even without Mr. Gaits, such devotion was dangerous. In her mind she carried on a conversation with Tom so he could understand, so he wouldn't think her tougher or stronger or saner than she really was.

I don't want to fire Emma, she said in her mind to Tom Clay. I need her, she said. Not just for Lily and Kat, but for me. She makes me feel double my size. Capable of anything I want to do. And look at ROSIE. Look what I've been able to do.

She's stark raving mad, she had Tom say to her. What are you going to do about it?

Talk to her.

That's a terrific idea, Tom said. And what are you going to say?

I'll start with asking her why she told Lily that her father had no legs.

She opened the refrigerator door. There was leftover dinner—chicken with broccoli in a sauce, half of a lemon cake which Emma had made, a quart of milk, orange juice, two eggs, Vermont cheese unopened, and strawberry jam. She took out the cake and cut herself a slice. Just as she was about to bite into it, she changed her mind, dumped it in the garbage, tied the top of the plastic garbage bag, and put it in the large green plastic bag so Emma wouldn't see she'd thrown it away and guess that Eleanor was suspicious of poison. What poison would you put in a lemon cake? And would she try to poison Lily and Kat as well? She needed an aspirin. There was no aspirin in the cabinet over the sink except baby aspirin so she took twelve and lay down in front of the fan in the hope sleep would overtake her quickly.

She was asleep when the telephone rang. It was two A.M.

"Elly?" Sara said in her soft, anxious voice. "I'm so sorry to wake you."

"Never mind, Mama," Eleanor said. "What's the matter?"

"I'm just calling about Jonathan. Have you heard from him?"

"Jonathan?"

"I thought you might have heard from him tonight. He's gone. He left after supper."

"Maybe he's out with friends."

"No. He's left. He packed."

"Left?"

"I actually thought he might have called you and asked could he stay."

"Well, he didn't," Eleanor said.

"He's very upset," Sara said. "Molly Saucer left."

"Molly leaves once a month. I'd have thought he was used to it and besides, Mama, he's thirty-two. He's got to grow up."

"This time she's left for good," Sara said, ignoring the remark about Jonathan's age. "She got married."

"Great."

"I don't even particularly like her. She wasn't one of my favorite waitresses at the hotel. But Jonathan loved her."

"Well, I think good riddance," Eleanor said. "What does Papa think?"

"He's gone to bed," Sara said.

"I'm sorry, Mama," Eleanor said. "Why don't you call Frederick? Jon may have been in touch with him."

"They're fighting," Sara said. "They've been fighting since Christmas."

"What about Nich-o?"

"I did call Nich-o," Sara said. "He has stomach flu."

"I'll call right away if I hear anything, Mama."

Eleanor got up. It occurred to her that Jonathan might very well have decided to come to Philadelphia. She slipped on a T-shirt and jeans, went down to the second floor to a classroom at the front of the house with a large bay window overlooking Gowen Avenue. She didn't turn on the light so she could see outside to check if by any chance Jonathan's blue Chevrolet was there, if he had been knocking on the first floor and she hadn't heard him all the way up in her apartment.

To her surprise, there was a car. She couldn't tell the color but the headlights were on. Without a second thought she went downstairs assuming it was Jonathan, actually pleased at the thought of company, especially Jonathan. She turned on the front porch light and opened the door. The person in the car had gotten out, although the headlights were still turned on.

"Jonathan?" she called.

When she got to the steps, she could see the person under the bright light of the street lamp and it was not Jonathan at all. It was Emma Gaits's father.

She slammed the front door, bolted it, dashed up the stairs, turned off the lights in the living room of her apartment, and stood at the window. He had gotten back in the car.

She called the police but by the time she went back to the window, he had pulled out from the curb and driven down Gowen Avenue. She saw him turn left at Stenton and within several minutes a patrol car pulled up.

"I'm sorry," she said when the policeman rang the doorbell. "He left." What could she tell him? What had Mr. Gaits done?

Sara called at 6:30. Eleanor was awake, sitting on the couch in the living room with a book, unable to read.

"Jonathan came home," she said. "I'm so sorry to have awakened you last night."

"S'okay," Eleanor said. "Where was he?"

"Drinking," Sara said. "And then he parked at Uncle Albert's and slept in the car."

"Tell him to blow up Molly Saucer's house. She isn't worth potato chips," Eleanor said.

For a moment she thought to tell her mother what had happened, but what was Sara to do about it and what truth was there in Mr. Gaits as danger anyway? He was probably a harmless middle-aged man with too much to say and too much time alone.

But she was going to talk to someone, she decided. First thing, as soon as she fed and dressed the girls, she was going to New York to see Amanda.

FIVE

ELEANOR LEFT BEFORE Emma Gaits arrived on Tuesday morning. She taped a note to the front door.

> I have gone on holiday for several days.
> I'll let you know when I get back.
>
> EM

She didn't know what she was going to do about Emma Gaits. She should fire her. Vamoose, she should say. Don't come back ever. But the situation was more complicated than that.

When she was small, Sara used to sing her a song she didn't understand. Still she didn't understand it.

> *Mama, mama, mama,*
> *Pin a rose on me.*
> *Two little boys are stuck on me,*
> *One is blind and the other can't see.*
> *Mama, mama, mama,*
> *Pin a rose on me.*

That was how she felt about Emma Gaits. Stuck on her. Or

else Emma was the one stuck. Either way, what ought to have been a clear and simple decision was not.

She drove to the Chestnut Hill local, parked, and caught the 7:40 train to the city.

Kat was crabby. Kat was often crabby, but this morning nothing was satisfactory. Not her bottle or her pacifier or the box of animal crackers Eleanor had in her bag or the Richard Scarry books. She threw them all on the floor of the train, took off her sandals, and threw them, and as Eleanor was picking everything up off the floor Kat took off her Pampers.

"Maybe we shouldn't go to New York," Lily said.

"We have to see Amanda."

"Maybe we could go tomorrow," Lily said, helping her mother pick up the things on the floor of the train.

"We're going now," Eleanor said, exasperated. "Amanda needs us."

Amanda was melancholy when Eleanor arrived at her apartment. She was packing to go to Ashland for the month of August and there were clothes laid out, unfolded, on her bed. The kitchen counters were dirty. The teapot was boiling for ice tea when Eleanor walked in the door, but there was no ice in the refrigerator. In the bowl on the kitchen table, peaches were rotting and there were ants dashing around the edges of the wooden fruit bowl.

"I suppose everything is a mess," Amanda said.

Kat collapsed on Day who was lying beside the couch next to Amanda and burrowed her head in his fur.

"It's a little messy," Eleanor said. She washed the counters, tossed out the peaches. "Maybe you should have a cleaning lady."

"I don't want a cleaning lady," Amanda said.

Lily sat down on the floor where Amanda stacked her books and opened a large one of nature photographs by Eliot Porter.

While the children were settled, Eleanor went to the market at the corner and bought lunch, more peaches, a bag of ice. By the time she came back, Kat had crawled across Amanda's belly and fallen asleep.

"You seem weary," Eleanor said, unpacking the groceries, cleaning out the refrigerator, making Swiss cheese sandwiches.

"I'm in a bad humor," Amanda said.

"Amanda doesn't like her artwork," Lily said from the floor where she was sitting against Day looking at pictures.

"Your sculpture?"

"What I don't like is in the backyard," Amanda said.

Eleanor looked out the back door. In the middle of the patio on a table was a new figure, smaller than the thick-thighed woman she had completed, cast, and given to Sara for the garden of the P Street house. This one looked like the figure of a large dog lying on her side. The flanks were broad at the thigh. The neck was thick.

"It looks like a dog, doesn't it?" Amanda said. "Like Day."

"A little like Day," Eleanor said. She made ice tea. "What's the matter with a dog?"

"Nothing whatever if a dog is what I had in mind," Amanda said. "But what I had in mind was a woman."

She moved around the apartment with relative ease, lifting a sleeping Kat, putting her down on the couch on her stomach, putting the chairs around the table for lunch.

"Have you come for the night?" she asked when she sat down.

"I have come with a problem," Eleanor said. "So I may stay longer. Maybe Wednesday or Thursday. ROSIE is closed until the first of September, so I'm free."

"Then stay all week and you can help me do my last book of photographs so I can finish that before I leave for Ashland."

"I'd like to stay until Sunday," Lily said quietly.

"Why Sunday?" Eleanor asked.

"Because Emma Gaits doesn't come to work on Sunday so it will be all right to go home."

Amanda furrowed her brow.

"And what's the matter with Emma Gaits?"

"Everything," Lily said.

"What was your sense of her when she was here?" Eleanor asked.

"I don't need eyes to feel her devotion to you," Amanda said.

Eleanor shrugged. "I suppose," she said.

But later, after lunch, Amanda had more to say. Lily was resting in Melvina's old room, Kat still sleeping, and Eleanor took a stool to the large table in the middle of Amanda's living room and spread out prints from her exhibit of women.

"What I would have said if Lily had not been there is that Emma Gaits is in love with you," Amanda said. "Isn't she?"

"That's what Tom says."

"Tom has some good sense about people," Amanda said. "What did he say?"

Eleanor told the story of Emma Gaits from the beginning, including the story about her father and the missing legs.

"Get rid of her," Amanda said. "Fire her and change the locks on the doors."

"I suppose I'll have to," Eleanor said.

"Of course you have to," Amanda said.

Eleanor stayed until Wednesday and then Thursday. She didn't want to leave. In the morning she'd make breakfast, get out art paper and books and records for Kat and Lily to play with in the garden, and then she'd sit with Amanda at the large table in the living room organizing pictures.

"Do you want the book to be chronological?" Eleanor asked, looking at a print of Lincoln Draper during the war, of Melvina in their kitchen on P Street before it was remodeled for the Small Hotel.

"Perhaps," Amanda said. "But I want it to be like memory as well so the book has a look of surprise and not nostalgia," she said, feeling the surface of a photograph of Lincoln. "I hate nostalgia," she said, "although I'd like to have a picture of my mother for the book."

"Maybe you should include one of her letters," Eleanor said.

"Maybe," Amanda said. She got up to make tea.

"I suppose you know that her mother was dead when she wrote those letters." She took two cups out of the cupboard, poured milk in a pitcher, got out spoons from the drawer beside the sink.

"Mama told me."

Amanda poured the hot tea and carried the cups across the room, without spilling, even walking with ease.

"There is one letter, I remember," she said to Eleanor. "In the bureau drawer next to my bed. You should look for the tape marked Christmas 1897."

Eleanor went into Amanda's bedroom.

"The tape recorder is beside my bed," Amanda called.

Eleanor brought the tape recorder and tape, put them down for Amanda, who turned on the tape and pushed fast forward.

"There," Amanda said. "Now listen."

I am no good at geography but I wish I could see where I am in relationship to Wales, to Rhyl, to New York where you are buried in St. Thomas R.C. Cemetery. Do I exist, I sometimes wonder, if you cannot see me?
Yr. loving daughter,

"You see?" Amanda said triumphantly. "We are the image of our mother's perfect dreams." She pushed eject and gave Eleanor the tape to put away. " 'Do I exist if you cannot see me?' You should put that on a page right after the title page."

"It sounds peculiar, doesn't it?" Eleanor asked.

"Everything true about people is a little peculiar," Amanda said.

Eleanor sat down at the table with Amanda.

"You put the tape back in order, didn't you?" Amanda asked.

"I double-checked," Eleanor said, amused. "You must know those letters very well. Do you listen to them before you go to bed at night?"

"From time to time," Amanda said, not wishing to confess that, in fact, she listened to them every night, one after the other, in order. "If I have trouble sleeping," she said. "I haven't had any trouble sleeping since you've been here."

"I haven't either," Eleanor said. "No nightmares. Not once."

Amanda left for Wisconsin the first Friday in August. Eleanor went with her to the airport by taxi, saw her off to Duluth, and then took the train from Penn Station to Philadelphia.

"I loved our vacation," Lily said happily when they were settled in the food car of the Amtrak train.

"So did I," Eleanor said.

"Did you, Kat?" Lily asked.

"No," Kat said. And they all laughed.

While Kat and Lily colored dinosaurs green in Lily's coloring book, Eleanor took out her tape recorder.

Something mysterious had happened to Eleanor with Amanda that week, sitting at the table with her photographs, the pictures of strangers mixed with pictures of Eleanor's own life as a baby with Sara, as a child in the garden of the Small Hotel, in her grandmother's familiar bedroom on the third floor of P Street, pictures intermingled with Flat Mouth and Amanda as a girl, a self-portrait of Sam Dane, her mother as a child in Greenwich Village dressed up like a Victorian doll. Eleanor felt a kind of safety in a family which had seemed for years to be disintegrating since she had discovered the empty bottles in Sara's linen closet. She wanted to thank Amanda for what suddenly felt like a gift.

This tape is to Amanda from Eleanor. Lunchtime, August fourth, 1972, just outside of Trenton, New Jersey, on the train to Philadelphia.

I was looking out the window as we flew by Trenton just now—too fast for my eye to quite take in the image in front of it, except in reflection after the image was gone. And I thought of your photographs for the book— how, if arranged in sequence, they could create the illusion of time in this century—like a motion picture in which the camera takes a still photograph and then a second and a third, each frame persisting in the eye until the next image arrives so the eye is tricked into seeing continuous motion.

Our lives have changed so quickly, your mother's and yours, my mother's and mine, faster and faster, from a still photograph to a silent film to a camera with ninety frames a second. It seems today as if there is only time to dip into the moment and briefly stop the motion.

Your photographs capture that sense of time, and reading through your book will seem, I think, like looking out the window of a train at the swift-moving world, then stopping at a station from time to time to read the signs.

SIX

AN OLD AND familiar anxiety overtook Amanda just as she stepped onto the plane for Duluth as the stewardess said "Good morning" in her sunny voice, took Amanda's ticket, helped her to the front seat in the coach section where she sat alone so Day could be at her feet.

"Can I get you anything?" the stewardess asked in the solicitous voice people reserve for the handicapped.

"Nothing," Amanda said with irritation. She felt around for her seat belt. She didn't like to fly since she had lost her sight. The whole experience felt sudden and unexpected, especially if the pilot was silent and gave no information over the intercom about ascent or descent or scenery or altitude.

But this anxiety had nothing to do with flying. These feelings were ancient, half a century in memory, and had to do with danger to children. She was flooded by tidal waves of terrifying possibilities.

It occurred to her that the door to the plane had not closed, that Eleanor was probably still in the airport and she could detain her. That is what she felt. A need to intercept an impending danger. She put on the light for the stewardess.

"Yes?" the stewardess asked.

What should she say? She hadn't thought it through. Get me off this plane. Someome must get my granddaughter. She's somewhere in La Guardia. Page Eleanor March before she catches a cab to Penn Station. She heard the doors closing ahead of first class.

"Can I get you something?" the stewardess was saying.

"Water," Amanda said meekly. "I need to take an aspirin."

The plane had begun its taxi to the runway when the stewardess returned with the water.

Amanda had treated the story of Emma Gaits like a story, someone Eleanor had read about with an unbalanced father, someone invented. Certainly Amanda had understood what longing Emma Gaits filled in Eleanor's life. After all, there had been those years, especially when she was small, when Sara, overspent emotionally by Jonathan's illness, was absent from Eleanor's life.

Amanda knew in her marrow about mothers. She didn't underestimate the cost of their absence in the lives of girls. What struck her now, as she sat in darkness, overconscious of the movement of the plane, was Mr. Gaits. It had been years since she thought about her own father—she was not by instinct reflective, easily bored by psychological considerations. But blindness had changed that. Now she was locked in the dark closet of memory and she thought about things. Her mind wandered down corridors that simply would not have opened when the sights of the world consumed her attention. Her father as a dark figure slid back to consciousness and she remembered clearly what it was like to lie in bed as a child and fear his nighttime arrival. She felt in danger, as if their lives as a family were at risk.

As the plane lifted over the Northeast, she thought of the story Eleanor had told her about Emma Gaits and her father as a true story. As fact, it was a story full of danger and she wanted to stop Eleanor from returning to Philadelphia, to protect her from what suddenly seemed to be real trouble. In Duluth, she'd call her in Philadelphia, call Tom Clay and ask him to go to ROSIE just in case.

By luck, the flight was easy and she didn't have to change planes. She was in Duluth by noon central time which meant it was one eastern so if Eleanor had caught the 9:30 train to Philadelphia as she had planned to do, she would be there by now and home. Amanda had a driver meeting her to go to Ashland, but she asked him to wait while she made several calls.

A woman answered at ROSIE.

"Is Eleanor March there?" Amanda asked.

"She's not," the woman said. "She's out of town."

"Who is this?" Amanda asked.

The woman hesitated. "This is her assistant."

"Emma Gaits?" Amanda asked.

"Yes, it is."

"This is Eleanor's grandmother."

"I'm so glad to talk to you," Emma said. "Where is Eleanor?"

"I thought she would be there."

"I haven't seen her for a few days."

"Please have her call me in Wisconsin when she arrives," Amanda said. "She should arrive soon and she has the number."

She called Tom Clay next. Matty's mother answered the telephone in a weary voice. Tom was out, she said. He wouldn't be back until supper.

Amanda felt a certain desperation.

Sara was at home. She answered the phone after several rings.

"Sara?"

"Mama," Sara said. Her voice had a familiar slippery quality.

"What are you doing at home?" Amanda asked.

"Hendrik is in New York."

"And where is Jonathan?"

"He went with him to talk to the people at the *Times* about crosswords," Sara said. "Where are you? I thought you had gone to Flat Mouth's today."

"I'm on my way," Amanda said. "I'm in Duluth. You're home alone?"

"Yes, they're gone until tomorrow."

"Drinking?" Amanda asked. She couldn't stop herself.

"No, Amanda," Sara replied, "I'm not drinking."

The driver asked her if she was ready to leave for Ashland when she hung up from the last call.

"So you're going for a nice holiday?" he asked pleasantly when he had helped her into the backseat of his car.

"I am ready," Amanda said. She settled into the seat. When she was in Wisconsin, especially there, she was desperate to see the long stretches of green fields, the clear lakes, the silver pines lined along the horizon. She thought too much without the distraction of sight, she told herself. Eleanor was fine. Of course she was fine. She was that kind of woman. Like Amanda.

SEVEN

THE FOURTH OF August was a lovely, bright, cool summer day in Philadelphia. Eleanor, pensive, homesick for the safety of the brief days with Amanda which had stirred in her a desire for childhood, arrived at one at the Chestnut Hill station.

She wasn't ready to go home.

"Let's have ice cream first," she said taking Lily's hand, "and then we'll go back to ROSIE."

They had huge bowls of vanilla with strawberries and whipped cream in the back garden of the deli on Germantown Avenue. No one else was there.

"Who's Kat's daddy?" Lily asked when she had finished her ice cream and the rest of Kat's.

When Lily had first asked about her father, Eleanor told her that she had very much wanted a child but she wasn't married. Lily had been satisfied with that for an answer at the time.

"Is Kat's father the same as mine?" she asked now.

"He is the same father."

"But Kat's not the same as me," Lily said with some disapproval. "Are you sure he's the same?"

"I am," Eleanor said.

She answered only the questions Lily asked, never more. That had been Amanda's advice.

Someday she would tell the children. Or perhaps someday she would be together with Tom. Since the trip to Amanda's, she wanted to marry. It was suddenly too difficult alone.

"Let's go now," Lily said, wiping her mouth with the napkin, climbing down from the chair. "Will Emma Gaits be at home?"

"No, she's not there now," Eleanor said. "And she won't be coming back."

"Good," Lily said. "I didn't like to listen to her father on the phone," she said.

"I wish you'd told me earlier," Eleanor said. .

"I was afraid to," Lily said. "I was afraid she was your best friend."

"Well, she isn't my best friend," Eleanor said. "She never was."

The house seemed to be empty when Eleanor opened the front door of ROSIE. She stopped downstairs to open the windows in the classrooms and the office, to clear the staleness in the air, while Lily went upstairs to the apartment with her small suitcase and Kat followed her one step at a time.

When Lily ran outside, Eleanor was in the backyard checking the garden, tended by a gardener who worked full time for the Episcopal church down the street.

"Mama," she called. "Guess what?"

"What?" Eleanor said brushing Lily's hair out of her eyes.

"Emma Gaits is upstairs."

"She is?" Eleanor said.

Lily took her mother's hand and they walked across the yard to the back porch.

"She's hurt," Lily said earnestly.

"Hurt?"

"She looks just terrible," Lily said.

Emma was lying on the double bed in Eleanor's room wearing Eleanor's robe. Her long blond hair was spread out in pale feathers on the pillow, her feet bare, her hands folded across her stomach. Her face was swollen and bruised the color of dark plums.

"What happened?" Eleanor asked.

She knew what had happened. She didn't even need to ask. She picked Kat up and sat down on the end of the bed.

"Where were you?" Emma's voice was weary and without accusation. "I've had an awful time since you left." She spoke slowly through thick purple lips.

"I was on a holiday," Eleanor said.

"You should have told me," Emma said.

"I told you I had left. I didn't want anyone to know where I was," Eleanor said. "You look terrible, Emma. You should leave Philadelphia." She took Lily's hand. "I'm putting the girls down for a nap and then we'll talk."

"Tom Clay called," Emma Gaits said. "He thought you were supposed to be home today."

"That's what I told him," Eleanor said.

"Your grandmother called too."

Eleanor carried Kat into her bedroom, took off her sandals, changed her diaper, and lifted her into her crib.

"What do you think happened to Emma?" Lily asked when she and Eleanor had gone into her room.

"I don't know," Eleanor said. "She looks as if she's been in a fight."

"Do you think her father did that?" Lily pulled down the covers and crawled between the sheets. "On the telephone, he used to say he would beat her up."

"You heard that when you were listening in?"

"That's what I heard."

Lily pulled some books out of the bookcase.

"Well, Emma is going to leave today," Eleanor said.

"When?"

"I'm going to talk to her while you and Kat are taking your nap," Eleanor said.

"Will you read me a story first?" Lily asked.

"One story," Eleanor said and she opened the book on her lap.

What Lily remembered later was Eleanor's hands against the book—her small brown hands, almost the hands of a child, against the blue book jacket and the black print.

The afternoon was late-summer quiet. There were few cars on Stenton Avenue. Gowen Avenue, in front of ROSIE, was empty. No one was on the streets at three o'clock in the afternoon. The shades were pulled in the houses, the trees barely moved in the light breeze.

The telephone was ringing in her bedroom when Eleanor walked in, but Emma Gaits had answered it.

Eleanor opened her backpack, took out her nightgown and hung it in the bathroom, dumped her clothes on the bed, and took hangers out of the closet.

"She's back, like I said," Emma was saying. "Do you want to talk to her?"

"For me?" Eleanor asked.

"My father," Emma said. "You can talk to him if you want."

"Tell him you'll be home shortly. In an hour."

Emma had her hand over the receiver.

"I won't."

"Give me the telephone then," Eleanor said coolly. She took the phone.

"Emma will not be working here any longer," Eleanor said and handed the telephone back to Emma.

"He beats me," Emma said. "That's what happened."

"Then you should go to the police," Eleanor said. "But you can't come here any longer."

"I have to stay here," Emma said. "He worse than beats me."

Eleanor hung her clothes in the closet, turned on the fan overhead. She felt an extraordinary calm.

"I have to stay," Emma said.

"When Lily and Kat wake up from their naps, we're going to the market. I want you to leave then," Eleanor said.

Tom had been right from the start. She should not have gotten involved. There was nothing she could do to save Emma Gaits. She took some dead flowers out of a vase and tossed them in the wastepaper basket. Outside, the cutting garden was full of dahlias. She would pick them before dinner. "What did my grandmother say?" she asked.

"To call her in Ashland tonight. And Tom will call back," Emma said crossly. She had gotten up and taken a skirt and T-shirt out of the paper bag she was using as a suitcase. She took off Eleanor's robe.

Eleanor went into the kitchen and opened the refrigerator. She had left in such a hurry that the leftovers from dinner last week were rotting on plates on the shelves and the milk was sour. She cleaned off the shelves. Emma came to the door of the kitchen.

"I'm going to take a shower," she said. "I suppose you'd let me borrow enough money for a few days to get on my feet so I don't have to go back to his house."

"Of course, you shouldn't go back," Eleanor said. "And you don't need to borrow. I'll pay you your salary for a month." Eleanor looked around for her purse with her checkbook. It wasn't in the bedroom with her backpack or in the kitchen. She must have left it in the car.

She went down the two flights of stairs, across the hallway, and out the door. Had she left it at the ice cream store? she wondered. She was on the front porch on the way down the steps when she looked up and saw John Gaits standing in front of her white Toyota, which was parked beside the house.

She stopped when she saw him. He stood squarely facing her, his legs apart, wearing a broad straw hat, a yellow dress shirt with the sleeves rolled up, khaki trousers. He looked like an ordinary man who belonged in the neighborhood except for the hat.

It was 3:15 in the afternoon and with the exception of

Sally Brand two doors down the street walking her Labrador puppy, no one was on Gowen Avenue.

John Gaits fired four shots in rapid succession from a handgun. One missed Eleanor altogether and was found later lodged in a pillar on the front porch. With the last one he killed himself.

LILY
AND
KAT

ONE

AMANDA ARRIVED IN Ashland in the afternoon on a day of extraordinary brightness. She could tell by the sun on her arms and face.

The driver stopped the car abruptly at the rooming house on Arch Street. "We're here," he said. Through the open window, she heard Flat Mouth's voice. The driver got out and she could hear them talking, but not what they said. Then the back door opened. Flat Mouth was there beside her, his body across her chest as he kissed her. And with a cold certainty, she knew.

"The driver will take us back to Duluth now and I have made reservations to Philadelphia," he said.

"You're coming with me?" Amanda asked.

"I am coming," he said.

On the trip to Duluth, Flat Mouth and Amanda didn't talk. He held her hand, running his hand across her palm, up and down her arm with great gentleness, the way he stroked the flanks and necks of his ponies. She didn't yield to his sweetness but sat erect, looking out the window of the backseat as if she could see.

Sara answered the phone just after five. She was lying in bed propped up on pillows with a Coca-Cola on her bedside table and a cigarette. She had been drinking. When the call came, she was vaguely sleepy and lightheaded. When she stood, she was unsteady on her feet.

It was Tom Clay who called. She had never met him but in the bottom drawer of her bureau where she kept her panties and slips was a stack of clippings in a manila folder. Regularly she read the *New York Times*, *Time* magazine, *Newsweek*, and the *Washington Post*. Every time there was a mention of Tom Clay, she cut it out and put it in the folder. She had not told Eleanor, of course. Eleanor would have been irritated at Sara's interest perhaps, or her sentimentality. Certainly she would have been defensive because they ought to have been married and weren't. But as short a time ago as June, Eleanor had said that they would marry eventually. After Matty. She could not make herself say after Matty died.

Tom Clay was in Newark when he called.

"I am going right over," he said. He said he had called Amanda in Ashland. She had not arrived yet but he had spoken with Flat Mouth and they would come straight to Philadelphia.

When she hung up the telephone, Sara was completely sober. She drank her Coca-Cola, called the hotel where Hendrik and Jonathan were staying in New York, and left a message for them to call. Then she called Albert.

"I'd like for you to drive me to Philadelphia," she said.

"Of course," Albert said. "Or I could get you on a plane, which would be faster, and then I'd drive up."

"I don't like planes." It was important for her to be careful, to arrive in Philadelphia safely.

She didn't call Nicholas or Frederick. They would be at work and she didn't want to tell them while they were in a public situation. That was actually the reason she waited to call, she told Hendrik later. She thought she would call on the highway, north of Baltimore, so it would be after six and she'd find them at home. It didn't occur to her that the news would be on the radio nationwide.

"I thought I was thinking very clearly," Sara said when she saw Hendrik later that night. "I should have thought it would be on the radio."

While she waited for Albert, she went into the bathroom and opened the linen closet where through the years she had kept liquor. Although she drank only when she was alone, she always had a bottle of gin and a bottle of bourbon behind the stack of towels and washcloths. Now she took them out, emptied them in the toilet, went downstairs and threw the bottles in the kitchen trash. And that not sufficient, she took the trash bins to the alley.

She'd never have another drink, she told herself. "I promise," she told God, as if for this moment she could pull him in for her defense, negotiate this favor.

She took responsibility for Eleanor's condition—"my fault," she said to a God to whom she had never before spoken. "I promise," she said aloud, washing her hands under the faucet, splashing her face with water. She took two breath mints out of the dish towel drawer. She was a good woman, she told herself. A very good woman, but the shame was too great. She held herself to blame.

She brushed her hair, still thick and shoulder length, not gray at fifty-three, but paler than the honey color she had had as a girl. She changed her dress to a navy blue linen, quite short, straight and stylish with a broad white collar. She put on navy panty hose, changed purses to a navy blue leather, and went downstairs, amazed at her self-possession.

It was not until they were at an Exxon station north of Baltimore where they had stopped to make the calls to Frederick and Nicholas that she realized she had left the house without any shoes.

Emma Gaits behaved with uncommon good sense. She had heard the gunshots, had gone to the window in the living room of the apartment. What she saw was Sally Brand running with her Labrador retriever puppy toward her house. Then she saw her father, who had fallen on his knees against a large tree. From the third-floor window, she couldn't see Eleanor at all.

First she called the ambulance and police. Then she checked the girls, who were still sleeping. When the telephone rang, it was Sally Brand, who said that Eleanor had been shot and was lying on the front porch. The man who'd shot her, Mrs. Brand reported, had shot himself, or so she thought, but she had run home and bolted the door and called the police. So she wasn't entirely sure of that information.

Emma Gaits made a decision then. She didn't go downstairs to check on Eleanor. Instead, she turned the radio to the all-music station and turned the volume up to drown out the sound of the sirens. She called Tom Clay in Newark and told him Eleanor had been shot by John Gaits and would he please come. She asked him to call Sara and Amanda and gave him their telephone numbers.

Tom Clay arrived first. He had driven from Newark first to Chestnut Hill Hospital and when he stopped the car in front of the house on Gowen Avenue at 6:15 P.M. on August 4, people were standing in small groups with their children and their dogs, talking in whispers.

"The girls are in Eleanor's room," Emma said taking the chocolate pudding off the stove, pouring it in little cups.

"What have you told them?" Tom asked.

"I have told them she is hurt," Emma said. "But they didn't see anything. They didn't see the ambulance take her away. I have asked the police not to let anyone upstairs until Sara and Amanda get here."

"Did you see her?" Tom asked.

"No," Emma said. "I stayed with the girls."

Lily and Kat were sitting on Eleanor's bed, Lily dressed in a yellow pinafore, Kat in diapers.

"Hello, pussycats," Tom said softly.

"Mama got hurt," Lily said quietly.

"I know." Tom sat on the bed and took hold of Lily's feet.

"I would like to see her," Lily said. "So would Kat."

"No," Kat said, looking at Tom suspiciously.

"Your grandmother is coming up from Washington to help and so is Amanda," Emma said.

Emma brought a tray of supper with chocolate pudding and milk and blueberry muffins, all their favorite foods.

"Thank you, Emma," Lily said, taking the dish of chocolate pudding although she couldn't eat it.

Kat pushed the tray away.

"Would you like ice cream, Kitty Kat?" Tom asked.

"No."

"Nothing at all?" Tom asked.

"No," Kat said.

The girls sat on Eleanor's bed all evening while the house filled with people, Albert and Sara, then Nicholas and Jonathan and Hendrik. Frederick arrived close to midnight. The family sat in the living room of the apartment, except Sara and Hendrik, who went to the hospital, and the girls, who would not move from Eleanor's bed.

Amanda and Flat Mouth arrived just after midnight. Jonathan was in the room with the girls when she arrived. She called out hello and walked through the door of Eleanor's bedroom where the children were sitting.

"See?" Kat said breathlessly to Lily and she held her hands over her eyes.

TWO

AT AMANDA'S INSISTENCE, Jonathan contacted a clipping service.

"Keep everything," she said to Jonathan. "Every report."

"Why?" Nicholas asked. "Who could bear to read them?"

"For Lily and Kat," Amanda said.

Jonathan read each article and filed them alphabetically according to the publication. There were the initial reports in newspapers all over the country. There were magazine pieces and a number of essays, several citing Eleanor as an example, a virtue of the sixties revolution.

From the front page of the *Washington Post*, August 5, 1972:

ELEANOR MARCH, 26 YEAR OLD HEROINE TO THE CHILDREN OF THE PHILADELPHIA GHETTO, KILLED ON HER FRONT PORCH. At 3:15 p.m. on Friday, August 4, Eleanor Steward March was shot once in the chest at close range by John Gaits, the father of her assistant, who then shot himself. Mr. Gaits, twice hospitalized for psychotic episodes, arrived by car at ROSIE, Inc., the school for children of the Philadelphia ghetto founded and directed by Miss March, at about 3:10 p.m. According to one witness, he got out of his car and was standing just in front of Miss March's Toyota station wagon when she came out on her front porch. According to Emma Gaits, assistant to Miss

March and daughter of the assailant, Miss March was going to the car to get her purse which she had left there earlier. Before she stepped down from the porch, Mr. Gaits fired four shots in rapid succession, the last one in his own temple.

"He was crazy," Miss Gaits said to a reporter. "He had told me he wanted to get rid of Eleanor because of my friendship with her but I never believed him."

According to a neighbor of the Gaits in Germantown, Mr. Gaits had been twice hospitalized for sexually abusing his daughter.

Eleanor March, daughter of Sara and Hendrik March of Washington, D.C., and the mother of two daughters, Lily and Anna Katrina, established ROSIE, Inc., in 1965 at the University of Pennsylvania. It was named for Rosie Kyle, a young black woman murdered by a white fraternity man in November, 1964.

From the obituaries:

Services for Eleanor Steward March who died of gunshot wounds on August 4, 1972, will be at 4:00 p.m., August 10, 1972, in the Great Choir of the Washington Cathedral.

From the *New York Times,* August 5:

Eleanor Steward March, founder of ROSIE, a program for poor black children established by Miss March, was assassinated at 3:15 p.m. yesterday on the front porch of ROSIE, Inc., also her home, by a gunman who then shot himself. Miss March is the granddaughter of the photographer Amanda Steward.

From the *Los Angeles Times,* August 5:

At 3:15 p.m. on Tuesday, August 4, John Gaits, a former mental patient who had a history of sexual abuse, shot and killed Eleanor Steward March, founder and director of ROSIE, a program for ghetto children established initially at the University of Pennsylvania by Miss March and adopted by several urban universities around the country. The 26-year-old March, mother of two daughters, had just stepped out of the front door of the house where ROSIE is located when Mr. Gaits, standing less than 25 feet away on the sidewalk, shot his handgun four times, hitting Miss March twice, once in the front of the head, once in the chest. She died instantly. He then shot himself.

From *Time* magazine, August 8:

LIVES OF THE SAINTS: A STORY OF HEROINES.

Eleanor March was eighteen years old, a freshman student at the University of Pennsylvania, when Rosie Kyle, a twenty-year-old black student from Butte, Alabama, was stabbed to death by a white fraternity boy just under the window where Miss March's room was located.

In April following the murder of Rosie Kyle, Miss March established ROSIE in her honor, a volunteer program in which college students work with ghetto children in reading, writing, art, theater and sports after school.

It is one of the ironies of the times we have lived through that eight years following the death of Rosie Kyle, Miss March had been murdered by a mentally ill white man with a history of incestuous sexual abuse and psychotic breakdowns.

From the *New York Times Magazine:*

ELEANOR STEWARD MARCH: MAY 1, 1946–AUGUST 4, 1972. A TRIBUTE BY TOM CLAY.

All over the news, they are calling Elly March a saint. I don't know what a saint is at any time or in our time—whether she's a saint because she did something about trouble in the world or because she died at 26 or because she was assassinated by a crazy man. But I would rather not give a name to what she did and who she was.

Eleanor March was a sunny child in a dark world and I can't bear to think that the days will go on without her.

There were editorials all year and Jonathan kept track, although as the year went on he could not read them any longer. They lost a sense of reality for him. His literal mind could no longer identify his sister within the stories.

And gradually as the year went on, the story of Eleanor March became a myth. People everywhere knew about her. There was no stopping the romantic alterations, no setting the record straight.

* * *

"What are you going to do with all these stories?" Sara asked Amanda one afternoon in late fall 1972, cooking dinner. "You have the good fortune of not being able to read them. You wouldn't even recognize Eleanor in them."

"We need records," Amanda said. She was sitting in the small chair in her bedroom in the house on P Street, her feet on Day's back, facing toward the open window. She sat that way often, as if she were a girl, as if she could look out the window and see the tops of the trees, the roofs of Georgetown. "Like photographs, they are part of the truth."

THREE

THE DAYS AND weeks after Eleanor's death went on and on. The days of late summer had more hours of light than the family could bear. There were long silences at meals. The garden overgrew. The dishes were left unwashed.

And gradually everyone came home. First Nicholas arrived in late August without the woman he had lived with and took an apartment on Dupont Circle. By fall he had joined a law practice dealing with issues of the environment. In early September, Frederick and Beatrice moved when the *Washington Post* offered him a job; they bought a small house around the corner from his parents. Bonita, who had come to Philadelphia the day after Eleanor's death, followed the Marches back to Washington, moved into her old room, and stayed until the weather got cold.

A family fortress grew around Lily and Kat. There were always people at dinner. Everybody cooked or stood around the kitchen talking. They made a ceremony of food, although for a long time no one was hungry.

Sara taught Lily to make sweets—cherry cobbler and apple cake with cinnamon and cloves, peach tart and blueberry flan. Lily would sit at the counter with an apron over her pinafore while Kat lay silent against Day's flanks, her eyes flashing at the people around her.

"I think Kat knows how to talk," Lily said to Sara one evening while they were cutting vegetables for soup. Kat was upstairs in Amanda's room with Day.

"You do?"

"I think she knows how to say quite a few words," Lily said.

"Has she spoken to you?"

"Not exactly," Lily said, "but last night after our light was out and I was sleeping, I heard voices and there was Kat very quietly in her bed saying 'El-ea-nor—Eleanor—Elea-nor.' "

" 'Eleanor' is a very hard word to say," Sara said.

"I know."

"So maybe she will start speaking to us soon."

"I hope so," Lily said.

But Kat didn't start to speak, except "No," and from time to time when she was lying on Day or in her bed, members of the family could hear her practice "Eleanor" in different ways. It was as if the name itself had melody, a nursery rhyme, a lullaby whose sound in her ears had the comfort of the familiar.

Sara was remarkable in emergencies. There must have been in her temperament the physiology of a bear whose temperature drops as he falls into his deep winter sleep. She could go months and years at reduced efficiency but in the face of trouble she found deep pockets of energy. She concentrated on Lily and Kat, easily, calmly, as if nothing were particularly out of sorts. She could spend hours in the kitchen making cookies or teaching them to sew or coloring or cutting out paper dolls as if she had no other interest than such play, no demands on her time.

At night, she turned to Hendrik. They slipped quietly into a love affair together after the lights were out, the house sleeping, withstanding the deep sadness between them with surprising sweetness.

The night Eleanor March died, the rooms of ROSIE filled with friends of Eleanor's and volunteers, teachers, children

from North Philadelphia and their makeshift families.
Even strangers. The tables were spread with casseroles.
There were kegs of beer in the back garden and the sweet
smell of marijuana hung in the air. People stayed all night,
into the next day and the next, camping out, stunned either
to silence or to speech.

Sara and Amanda sat in Eleanor's kitchen at the table
and made decisions.

They would take the girls to Washington.

"I'll put them in Eleanor's old room next to Melvina's.
I'll paper the wall in tiny flowers," Sara said desperately.

Amanda would move to Washington, sublet her apartment at least until Christmas, maybe longer.

Tom Clay had to agree. He had no claim on the girls, he
said. Besides, his life at the moment with Matty ill would
be terrible for them. He seemed brisk, competent, and
straightforward. And devastated.

"I wish he would die of sadness as proof," Amanda said
to Flat Mouth.

Tom stayed on in Philadelphia with the Marches for the
four days that they were there. At night, he slept in
Eleanor's bed on the side where she had slept, next to the
telephone.

"Tom is sleeping in Eleanor's bed," Sara said to
Amanda after the first night.

"I heard that he was," Amanda said.

"I mean he is sleeping where she slept." Sara was
pleased to see Tom there. Somehow it affirmed his affection for Eleanor. "He must have actually loved her."

"Of course he loved her," Amanda said. "You know that."

"I didn't ever know that," Sara said. "Not absolutely."

At first Emma Gaits helped in the house, silently, apologetically. She kept the refrigerator full and the dishes
clean. But on the morning of the third day, she told Sara
she was going to the market for milk and bananas and she
never came back.

"I hope we never hear from her," Sara said.

"We won't," Amanda said. "I'm certain of it."

On the fourth day, Flat Mouth returned to Wisconsin and the Marches finally left for Washington. Amanda, Lily, Kat, and Sara on the train, Hendrik, Nicholas, Frederick, Jonathan, Jane, and Albert by car. They were edgy, conscious of each other's shortcomings, ill-tempered, and that is how they limped through the first winter, their moods like weather. There were long silences, unrelenting exhaustion, but they were steadfast in their resolve to make a life for Lily and Kat without disproportionate sadness.

FOUR

THE NIGHT FIONA'S daughter appeared out of nowhere was a warm stormy night in February. The winter of 1973 had been a mild winter with days of rain, and this night was no different, but the rain was steady and heavy, accompanied by thunder, unsettling in winter.

"If only it were cold," Sara said that night to Hendrik. Lily was sleeping between them as she did from time to time.

"I'm having a little difficulty getting to sleep," she'd say, apologetic, knocking on their bedroom door in her bathrobe and slippers. "Kat's left again."

Kat left often. She took the pale blue wool blanket off her bed, dragging it behind her down the hall and up the stairs to Amanda's room, where she slept under Amanda's bed.

"She can't sleep under the bed, Amanda," Sara said.

"That's where she wants to sleep," Amanda said.

"It's winter," Sara said. "She'll catch a cold."

But there was no arguing with Kat. Finally Sara got a sleeping mat and put it under Amanda's four poster bed so the nights when Kat decided to sleep there she wouldn't be sleeping on the hardwood floor next to Day.

"I don't mind the mild weather," Hendrik said running

his fingers through Sara's hair, which she had cut short since Eleanor's death. With her short hair and clear ivory skin, she sometimes looked like a girl. "I just wish it would stop raining. Even Amanda says she feels the gloom through her skin." He licked her fingers, running them along his lips.

The sudden passion in Hendrik, the depth of her own response, surprised Sara. They made love that year as if they had just met. On some of the nights that Lily slipped into their bed and slept between them, they reached across her for one another and Sara fell asleep dreaming of sex.

This night, however, they were lying awake waiting for Fiona's daughter to come. Her name was Anna Jermyn Brown.

She had called that morning to say she was in Cleveland and driving east if this was, as she thought it was, the home of Amanda Steward who was the daughter of Anna Jermyn Steward who was the daughter of Maria Jermyn, her grandmother. By her calculation Amanda Steward was her first cousin and Fiona, her mother, was Amanda's mother's sister. So perhaps there'd be room for her to spend the night. She was traveling on business.

"You've never mentioned Fiona," Sara said.

"I didn't know her," Amanda said. "I knew about her from the letters my mother left. She was my mother's younger sister."

"It has taken her a long time to get in touch," Hendrik said.

"She said she just learned about me this fall," Amanda said. "She read the articles about Eleanor's death in the Madison, Wisconsin, newspaper where she lives and thought when my name was mentioned that she should get in touch."

"I hope she is just passing through," Hendrik said.

"We'll see," Amanda said, pleased by the news of a cousin. "Maybe we'll like her."

Fiona's daughter arrived at two in the morning in a driving rain and rang the front doorbell. Amanda was sleeping and Hendrik had fallen asleep with his bedside light on, so

Sara went downstairs and opened the front door to a gray-haired woman in her sixties with tiny black squirrel eyes and a small pinched face peering out of the hood of a cape.

"I am Fiona's daughter," she said, "Anna Jermyn Brown." She took off her cape. "I had a time finding this place," she said in a heavy midwestern accent. "There's nothing but circles in Washington. Do you have a cup of coffee?"

Sara turned on the downstairs lights and went into the kitchen.

"I drove all the way from Cleveland—eight hours—without stopping, and the trucks on the turnpike were awful."

Sara turned on the faucet to fill the pot, opened the refrigerator, and took out some blueberry muffins.

"You're the mother of the girl who got murdered. That is how I found you. Reading that terrible story in *Time* magazine. It said that your daughter had a grandmother called Amanda Steward who is a famous photographer and I thought to myself . . ." She sat down at the kitchen table and lit a cigarette. "Amanda Steward. I know that name. And then *click click* in my brain—I remember a picture I have of my Aunt Anna who I never met because she died before I was born but my mother Fiona told me about her—and there in this picture is my Aunt Anna Steward and her daughter, Amanda, so I put two and two together when I read that story and then I waited six months to get up the nerve to call." She blew the smoke through her nose. "And here I am."

"I thought you came on business," Sara heated the blueberry muffin, got out a coffee cup.

"I did."

"My mother's asleep now but we have a room for you upstairs," Sara said. "Do you have luggage?"

"Just what you see here," she opened the satchel, which was her purse, took out a small bottle of dark rum, and poured it in the coffee.

"Fiona died in sixty-nine," she said, "and I had a brother who died when he was ten when the tractor on our farm turned over on him, so it's only me and Amanda left now as far as I know."

Sara poured herself a cup of coffee. "Do you happen to have the picture of my mother and her mother?"

"Of course I do," Anna Jermyn said. "How was I to prove we were related without it?" She reached into her satchel, pulled out some aspirin, a pair of underpants, a hair net, a wallet, a pink and fuchsia chiffon scarf, and an envelope with PIX written on it. She opened the envelope, which had a stack of photographs, mostly old, five by sevens, mounted on cardboard. "See for yourself."

Sara found the one immediately in the middle of the stack, a picture which showed a woman around thirty, fair, quite lovely, and familiar to Sara. Standing on her knee was a tall, dark, solemn child with black eyes and black hair in the shape of a yarmulke on the top of her head.

"My mother has never seen a picture of her mother," Sara said. She could feel a sob starting in her stomach.

"I'll show her in the morning," Anna Jermyn said.

Sara rinsed her coffee cup in the sink, stood with her back to Anna Jermyn. She took a deep breath. Certainly she didn't want to cry.

"Amanda is blind," she said and turned on the faucet full force.

FIVE

ANNA JERMYN BROWN had come for money. Ten thousand dollars was what she had in mind, but she kept that news secret for several days and when she brought it up, it was only with Amanda.

The morning after her arrival, however, she slept late. Most of the day had gone by the time that she came downstairs to the kitchen for fresh coffee and a piece of toast. Amanda was there sitting on the rocker while Jonathan tested her on crosswords. Kat was lying against Day in her

Osh-Gosh overalls and bare feet, and Lily was making chocolate chip cookies on the counter.

"I hear you have a picture of my mother," Amanda said.

Anna Jermyn put her finger in the chocolate chip dough and licked it.

"Mmm," she said. "I do. I showed it to Sara last night."

"Do you have it now?" Amanda asked.

Anna pulled it out of her pants pocket. She wore men's trousers and a striped oxford button-down shirt. Her gray hair was short and curly, her small face, lightly wrinkled, had been the face of a pretty girl, pretty in a sweet way, now pinched with years of bad luck.

"I'll show it to Amanda," Lily said taking the picture and looking at it under the overhead light in the kitchen. She washed her hands and took the picture over to Amanda, fixing herself a place between her grandmother's legs.

"You have a little bit of black hair on the top of your head and very long arms," Lily said.

"Can you tell it's me?" Amanda asked.

"Easily," Lily said. "You have the same black eyes and you look very serious and your bones are sharp. You have on a long white dress with lace at the neck."

Kat got up from her bed on Day's belly and climbed on Amanda's lap to look at the picture.

"Your mother is sitting down on a chair with a high back and fancy carved wood. She looks like Mama Sara, doesn't she, Kat?"

"No," Kat said earnestly.

"She means yes," Lily said. "She has brown hair probably and it's pulled behind her ears. But her eyes look like Mama Sara's and her face has the same shape. Don't you think so?" Lily asked Anna Jermyn, who had taken a chair from the breakfast table and sat with her feet up on another chair.

"They look exactly alike to me," Anna Jermyn said, pleased with developments.

Jonathan took the picture from Lily.

"Do you remember her at all, Amanda?" he asked.

"A little," Amanda said. "But I only began to remember

what she looked like when Sara grew up and had what I believed must have been my mother's face."

"It's uncanny," Jonathan said.

Sara walked in the kitchen with her arms full of marketing.

"Did you see this, Mama?" Jonathan asked.

"I saw it last night," Sara said. "She looks like you too, Lily." She ruffled Lily's hair.

"I would like to have this picture," Amanda said.

"We could copy it," Jonathan said.

"Of course," Amanda said. "We could copy it for Anna Brown. But I would like to have the original."

"But you can't see it, can you?" Anna asked, not unpleasantly.

"I tell her what she can't see," Lily said quickly.

Amanda hesitated. "I'd be happy to pay you for it," she said.

Anna made a low sound in her throat like a hum and poured more coffee. "I'll take it under consideration," she said.

"Do you remember what I look like?" Sara asked Amanda that night in her mother's room before she went to bed.

"Of course," Amanda said brusquely. "I remember exactly how you looked the last time I saw you, unless your hair has fallen out."

Sara sat down at the edge of her mother's bed.

"Your newfound relation has come for money," Sara said. "That's what Hendrik says."

"That's fine."

"Why not just have a copy of the picture, Mama? Don't get involved with her."

"I want the original," Amanda said.

"It may be costly."

"So I'll pay," Amanda said.

Sara brushed her hair in her mother's mirror, pulled it back off her face like the woman in the picture, assumed Anna Steward's beatific expression.

"I wonder," she said to Amanda. "Why is it you have no pictures of your mother at all?"

"I was wondering the same thing," Amanda said. "It occurred to me that my father may have destroyed them."

"Destroyed them?"

Amanda felt through her closet for a sweater. "He couldn't bear the past unless it worked out perfectly," she said. "And of course it never does."

Once more that night, Sara went upstairs. Amanda's light was out and Kat had just slipped under the bed with her blue blanket.

"Mama?" she asked. "Are you asleep?"

"No," Amanda answered.

"Don't pay just anything," Sara said. "Hendrik is afraid that you will."

"Hendrik is afraid I'm sentimental in my old age," Amanda said. "He doesn't know that I've always been sentimental."

Anna Jermyn Brown said ten thousand dollars would change the course of her life, which had been full of reversals since Fiona died. She could go back to Wisconsin and pay her debts and rent a nice place on the lake. She was not grateful. That pleased Amanda particularly. It made Anna Jermyn feel like kin. In exchange, she told Amanda everything she knew about Fiona and Anna and gave her the picture.

"You think you'll hear from her again?" Hendrik asked that night at dinner after Anna had left.

"I don't care if I hear from her again," Amanda said sharply. "She was a gift."

"An expensive gift," Hendrik said.

"I could afford her," Amanda said.

Amanda asked Sara to put the picture in her room on the table with the pictures of Flat Mouth and Grandmother Yellow Flower's beads and the G. C. Murphy feathers. The picture changed her room. Whether she could see it didn't make a difference. Its presence made her very happy. Someone behind a lens in 1902, perhaps 1903, had borne witness to an afternoon when she stood on her mother's knees and put her arm around her mother's neck.

SIX

Kat was still not speaking in August 1974, and she was almost four years old.

Hendrik insisted on a speech therapist who came three times a week and had her make sounds with the piano and violin which at first she refused to do. When, however, it became clear that the speech therapist was going to stay the full hour of every lesson whether she made any sounds or not, Kat followed the scale of the piano with her voice. Still she did not use words although she imitated the tongue movement and throat sounds the therapist required.

"Don't make an issue," Amanda said after dinner one night.

"It is an issue," Hendrik said. "She won't be able to live an ordinary life." He took a letter out of his pocket and put it on the table. "She can't go to school."

"We have a letter which says she can't go back to nursery school unless she has learned to say more than 'no,'" Sara said.

"Why didn't they tell you that in June?" Amanda asked.

"They did," Sara said. "They said they'd wait until the end of the summer and then see how well she was talking."

"Why didn't you tell me this?" Amanda asked.

"We hoped she would be speaking by now," Sara said. "We thought surely she would be."

"That's not what I asked you," Amanda said crossly.

Hendrik hesitated. "We didn't tell you because I think you are in collusion with Kat."

"Just a minute, Papa," Jonathan said.

"I'm not criticizing Amanda," Hendrik said. "I think you are admiring of her stubbornness—and so she thinks it's a good thing not to talk. After all, you told me that you didn't talk for a while."

"I am admiring of her stubbornness," Amanda said.

"Read the letter to us," Jonathan said.

"I will," Sara picked up the letter.

Dear Mr. and Mrs. March,

We appreciate your cooperation in letting us test Anna Katrina last Thursday. Unfortunately, she continues to be non-verbal. As I'm sure you understand, the teachers and in particular the other children in the class find her constant repetition of "No" hostile.

Amanda held up her hand. "Don't read anymore," she said. "Of course she's hostile. Her mother is dead. Forget school. Take her out. She shouldn't be in school among such stupid people."

"The point is that we're trying to give her a normal life and she has to go to school, Mama," Sara said. "She needs friends."

"Like the woman who wrote that letter?" Amanda asked. "With such friends, she's better off mute."

In the middle of the argument, Lily came downstairs and stood by the chair where Jonathan was sitting.

"Kat is locked in the bathroom," she said quietly. "She was sitting on the steps listening to your argument and then she had to go to the bathroom. And then she locked herself in."

"How do you know she was sitting on the steps?" Hendrik asked. "You were supposed to be sleeping."

"I was sitting on the steps too," Lily said.

They had to call the fire department to unlock the bathroom door and when they finally broke the lock and went into the bathroom, Kat was sitting in the bathtub with Sara's makeup, her lipstick and blush and mascara and eye shadow painted in Indian designs on her cheeks and forehead.

"I'll fix her," Lily said quickly. "I'll wash her face." She reached into the bathtub and took Kat's hand. "Please," she said.

Lily helped Kat out of the tub and sat her down on the toilet seat. At four, she looked like a miniature Eleanor, with black curly hair in a cap around her small face which would, when the baby flesh disappeared, be the angular face of her mother. Lily soaped the washcloth.

"Close your eyes," she said scrubbing the lipstick off her forehead. "You make me so cross, Anna Katrina," she said. "I'm sure you can talk. I'm sure you can say everything that I can say almost. And you just won't." She rinsed the washcloth and scrubbed the green eye shadow in circles on Kat's cheeks. "And now, did you hear? You won't be able to go to school because you won't talk. It makes people very cross." Lily reached into the medicine cabinet, took down a jar of Nivea and rubbed it on Kat's lips, which were brightly colored with Peaches and Cream lipstick, Sara's favorite, now in pieces on the pale yellow bathroom carpet. "Everyone has tried their best," Lily said. "They've done everything they could and they're old to have two new children. We're very lucky, Kat," Lily said, finishing with Kat's face, picking up the pieces of lipstick on the carpet, and scrubbing the carpet with a washcloth and soap. The lipstick wouldn't come off. In fact, it spread into a larger circle beside the toilet. "Now look," Lily said, crying in frustration. "We could have been orphans."

When Lily looked up, Kat was crying. She sat on the toilet seat, her hands folded in her lap, tears running over her round cheeks.

"Oh, Kat," Lily said, picking her up. Kat wrapped her arms around Lily's neck, her legs around her waist, and burrowed her face in her shoulder. "I just wish you'd be a little good."

And she carried her to the blue flowered bedroom which Sara had made perfectly for them with white wicker rockers and Victorian dolls, a soft blue carpet and matching bedspread and curtains, a blue flower bower overlooking the back garden.

"Would you like to sleep with me?" Lily asked, pulling off her spread, crawling between the sheets.

"No," Kat said quietly. She climbed between the sheets next to her sister and fell immediately to sleep.

SEVEN

MATTY CLAY DIED in October 1974. Sara read a notice about her death in the *Washington Post*: "Matty Clay, wife of civil rights activist Tom Clay, died at 37 after a long illness." Hendrik read it in the *Times* where there was a longer story on the obituary page.

Tom had seen his daughters several times since Eleanor's death although not in the last few months. They called him Uncle Tom, although Lily knew he was her father—she had asked Sara in the fall after Eleanor's death. But that's all she wanted to know and if Sara brought up the subject, she said she liked to think of him as her Uncle Tom.

In January 1974, when Matty became terribly ill, Tom resigned as director of ROSIE to stay with her and in the summer ROSIE closed for lack of funds. There was a small notice in the *New York Times*, the same issue which included the news of the resignation of Richard Nixon as President of the United States. Eleanor's name wasn't mentioned. Sara and Hendrik read the story but at first they did not mention it. They seldom mentioned Eleanor at all, seldom could bear to mention her. If they thought too much about her, their individual anger, Sara's depression, Hendrik's bombastic bad temper, would begin like acid to burn the edges of their marriage.

The closing of ROSIE, however, set Sara off.

"I can't stand it," she said to Hendrik. "Everything that happened in that whole generation is closing down. They're not even thirty."

"Don't read about it," Hendrik said. They were lying in bed and Hendrik was working on the final revisions of a new book about the German character.

For days after the notice in the *Times*, Sara couldn't get out of bed in the morning, as if ROSIE and Eleanor were one. She was hung over although she had not had a drink since the afternoon of Eleanor's death. She felt terminally ill, a cancer which would express itself too late for curing.

"You could get bitter," Amanda said sitting beside her daughter's bed during the summer weeks that Sara was too depressed to get dressed.

"I am bitter," Sara said. "That's what has happened to me. I wish I'd been brought up with a God. Any old god. Just someone for days like this."

"Well, you weren't," Amanda said.

"What I'm left with is not enough," Sara said.

"It has to be," Amanda said.

And gradually the weight lifted. By September Sara was going about her days again.

The morning in October that Matty Clay's death was announced was warm and sunny with the crisp smell of autumn in the air. Sara and Amanda walked Lily to Wisconsin Avenue to pick up the school bus, Sara's arm linked through Amanda's as they crossed the slippery, mossy brick sidewalks of Georgetown.

"He can't have them," Sara said on the way back down P Street after the school bus had picked up Lily.

"He's shown no signs of wanting them," Amanda said.

"Because she's been sick," Sara said. "Now he'll want them."

"If he wants them now," Amanda said, "it's too late."

"I hope," Sara said. "I would hate a fight."

Hendrik was sitting on the front steps with Kat reading the paper when they came home.

"Tom Clay called," he said to Sara. "He wants you to call back as soon as possible."

EIGHT

AT THE LAST minute, Amanda went with Sara to meet Tom Clay in New York. Lily and Kat went too, but they were the point of the trip and had been expected to go all along.

Since Tom's initial call, the plans had changed daily. He had said to Sara that he wanted to see the girls as soon as possible; he wanted to discuss the future.

"How did he sound?" Amanda asked.

"Polite," Sara said. "He always sounds polite."

He was willing to meet them anywhere, but Sara said no to Philadelphia. She could not bear to go to Philadelphia at all. On the few occasions she and Amanda had gone to New York, they flew so she could avoid the stop at 30th Street Station, the sight of the Schuylkill River swinging out toward Mount Airy.

Tom suggested coming to Washington.

"I don't want him here," Hendrik said. He could not forgive Tom his ultimate failure to Eleanor.

Finally they agreed to meet in New York. At first it was going to be Sara and Hendrik taking the girls, but at the last minute Hendrik would not go.

Since her death, Hendrik had begun to speak with the same heavy German accent he had when he arrived in America, as if to secure himself in the familiar language as protection against reversals of fortune. In the afternoons after they had both finished writing, he and Albert spent hours together walking the streets of Washington. In the evenings, he was more gentle than Sara had ever known him to be even in the flush of their early romance. But subdued. Sometimes he helped with dinner and he always read to Lily and Kat before they went to bed. He didn't work in the evening as he had done when his own children were young. The father which Lily and Kat would remember in Hendrik was a different man than Eleanor's father had been.

The subject of Tom Clay came up frequently. Especially the question of whether he would want to take the children eventually.

"They are not his to take," Sara would say. "We have the notarized paper Eleanor left."

Hendrik shrugged. "We should see a lawyer," he said.

But they never got around to seeing a lawyer.

The Thursday after Matty's death was cold and rainy. They traveled first class because of Day, and that morning they were the only passengers in first class so Lily and Kat sat on the swivel seats at one end of the car and Sara sat next to Amanda at the other. Perhaps the shrouded day or the nature of the occasion or just the rain against the windows made them particularly comfortable with each other, confessional.

"You have a life I haven't felt in you since you were a little girl," Amanda said.

"I don't drink any longer," Sara said with a rare directness.

"That's not what I mean," Amanda said.

"It's what I did for a long time." Sara took off her wet shoes, put her stocking feet on the heater on the floor of the club car.

"I smothered you. It was extremely stupid of me," Amanda said. "I used to tell Hendrik that we left you no room for a life."

"You were not an easy mother," Sara agreed. The truth seemed easy that morning as it rarely was. She wanted to tell Amanda she was also proud of her but to say anything seemed insincere. Instead she lifted her mother's long slender hand, bumpy at the joints, and lay it against her cheek.

"I like being a mother," Sara said. "In a way, I feel I'm good at it even though I slipped out of my own children's lives early."

"You are good at it," Amanda said.

Sara took two fashion magazines out of her satchel. She no longer read books, only magazines, and, like Amanda used to do, she only looked at the pictures, lingering over the shapes of clothes, imagining herself in them.

"Tell me what you see?" Amanda asked, as she often did when they were out together.

"A green suede suit with a short straight skirt." Sara laughed.

"Don't bother to tell me," Amanda said. "Tell me if you ever loved Albert."

The subject of Albert had never come up, although surely Amanda suspected. Sara had herself almost forgotten—they were all such good friends again, especially Albert and Hendrik. Only occasionally, unexpectedly, the memory of feeling flew by, dipped toward her like a young bird that had lost its bearings.

"Albert actually loved me. I loved that in Albert. For Hendrik, I'm sure you remember, I was the mirror of his own reflection," Sara said.

"Perhaps Albert would have been a better man to spend a life with," Amanda said. "But who would have known, to meet him in his miserable humor?"

"Whoever knows?" Sara said. "There's such a lot of guesswork between men and women," she said.

Lily came up the aisle and leaned against Sara.

"Kat wants to know what is going to happen with Uncle Tom."

"We don't know, darling," Sara said. "He wants to see you."

"How do you know that Kat is worried if she doesn't talk, Lily?" Amanda asked.

"I know what she thinks," Lily said earnestly. "I know she's a little worried." She took two cookies out of her grandmother's satchel and went back to the seat with Kat.

Lily walked down Fifth Avenue holding Tom Clay's hand. Kat walked next to Lily, her hands deep in her overall pockets. She refused to hold Lily's hand. Sara and Amanda stayed at Amanda's apartment.

It was gray in New York but not raining. The streets were crowded so Tom wound Lily in and out of the ribbons of people on the streets and Lily grabbed hold of Kat's overall straps so as not to lose her.

Lily was imagining Tom as her father.

"So Daddy and I are going to lunch now," she was thinking, "and then we'll go to the zoo and maybe get ice cream and for dinner I'll wear my new rust-colored corduroy jumper and my hair long with a ribbon."

Years later she would remember that moment for the simple pleasure of it, the familiarity.

"I used to walk along the streets of Greenwich Village," she would think to herself from time to time, "holding my father's hand." Although it never happened again in quite the same way.

They went to a tiny French restaurant on 10th Street off Fifth Avenue at which, Lily told Sara later, they had long bread on the table without a plate and Tom let them drink some of his red wine. They sat in dark booths with red-and-white tablecloths at the back of the restaurant. The walls were glossy and the room smelled of stew.

Lily remembered what Tom said exactly. Through the years, she told Kat again and again precisely the order of the words as he spoke since Kat, as it turned out, remembered stories as they happened only through the high-pitched filter of her mind.

Tom rested his chin in his hands.

"I met your mother eight years ago on the twenty-first of August when she was twenty and a student at the University of Pennsylvania and I was married to Matty."

"Mama told me," Lily said. "She told us," she corrected herself although Kat had been too young to be told stories.

"I loved her very much but because I was married and had a little boy, we had to have a secret life."

Kat put her hands over her eyes.

"Do you understand?"

"No," Kat said.

"She understands," Lily said. "We understand."

"You know then that I am your father."

"And Kat's father too?" Lily asked.

"I am Kat's father too."

"Mama told me," Lily said.

"But I couldn't live with you because I was married to someone else."

Lily wanted to ask why he didn't live with them anyway but she held her tongue. There were a lot of questions she thought about later when she was lying awake in her own bed.

"Before your mother died, she wrote a letter asking Amanda and Sara to take care of you if anything happened to her."

"She told me," Lily said. "She told me everything."

Kat peered at him from behind her fingers.

"Now, since my wife has died, I could take you. It wouldn't be as complicated as it was before."

Lily had been afraid of this. She wanted a father certainly and it was perfectly fine for Tom Clay to be her father, although she hated his eyeglasses and wished he would not dress in blue jeans. But she didn't want to live with him.

"We're very happy with our grandparents and Amanda," Lily said. "You could come to visit us as much as you like. Every week if you want. Anyway, we can be a bother."

He drank the rest of his wine and ordered another glass. "I am going to visit," he said, "and I hope you'll visit me. I'm sending your grandparents some money every month to pay for your college and for trips," he began.

Lily lost interest in the particulars and she didn't remember the other things that he said that afternoon, but she knew he continued to talk for some time while she and Kat got sleepy after the long emotional day.

And suddenly, he was crying. He put his head down on his arms and he was sobbing.

What Lily remembered about that moment was Kat, who put her small hand on Tom Clay's long dark hair, patting it lightly. Then she leaned over and kissed his wet cheek.

On the train, Lily sat in the chair with Sara and Kat leaned against Day.

"Do you want to know what happened?" Lily asked Sara.

"Of course," Sara said.

Kat looked up from the floor and turned toward Amanda.

"He told us he's our father," Kat said in a small, clear voice. "And then he cried."

Sara looked over at Lily whose face had a vanishing flicker of surprise and then at Amanda. She picked up her fashion magazine and pretended to be lost in hairstyles. Not one of them, including Kat, who had covered her eyes with Day's long golden fan tail, remarked on the fact that Kat had finally spoken.

NINE

EVERYONE WAS COMING to Kat's tenth birthday. That Sara had promised. But on the morning of her birthday, Kat woke up early with misgivings. Maybe Frederick hadn't made it back the night before from Ireland where he had gone with Beatrice to see her parents. Maybe Nicholas still had the flu or his new baby girl, named for Eleanor, had a cold and Nicholas's worrying wife would refuse to bring her.

Kat hated the responsibility of birthdays, the rising hopes. She knew Tom Clay had arrived from Raleigh where he had moved after Matty Clay died. He was staying with friends and had called the night before to say that today they would go out to lunch and walk the Billy Goat Trail. She went to the bathroom, peered into Lily's flower garden room, but Lily was still sleeping, on her back, her eyes open, only the whites showing as usual.

Upstairs she knew Amanda was up. She got up early to work on small pieces of sculpture, abstract forms. A card table was set up in the middle of her room and she sat in a folding chair and worked in clay. There wasn't sufficient space to work on large pieces and she had lost an interest in the way things actually looked. Her memory of what she had seen sufficed. So she had begun to work in shapes, mostly inexact circles punctuating the centers of blocks of clay. What she liked especially was the feel of the clay—to work a piece of clay until the wet surface was absolutely smooth.

When Kat went upstairs, Amanda had already been working for more than an hour. Day, kept on since retirement, was lying on her bed, taking liberties, and young Day, newly trained, overzealous in his duties, stood up when Kat walked in the room and growled.

"I hate birthdays," Kat said lying down on old Day's back.

"Well, happy birthday anyway," Amanda said.

"Maybe no one will come to the party."

"I'm sorry to say, everyone will come," Amanda said.

In the misty November sun, Amanda looked older, her face lined, sunken between the bones. She had stopped wearing sunglasses and wore instead a long purple scarf, sometimes a forest green one, tied around her head. Nothing to disguise her vacant eyes. This morning she wore a purple scarf, improperly tied, and this small imperfection in her grandmother made Kat angry.

"Is eighty old?" Kat asked.

"Not particularly," Amanda said, irritable with her family's concern about age, as if her inevitable mortality were an act of will, a decision for failure.

"How old would my mother be if she were alive now?"

"She would be thirty-six."

"And how would she be at thirty-six?"

"Like she was at ten."

"Tell me," Kat asked. "I want to know everything about her."

She knew that Jonathan had saved the stories about Eleanor's death and that they were kept in Amanda's room.

"We'll keep them in Amanda's room because she isn't able to read them and the rest of us can't stand to," Sara had said.

Lily wouldn't read them. Amanda had told her the articles were there whenever she wanted to see them but Lily had never been interested. Lily's room was free of photographs as well, nothing from the past. She liked to keep fresh flowers in a small vase on her bureau, school pictures in color of her friends, changed every year, the old pictures thrown out, pictures of the family as it now was. There was no picture of Eleanor and no picture of herself before Eleanor died.

"I don't like the past," she said simply to Amanda. "It's over."

"But it's not over," Amanda said. "It's never over."

"Anyway," Lily said, "I don't want to read old newspaper stories."

Kat did. She sat in Amanda's bed all morning reading the stories about Eleanor's death until Tom Clay arrived to take her to the park.

"Can you remember how she looked?" Kat said.

"Exactly."

"Like her pictures? I have a lot of pictures of her in my room which you took. Even one when she was ten."

"She looked like her pictures—yes," Amanda said. "But not like them either. Your mother was very hard to photograph. Her face changed expression so quickly I had trouble capturing her."

Amanda put her arm around Kat's waist, still plump with girlish flesh.

"Your mother lived with a sense of urgency," Amanda said.

"I am not in a hurry," Kat said. She put the stories back in the folders and dropped them in the file box in Amanda's closet.

Everyone was at the party. Frederick and Beatrice came back from Dublin with colds and news that Beatrice was having a baby, to everyone's surprise since she was almost forty, beyond bearing children, they thought. Frederick had softened with either age or Beatrice. Like some angry, disappointed men, like Hendrik, he had grown sentimental.

He cried easily, especially at movies or feature stories about bad luck.

In a rare outburst at one of her children about another, Sara told Jonathan she hated Frederick's new public show of emotion.

"Mean boys grown up can be like that," Jonathan said.

"He wasn't a mean boy, Jonny," Sara said.

"I love Frederick, Mama, but take it from me, he was a mean boy."

Jonathan had finally moved to his own apartment near Georgetown University but he still used the shed in the back as a study, often working late, and several nights a week he'd eat with the family. Nicholas had married an impeccable young woman named Charlotte, whose father was a former Secretary of State. He had developed an admirable law practice, half private and lucrative, half public interest. They lived a life of carefully laid-out plans, of ease and predictability, in a house whose surroundings were repeated from glossy magazines.

"Is Nicholas still as beautiful as he always was?" Amanda asked Sara one day.

"He's very handsome," Sara said.

"Such a shame to be quite so good as he is," Amanda said. "Even when he was little, he never colored out of the lines."

"Perhaps that had something to do with those years," Sara said. "Those years" was the name Sara had given to her drinking. "He's overcautious."

She and Amanda talked frequently about the way things turned out and how they might have been different. It was a subject which interested Sara specifically.

"He was born like that," Amanda said. "I don't believe in environment. Born good and Freddy was born a little mean and Jonathan was born sweet with a little help from early intimations of mortality."

They laughed.

Eleanor's name was almost never mentioned.

Albert was at the birthday party with Jane—his early self again. The Billy Tudor books which he turned out once a year were less successful than they had been since the book market was flooded with spy books. He was satisfied with his turn of fortune. It fulfilled his expectations. Hendrik, the more successful brother for all the years when they were children, had finally, with the publication of *The German Character*, achieved the critical acclaim he wanted as well as money for the first time in many years.

"We can afford to buy the house from Amanda," Sara said one night before they turned off their lights.

"That makes no sense to me. We will inherit it when she dies."

"She's not going to die for a long time," Sara said, suddenly overwhelmed with the possibility.

And for the first time in several years, she left the room and spent the night in the living room, unable to sleep, looking at the pictures in the fashion magazines she kept hidden under the couch.

At dawn, Hendrik came down and apologized.

"Of course we'll pay." He sat down next to her on the couch. "The trouble I have being American is money," he said. "Everything is money. It's very un-European."

"But we aren't European," Sara said.

"I'll write a check to her today."

"No," Sara said. "Do it in a ceremony. Do it at Kat's birthday party so with everyone there, all the children, we acknowledge that she has been generous."

Kat sat next to Lily, who had chosen an outfit for Kat to wear to her party, one of Lily's, too large since Lily had grown tall and leggy, but Kat was very pleased to look like Lily whom she thought the most beautiful girl she had ever known and the kindest.

Amanda sat on the other side of Kat. The familiar voices gathered together for the first time in many months were comforting to her ears. She wanted to listen.

"Do you remember when I only used to say 'no'?" Kat was saying, touching Amanda on the arm to get her attention.

"Of course I remember," Amanda said. "We were all very worried."

"I used to love to listen, especially to the family at dinner, like now," Kat said.

"And isn't it funny to hear the way everyone talks always the same way," Amanda said. "Just like a play. Hendrik always complains about America and Albert says America is the same as always and Sara asks Beatrice how she is and Charlotte how she is and tells what new thing has happened to Jonathan as if he can't talk himself."

"I know," Kat whispered back. "I'm just glad you didn't leave us in Philadelphia."

"You're quite right," Amanda said reaching for Kat's hand. "It would have been a big mistake to leave you in Philadelphia to take care of yourselves."

And they both laughed.

Hearing the voices of her family, clearer since she couldn't see them, she had an unaccountable sense of triumph, as though the people gathered around the dining room table were her work, and remarkable. A flickering moment of pride which gave way, even before the tears filled her throat, to the truth. They were an ordinary American family, of course, and what was extraordinary about them, captured in the familiar voices she heard, was their survival like that of a lot of families in a country without a past, in a century that had moved with the speed of sound.

Albert had brought champagne. After the toasts to Kat were done and the presents opened, the chocolate birthday cake made by Lily gone, Hendrik went to the study to get the speech he had written to Amanda.

The telephone call from Flat Mouth's wife came while he was opening the middle drawer of his desk.

"We are at dinner," he said.

"It is important she call me back as soon as possible," Star said.

She didn't tell him the nature of the call and he didn't want to ask what had happened to Flat Mouth, as he told Sara later. So reluctantly, putting the speech in his inside pocket, he went back to the dining room.

"You have a telephone call," he said to Amanda.

"Flat Mouth?" Sara whispered.

"Something has happened," Hendrik said. "His wife is on the phone."

"Trouble?" Jonathan asked, leaning across the table to his mother.

"Flat Mouth," Sara said. She looked around the table. "Where's Kat gone? And Lily."

But Kat had slipped away after Lily, following Amanda to the study.

TEN

AMANDA SAT ON a bedroll in Flat Mouth's tent, her back against Day, the soles of her feet against the soles of his feet. It was a late November evening and a heavy wind battered the sides of the tent. Flat Mouth lay on his back with his eyes closed, but he was not sleeping.

The night of Kat's birthday, Star had called Washington at Flat Mouth's request. She was glad to have Amanda at Bad River, she said, glad for her friendship with Flat Mouth, for her help in cooking the meals, allowing her to slip in and out, sometimes for hours, occasionally at her daughter's for the night. The tent was too small for three people and a dog, whose strong canine smell dominated, especially when it rained. That and the odor of an old man dying of cancer. But no one complained about the inconvenience.

Flat Mouth was talkative. What he wanted to do was go over his life, his life with Amanda especially, slowly, sequentially, lingering over each major event.

"You'll stay until I die," Flat Mouth said. "Star is agreeable."

"Maybe I'm not agreeable," Amanda said.

"You are," Flat Mouth said. "For a difficult girl, you have always been agreeable."

He had had cancer for a long time but he had told no one, certainly not Amanda. The cancer had grown slowly but now, as he said, "I could lose consciousness quickly. And then I wouldn't have the opportunity to tell you the things I want you to know."

"Why didn't you tell me when I was young?"

"I didn't want you to know them then," he said simply.

One of the things he wanted to talk about, to Amanda's surprise, was her work. She didn't know he had paid attention.

"I thought you knew only the pictures I did of you," she said.

"That is not how I am, A Man," Flat Mouth said. "You know me better than that. I have always paid attention."

This particular November evening, he was talking about time.

"You have understood time, especially in this century, except at Bad River. How fast it moves, how much faster than it used to move. That is in your work."

Amanda had not thought often about her work since she lost her sight. Occasionally she wondered about her last book—how it would look, if in fact it would ever be published as a book, whether anyone would have the time to put it together.

But Flat Mouth was right. Time used to stretch out in a long ribbon, linear, day after day with very few surprises. Now lives were led in short takes, fixed in place like the pictures in photograph albums, occasions, birthday parties and Christmas dinners, graduations. What she had tried to express in her work, although she did not understand it at the time, was a narrative of disconnected epiphanies, to capture a sense of continuity in a world whose definition was change.

She had been lucky to keep Flat Mouth on the horizon all her life. Lucky and smart. She looked at him now, his eyes closed, his gray hair thin as silk thread on the pillow, his legs crossed at his ankles, his feet barely gnarled from eighty-four years of walking often without shoes. Strange about feet, she said to him. The way a person counts on the feet to remain the same.

When the wind picked up, howling through the teepee, Day got up, walked over Flat Mouth, growling at nothing.

Flat Mouth was restless. Star was at her daughter's, would not be back until morning and, for a while into the night, Amanda was uncommonly frightened. Here they were, she and Flat Mouth, two old people with infirmities and a dog. What could they do against a catastrophe?

"What kind of catastrophe are you thinking of, A Man?" Flat Mouth asked.

"Perhaps a tornado."

"That would be fine. I wouldn't mind a tornado," he said. His voice was thick as if he had been drinking. "What are you worried about?"

She hesitated. "I'm worried about what I would do if you died now on this windy night with me alone."

"I won't die," he said. "I'll wait for a more convenient time." He reached out for her. "Maybe you could sleep beside me," he said.

"Maybe," she said, feeling her way to the top of the bedroll where he was lying, fixing a place for herself beside him, the place where Star usually slept.

"Thank you for taking the pictures of me, A Man," Flat Mouth said. "I feel better to have them."

Amanda laughed.

"But that was years ago," she said.

"Of course. And now I have them," he said. "You see? That is what you knew by instinct. Time is always now if you are careful not to let things fall off the earth. You have been excellent at your work."

"Thank you, Flat Mouth." She bunched up the bedroll behind her for a pillow, settled next to Flat Mouth, and took his hand. "Now don't be so stupid as to make me weep."

Sometime in the middle of the night, the wind stopped and it began to rain. The sound of rain against the side of the tent had the effect of rocking.

In the morning, Flat Mouth did not wake up. He was not dead. She could feel the warmth of his hand, but sometime during the night he must have fallen into a deep sleep.

As she had promised, she stayed the few days until he

died on the last day of November. And then, with Star's help, she got her things together and flew home.

On the airplane she made the decision to move back to New York. She was almost eighty-one, in good health except for her eyes. But more than likely, if she remained in the company of so many people, she would allow herself to slip. She should be alone without help to keep the machinery for survival in good shape.

ELEVEN

IT WAS A warm December Saturday. Sara and Hendrik were in Montrose Park walking old Day, now Kat's dog, with Lily and Kat, who were in mourning.

Lily linked her arm through her grandmother's. "I don't know why she had to leave."

"She didn't have to, darling," Sara said.

"That's worse," Lily said. "That means she wanted to leave."

"She'll be home a lot. Weekends and holidays," Hendrik said.

"It's dangerous to live alone," Kat said ominously. "People die of it. I read that in the paper."

"Animals go off and die alone," Lily said morosely.

"She's not gone off to die," Sara said.

"Then why did she go?" Lily asked.

"I'm not entirely certain," Sara said. "I'm just certain she thought it was the right thing to do."

Amanda had been adamant.

"It's been the three of us for years. Besides," she said, "it's your house now."

Hendrik had paid for the house through Amanda's accountant since she had refused to take the check, which was not in any case the present market value. Not even the cost of the house when he had moved in more than forty years before.

"That was a gesture, Amanda," Sara said. "Not an actual transaction."

"I feel differently living here now," Amanda said.

"You shouldn't," Sara said.

"What does that mean?" Amanda said crossly.

For the first time since Eleanor's death, they fought.

"You made the decision to move to New York before Hendrik paid for the house," Sara said. "We should have paid. You made things possible."

But that night Amanda would not come down for dinner. She blamed a headache although, in fact, she was brooding.

The money from Hendrik had unsettled her. Most of the night, she sat in the chair by the window, the window open to chilly air, her feet on the sill.

Late, it must have been late for the house had been quiet for some time, she heard footsteps coming to the third floor and then a knock.

"Amanda," Hendrik said.

She didn't hear him open the bedroom door.

"I'm sleeping," she said.

"You aren't sleeping," Hendrik said. "You're sitting on the chair with your feet out the window and the air freezing."

"I can't sleep," Amanda said.

Hendrik walked in the room, walked over to the window, moved her feet gently, and closed the window.

"I'll take the money back if you'd prefer," he said.

"I prefer," Amanda said. "What is it you want to pay for? Already I have put the house in your name for taxes."

"We want to pay for the use of it all these years," Hendrik said. "Sara feels strongly." He sat down on the bed. "I have never understood Americans and money. Here money is love, love is money. It is much better to be poor."

"Don't worry about America anymore, Hendrik. You've been here too long to worry." She got up, reached in her closet for a sweater. "Is the light on in my room?" she asked. "It feels that way."

"The light is always on," Hendrik said grumpily. "Night and day. You shouldn't live alone. The house could catch fire. I'll take the money back and live as, whatever you call it, your charge."

"Good," Amanda said. "And I'll go to New York where I would have gone anyway, money for the house or not, where I can keep my lights running night and day."

"Oh Amanda," Hendrik said. "When will you be old enough to stop fighting? Ever?"

"Soon," Amanda said.

In bed, Hendrik pressed his face against Sara's arm.

"I don't understand your mother, Sara. I don't understand her at all."

"Of course not, darling," Sara said. "I don't either. No one does."

"You do. Yes, you do," Hendrik said. "All of you women in this house understand each other perfectly. It's very difficult." He rolled over on his back.

Lily had sat in Amanda's bedroom and watched her pack, watched her feel through the closet for trousers which she still wore exclusively, through her drawers for sweaters, folding them to pack.

"See?" Lily said. "I'm not helping. You could stay in Washington all the time and I promise I'd never help."

"Your hair looks funny the way you've braided it," Kat said.

"Maybe I should cut it," Amanda said.

"No, you should never cut it," Kat said. "I should braid it."

"Tell me really why you are going," Lily asked.

"After your mother died, I told Sara I'd stay until Christmas and I've stayed eight years," Amanda said. "I have to find out whether I can still take care of myself."

"Well, you can't," Kat said. "Your sweater and pants look terrible together. You will probably look funny whenever you go out in New York City."

"I probably will."

"Or you won't go out in New York at all."

"I'll go out and you'll come see me and we'll go out together."

She sat down on the chair next to the window and put her feet on young Day's back.

She had been thinking of making a sculpture when she got to New York and she had in mind a figure of a woman sitting on a straight-back chair—her arms forward on her knees, her elbows unbending, her right ankle across her left knee, a mannish posture. But the figure as a whole would have grace and presence. She could work in the center of the living room on 13th Street.

"For eight years you children have filled the corners to the ends of my fingers. But you don't want the responsibility to be my life," Amanda said brusquely. "You want me to fly so you can fly too."

"That's not true," Lily said.

"It's true," Amanda said. "And it's not so bad."

In Greenwich Village, Amanda took pleasure in the order of her day, living by the radio so she'd know the time and news, so the small apartment would be filled with the sound of voices. She got up early, walked to Fifth Avenue and had croissants and coffee at the bistro on the corner of 13th. She worked on sculpture until lunch, which the cook at the bistro had made her at breakfast to take home—a sandwich, ham with mustard, sometimes turkey, always a smooth egg custard. In the afternoon she walked the same route every day and gradually the people on the street would speak, knowing already if they were from the neighborhood who she was. "Amanda" they called her, never Ms. Steward, and it pleased her especially to be in the company of friends although she knew no names.

Later, she turned on the tape recorder.

This is for Sara and Lily and Kat. It's Monday, the fifteenth of December.

I have been thinking about the book of photographs from my last exhibit which I began to put together with

Eleanor. I'd like them strung together like a story so the feeling will not be of the random moments in a person's life disconnected from any sense of continuity—but more or less the continuity of a woman's mind, where the narrative is not linear but three-dimensional and has to do with the imagination's capacity to connect pictures—of Lincoln Draper in Château-Thierry in 1918, with Eleanor and Lily, nose to nose, in the garden of P Street the summer after Lily was born.

I don't want the narrative to be linear because the mind isn't—otherwise what a desperate life it would be day after day to the end.

At night after supper, which was always ice cream, usually vanilla with dark chocolate sauce, and a pot of tea, Amanda would lie on the couch in the living room, heavy with the damp earth smell of clay, and listen to Anna's letters read in her own voice.

TWELVE

LILY AND KAT made tapes to send to Amanda as their mother used to do, every week except the one week a month, gradually one every two months, that Amanda got on the Metroliner with Day and came to Washington for a few days.

Hi Amanda, this is Lily and it's March 15, 1981. I finally read the stories about my mother kept in your closet. Tom was here and he wanted to read them and he wanted me to read them with him so I did because I couldn't think of a way to get out of it. He got very angry even though he had read a lot of the stories when she died. "These stories are not your mother who I remember as sunshine and daring," he said to me. "Who is a person anyway?"

It was the wrong time to ask me that. Since I became

thirteen, I wonder all the time about myself. Whose hands are these at the end of my arms? Whose hips, since mine are spreading and I look like a garage. Kat thinks I'm strong and even-tempered. That's a joke. Turned inside out, I'm vanilla pudding, the runny kind. My teachers think I'm good as gold but at night the pictures on my brain are not the thoughts of a good girl.

What I remember about my mother is cozy. I think of her as a child and that we played together and were about the same size. Once you said to me that memory is strange and unreliable. So I don't know who Eleanor March was either, any more than I know myself. You are the only real person I know who doesn't change day after day as if you knew everything when you were born. Or is that because you are old?

I'm getting fat. Kat says so.

I think I'll be a doctor. I'll tell you about that later.

Good night, sweet prince.

This is Kat, of course. It's the Fourth of July and there's a party here with all the relatives and I'm in your room in what kind of mood you can guess.

Why didn't you come in June?

I hate Lily. It just started yesterday when she put pictures of the awful boys in the ninth grade in picture frames on her dresser and bought eye shadow at the drugstore so she looks bruised in the face like an abused child.

Mama Sara says you're going to Wisconsin in August to visit Flat Mouth's wife. Isn't that a little weird? This whole family is a little weird. Mama Sara probably didn't tell you so as not to cause trouble that Jane left Albert and moved to Hong Kong with a new job. So now Albert spends most of the nights at our house in the room next to yours and smokes his terrible cigarettes and has trouble with his stomach.

I guess you remember my birthday is November 8 and I hope you plan to be here, or else.

This is Kat and it's February 7 and I've gone to bed for my life. I'm in your bed and old Albert's in the john as usual and I'm not answering the telephone, which is ringing at this very minute for me from the drama teacher who cast me in the lead of Oklahoma! *on February 1. Since the cast was posted on the bulletin board, I've been too sick at my stomach to get out of bed.*

Sara says I have stage fright and I'll get over it and what I have to do is go to school and play in Oklahoma! *What a waste, Lily told me. I have this beautiful voice and could be an opera singer. Fat as buffaloes is what Jonathan says of opera singers. Lily says she's very disappointed in me. She looks at me with a long sorrowful face as if she's just had news of a death. I could pulverize her when she acts like my mother and a saint.*

In my daydreams, I am an opera singer, of course, but all the endings of the operas in which I sing are happy endings.

Hello, Amanda. This is Anna Katrina March speaking to you from bed. You are coming for Lily's sixteenth birthday party and coronation and I want to tell you in advance that I'm still home from school with stage fright. Every time the subject of school comes up, I throw up. Once I broke out in hives and had to go to emergency at Georgetown Hospital. Sara is going to try to get you to do something about it, but you can't. Even you can't.

This is what I think. There are people who are the lead in school and then kaput. And there are other people growing in silence underground who suddenly burst through the earth in brilliant color. That's the person I am. I don't want to go back to school ever. I certainly don't want to explain to that limp-brained drama teacher that she has ruined my life by giving me the lead in Oklahoma!

I can't wait to see you. I should tell you in advance how I look. I'm quite tall—five feet six and thin—bony is how Lily describes it. I have grown my hair and it's a black curly bush down to my shoulders, and I dress like you do in trousers and sweatshirts to hide my breasts. I tell you all this so you can imagine me.

Lily is beautiful. Even when she's driving me crazy. I know that she's beautiful and everyone loves her. Albert, it turns out, has cancer and everyone hates Jane for leaving him.

Hugs and kisses and a thousand balloons to the one and only Amanda Steward.

p.s. Mama's told me that Flat Mouth called you 'A Man.' I'd like to be a man sometimes instead of a woman. Then I could do what I please.

This is Lily and it's Saturday afternoon, the fifth of October in 1985. Last night at dinner, we talked about you through dessert. Everyone was here. Nicholas and Charlotte and Frederick and Beatrice and Jonathan and his new girlfriend called Cassandra who is a waitress on roller skates at a new restaurant on Wisconsin Avenue. Mama Sara said you are getting too tired to come to Washington and we should come to New York once a month. That after all you'll be eighty-six on January first and it's too much. Jonathan said that you should move back here. That it's not sensible for you to live alone, and then Cassandra told a terrible story which ended badly about her grandmother living alone, but as you can imagine Cassandra is the sort of woman with a tragedy for every social exchange.

I didn't say anything at the time but it occurred to me that if I get into Columbia where I've applied pre-med, I could spend half my time with you. I'd turn Melvina's room into mine and that way I'd get more work done than if I were in a dorm and we could be together. Please think about it. I applied early to Columbia.

Kat treats me as if I'm a criminal passing through the house. Mama Sara says it's because I'm leaving and Kat's bereft. I'd hate to see how she'd behave with a real tragedy.

Kat had her first recital last week and she's astonishing. She still can't sing onstage. They put up a screen and she slips through the back curtain so you can't even see her feet under the screen. But she sings like an angel—if you can believe there's any angel there at all.

Mama Sara probably told you. I heard from Colum-
bia yesterday and so we'll be half-time roommates in
September if Kat hasn't put cyanide in my tea before
then.

Good morning, Amanda. It's the first of February and
this month Lily will be eighteen and then she will leave
forever to seek her fortune which will be sour cream if
there's any justice in the world. As a roommate, you will
find her one hundred percent self-centered and it's very
lucky you can't see because if you could, you'd be
treated to hours of watching her brush her shoulder-
length honey-blond hair into a thick curl and stand side-
ways in the mirror, holding her breath to see if her
stomach is still flat as paper.

These are the things that are happening in the next
few months. We are having an eighteenth birthday party
for Lily with champagne and boys. Then in June right
after she graduates, Tom Clay, our father who art in
heaven, is taking her to Paris for a graduation present
and they're biking around the south of France. I cannot
wait until she leaves but I extend to you my sympathy
which sentiment you will understand soon enough.

Dear Amanda,

Kat had her first recital without standing behind a
screen. She sang Mozart's "Deh vieni, non tardar" and
Tatiana's letter scene by Tchaikovsky. And she was wonderful, wonderful.

I have been thinking quite a lot lately what kind of
life I will lead. I want to be a doctor and I think I'll be
a good doctor. But I also want to have an ordinary family with a father and children and only the necessary
risks of chicken pox and strep throat. Kat will find
enough danger in the world to satisfy this generation's
need for adventure.

The man—you knew there was a man, didn't you, with
such confidence I am showing in domestic
tranquility—in any case the man I met this summer is a
resident at Georgetown University Hospital. Jonathan
says he's too serious and not sexy, but what does Jona-

than know? I think he's serious and sexy. This morning Kat found the notebook I've been keeping with designs for wedding dresses and children's names just so I'll be prepared in the event of an emergency. Kat drew a picture of a bride in a pinafore—remember how I used to refuse to wear anything but pinafores?—"Mrs. Benjamin Callahan in the rose garden following her wedding to a Freak," she wrote. Benj Callahan. That's his name. He's twenty-four, which doesn't seem too old for me, do you think? Jonathan Abbott was quite a lot older than you were, wasn't he?

You probably didn't hear on the radio but it was in the Post *this morning that Emma Gaits—remember?— was found dead in the house where she grew up in Germantown and the assumption is that she killed herself. They mentioned about Mama. I remember Emma Gaits's long thin hair which smelled like lemon and she chewed the skin around her fingers so when she read a story to me, her fingers sometimes bled on my books.*

I'm bringing some posters for Melvina's room and an Indian rug.

Hi, Amanda. Here is Kat's last recital which I promised to tape but Jonathan had trouble with the tape recorder and we missed the beginning. So I'll tell the beginning which left us all—Mama Sara, me and Hendrik, Frederick and Beatrice, Jonathan and Cassandra, Nich-o and Charlotte—all but Albert who is back in the hospital— weeping.

She had been asked to introduce her recital with a story about her beginnings in music—and this is her story as she told it: "My mother, whose name was Eleanor, died when I was two years old and for a long time, in fact until I was almost four, I refused to say anything but 'no.' My sister, Lily, tells me, however, that I used to sing myself to sleep at night and this is what I sang." And she sang it:

"ELEANOR—ELEAN—NOR—E—LEA—NOR— EL—EAN—OR."

THIRTEEN

AMANDA DIDN'T GO to Washington for Christmas in 1989.

Lily, in her last year at Columbia and living with Benjamin Callahan, said Amanda was too tired, uncertain of her ability to get around.

Day was getting old, sometimes unreliable, but she refused to get a new dog.

"Day's fine," she said to Sara.

"He misses streets. Sometimes he forgets to stop," Sara said.

"So," Amanda said, "we're both old."

Kat, who lived with Amanda during the time Juilliard was in session, said Amanda was not tired or uncertain. She was staying in New York because she wanted to finish her introduction to her book of photographs and decide on a title.

"Also," Kat said, "she has to finish her sculpture."

"She's been working on that same thing for almost ten years," Hendrik said.

"She's slow," Kat said. "And she keeps starting over."

In the fall of 1989, the iron curtain had lifted and the Second World War was finally over. The Berlin Wall was down. Eastern Europe, long under the dark shadow of the Soviets, was declaring freedom, country after country.

Hendrik was a European once again.

"So, America," he said, his accent thick with German, "you are going to be beaten at your own game of democracy."

"You are American, Hendrik," Sara said. "Remember?"

"Austrian to the marrow of my bones," he said. "And Jewish."

"Like most Americans," Sara said.

They were in the kitchen Christmas Eve—Hendrik in

the rocker with a beer, Kat and Lily breaking the stale bread for stuffing, chopping onions.

"There will be eighteen for dinner tomorrow," Sara said taking pleasure in naming them, a sense of accomplishment. "Frederick and Beatrice and Maud and Beatrice's sister, Nich-o and Charlotte, Elly and Madge, Jonathan and maybe Cassandra, if they make up by tomorrow, Kat, Lily, Benjamin, me and Hendrik, Pamela, and Susanna with her new boyfriend."

"Albert would have particularly enjoyed this Christmas," Hendrik said morosely.

"Albert never enjoyed any Christmas, darling. And you know what he would have said about Eastern Europe."

"He would have been extremely pleased."

"He would have said in that raspy cigarette voice," Kat said, " 'A united Germany will be the end of the world. And watch out. A united Germany is what we're going to have.' "

Jonathan came flying in late in the evening and by his demeanor it was clear that Cassandra was relenting and would most likely be at Christmas dinner.

They finished in the kitchen before midnight, wrapped the last presents, draped the tinsel and hung candy canes on the Christmas tree, put up the stockings, which the children, now Kat and Lily, always filled, and a little reluctantly, although it was late and they were all, except Sara, drifting with wine, they went up to bed.

Kat put on her nightgown and knocked on Lily's door. Benjamin sat on the side of the bed reading a magazine and Lily was wrapping a package in silver paper on the end of the bed.

Kat moved Benjamin's feet and sat down beside her sister. "What do you think is the matter?" Kat asked.

"It doesn't feel like Christmas, does it?" Lily said.

"Amanda?" Kat asked.

"Amanda." Lily nodded.

FOURTEEN

THE DAY BEFORE New Year's Eve was particularly cold, but Amanda opened the windows overlooking the back garden because the living room felt too hot and she seemed to be having trouble breathing.

She had not eaten. There were juices in the refrigerator, a quart of milk, a half-finished bottle of red wine, but that morning she had not felt like walking to Fifth Avenue for croissants. Mr. Harvey, the owner of the shop, had called when she didn't come in as usual and said he'd bring her supper as soon as the shop cleared of customers for a while but she wasn't hungry for the ham sandwich he brought and ate only a spoonful of custard.

Sara was coming with Lily and Kat. They'd be in New York by dinnertime.

"We'll stay through your birthday," Sara had said. "Kat is making angel food cake."

"What I'd really like is lemon cake with chocolate icing," Amanda said. "And all the candles lit. Ninety of them and one for good luck."

By late afternoon, she felt less tired and worked on the seated woman. The sides of the face, an angular face with high cheekbones, didn't seem to match exactly. She felt her own face. It was difficult to tell. She flattened the cheekbone and the eye on the clay woman. In the morning, she'd do the right side of the face again. Maybe now it would be better to lie down and work on the introduction to her photographs, which was almost complete.

Perhaps she should eat, she thought. Chocolate milk. That was what she wanted. There was chocolate syrup in the cupboard. She poured a glass of milk, turned on the tape recorder.

It's December thirtieth in the afternoon and soon you'll all be here but I want to put this down for who knows what I will remember to say with the excitement when you come.

The name of the book finally came to me this afternoon while I was working on the mismatched cheekbones of my clay woman. It seems the right sort of name for a book of photographs covering a lot of years, mainly of women and girls, some men and little boys of course. But the point of view is that of women. So I'd like to call it Daughters of the New World. *There'll be the title page and the letter from my mother and then the introduction, which is finally complete on these tapes. Do you think it would be too sentimental to have a small reprint of the old photograph Anna Jermyn brought of my mother and me?*

The tape continued to play and Amanda continued to speak into it, aware of a sudden and profound weakness and initially aware that the words she spoke made no sense.

FIFTEEN: JANUARY 1, 1990

THE SILVER WINTER sun fell between the slender buildings on West 13th Street, sifted through the soot-gray windows. Lily and Sara worked in filtered light, Day under the table, and in the kitchen Kat was making chocolate fudge sauce in the double boiler. The apartment smelled sweetly of lemon cake baking.

The Seated Woman had been moved to a corner of the spare whitewashed living room and a large pine table was in the center of the room where Amanda's photographs were spread. The tape recorder was on and Amanda's clear deep voice, unshaken by age, was playing, a little at a time, so Lily could transcribe the introduction to *Daughters of the New World.*

Sara was arranging photographs.

"What do you think?" she asked Lily, holding up the first picture Amanda had taken of Melvina seated in the rocking chair in the kitchen of the house on P Street, the promise of a smile around her lips. "Should she go first?"

"You should go first," Lily said. "That picture of you during the Depression with Bonita hiding under your dress so all we can see of Bonita is her plump legs."

"Then Melvina?"

"Then Eleanor," Lily said. "You and Mama in front of the Small Hotel. Then Melvina and maybe that picture of your father in the war."

Kat finished the fudge sauce, dipped her finger into the chocolate, and licked it.

"Did you look at Amanda's woman carefully?" she asked Sara.

"Well enough to see that she's unfinished," Sara said. "The right cheek and eye haven't been done at all."

"The funny thing is that she was finished when I left to come home for Christmas. Completely finished. Only the right eye was a little off center and the cheekbone didn't match the other cheekbone."

"She must have flattened it," Lily said. "It was finished when I saw it too and it was good, especially the body. But it doesn't look a bit like Amanda."

"Is it supposed to?" Sara asked.

"She was her own model," Lily said.

Sara laughed. "She was always her own model," she said.

In the kitchen, Kat put the lemon cake on a plate and spread the shiny chocolate icing on the top, around the sides. She counted ninety-one candles from the boxes of yellow birthday candles and put them in concentric circles around the top of the cake.

"Now," she called. "I'll need your help lighting them." She put the cake on the table beside Lily and they each lit candles until all ninety-one, burning swiftly down to the icing, were lit.

"You sing," Lily said.

"Not just me," Kat said. "We'll all sing." And she began:

> Happy birthday to you
> Happy birthday to you
> Happy birthday, dear Amanda,
> Happy birthday to you.

"Make a wish, Kat," Lily said.

"We'll each make a wish," Sara said.

"Do we keep it a secret?" Kat asked.

"I think we should," Sara said.

"Ready?" Lily asked.

"Ready."

And together, their heads bent over the multitude of flickering lights, they blew out the candles.